ROME

THE ART OF WAR

www.transworldbooks.co.uk

Also by M. C. Scott

HEN'S TEETH
NIGHT MARES
STRONGER THAN DEATH
NO GOOD DEED

BOUDICA: DREAMING THE EAGLE
BOUDICA: DREAMING THE BULL
BOUDICA: DREAMING THE HOUND
BOUDICA: DREAMING THE SERPENT SPEAR

THE CRYSTAL SKULL

ROME: THE EMPEROR'S SPY
ROME: THE COMING OF THE KING
ROME: THE EAGLE OF THE TWELFTH

For more information about M. C. Scott and her books,
see her website at www.mcscott.co.uk

ROME

THE ART OF WAR

M. C. Scott

BANTAM PRESS

LONDON · TORONTO · SYDNEY · AUCKLAND · JOHANNESBURG

TRANSWORLD PUBLISHERS
61–63 Uxbridge Road, London W5 5SA
A Random House Company
www.transworldbooks.co.uk

First published in Great Britain
in 2013 by Bantam Press
an imprint of Transworld Publishers

A CIP catalogue record for this book
is available from the British Library.

ISBNs 9780593065464 (cased)
9780593065471 (tpb)

Addresses for Random House Group Ltd companies outside the UK
can be found at: www.randomhouse.co.uk
The Random House Group Ltd Reg. No. 954009

The Random House Group Limited supports the Forest Stewardship
Council (FSC®), the leading international forest-certification organization.
Our books carrying the FSC label are printed on FSC®-certified paper.
FSC is the only forest-certification scheme endorsed by the leading
environmental organizations, including Greenpeace. Our paper-procurement
policy can be found at www.randomhouse.co.uk/environment.

Typeset in 12/15pt Sabon by
Kestrel Data, Exeter, Devon.
Printed and bound in Great Britain by
Clays Ltd, Bungay, Suffolk.

2 4 6 8 10 9 7 5 3

MIX
Paper from
responsible sources
FSC® C016897
www.fsc.org

For Bill and Mark,
with many thanks

CONTENTS

EVENTS LEADING TO
THE YEAR OF THE
FOUR EMPERORS

AD 54   Claudius dies. Nero takes the throne

AD 62   Seneca retires. Nero's wife Octavia dies

AD 65   Pisoan conspiracy exposed. Seneca forced to suicide

AD 66   Corbulo forced to suicide

AD 67   Vespasian leads Judaean legions against Galilee

AD 68
8/9 June   Nero forced to suicide. Galba takes the throne

AD 69
15 January   Galba slain, Otho takes the throne

AD 69
16 April   Otho's suicide. Vitellius takes the throne

AD 69
July 1 – 3   Vespasian hailed as emperor by eastern legions

ON THE USE OF SPIES

Knowledge of the enemy's dispositions can only be obtained from other men. Hence the use of spies, of whom there are five classes:

1 **Local spies** – Having local spies means employing the services of the inhabitants of an enemy territory;

2 **Internal spies** – Having internal spies means making use of officials of the enemy;

3 **Double agents** – Having double agents means getting hold of the enemy's spies and using them for our own purposes;

4 **Doomed spies** – Having doomed spies means doing certain things openly for purposes of deception, and allowing our spies to know of them and report them to the enemy;

5 **Surviving spies** – Surviving spies are those who bring back news from the enemy's camp.

Sun Tzu *The Art of War*

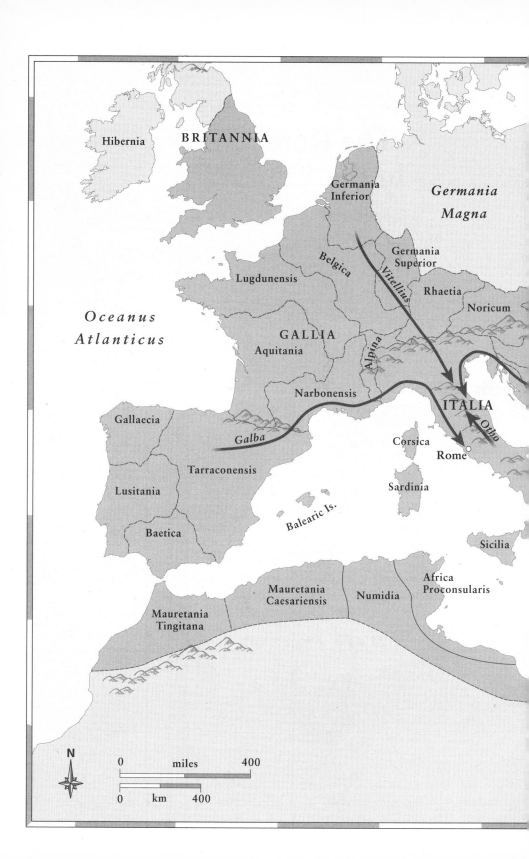

The Roman Empire in the 1st Century AD

Sarmatia

Pannonia

Oblia

Tyras

BOSPORUN KINGDOM

Dalmatia

Mucianus

Moesia Superior

Moesia Inferior

Illyricum

Pontus Euxinus

Thracia

Macedonia

Bithynia

Pontus

Mucianus

Epirus

Armenia

Cappadocia

ASIA

Galacia

Achaea

Lycia

Cilicia

PARTHIAN EMPIRE

Creta

Antioch

Assyria

Cyprus

SYRIA

Mesopotamia

Mare Interum

JUDAEA

Cyrenaica

Alexandria

Arabia Petraea

Arabia Magna

Aegyptus

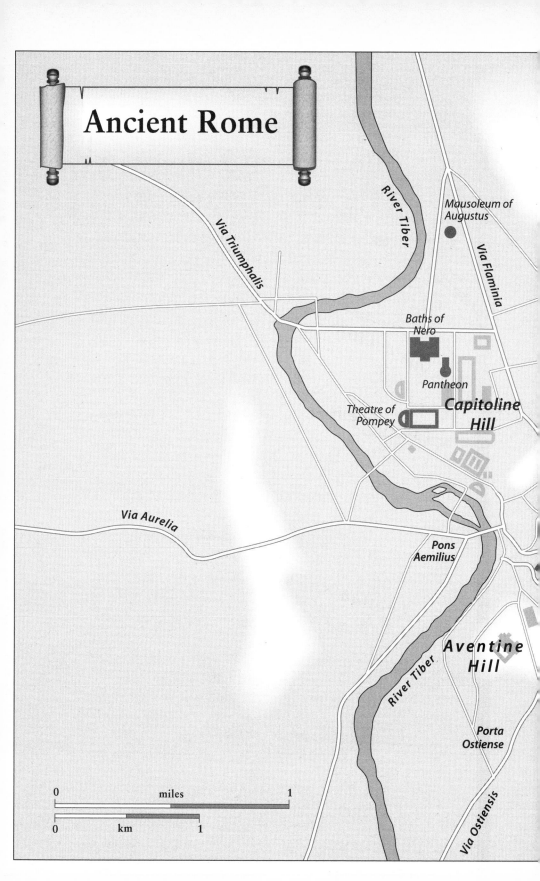

Ancient Rome

River Tiber

Via Triumphalis

Via Flaminia

Mausoleum of Augustus

Baths of Nero

Pantheon

Via Aurelia

Theatre of Pompey

Capitoline Hill

Pons Aemilius

Aventine Hill

River Tiber

Porta Ostiense

Via Ostiensis

0   miles   1

0   km   1

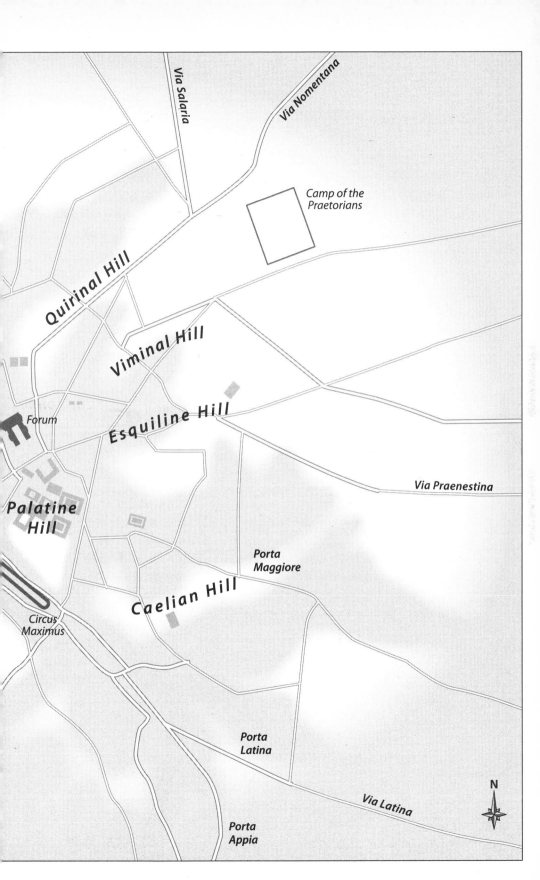

Antonius Primus' route to Rome

Germania
Superior

Rhaetia

Noricum

Pannonia

Carnuntum

Alpina

Cremona

Ravenna

Illyricum

Dalmatia

Corsica

Narnia
Rome

ITALIA

Sardinia

Mare
Internum

Sicilia

Africa
Proconsularis

Numidia

N

0   miles   200

0   km   200

FOREWORD

On 9 June AD 68, in the thirteenth year of his reign, the dangerously dissolute Roman emperor Nero Claudius Caesar Drusus Germanicus died by his own hand, having been named an 'enemy of the state' by the senate, and thereby ending a dynasty that had ruled Rome and her empire for close to a century.

There followed what has become known as the Year of the Four Emperors, but was, in fact, eighteen months in which four successive men, generally with several legions behind them, claimed the title of emperor.

The ensuing civil war ripped the empire apart, setting legion against legion, brother against brother, father against son. Most of the destruction occurred far afield in battles prosecuted by absentee emperors who ruled Rome from the relative safety of their legionary encampments.

But in June of AD 69, Vitellius, the third man to claim the title, entered Rome at the head of sixty thousand legionaries. Thus, as his opponent's legions marched closer, the nightmare of civil war threatened the capital itself . . .

PROLOGUE

There follows the evidence as related to me concerning the spy Pantera and his role in the conflagration, both literal and metaphoric, that has assailed Rome in the past year.

The spy cannot speak for himself, and so, at the emperor's insistence, I have interviewed all those available to me who might shed light on his culpability, from the emperor himself to those in custody awaiting execution.

Time is short, for which reason, I have presented here an unedited transcript of the interviews as they were spoken to me. I offer no apologies for the coarseness of the language in places, nor the obvious imprecisions in memories of those who were involved.

The names and ranks detailed are those held by the relevant individuals at the time the events occurred, and are not necessarily those they hold now.

This is a true and accurate representation, from which the truth may be deduced.

This I swear in the name of Isis, for I am her Chosen, and must remain impartial in the affairs of men.

Hypatia of Alexandria

PART I

LOCAL SPIES

CHAPTER ONE

Judaea, June, AD 69

Titus Flavious Vespasianus – Vespasian

It began, as it ended, with the scent of wild strawberries.

Sharp, sweet, erotic beyond words, it was the scent of Caenis, of her skin, her hair, of the flat channel between her breasts and the ambrosia-sweat that dripped from them on to my face.

It surrounded me, carried me far from myself. I swept my thumb up and round and brought it to my lips. My eyes sought hers to share my tasting of her. She was kneeling over my hips, drawing me inside with the chaotic abandon that had never failed to startle me when the rest of her life was so ordered.

She smiled and was fierce: a tigress; she was wild: a harpy; she was perfect: Athena, or Artemis, or the bright god-woman of the moon who spins her foam down to seduce poor men who cannot stand against her.

I couldn't keep still any longer. However hard I tried, I couldn't keep my eyes open, either, to see if she had met her climax as I met mine. Later, of course, I would find out. Later, I would attend to her need. Later, when I could bear to—

'My love . . .' She leaned forward on to me. Her breasts were heavy on my chest. Her lips kissed away the sweat from the sides of my eyes.

She was resting on her small, sharp elbows and her hair fell on my face, tickling my cheeks. She swept it up, and hooked it over her ear. 'Must you go?'

Lost in the undertow, it took me a moment to understand her question. I had to drag back memories of who and what and where.

Slowly . . . we were in Greece, on the island of Kos, in exile for the sin of sleeping under the spell of a song.

The sleep was mine. The song had been the emperor's and Nero was not kind to men who offended him. Only a year before, Corbulo had been forced to suicide for no greater crime than being a good general, loved by his legions; I was only alive because I had no money and posed no threat and had not, until that point, mortally offended the emperor.

And so we had run away to Greece together, Caenis and I, and through the long winter we had awaited the messenger who would order me to fall on my sword and surrender my pitiful estate to the crown.

But then Nero's messenger finally came, and his order was not the one we had so feared.

Far from being required to fall on my sword, I, Vespasian, had been given command of the Judaean legions, with a remit to subdue the insurgents who had taken Jerusalem and stolen the eagle of the XIIth legion. If I failed, of course I would have to die, and even if I succeeded there was every chance that I might still face Corbulo's fate, but for now, I was safe.

Duty said I must go, but, more, I *wanted* to: war was my

lifeblood, the hard matter of my bones, the joy of my ageing days, and no amount of love could hold me back from it. I tried to speak, to tell her so softly, and could not.

Nearby, a man groaned. I am shamed to say that it took me some time to realize that the voice was my own, and that it bounced back to me soft with the echoes of goatskin, not crisp from a plaster wall; that the scents around me were not of strawberries at all, but the autumnal fragrances of the legionary encampment: old fire smoke, men's sweat, honed iron and rusting armour.

Everything was rusted here, in Judaea, because I was *here* in my tent, not *there* on Kos, and *here* was . . . a mile south of the Syrian border, and more than a year had passed since I had last lain with Caenis.

I was a general in command of Nero's armies: three legions were camped with me and two more with Mucianus half a day's march away.

I had been wounded twice in the past year. I had led the charge from the front more times than I chose to remember and I had won back a province as I had been ordered to do; all but Jerusalem was once again under Roman rule and death had not taken me yet.

I tried to open my eyes, and failed, and in the moment's half-held breath between sleep and true awakening I knew two things: that I was alone in my bed – my act of emission had been solitary and wasted – but I was not alone in my sleeping quarters. An intruder was in there with me and he had not come with kindness in his heart.

I was not armed, that was the hard part. My sword was on my kit box at the far side of the tent, and might as well have been in Greece. A knife hung from the crossed poles of my camp bed, closer, but still too far away for me to reach it without being seen to move.

Beneath the thin linen that covered me, I was naked as

a child, with the stain of my own lust fresh on my loins. A shadow stood poised in the grey-milk light to my left.

What I did next was all instinct. I bunched both hands into fists, took a deep, rollicking breath, rolling a little, as a man does in disturbed sleep. For good effect, I whistled and grumbled on the exhalation.

And then I shouted.

'*Haaaaaaaaaa!*'

It was more of a scream, really. On the battlefield, I would have been ashamed of its pitch; my men knew me as their general who roared like a bull.

Here in the close confines of the tent the noise crashed around, coming from all places at once, and it was powerful enough to scare a man who was already on the edge of his fear.

I couldn't sustain it long, but it gave me time enough to hurl myself off the bed and tumble across the floor away from the deadly shadow.

I hit my head and scrabbled for my pack, which had to be close. My hands closed on cold metal: the long thin plates of the banded legionary armour that has come into use these last few years.

You have to understand that in battle I wear what my men wear, and usually I am glad of it, but this once, a general's solid breastplate would have been better. I fumbled for a weapon, but the shadow charged at me, snarling.

'No!'

I jerked aside, and felt a blade sting as it skittered over my ribs. I was bellowing like a bull now, no words, just a noise that might keep this hound of Hades away from my throat long enough for me to find . . . *ha!* The hilt of my gladius. This, too, was what the men carried into battle, and it was perfect: short, savage, sharp enough to gut a man.

I thrust it forward, kneeling, and felt it slide across a leather jerkin, but I had already punched my left shoulder and fore-arm forward in a following blow. Perhaps a year ago I could not have done this, but I was battle fit by now, my body as much of a weapon as my shield. I felt muscle yield, the impact of bone, solid against me, the slide of leather. I drew my arm back for another thrust and—

A sudden flare of firelight, dazzlingly bright. Shapes shifted within it, and even as I wrenched my head away I felt the body beneath me flinch under a blow I had not delivered, felt hands grab past me to hold arms that were not mine, heard a voice I knew, but could not immediately place, shout, 'Alive! Keep him alive!'

Thus, rescued, I, Titus Flavius Vespasianus, senator, second son of a tax farmer and current commander of the armies of Judaea, rolled away, and sat up.

On the far side of my tent was a flurry of contained violence, in which I took no part.

CHAPTER TWO

Judaea, June, AD 69

Vespasian

'My lord?'

I was sitting hunched on a folding camp stool in front of a brazier in the outer, more public, section of my tent.

My hands were wrapped round the old silver mug that was my grandmother's gift when I first left home. I've had it with me on every campaign since Britain; I have it still.

It's my mirror as well as my drinking vessel. Once in a while, it shows me a handsome man, flushed with victory. That night – I suppose it was morning by then – a ruddy-faced farmer stared back at me with haunted eyes, cheeks too broad and chin too sharp, hair grey as a winter's dawn and two fat brows creeping to kiss in the folds of a frown.

I had faced death in battle so often that I had come to think myself immune to fear. That morning, I had learned that I was not.

Sweat ran like rain off my face, while the rest of me was shaking with cold and fright. I wrapped my arms about my ribs, testing the bruises and the long line of the knife cut, and discovered that someone had draped my campaign cloak about my shoulders.

For decency's sake, I should have pulled it tight and belted it, but I made a decision a long time ago not to hide myself from my men, and so I let them see for themselves the crusting on my thighs and the shivers that racked me, and the heavy, hollow breathing, like a horse that had just lost its race.

It wasn't enough though; they were waiting for more and the press of their patience was giving me a headache.

I looked up, squinting against the brazier's heat. 'Demalion?'

Demalion of Macedon had been my personal aide for the past two years. He was the only man I knew who would have had the compassion to think of a cloak at a time like this.

Demalion is tall and dark of hair and would be heart-breakingly comely were he not so weighed down by old grief. When I first took him on as my aide, I promised myself that if I ever saw him smile, I would open the flask of Falerian I had brought with me when I left Caenis.

'My lord?'

Not tonight, evidently, for the man who stood just beyond the rim of the fire's red glow was not smiling, and was not Demalion.

If Demalion was striking, Pantera – the spy, whose name meant 'leopard' – was the kind of man who could blend into the background in a crowd of two.

And, of course, he was the one who had broken into my tent and led the capture of the assassin; I should have known him sooner.

What can I say of him? If you know Demalion's story, you will know how Pantera and I first met. After the re-formation of the XIIth, he joined me for some of the Judaean campaign and I made use of him, or him of me; I never knew which, although in an odd kind of way I trusted him more than many of the men around me.

He was a spy, subterfuge was his world, but he had a kind of integrity that seemed real to me and I believed that he spoke the truth when he chose to speak.

He wasn't saying anything just then. He was simply standing on the other side of the fire, a shadow beyond the rim of light, with nothing exceptional about him. He was of middling height, of middling build, with hair of a middling brown and middling skin tanned by wind and sun, neither as dark as the Syrians nor as pale as the northmen of the Germanies.

It was only when he moved that he set himself apart: despite all his injuries, he had a feline grace about him that had my hair standing on end, such as I have left.

'Pantera,' I said. No joyous reunion this, everything quiet; he demanded that, somehow. 'I thought you were in Rome?'

'I was. I left at the end of April.'

Which would have been when he heard news of Otho's death; when Vitellius was acknowledged emperor.

I didn't ask why he had left then, nor why he had come to me now; the answers were obvious, and I hated them.

Even so, to have travelled from Rome to our camp in two months was impressive, but I couldn't find anything to say that didn't sound patronizing and so instead I tipped my head towards the tent flap, and the growing sounds of chaos outside.

'Where's Demalion?'

'Making the assassin ready for questioning.'

Two questions answered, and neither of them had I asked: yes, the intruder was an assassin; yes, he had survived his capture. Such economy of thought.

'A centurion?' I asked, but it was more of a comment than a question. It's always the centurions who are sent to do the dirty work; they make the most dedicated and efficient killers.

In any case, this one was hardly the first. Galba had sent one to kill me when he first made himself emperor just after Nero's death. Otho, his murderer and successor, would no doubt have got round to sending another if he hadn't been so busy trying to fend off Vitellius. And now Vitellius, or more probably Lucius, his younger, more ambitious, more ruthless brother, had sent yet another to accomplish what the others had failed to do.

Truly, any questioning was only for the men, to assuage their need for retribution; we knew the answers, or so I thought. My only real doubt was whether, without Pantera, he would have been stopped in time.

But the legions expect certain things, and there are rituals that must be observed, not least by a general whose life has been saved by the diligence of his staff.

I set down the mug and lumbered to my feet when I would have just as happily gone back to bed. 'What do I need to know before we go out there?'

That was the thing about Pantera, you could ask him these things and expect a decent answer.

'Not a great deal. His name is Publius Fundanius. He was a local man, a Syrian, recently promoted to the third cohort of the Tenth. Seneca always said that the best agent was the officer of the enemy you turned to your own ends, but the second best was the local man, who knew the lie of the land and could chart his way about it. With this man, Vitellius had both woven into one; a local man who was also an officer in your ranks.'

'What did they offer him?'

'A commission in the new Praetorian Guard.'

'But he isn't Roman.'

'That doesn't matter any more. The new emperor is in the

31

process of turning the entire First Germanica and the Fourth Macedonica into Guards.'

'Hades, is he?'

That was news, and there was little enough of that from Rome just then. I was like a starving man shown a roast goose, desperate to rip it apart with my bare hands.

'He's taking risks, isn't he? The men of the Macedonica are raised from the barbarian tribes around the Rhine. They may be citizens, but only because their grandfathers fought for Caesar and their fathers for Tiberius. The Germanica are worse. If you're going to pay your Guard twice what you pay everyone else, you'd have thought you'd take care to choose them wisely; at least pick real Romans. In any case, Rome has nine cohorts of the Guard already; how many does a man need to make himself feel safe?'

Pantera smiled, just a little. Have you ever seen him with a smile on his face? He was a different man, suddenly; younger, with a spark like a street urchin.

He cocked one brow and said, 'He's made sixteen new cohorts of the Guard and four Urban cohorts, each of a thousand men.'

'That's twenty thousand men!' You could have heard that shout in Syria. 'Is he insane? Rome will burn, those parts that have not been pillaged!' And then, 'What's he doing with the old Praetorians, the ones who supported Otho?'

'He decommissioned them; paid their pensions and ordered them out of Rome. Also the astrologers: they have to be gone by the first of October, on pain of death.'

I wanted to sit down, to call for wine, to bank up the brazier and pepper Pantera with questions about Rome and her new emperor. What was Vitellius doing with his power? Was it true that he was driven by his brother, that Lucius was the real power behind the throne?

But outside, a man gave a single, quiet order and another

voice was choked off in the kind of noise that only animals make, or men in great pain.

I stood and Pantera handed me my belt and made me presentable, as Demalion would have done.

'I suppose,' I said, 'we'd better learn what we can from our nocturnal visitor and then kill him before half the camp tries to tear him apart with their bare hands.'

CHAPTER THREE

Judaea, June, AD 69

Vespasian

'Say it.'

It was only just after dawn. The day was milk-white cool, a faint mist draped along the horizon waiting for the sun to burn it off.

The Syrian assassin hung by his wrists from the whipping post that had become both more and less than that.

Pantera stood nearby, his face and tunic mottled with blood. I saw his hands make a small, sharp movement and there was a pained, inaudible mumble that ended in a grunt.

'Louder. Who sent you?'

'*Lucius Vitellius!*'

The name bounced off the silence. Half the camp had heard what had happened and had come to watch. They were standing in lines, armour bright, glaring hatred at this man who had been their friend.

There was nothing more to be learned. My mouth was dry and my spit had the iron-sweet taste of another man's blood. How many men had I killed in battle, without pause for thought? How few had I killed like this, hanging by their wrists from a high hook, drained of all that made them men?

It could have been worse. Fundanius might have been a traitor and a failed murderer, but he had not lost his eyes to hot irons, or his fingers to a dull, serrated knife; his skin had not been peeled slowly from his back, nor his limb bones crushed and wrenched from his torso.

In honesty, there had been no need for more than a cursory beating and even that had been as much to satisfy his pride as to appease the rage of the men.

He had nothing to gain by lying and all he could tell us was what we already knew: that a successful general on the eastern borders of the empire was deemed a mortal threat to the men who now ruled in Rome.

I was not safe in Judaea.

Pantera knew it, had known it from the moment Vitellius had taken the throne.

Like Corbulo, I had been too successful. I had subdued the rebels in Judaea as I had been ordered to do and now I commanded the absolute loyalty of three victorious legions plus the goodwill of at least five others.

Vitellius, by contrast, was an indolent hedonist who had happened to find himself at the head of four Germanic legions at a time when their generals needed a figurehead to put on the throne, and even then they'd offered it to someone else first, and been turned down: Vitellius was everyone's second choice, and the world knew it.

And so now that world was looking to the east, to the eight legions of Judaea, Syria and Egypt, to see if they, too, would choose to name their own emperor.

Out there on the parade ground, with the milk-dawn sun just colouring our flesh, I was surrounded by the men of those legions, who knew exactly the power they held.

The ones nearest to me shifted and shuffled when I looked at them. Demalion caught my eye and didn't look away. He thought his face was closed, when in fact expectation was written all across it, and he was hardly alone; the same look was printed on the face of every officer I could see.

A centurion had been sent against them, Roman against Roman, and it offended their sense of the world even as it churned their blood to battle froth. They wanted vengeance and restitution and action; before all of these, they wanted blood.

The assassin sensed their mood. He lifted his bruised head and spat a few spiteful words at Pantera. Even at this distance, half a dozen paces away, I could hear the venom in his voice, if not the detail.

I thought it a last foul defamation, 'Fuck you all and may you rot for ever,' the kind of thing condemned men the world over say to their executioners before sentence is carried out.

But Pantera was interested, suddenly, in ways he hadn't been before. His face grew still. He asked a question and got another spit-thick answer which was clearly not enough. With barely a nod, he reached back to the brazier, selected an iron and slid it into the fire's red heart.

He pumped the bellows himself. The heat sent the nearest men back a pace. Everyone was still now; this was more than just the routine questioning of an assassin.

With a look of weary distaste, the spy slid his right hand into a leather glove and lifted the iron from the fire. The tip was white hot.

The assassin's skin blistered along his cheekbone in a line towards his eye. The smell of singed flesh tickled the air. Pantera's lips moved, but it was impossible to hear his question over the high shriek of his victim. The iron moved away. The question came again, and this time Fundanius drew breath to answer.

I think I stepped forward. Certainly I leaned closer to listen, to ask my own question.

'What did he—'

'*Lord!*'

Pantera and Demalion dived at me together. They collided in a crack of bone and flesh and brought me down, held within the solid shield of their bodies.

Above, a flash of silver caught the sun. I heard a grunt tinged with triumph and then, amid the sudden uproar, a howl of defeat that sent bile shooting sour up my throat.

I know the sound of a cohort shocked into fury. There were only two possible reasons to hear it now and I wasn't dead, which meant . . .

I shoved myself free, rolled to my feet, spun round to the whipping post.

Publius Fundanius, failed assassin, hung limp from his wrists, a squat-bladed throw-knife lodged in his throat. Blood traced a faltering arc from the wound; even as I watched, it slowed to a dribble.

He was gone beyond reach: dead; slain to secure his silence.

'Who did this? Hold him! Bring him to me now!'

Rarely have my men seen me angry. They fell back before the force of it.

'*Now!*'

It is not hard to find a traitor who throws a knife when he stands in a row with loyal men on either side, before and behind. Before the echoes of the last word had become dust in the sand, the crowd parted and two centurions dragged a third between them.

'Albinius?'

I would not have believed it, and yet could not do other-wise, for a wide, scarlet gash marked his throat, still leaking blood, and his own right hand was scarlet to the wrist.

'Albinius?' I said again.

I *knew* this man. True, he was a Syrian, but he wasn't some new conscript, brought in under duress and hating us for it; he was a volunteer of fifteen years' service, a cohort commander. He had fought at my side for the past two years. He had led, come to think of it, the third cohort of the Xth legion, into which Fundanius had so recently been promoted.

He was not dead yet; he had killed his co-conspirator cleanly enough, but, as with many others, his courage had failed him when it came to killing himself.

I took his ruined face by the chin, ungently lifted it. His eyes were losing focus, but they came to rest on my face. He smiled, and there was in it no shame, or apology, but a tinge of triumph and such loathing as I have only before seen on a battlefield, and then rarely.

'Albinius, why?'

He shook his head and tried to speak, but the words whistled shapeless from the cut edge of his windpipe.

He could not have told us anything even if we could have kept him alive long enough to force from him a name, or what he had been paid, how much and in what coin, to per-suade him to betray his general so completely. By his own hand, he was beyond revenge, or use.

The men were restless, needing blood, and, now, I could give them what they wanted. My gladius floated to my grip, light as a wheat stalk. With barely another thought, I drove it into Albinius' chest, striking just below the left nipple, aiming up and in and back towards the point of the right shoulder, as I had been taught too many years ago to remem-ber.

As it always does, my blade jammed between the ribs and I had to use both hands to wrench it free. Blood bloomed bright about the wound in his throat, foaming on the final breath.

The traitor's eyes glared their last light, and grew dull.

I said, 'Leave the carcasses outside the gates for the jackals. No honours.'

The men about me saluted in silence, but they didn't rush to do my bidding. Instead, the expectation I had read earlier on the faces of the officers was multiplied right along the row.

If I didn't act swiftly, they'd hail me imperator, there, on the spot, and I'd have to execute them all for treason, or lead them into civil war.

I turned back to Pantera. He was waiting a pace or two behind us, apart from the centurions, the tribunes and the legates.

In that short time, he had rinsed his face, his hands. Only his tunic was bloodstained. His expression was bland. It was over a year since he had sat in my tent and told me I could be emperor. Then, I had laughed in his face.

'We need to talk,' I said. 'Find Titus and Mucianus and tell them—'

'They're in the command tent, lord, awaiting your presence.'

'Oh, Hades, do you never stop? Bring Demalion then. He can guard the door.'

CHAPTER FOUR

Judaea, June, AD 69

Vespasian

The sun was up by then, not far enough to broil the day, just a cherried orb on the eastern horizon that stained the light in the tent to blood.

Not counting Demalion, who stood within the door flap, we were four who gathered around the table inside to talk treason, taking watered wine in our campaign mugs, eating brown olives, and small silvery fish, caught by their millions on the coast and dried on rocks in the sun.

I was the oldest, the greyest, the one who, seemingly, must carry the conscience for this treachery we planned.

The youngest, not yet thirty years old, was Titus, my elder son, the light of my life, my legacy to the world. I wouldn't say that in his brother's hearing, of course. Domitian knows, but he doesn't need to hear it said aloud.

Unlike his younger brother, Titus has been gifted an honest, open face, an athlete's never-ending grace, buoyant chestnut hair and a lively eye. If he is not beautiful – and let us be honest, he is too short to be beautiful, his face too round – he has the glorious vivacity of youth that sets lovers trailing after him by the score.

Already a legionary legate, commander of the XVth Apollinaris, with the path to senator and then consul laid wide before him, my son, Titus Flavius Vespasianus, had most to lose.

Mucianus, former consul and now governor of neighbouring Syria, might be a decade younger than I am – it's hard to tell his age with any accuracy any more than one can tell his exact parentage – but he was one of the few competent generals left alive after Nero's predations on the senate.

Unmarried, childless, he was quite evidently lost to Titus' smile, though I would wager my entire estate that the boy had not lain with him, and never will: Titus is made for women to exactly the same degree that Mucianus is not.

Even so, lust and ambition make for a heady wine and they had combined to transform this lean, driven man from the rival he once was to the kingmaker he wanted to become.

He had commanded the three Syrian legions during the recent Judaean war: the IVth Scythians, the VIth, and the newly reformed XIIth. They loved him just as my legions loved me and would have marched into Hades if he'd asked it of them. Just then, Mucianus was minded to ask them to propel me to the throne in Rome if only I would stop being obstinate and accept his offer.

And then there was Pantera, who was playing the role of secretary, a fiction that was laughable. Pantera was the one who had first suggested this path, nearly two years ago. Pantera was the one who had induced the Hebrew prophet to hail me the inheritor of their Star Prophecy that said a man would arise in the east and become lord of the whole world.

But it was Pantera who was so carefully not speaking now,

leaving Mucianus to make his points for him, which he was doing, I have to say, with the zeal of the newly converted.

'Vitellius is an incompetent idiot who excels only at eating and drinking, usually at others' expense. He wouldn't be emperor if the Rhine legions hadn't put him on the throne and even then they wanted Rufus first. He's a profligate wastrel who makes Nero look restrained in his spending. He'll bankrupt the empire, and reduce the senate to a bunch of drooling fools.'

'There are those,' said Titus idly, studying the tilted surface of his wine, 'who will say Nero accomplished that many years ago.'

Mucianus stopped. He tapped his long finger to his lips. His thoughts were so clear, and so graphic, that I didn't know whether to laugh aloud or drag him outside and flog him.

I could do neither, obviously. Addressing them both, I said, 'I am the second son of a tax farmer. My brother was the first senator in our family and he makes it universally known that I only followed him into public service at our mother's insistence. Since Octavian became Augustus, there has never yet been an emperor who was not of solid senatorial stock. Drooling idiots or not, the blue-blooded men of the senate won't have me.'

'If you'll forgive my saying so,' Pantera said, quietly, from the farthest end of the table, 'there have been three emperors in the past twelve months and the premium on ancestry has fallen noticeably with each one. If we delay, it is not Vitellius we must fear – incompetent and indolent as he is – but his brother Lucius. He is twenty years younger, more ambitious, more intelligent and more ruthless than any of his recent predecessors. If Lucius gains open control, there'll be more than two assassins sent against you; there will be dozens. With respect, you can't afford that, and if you won't fight on your own behalf, then do so for the people and the senate of Rome.

They want – and deserve – a leader who can set the empire back on its feet, who will rule with compassion, not caprice or cruelty, and who can count higher than ten without having to take off his boots to number his toes.'

Delivered of this speech, Pantera looked me clear in the eye. 'My lord, you have six legions here, and two more waiting under Julius Tiberius in Alexandria. He will have them swear their oath to you the day we give him the word. With all that help, you can be emperor. The question is, do you want to be?'

'Do I have a choice?'

It was a genuine question; I still thought I might wriggle out of it.

Mucianus answered. 'Not if you want to live, no. If those two are the only ones in your army in Lucius' pay, I'll eat my belt. We can hunt for traitors, but they won't give themselves away easily, and all we can be sure of is that Lucius will know soon that his men have failed. He will send others, or Vitellius will send orders for you to fall on your sword. Either way, you will die. The only chance to live is to take the field against them both. The choice, such as exists, lies in how this may be done. There is a way without bloodshed. Or there is the havoc of civil war.'

'Without bloodshed? Are you *insane*?' I slammed both palms on the table, and to hell with who might be listening outside. 'Vitellius may be an idiot, but his brother and his generals are not. They have four legions camped in Rome, eating at the city's heart like so many locusts. You told me yourself that they have *sixteen thousand* newly made Praetorian Guards. They have the massed naval fleets at Ravenna and Misene with their men in dock over winter and nothing better to do than pick their noses and fuck the local whores. They'll march when they're called to and be glad of it, particularly if Vitellius offers to make them into full legions. On top of that, he has legions scattered through the Balkans and the Germanies, any or all of which could block our route to Rome and may well do so. How, exactly, do you plan to take them on without bloodshed?'

'With minimal bloodshed, then.' Mucianus gave a merchant's shrug. 'Vitellius will have to relocate some of his legions before winter. Rome can't sustain those numbers for long: the people will revolt against feeding so many mouths.'

'He won't send them far.'

'He won't, but then we don't want him to. If you go to Egypt, you can threaten to choke off the grain supply to Rome. Shortages would be blamed on Vitellius and there would be riots. That'll maintain pressure on him, whatever else is going on. I, meanwhile, will march at the head of as many men as Judaea can spare – I think probably five legions – while your son Titus' – Mucianus flicked his long lashes at the boy, who had the grace to smile – 'Titus will remain here with command of those legions left behind. He will prevent a renewed insurgency and then complete the defeat of Jerusalem when you are safely made emperor. Thus you and he will be kept safe from harm and guilt while the war is prosecuted, and you can return to Rome bringing peace with you when the war has burned itself out.'

'And Pantera?' I asked. All eyes turned to the head of the table. The man was not a soldier, but none the less . . . 'What will you do?'

Pantera laid down his unused quill. He stretched out, languid as a cat on a bough. Only his eyes betrayed him, for they were not languid at all.

'I will come with you to Alexandria and introduce you there to those who can help your cause. The fellowship of Isis, I think, will support you, and others whose loyalty is un-shakable. After that, I will travel to Rome and work towards your ascent to the throne. To that end, I will bring to you the services of Seneca's spy network. We will need spies local to Rome; men and women who are so embedded in the fabric of society that their presence is taken for granted. We need freedmen, tradesmen, whores, taverners, ostlers, equestrians, senators and their women, all pulling in the same direction, all united by trust. Seneca created such a network and there is nothing in the empire to match it.'

I ran my tongue around my teeth, found a fragment of fish, and chewed on it until the salt burst on my tongue.

'Seneca is dead,' I said. 'He set himself against Nero and paid with his life.'

'His legacy lives on.'

'Under your command?'

'Under his successor, the new spymaster, known as the Poet. We have discussed your cause and the network will support it.'

'Really? And you only thought to tell me now?' I chose temporarily to forget that he had only arrived in the night, and had found himself in the middle of an assassination attempt.

I paced the floor; it helps me think. 'Why? Why are you doing this? You've been pushing me towards outright treason since you first brought back the Eagle of the Twelfth. Why?'

'Seneca's final request, his order, if you like, to those of us who served him, was that we find a man worthy of the empire and set him on the throne. In our opinion, you are that man.'

'The only worthwhile man in the entire empire?' Disbelief must have shown on my face. 'You can't be that desperate!'

Pantera said nothing, only blinked in a way that, beyond all reason, reminded me of my dream, and so of Caenis.

I turned on my heel. 'Come with me.'

Titus and Mucianus rose, but I waved them back, and poked Pantera with the heel of one hand. 'Only you.'

I needed to be alone and we couldn't go out the front; half the army was waiting there. So I pushed through the back flap of the tent into the small space outside where the night guards squatted to relieve themselves.

Pantera followed me and, with care, he and I negotiated a path to the centre, holding our breaths against the stink.

Above, a solitary hawk rode the winds, or perhaps it was a carrion bird, come to feed on the two dead men; at sixty, my sight is not what it once was.

I watched it a moment, seeking calm, and then looked again at the waiting spy. I had no idea, really, who this man was. I didn't even know if he was a Roman citizen. But I knew what he could do. I learned a long time ago that men are best judged by their actions.

'What did we lose?' I asked. 'What was the assassin about to reveal that was so dangerous to our enemies that Albinius had to expose himself to kill him? What did he say that made you heat the irons?'

'He said, "They hate you. They will see everything you care for destroyed."'

'Everything *you* care for? You? Not me?' That made the hair stand proud on my neck, I can tell you. I said, 'I thought you were secret? I mean, obviously people know you exist, but I was given to understand that nobody outside a select few knew you were a spy.'

Pantera's gaze was lost on some distant horizon. 'It's possible that Nero kept notes and they have been found.'

'Nero?' No one shed tears when that one died; maybe we should have done, seeing the mess it left us with. 'What did he know?'

'Too much. He was one of Seneca's protégés; he always knew more than was safe. I'll learn how much more when I get back to Rome.'

'You still plan to return?'

'If I stay away, Lucius and Vitellius have won before we start.' Pantera's smile was dry, no humour in it, no sudden vivacity. 'With or without me, the legions will put you on the throne. You don't need me, but I may be able to smooth the way. With your permission, I would like to try.'

He talked as if it were a given that we would launch this war. His eyes came to rest on my face, full of surmise.

I said, 'I have one condition.'

'Name it.'

I dragged the ring from my finger, the only one I ever wore. I have it back now. It looks cheap, it *is* cheap; gold and silver mixed, with the emblem of the oak branch on it. It looks like nothing, but everyone who knows me, knows it.

I held it out to him. 'See my family safe. I cannot bring them out of Rome: to endeavour to do so would make them immediate targets. And in any case, they won't leave.'

That was true. I have never had the authority over my family that I have over my men. Pantera knew that, I think.

'So do this for me. Go straight to Rome and act in my stead to see them safe. Sabinus, my brother, is prefect of the city. We have never had an easy relationship; he's a politician and I am a soldier and he will hate this, whatever he says, but he *is* my brother, and I would not have him hurt by my reckless-ness. Domitian, my second son, is only eighteen and a quiet boy, not made for war. He lives with Caenis, freedwoman of Antonia, and she is . . . if you know anything about me, you know what she is.'

Softly, 'I know.'

'Then know this: Lucius must not be allowed to kill these three out of hatred of me, for if I am emperor and any one of them has come to harm, all the power in the world will not repair their loss. Do you understand?'

He looked me squarely in the eye. 'I do.'

'Do you accept?'

'I do. I will protect these three with my life. And I will make sure that Seneca's network of local spies in Rome and its immediate provinces smooths your path to the—'

'No! Listen to me! Do you know what it means to love?'

It was the dream that drove me, and the sense of things sliding out of control. I gripped Pantera's arms, high, by the shoulders.

We were face to face, an arm's length apart. I could see the detail in his face, lose myself in the turbulent oceans of his eyes.

The emperor Tiberius once famously said that taking rule of the empire was like grasping a wolf by its ears; dangerous beyond comprehension, but impossible safely to let go.

Here, now, in the foul latrine space behind my own command tent, I found that I had grasped a leopard by the shoulders and I was not at all sure of the consequences.

I waited, and in his face I saw a wall brought down, a closed door opened. Where had been a mirror was now a glass, and what I saw through it was my own fear made barren. I saw who I would be if Caenis were to die, or Domitian; if I were betrayed by those I loved. The vision left me colder than the assassin's touch.

'I had a wife once,' Pantera said, and his voice was a husk. 'And a daughter.'

Had. I didn't want to ask, and must. 'What happened?'

'I killed them both, that the enemy who had defeated us might not take them as slaves. My daughter was three years old. I cut her throat while she lay in her mother's arms. And then I killed the woman I loved.'

What could I say? I stood silent, and after a while Pantera took my two hands in his own and lowered them from his shoulders.

Formally, he said, 'I have no brother, but know what it is to love a man as if he were that close. I might have killed my own daughter, but I have another still alive. I have never seen her, and she is raised as another man's child, but even so, I understand some of what you mean when you say Caenis, Domitian and Sabinus are dear to you.

'I swear to you now that I will protect the lives of these three with my own, or I will answer to you when you are emperor.' He shifted a little, listening. 'And now, my lord, I think you must dress, and go out to meet your legions.'

This once, he was late, for I had already heard it: the susurration of a thousand sandalled feet scuffing over sand, the hush of men trained in silent assault.

I was not under assault any more, but I had heard this sound so often in the pre-dawn dark of a raid on a village, or a town, or a cluster of caves in the desert, that it raised battle blood in my veins.

An unexpected flap of tent skin made me jump: Demalion was there, and Hades take him but the lad was smiling. Not broadly, not with Titus' ripe humour or Pantera's scarred irony, but the sweep of his mouth was unquestionably up instead of down, and it was this small miracle, with its promise of a flask of Falerian, that told me I had crossed my own Rubicon; that there was, in truth, no going back.

Demalion carried my tunic over his arm, and my armour pack, and my silvered greaves and the enamelled belt, worn through to the bronze beneath with three decades' wear. With his help, I dressed as fast as I have ever done, and then I lifted the tent flap with my own hand.

I looked left and right, to Titus and Mucianus who had come to join me. Behind were Pantera and Demalion.

'Shall we go to meet our destiny?'

Outside, the day felt newly minted; sharp, fresh, not yet too hot. My men were standing in parade order, line upon line, in their hundreds, their thousands, in their shining, dazzling tens of thousands: the IIIrd, the Xth, the XVth, that were my own, plus the IVth Scythians, the VIth Ferrata, and the ill-fated XIIth Fulminata commanded by Mucianus.

There was a moment's lingering stillness as each man took a breath and the suck of it rippled soundlessly back from the front lines to the rearmost.

It held one last, long heartbeat, and then the morning split asunder, rent by a wall of sound as, with one voice, thirty thousand men hailed me in the word that made me their ruler.

'*Imperator!*'

PART II

INTERNAL SPIES

Chapter Five

Rome, 1 August AD 69

Sextus Geminus, centurion, the Praetorian Guard

It was raining on the morning of the lead lottery that was my first true introduction to Pantera; the kind of torrential rain that felt as if the gods had upended the Tiber and were pouring the result on to our heads; the kind of rain where you were drenched to the skin as soon as you stepped out of the door; the kind of rain that everyone said was a bad omen.

But still, it was only rain; nobody was dying, and in any case, we were legionaries: if we were ordered out of barracks, we went.

Vitellius had given the order. He didn't believe in the power of omens and he wasn't going to cancel his precious ceremony just because the sky was weeping, so we were called to parade in the forum at the second watch after dawn and had to stand in our cohorts, listening to him read his speech.

We should have known it was bad then. I mean, really . . . we'd just marched the length of Italy, and risked our lives half a dozen times to put him on the throne. We'd fought other legions, just as good as us, when the men in them were our brothers, our fathers, cousins, friends and lovers. We'd killed men we admired and marched over their bleeding bodies in his name. Was it so hard to say thank you?

I've done it without notes, he could have done the same. But no, he had to read from his sodden scroll and we had to stand and watch it disintegrate in his hands. When he was done, we had to about-face and slow-march to the top of the Capitol.

There are three routes up that particular hill. If you're feeling fit, there's the Hundred Steps on the north face that take you straight up to the north gate, but it's a stiff and savage rise. If you want something slightly less vicious, there's the Gemonian steps on the southwestern aspect. That's the place where the bodies of executed criminals are exposed before they're tipped into the Tiber.

And then there's the long, slow, winding path that takes you up the south slope on to the Arx and then across the saddle of the Asylum before you reach the Capitol proper and the temple of the three gods.

This was the new emperor's opportunity to display his victorious troops to his city, which meant we had to take the slow route so that the masses could line the streets and cheer. They did, of course; to do anything else risked being arrested for sedition.

He'd already banned the astrologers, which did nothing much beyond ensuring that every street corner was decorated with graffiti telling in detail how the stars predicted his death. Everyone read it and half believed it, but nobody wanted to be next in line for exile, so the plebs turned up in force and stood in the driving rain to cheer us as we marched out of the forum.

I hadn't been back in Rome for long and it was interesting to see what had changed. Nero's giant statue was still there;

Galba had taken it down and Otho had put it back up again. I think Vitellius couldn't decide whether he wanted to make friends with the senate, who hated Nero, which meant he'd have to take it down, or with the people, who'd loved him, and wanted it to stay. I don't think the fact that it was still there meant he sided with the people, more that he was just really bad at making decisions.

So we passed Nero, and remembered not to salute as we'd done when we were last in Rome, and on we marched up the hill, past the statue of Juno Moneta and on towards the mint, where you could feel the blast from the furnaces even through the rain.

The coiners had been working night and day since we came back to Rome, melting down coins of the other emperors ready for reminting. Vitellius had only just got round to sitting for the celators so it was only the newest coins that had his image on.

It wasn't a bad likeness. If you only look at his face, he's a good-looking man, taller than any of us by half a head, with a strong nose and a bald circle on his pate that can look quite stately at times.

He was lame, though, which is less than ideal in a general, and it wasn't as if it was an injury gained in the field; he'd broken his thigh bone in a chariot accident, which is about as stupid as it gets, really.

So we passed the mint and the coins in my pouch jingled in sympathy with those being put to the fire, and my guts griped, and if I could have walked off down the path I would have done.

Why? Because the whole thing was a mistake. If you're going to follow someone all the way to Rome, you have to make sure it's the right man, and Vitellius was never that.

I said so in January when the whole thing started about not renewing our oath to Galba and swearing to Vitellius instead. I argued as long as I could, but there's a point when loyalty to the old regime becomes treachery to the new and I had my men to think of.

So I swore with the rest of them and after that . . . when it comes to the edge, a man's word is his only coin. If you can't keep an oath, you're no better than the barbarians.

On we trudged, past the row of dilapidated priests' dwellings, each leaning on the next like an old man in want of a stick, and on, shuffling in through the vast and ancient gates of the temple, which has been home to Jupiter, Juno and Minerva since the time when Rome was too poor to build them a temple each and had to house all three under the one roof. Later, when there was gold enough and more to spare, nobody was about to offend two out of the three most revered deities in the city by rehoming them elsewhere.

So we were left that day to wait under the combined gaze of the three, each one cast in bronze, three times life-sized, standing amongst the columns in mute tolerance of us mortals who milled around their feet.

It was cold, then. We had stopped marching and the rain sank into our bones. I was a stinking mass of fulled wool and wet linen; a drenched dog would have smelled better.

The priests had lit extra braziers against the cold, and were burning incense on them by the fistful. I breathed in feathers of blue smoke that tickled my nose to the edge of a sneeze until, eventually, we officers were summoned forward into the central sanctum. In there, I didn't sneeze at all.

Since I was a boy, I have been struck silent by this place, by the weight of empire bearing down on the roof beams. Built by the good king Tarquin at the founding of Rome, dedicated by the hero Horatius, a shrine of some sort has stood on this site since the city was no more than a spark in one man's imagination.

Legend said that if the temple were to fall, Rome would fall with it: everyone knew this. Nobody, of course, expected it to happen.

'Sextus Geminus! Formerly of the Fourth Macedonica!'

My head snapped up; it does when you hear your own name. I looked to the altar and there, staring at me, was Aulus Caecina, legionary legate of that very IVth Macedonica, the general who had driven us through the Alps at a time when everyone else said winter had made the routes impassable. If any one man made Vitellius emperor, it was him. I have never quite known how to be in his company, and knew now least of all.

At least he was alone. There were priests on either side of him, of course, but no other officers. I had been afraid that Lucius might have been there; seeing Caecina alone was the first good thing that happened that day.

I did what eighty-three men before me had done, and seventy-six did after. I took eight good paces forward, knelt before the bright, hot fire, and stretched out my left hand.

A priest standing at Caecina's right side thrashed the air about my head with a laurel branch, sign of victory. Another priest, smaller and broader in the beam, glanced down at his notes, filled his lungs and bellowed, 'Sextus Geminus! First centurion, fifth cohort, the new Praetorian Guards!'

So that was my new rank. It was the same as the old one, except that the Guard was . . . the Guard. Better paid, kept in Rome, responsible for guarding the emperor's life with our own.

Caecina was talking to me, genially enough.

'. . . so thoroughly deserved. I never saw a man swing his century faster to face a new enemy. This is small recompense for your dedication and valour—'

He was good. He caught my hand and slid on a silver arm ring, which was my reward for my part in the battle at Cremona. He pushed it up beyond the elbow with the same kind of deft, impersonal precision the priests use when they cut a bull's throat.

It was his words that mattered far more than what he did. There was a point in the assault on Cremona when I'd turned three centuries round to face an assault on our right flank and he remembered it as if he'd been there in the mud and the slaughter, hearing every cursed command.

Very likely, he remembered something equally relevant for every one of the hundred and fifty-nine men with me; it's who he was, and that kind of care for his men was one of the reasons we'd mutinied against Galba when he asked us to, and then followed him to the brink of civil war and back.

Like Corbulo, like Vespasian in the east, Caecina was a soldier's soldier and we all respected him for it. What the rest didn't know was what he was like behind closed doors. Nor had I until the night before.

The trophy ring fitted perfectly. Cool silver hugged my flesh, so that I could feel the hard, fast throb of my veins against it. My whole body was shuddering, finely, like a leaf; if anything was going to happen, it had to happen now.

And it did.

As Caecina stepped back, the priest threw more incense on to the altar; much more than before. A broad fan of smoke splayed out, cutting us off from the line of waiting men behind.

I was alone then, with the priests and the altar and this man who remembered everything. I swallowed and heard my own larynx pop. Caecina looked at me as if I'd farted.

From his side, the bass-voiced priest bellowed, 'Choose! And may the gods guide your hand!'

A black silk bag was thrust forward at waist height. As each man had done before me, I slid my hand through the bag's narrow mouth, and felt—

Nothing.

I panicked, I will admit that now, to you. This was a lottery. I was eighty-fourth in a line of a hundred and sixty men. I was expecting to feel seventy-seven tokens of folded lead from which I was required to select one. For nearly a day, I had been steeling myself against this moment.

But now it was here, my hand closed on empty air. In shock, I looked up at Caecina and read on his face such intensity of cold, flat anger that I shoved my hand back in again, fumbled about and – there! – felt a single filet of lead lying in the bottom, tucked into a corner hidden by the overlying fabric.

It was the length of my thumb, folded over at either end and sealed in the middle with wax, and when I drew it out I saw that the wax was black and that the imprint of a chariot stood proud on the matt surface. Vitellius was favouring Nero, after all: the chariot had been his emblem, too.

I didn't break the wax seal; my orders – all our orders, given to us in the officers' quarters just last night – were to wait, and open them later, in private.

I held the tab out on the flat of my palm to show I had taken it. Caecina, restored to good humour, nodded briskly and I took my eight paces back and that was it: over.

It wasn't over, of course, it was only just beginning, but it felt like a huge step taken. I wasn't alone in feeling heartsick, I think; it was on other faces as we shuffled on sideways and sideways and watched each man take his eight steps forward and pick his lead from the lottery.

There was a tedious similarity to the proceedings broken by small differences in the rewards for our endeavours; Juvens, three men after me, was awarded a spear for personal valour, not an arm band, and Halotus, who came eight after him, was given on behalf of his entire century a disc to display on their standard.

Whatever he was awarded, though, each man at the same

time took a folded token from the black bag and stepped back, keeping the seal unbroken.

The lead grew warm and soft in the waiting. I kneaded it between my fingers; by the time the lottery came to an end, it was an acorn, which once had been a small, flat lozenge.

'Gentlemen!' Caecina held up a hand. His voice was high for a man's, sharp and clear. 'You each have a tab and, on it, a name. You know what to do. Know as you do so that we are, once again, a nation at war with itself.'

That got our attention: I had heard the news the night before, but my fellow officers had not. All along the row, we stood more upright, our eyes fixed on our general.

Caecina pitched his voice well; he knew how to play a crowd. 'We have news from the east. On the first of July, the prefect of Egypt swore his oath to Vespasian as emperor. His legions did likewise and they were followed by the legions of Judaea and Syria respectively. He is appointing senators, prefects, praetors. He is minting coins in his own image and collecting taxes in his own name. He is choosing senators and consuls to serve his version of Rome and he is recruiting armies to march at his command. In short, he is behaving as if he were already emperor and we the traitors standing against him. He is preparing for war and we must be ready to fight.

'Eight legions are ranged against us. There will not be any more, because our emperor is loved by his men, but they are enough for us to show once again that we are the best the empire can command.

'Go now, and prove yourselves first with this one assignment. And then, next spring, we will march against the traitors.'

Chapter Six

Geminus

Dismissed, I had no further duties until I took command of the watch at dusk.

Outside, the rain had eased; we were greeted by grey skies, but the gods were no longer weeping. My fellow Guards surged in a pack towards the barracks on the Field of Mars at the back of the Quirinal hill. All the chatter was of Vespasian's eight legions and where and how they might be beaten, which was pointless, because we all knew that even if they'd set off on the first day of July with their oaths to Vespasian still hot in their throats, it would take them half a year to reach Rome and they'd get here in the middle of winter when nobody fights.

I didn't want to hear a hundred men explaining the unlikely detail of how they'd smash the enemy lines single-handed, so I drew back from the rest to take short cuts that turned out to be long cuts, but meant that I was alone and nobody was asking questions, and I was free to learn my way around Rome again.

I grew up here. Rome was my birthplace and my home, but I joined the legions when I was nineteen and that was twelve years ago and I'd only been back once, just before the fire, and that disaster had changed everything.

We lost four out of fourteen districts and Nero's building programme afterwards was as radical as any we'd seen. He set statues where once were eighteen-storey slums, and slums where once were temples, so that there were areas of the city that felt completely alien to me as I walked through them. Only the seven hills were unchanged; their outline was – is – moulded on my soul.

That day, with the lead lottery done, I came down the Capitol and made my way through the forum. From there, I turned left up the Quirinal, at least notionally heading in the direction of the Guards' barracks.

This hill is not like the Palatine, home to senators and equestrians and merchants who have too much gold and need to show it off. The Quirinal is a thrifty place that offers residence to impecunious senators, bad gamblers, and the recently arrived who have not yet carved a place for themselves elsewhere.

I like it there; I always have. Free of my colleagues and their inane battle fantasies, I walked faster up the hill.

The Quirinal is like the rest of Rome in that money and status buys you height. As the hill rose, shabby shop fronts gave way to marginally more prosperous dwellings. Villas lined the road, and tucked away to one side halfway up were three parallel streets of small, neat houses funded by the imperial coffers for the widows of fallen generals, and then beyond them the bachelor homes of impecunious but worthy men who had lost their wives: in Rome, few things are left to chance and this proximity was no accident.

I came to a forked junction and took the left-hand path, which led to one of the widows' streets.

Here were flowers outside the doors, and the doors themselves had legion shapes carved on them: a Capricorn, a Taurus, a Thunderbolt. The women did not grieve openly for their lost menfolk, but the signs were there if you knew what to look for.

I had gone barely ten paces when I heard light footsteps behind me. Six months on campaign and you don't take these things lightly. I snapped round, blade sighing free.

'Juvens?'

Marcus Decius Juvens was standing just out of striking distance, a half-smile on his face, his head cocked to one side. He was a good man. I let drop my hand. 'What are you doing here?'

'I saw you go off on your own and wondered why.'

'Why d'you think? Did you hear the Runt saying how he'd disembowel Vespasian and all his armies at a single stroke? Or Arminios swearing on his Germanic gods to stand at the gates of Rome and slaughter anyone who tried to come through after the ides of September? Pointless bloody nonsense.'

'But harmless all the same.' Juvens looked like Julius Caesar's more cheerful younger brother, which he claimed was all good breeding and it might have been true. Certainly, he was from ancient patrician stock so refined that he could quote his ancestry for the past eighteen generations without pausing for breath.

Unfortunately for all concerned, his grandfather had lost the family fortune, and although his father had made half of it back, he had been careless enough to become entangled in Piso's conspiracy against Nero and so, along with fifty others, including Lacan, Seneca, and Piso himself, had been forced to suicide. Juvens senior's estate, such as was left of it, went to the crown.

He had two sons, of whom the elder, now penniless, subsequently tried to have himself elected consul and was so soundly beaten in the ballot that he retreated into self-imposed exile in Iberia. Our Juvens had survived by virtue of being the second son, too insignificant to be noticed. Scraping together loans at extortionate interest, he bought his commission and bribed his way to one of the furthest legions from Rome: the IVth Macedonica, stationed on the Rhine.

It was a risky strategy; at least half of those who buy their way to a junior commission find themselves dead with a blade in the back at their first skirmish, but Juvens was bright enough, wild enough, hard-drinking, hard-gambling, hard-whoring, hard-fighting enough to be loved by the men before we ever went into battle together.

They owed him money, too; Juvens' luck at dice was legendary. He paid off his debts in full within his first year. By the time we came back to Rome, rumour said he was almost as rich as his grandfather had been in his pomp.

None of that mattered, at least not as far as I was concerned, because Juvens had proved himself in war. In the past six months he had more than earned the spear Caecina had just given him for personal valour. He was an exceptional commander with an outstanding eye for a battlefield. I had fought twice at his side and would have been happy to do so for the rest of my life, although at that moment, standing like a fool in the widows' street with my blade half drawn, I wasn't sure the sentiment was returned: Juvens seemed to like everyone equally, which couldn't be true.

In blithe disregard of our orders, he asked, 'Who did you draw in the lottery?'

'I don't know. I haven't opened the tab yet.'

The first part of that was a lie, as you'll learn, and I'm sorry for it, but the truth was that we shouldn't have been discussing it at all: an open street is the very opposite of 'private'.

I said, 'You?', which made me equally guilty. It was a day when convention didn't count as much as it had done, when the rules had become suddenly flexible.

I live by rules, I'm not used to bending them. But I wanted to find out if Juvens would be happy to have me at his side in the coming days; I thought I was going to need some friends I could count on and I didn't have many. Allies? Yes. Drinking partners? Plenty. Men I could go whoring with? More than I could count. But friends? I had none I could name. Except perhaps Juvens, who studied me a moment, grinning, and said, 'Trabo.'

'Fuck, no!' I whistled. 'He'll kill you.'

'Probably.' Juvens looked ridiculously cheerful; he'd always had a wild side. 'I have to find him first, but if it's true he took an oath to see Vitellius dead, he'll have to come to Rome to do it. I'll know him when I see him.'

'And then you'll kill him. If you can.'

Because this was what the morning's lottery in the temple had been for: to convey the orders for the execution of a hundred and sixty 'enemies of the state'.

Arriving in his predecessor's palace, Vitellius had found a document in the archives, signed by a hundred and twenty officers and men of the old Praetorian Guard, asking to be recognized by Otho for their part in the murder of *his* predecessor, the emperor Galba.

Vitellius – or at least his brother Lucius – would happily have cut Galba's throat with his own knife, if someone else had held him still. But it had been done by the Guards, whose duty was and is to defend any emperor's life with their own, and no emperor was going to feel safe in the company of men who had already been suborned into killing one of their charges and might equally do so again. Which is why they had all been dismissed and the new Guard raised from those of us whose loyalty had been demonstrated on the field.

Thus it was that on that day, the day of our investiture, each of us hundred and sixty new centurions had been given the name of one of the transgressors – there were plenty to go round beyond the hundred and twenty of the old Guard – with orders to kill on sight.

If it were only that, I might have been happy, or tranquil at least. But it was not. The emperor's brother, Lucius, had called me into his office the night before and that was when my life had changed for the worse.

It was the last hour of the dusk watch and I had been walking past Caecina's quarters in the barracks above the Quirinal hill when I heard him call my name.

Turning, I had found the general standing in the doorway, beckoning me. I followed him into the legate's office, and there, seated behind a small table next to the only brazier, was Lucius Vitellius. Even then, he was considered the most dangerous man in Rome. The emperor, as we have said, was pot-bellied, lame and prone to drinking through the night. Darker and more saturnine, his brother Lucius was abstemious, fast as a snake and twice as vicious.

I knelt so fast I cracked my knees on the marble floor. I had no idea if I was actually required to kneel before the emperor's brother, but you'd have to think it wise at least to begin there.

A moment's silence followed, and then a sigh. 'Get up, centurion!'

The voice was soft, rolling, almost friendly. I have heard inquisitors speak like that before they break a man. Rising, I kept my eyes on the floor.

Lucius said, 'You were in Rome on the night of the fire five years ago, is that correct?'

'It is, lord. I was sent back from my legion by—'

'Thank you, we don't need details. We need someone who can identify the spy, Pantera, also known as the Leopard. He was with Nero on the night of the fire. I am told he controlled much of the defences?'

I was about to deny any knowledge of who did what – that night was a flame-filled horror of which I remember mercifully little, although my dreams since have been plagued by the stench of burned flesh, and the sound of children screaming – but there was a moment after, in the strange calm of the morning . . .

'Lord, does he bear a scar on his face above one eye, and is he stiff in the left ankle?'

Lucius glanced at Caecina, who nodded.

They both stared at me, so I went on with what I knew. 'I was with Nero in his flower garden at dawn the following morning. I was on duty there. He and this man – Pantera – had a . . . discussion . . .' Do you say to the emperor's brother that a man argued with an emperor and did not die for it? Nero was different then; there were still people who were not required to kneel in his presence.

I took a glance at Lucius and decided these were details he didn't need. In fact, now that I studied him properly, he looked like a man who'd had little sleep with no promise of more to come.

His hair hung black to his brow and there were dark circles under his eyes. If he'd been shaved, it was not in the past day. It was said that the emperor planned to leave Rome soon, to escape the stench of a city in summer, the press of an empire's attention, the constant clamour of those who craved his smile, his word, his law.

In his place, it was said, he planned to leave his brother to carry the weight of the empire, and what man can say that wasn't the worst of burdens?

Not my business. They wanted to know about Pantera and so I told them what I knew.

'There was a boy Nero wanted that the others didn't want

him to have. Pantera bought him with a promise.'

'What kind of promise?'

Caecina asked that, and this was not the affable general, the man-amongst-men who led from the front all the way from the Rhine, beloved by his officers and men alike, and known for his leonine courage and humour. This Caecina was angry, clearly, but it wasn't clear with whom. He radiated a kind of hard, brittle danger; nothing so crude as a blade in the belly, more the threat of crucifixion, or worse.

I was always taught that, if in doubt, it was safest to fall back on formality. Crisply, I said, 'In return for the boy's life, Pantera promised to find the man who set fire to Rome, and to kill him.'

Lucius lifted a lazy brow. 'Did he succeed?'

Caecina said, 'We believe so, lord. He killed the arsonist, and then, later, helped to return their stolen eagle to the Twelfth legion.'

Listening to that, I thought Pantera sounded exactly the kind of man who should have been helping to rebuild Rome after a year of civil war. I didn't say it, I'm not prone to suicide, but it must have shown on my face.

In a voice that crackled at the edges, Caecina said, 'Pantera has given himself to Vespasian. We have reason to believe he has committed Seneca's entire network of agents to the traitor's cause.'

Standing, Lucius walked around the desk. He was nowhere near as tall as his brother, but far leaner. Fitting his shoulders against the wall opposite, he fixed his gaze on me.

'Vespasian is en route to Egypt. Mucianus is marching towards Rome with his legions. He will take six months to reach us, or at least to be close enough to do us harm. In that time, we must make Rome secure. Do you understand?'

'Yes, lord.' Only an imbecile would fail to grasp that much.

'Good. In order to bring about this security, we are

creating the new Guard, as you know. Tomorrow's investiture ceremony will include a lottery, in which each of the new centurions will draw the name of an enemy of the state, apparently at random. You will draw Pantera's name; of those we trust, you alone can identify him.

'Your fellow officers have orders to kill their target on sight. You, however, will do your utmost to bring Pantera and his accomplices to us alive in order that they may be questioned. Failure to do so will be seen as complicity with his cause. Is that clear?'

'Yes, lord.'

'Then go. Pantera's ship docked at Ravenna last night. When we know where he's going, you will be informed. You may choose two or three good men to accompany you, but you will be circumspect in what you tell them. It goes without saying that this conversation has not happened. Do you understand?'

'Lord.'

I backed out of the doorway, bowing as much to hide the sweat on my face as out of respect for the two men inside.

That was the night before the lottery. I had lain awake through the hours of darkness wondering how they were going to rig it so that I chose Pantera's name and by noon I had found out – and I dared not speak of it to Juvens, who had just drawn the name of the man most revered in all the legions.

Everyone has heard of Trabo, tribune of the Guard, but I can perhaps give you a soldier's perspective. What marked him out was that he was one of us; an ordinary soldier who became extraordinary.

He didn't come from a senatorial family. His father was barely an equestrian, although he had been a centurion with the VIth, and there was a great-grandfather back somewhere down the line who'd won a neck ring for valour serving under Marc Antony in the wars of the Triumvirate, but that was it.

Trabo joined up at eighteen and from the start he was . . . you'd want to say unique, but the point is that he wasn't. He was one of us but he was just that little bit better than all of us at everything.

He could run a little faster, jump that hand or two higher, fight harder. When we put on displays for the generals, his javelin was the one that flew farthest and hit the mark most cleanly. If he'd lived in the old days of Greece, he'd have been an Olympian. In the legions he won silver to put on his belt or about his neck or on his arms, and by his mid-twenties he'd won pretty much every award there was to win and was heading up the ranks.

He made centurion at the ridiculously young age of twenty-five and nobody thought it was ridiculous in his case. He was promoted to the Guard at thirty, which was almost unheard of, but nobody begrudged him his place; he was Roman, you see, and that mattered. I'm Roman, too, but half of my men are Rhinelanders. It wasn't right, making them Guards.

But that's a different story. Trabo rose up the Guard ladder in the same way he'd risen up the legionary one and he was a tribune by thirty-five; the youngest for generations, perhaps the youngest ever. He was fiercely loyal to Nero and men said he wept when the boy stabbed himself in the throat. Then Galba took Nero's Guard as his own when he took the throne, and by all accounts Trabo was as loyal to his new emperor as he had been to his old.

But he was also a friend of Otho's. Otho had been a member of Nero's entourage and Trabo had stood guard over him, which, in practice, meant he'd gone drinking, whoring and gambling with him but not had any of the drink, the girls or the money. Well, not as much as Otho had.

For all that, they were both men of principle, both were

active, both understood where Rome needed to go and that it wasn't in the direction Galba was pushing it. When Galba named that mewling catamite Piso as his heir, Trabo was at Otho's right hand to make sure the mistake was rectified swiftly: Piso died first, but only by a matter of hours; Galba was gone soon after.

Would I have done the same? I think I might. It's not laudable: a man should be loyal to his superiors, but Galba was a disaster and everyone knew it; he had to go.

Otho would have been a good emperor. If I hadn't already committed to Vitellius, I would have followed him happily. I don't regret it; you can't choose your generals, but you can make the most of what they give you and offer unswerving loyalty in return.

Anyway: Trabo was a legend, a good man with a solid heart, the build of an ox and the skills of a trained killer. Trying to catch him single-handed might not have been a suicide mission, but it was close.

If one man could do it, that man was Juvens; he was the closest we had to our very own Trabo. And so you had to at least consider whether he, too, had slid his hand into a lottery pouch that contained only one tab of lead.

Our eyes met. Neither of us spoke, but on an impulse I said, 'Do you want help?'

'I was hoping you'd say that.'

We were away from the widows' houses by then, on a connecting street with only the windowless backs of buildings looking on to it. We were alone, and Juvens was walking backwards down the centre of the street where he was less likely to tread in the piles of mule dung.

His wild, reckless grin was gone. 'If we're going to be partners,' he said, 'you'd better open your tab. I'll look the other way.'

I knew what was on the tab, and if I was right, Juvens

knew that I knew. But we had to keep up appearances. *It goes without saying that this conversation has not happened.*

And so, in an odd kind of privacy, and not at all as I had imagined, I stood in a middling alleyway between two sets of mildly well-off villas, broke the black seal with my thumb and folded open the much-kneaded lead to reveal the name inscribed within.

'And?' Juvens was at my side. 'Anyone difficult?'

'Sebastos Abdes Pantera.' It was the first time I had spoken the spy's full name. It felt jagged in my mouth.

Juvens' frown was all confusion and surprise; you could tell he'd been expecting someone better known, or even known at all. 'A friend?' he asked.

'No, a spy. He helped keep the fire from consuming all of Rome.'

'One of Nero's men?'

'We have to suppose so. I've only seen him once. He won't know who I am.'

I didn't know Pantera then, so I believed that. Even so, my fist closed tight on the lead, squeezing it small.

'I would offer to swap,' Juvens said, 'but . . .'

But that would be treason. I smiled, thinly. 'I appreciate the offer. And I'll still help you with Trabo. I promise you, he will prove the simpler to kill.'

CHAPTER SEVEN

Rome, 3 August AD **69**

Quintus Aurelius Trabo

I hadn't met Pantera before that day, and I wouldn't say my life was incomplete without him.

I heard about the lottery soon after it had happened; everybody did. By the evening of the next day, a dozen different stories were circulating of who had drawn what name, and by the day after that, the complete list was making its way north up the Flaminian Way.

Word reached the drovers sometime after we crossed the river Nar, about a day short of Rome in the cart I was in. Men were reciting names of the hunted and their hunters and mine was first on everyone's lips. Set against me was Juvens; the best officer in Vitellius' army.

So I knew then what kind of calibre of a man they'd put on my tail. It felt like an honour, and did nothing to stop me from heading into Rome. I knew I could beat him: he wasn't that good.

It stopped raining that day, I remember, the day I came

back to Rome. They'd had three days of torrential rain and then the gods unleashed a blistering sun that lifted a haze off the mud and set the flies dancing in their millions.

It would have been easier if we'd been able to move a bit faster, but every man and his mule was on the road, making the most of the weather to bring the smallest bit of mouldy corn and mildewed leather into Rome while there was a profit to be had.

The emperor Vitellius had sixty thousand mouths to feed in a city already starved by last year's abysmal harvest, and anyone who could cut his crops ahead of his neighbour was likely to see his wheat worth its own weight in gold; at least, that was what we thought.

Rome needed wool, too, so I was a carter's assistant, driving a team of four oxen yoked to a frame with wheels tall as two men, and slung between them a cart that carried forty bales of wool.

What did I look like? Well, not a tribune of the Guard, that's for sure. It had been four months by then since Otho died; that is, since he took his own knife and killed himself so that other men might not have to die in his stead. There never was a man like Otho and I grieve for his loss with every waking day.

Me? Yes . . . I was perhaps a little taller than the average carter's assistant, a little broader in the shoulder. All right, a lot broader. I wasn't going to let my battle fitness go just because I wasn't training every day in the Guard; there are ways to stay fit that don't involve wearing lead weights and running up the hills of Rome.

I was dressed like a carter, that's what counted: a fifth-hand woollen tunic, good strong boots, a hat with a broad brim – and a beard.

The Guard is ever clean-shaven; that beard was my best disguise. My belt was a good one, too: a hand's breadth of ox-hide that would have cost a fortune in leather-starved Rome where the sacrifices were flayed and their hides sent straight to the tanners and from there straight to the legions.

In any war, the makings of armour become as scarce as food, and this war had grumbled on for over a year now; everything was in short supply. So if nobody looked too closely at the face behind the beard of the carter's assistant, it was because they envied the breadth of my belt, or were already trying to estimate the worth of the eighty bundles of unwashed fleece in the cart behind, or had been knocked back by the stink of raw lanolin that had the flies dancing in ecstasy for a full three yards all around us.

The carter didn't know who I was, of course. He didn't want to find out. We parted as we had joined, with a handshake and a nod, not long after the cart had passed through the gate that lies north of Augustus' tomb.

So that was me, Quintus Aurelius Trabo, formerly a tribune of the Praetorian Guard, now an outlaw with a price on my head, coming home.

So much had changed since I had left, and so little. It was spring when I marched out of the city in the van of Otho's legions, barely two months after Galba's assassination.

I've searched my conscience over my part in that and I'm not ashamed. It was bloody and vicious and brutal, but even now, I wouldn't undo any of it. The old man was a martinet, a throwback to the old days of the Republic, a disaster in the making.

Otho, on the other hand, knew how to think, and when to act. He was young, not yet quite forty, and had the resilience, courage and foresight that Rome needed then and, if you'll take my opinion, she still needs now. He was generous with his money and intelligent about how it was spent. He had honour and battle sense and the ability to talk up or down to the idiots in the senate when they needed it.

When he died, my world died with him, and I'll admit now that I thought hard about joining him in his honourable oblivion. I might have done it, too, but he had given me a letter to deliver and told me not to return to Rome too soon, to allow some time for things to settle. I knew what he was about, but I promised him I'd do whatever he asked and keeping that promise was one of the two things that brought me back.

The other was just as important. You'll have heard the rumour that I took an oath over his still-warm body to avenge him? It's true. That was the reason I carried a knife in the top of each boot and enough gold in the back of my belt to fund a small army, which was exactly what I planned to do.

It was early evening by the time we reached Rome. We'd set off at dawn, but the road had been so bloody slow we'd lost the best part of a day travelling less than ten miles. The first thing I saw when we were through the gates was the way the low sun glanced off the slow summer waters of the Tiber, lighting up the city. A weaker man, or one with less business ahead of him, would have wept at that.

I left the carter more or less at the place where the fire started five years ago. Then, it was all old wood and straw; it's not at all surprising that it went up in flames. Now, the streets are wide apart and there are water butts at every junction, and gongs to call the Watch if anyone sees so much as a spark.

I wandered round, getting my bearings, and struck off towards the Quirinal, and the Guard barracks that sits at the back of the hill. It had been my home for ten years and I wanted to be near it, even if I couldn't go in. Plus I had

Otho's blessed letter to deliver. I'd promised that I would do everything I could not to endanger the recipient, so I planned to reconnoitre on the first day, to see if the address was being watched. Daft as it seems now, I hadn't thought other people would be doing the same.

I listened as I walked; the talk of the streets is always interesting. They were still talking about the lead lottery, of course, or the death lottery as it was becoming known, but there were those, even amongst the merchants, who were still harking back to the fact that the emperor had made Guards of men who were not born and bred in Rome, as if this somehow diminished their own worth – the carters, the drovers, the merchants – as citizens of a great city.

This is old news now, and people are used to it, but back in the summer men were still reeling over the thought that it was possible for the legions to name an emperor outside the city and then give him his prize. That had never been done before, see, and the opinion of the gutter was that it wasn't a clever thing to have done then. Not any of it.

Everyone hushed up when the Guard came, and fuck me but there were a lot of them – far more than there had been in Nero's day. They were patrolling in their eights, one after another after another, looking uncomfortable, out of place in a city that wasn't their home, amongst people who fell silent whenever they walked past.

But they passed by, that's the point. They were hunting Trabo, tribune of the Guard, and none of them cast a second glance at a bearded carter. I grinned at them like a fool and they stared right through me and walked on. I know how slaves feel, now. There's a power to that invisibility if you can harness it.

To be safe, I pulled my hat down so the brim shaded my face and struck off through the evening crowds. In summer, the streets fill up at this time; the day's trading is largely done and the vendors are winding up their awnings and taking their stock into the back rooms to lock it away for the night.

For me, the big difference was that this evening was the first time I'd been in Rome when nobody knew who I was. The crush wasn't nearly at its height, but even so I was having to push my way through a solid wall of flesh when for the past ten years crowds had just . . . parted.

I had to remember not to shove the bastards aside in the emperor's name. I was talking to myself in my head: 'Stoop, round your shoulders, smile, back away, don't push, *don't* push. Don't hit him, either. You can't afford to start a fight.' It was frustrating, I can tell you. I'm not slippery like Pantera, I'm not naturally given to double-dealing and lies, but I found that if I treated it like a game, it was bearable.

At a certain point, with the sun low on my right, I finally turned up the first shallow slopes of the Quirinal hill.

The stench of dung and rotting vegetables, of old fish and dead dogs, lessened a little as I went up, or I told myself it did, and if it was mostly a lie, I was glad of it.

The taverns here were cleaner, their inmates increasingly more freedmen than slaves, more officers than men. In all senses, the crowds were more colourful, and more than a little drunk. I turned right into a narrow side road lined on either side by neat houses in white limed brick.

Small, self-contained, with few rooms and fewer slaves, these were the widows' houses, paid for by a gift of Augustus that no emperor had dared revoke. Summer flowers bloomed in tended troughs outside swept doorways. There was no great wealth displayed, but there was a delight in order that made my heart sing.

Each door was marked with a sign that identified the legion or emblem of a departed husband. Eighth along on the left a pair of oak leaves was engraved above the lintel: that was the sign I had been given. There were no Guards outside, none obviously watching. I walked on past to the western end of the street and the Inn of the Crossed Spears.

It'd always been a favourite of the Praetorian Guard and clearly still was. It was heaving with men in uniform and men who had only just shed their uniforms. And tonight, of all nights, the management had hired a troupe of acrobats, which meant, in turn, that all the charlatans of the street had slunk out of their hiding places and come to make the most of off-duty men with ready money.

There was an astrologer, one of the many who hadn't fled the city yet. Not far off was a salt-haired, owlish little dream-teller, and beyond him an ice-blonde Nordic woman who dealt in philtres and curses, ready to etch the name of a rival on a slab of lead to be thrown into an open grave that ill fortune might follow the one named, just as ill fortune followed those named in the lead lottery two days before in the Capitoline temple.

What I discovered in this inn, listening to the men talking, was that a dozen of those named in the lottery had already died, men who had been less careful when they returned to Rome, who'd probably been there for months and thought themselves safe.

Each name branded itself on my liver, each death was like wood hurled on to the fire that burned in my heart, sending it roaring until my blood fizzed in my ears and my head rang. I made myself breathe slowly, look around, smile, join the jokes.

I passed the dream-teller and threw a coin, laughing, and then, in a flush of pretend goodwill, bought a drink for myself and three junior officers of the Guard who stood in a cluster nearby. They were strangers to Rome, these men; they didn't know me, and I didn't know them, but I knew their like and how to play them with the right mix of deference and reverence, and the offer of wine; I was them once, or their like.

The risk seemed to work, for the officers clapped me on the shoulder and bought me a drink in return, and I had that giddy feeling of unnatural luck, as if the gods had cloaked me in more than simply four months' growth of beard and a worn leather hat. I accepted the beaker of raw wine that was pressed on me, though I spilled more than I drank, and I used the centurions as a shield while I kept my eye on the oak-leaf door halfway along the widows' street; I could just see it from where I stood without straining.

Presently the centurions went on their way. I was heading back to buy another drink when a hand caught my wrist.

'Do you dream of oak leaves, carter?'

It was the dream-teller. Small, dry, with a face like old driftwood crusted with salt-white hair, the man was impossible to age. I shook his hand off my arm and would have struck him, but I remembered who I was: a drunken carter.

'I dream of wine,' I said, thickly, 'and then women.'

'Do you so?' Sharp eyes stitched across my face, pinning the lie. 'When you are ready to dream of oak leaves, come and find Scopius and he'll tell you the fortune they bring.'

I was a carter; my only need for fortune was in good sales. Tugging on my hat, I forced a grin.

'I'll be gone before that, old man, while you'll be lucky if you're still alive. All soothsayers are to be out of the city by the first of October, or they'll sew you in a sack with a snake and a dog and throw you in the Tiber.'

'They won't sack me.' Scopius had the gaze of an owl, if an owl had eyes the colour of a dusk sky. 'I'm a dream-teller, not an astrologer. I know nothing about the stars, only about the dreams that grow beneath them. Come back when you're ready, *carter.*'

It was the edge he put on that last word that destroyed my evening. If he knew, who else?

Alert now, with an itch between my shoulder blades, I turned away and pretended a fascination with the acrobats.

In the short time I had been distracted, they'd stretched a tightrope across the street from one wall to the other, and now they were dancing along it, leaping up on to each other's shoulders, building a six-man pyramid with the lower three all balanced on the rope.

I thought at least the small one on top and definitely the blonde one in the middle row were girls. Looking more closely, I became sure of it; their tunics were short about the thigh to let them move freely, and belted tight. Their breasts were not full, but they were there, pliable, and firm and lovely.

The top girl, a dark-haired androgyne, leapt high into a neat-tucked somersault and I don't think I was the only man suddenly to think of bedding her. It was five months since I last had a woman and here was one, near naked, athletic as you like, almost within reach. I thought of the gold in my belt, and what it might buy me. There were houses in Rome, one on the side of the Capitoline in particular, that I had heard of, where you had to show your fortune even to get into it, but once in . . . there was nothing you couldn't do, if you were prepared to pay for it.

I had to think of the war and Otho's death to drag my mind away from that and from the acrobat girls. I got myself another drink and sat down at the entrance to the courtyard to watch the door with the oak leaves carved above the lintel.

It was a lifetime's instinct, I think, that told me I was not the only one interested in it.

CHAPTER EIGHT

Rome, 3 August AD **69**

The lady Jocasta Papinus Statius

I saw Trabo before I saw Pantera, and yes, I knew him. We had played together as children, my brother had been in love with him for years; I recognized him immediately. He didn't recognize me.

I was in the courtyard of the Inn of the Crossed Spears. Pantera had sent a message to say he was back in Rome, and that we needed to meet.

How well did I know him? Did anyone claim to know that man? I had met him twice before that I knew of. Seneca did his best to keep his better pupils apart so that none of us, if taken, could reveal the identities of the others, so we only met after his death. The meetings hang in my memory, all of them.

The first was in spring, the bright time of flowers, in Nero's reign, soon after Seneca's forced suicide. Gone with him in the same failed conspiracy were Lacan and Piso and Piso's wife and fifty other good men and women who had cared about the future of Rome. The city was brittle as winter ice with the shock of it. Men talked in whispers, women planned for widowhood and everyone crept from dusk to dawn like mice under the eye of a starving cat, wondering where Nero's paranoid gaze might fall next.

Pantera had been in Judaea. At my summons, he came to the house of Seneca's widow, the small, quiet woman who had been restrained from killing herself alongside her husband and now walked in the misery of the recently bereaved. She opened the door to him and then went outside, to see who might be watching, and to give us privacy to talk, that she might not hear what we had to say about her late husband. He had shared many things with her, but even so, there were some matters she was better off not knowing.

So we were alone in Seneca's spare, quiet house and I'm sure I was not the only one for whom it was full of memories.

The small central atrium had no columns, and only four shuttered windows to the outside with two rooms off. I had arrived first and arranged the room as I needed it, then gone to stand by the window, with the morning sun coming in over my shoulder.

That day, when he walked over the threshold, I saw what he wanted me to see: an unremarkable nobody with a stiff left ankle. I knew from what I'd been told that he had been questioned in Britain and had more scars about his body than you could count, but they were all hidden under a tattered tunic. He was clean, he was presentable, and you wouldn't have noticed him if you'd passed him in the street.

He stopped in the doorway and I watched him make the same assessment as me. Seneca always taught us it was best to stand in shadow, but if that was impossible, then to keep ourselves in bright light: each allows you the advantage of seeing before you are seen.

Pantera was of the shadows, I was of the light. That has

been true all along. My feeling is that if you can't be invisible, or don't want to be, then you do everything you can to draw attention to yourself. That way, people see those things to which you guide their eyes, not the things that you wish to keep hidden.

With that in mind, knowing the importance of a first meeting, I was dressed in fine white linen, and my hair was bound up on top of my head. The three gold pins that adorned it bore butterflies jewelled in scarlet and amber, lapis and green. I wore no other jewels, nor any make-up; on walking into the room, his gaze and his attention were caught by the glitter of those pins.

Any normal man would have seen them first, and then the shape of my body beneath my shift. Later, when asked, he'd have said I was tall and dark-haired and wore gold pins with butterflies on my head. He would have described my figure in detail. If he was particularly attentive, he might have said that my shift was white.

Pantera was not a normal man. He glanced once at the pins and then his eyes stripped me from head to toe and back again. You might think that was nothing extraordinary, but the point is he wasn't looking at my body, rather at what my shift might conceal, and when he was done he let his gaze rest on my face, on my eyes, whence danger might first be signalled.

He, too, had been asking around the city for information about me, and because I was . . . who I was I had been able to control what he had heard, and those bits I could not control I at least knew about.

He knew, therefore, that I was considered attractive, but was too wilful to be truly beautiful; that my brother was famous for his poetry but I believed myself the better writer and passed off my own work as his – that's true, by the way; that I was a widow and childless, although nobody knew the cause of my husband's death. Bloody flux, poison and a dagger in the night had each been mentioned, at which Pantera had remarked that any man would have to be particularly unlucky to fall foul of all three. None of his informants had laughed.

From another source, he had heard a whisper that I had been to the poison school set up by Nero after the death of Britannicus, and had been a willing and able pupil there. Another rumour said I was Nero's mistress and that he was planning to marry me when I fell pregnant.

Nobody mentioned that I had been a pupil of Seneca's, but that's because so few people knew about Seneca's spy network, and not even those who belonged to it knew the identities of their fellows. And nobody else in the world was privy to Seneca's private code, which I had used when I summoned Pantera here.

So that was our first meeting.

I tried to read his face: puzzlement, curiosity, hope, discovery, anger . . . all were there, but it was the sense of a watching intellect that was arresting, and brought to mind what I had been told of him.

He is wounded, but he is still the Leopard, still dangerous. His eyes look through you, until they don't. That's when he'll kill you.

Seneca used to say that to anyone who would listen and Pantera never took the time to contradict him. So I watched his eyes, watching mine, and I waited.

We both waited. Seneca taught all his students not to speak too early in any conversation, to let the other party make careless admissions on first greeting. Evidently, we had both been good students: the silence hugged us, gathering the scents of willow and running water, the sounds of birdsong; it did not break.

When it was clear that I must move first, I drew from

my sleeve the scroll I had secreted there. It was sealed with undyed beeswax on which was pressed Seneca's mark of the counting stick. I laid it on the farthest edge of the small cherrywood table that was the room's only furniture, next to a lit candle in a plain silver stick.

I said, 'He wrote this for you on the day he died.'

Naturally, Pantera expected it: why else would he have been called to Rome, to this house, at this time, if not to hear his mentor's last request? But he opened the letter slowly, not sure, I think, that he was ready to read such a thing in my presence.

His relationship with Seneca had been complex, and although I believe the greatest rift had been healed soon after he returned from Britain, there must have been a lot that had never been spoken.

I watched him scan the first lines.

From Seneca to the son of his soul, with love, greetings . . .

And so there it was, in black and white, *the son of his soul*. Pantera glanced up, wondering if I had read it, but I, of course, was looking out of the window at the stream, not at him.

I could hear his thoughts in my head as if he breathed them in my ear: *I never loved him as he wanted, and hated him for wanting it. But he was Seneca; how could you truly hate him?*

He didn't speak aloud, just read on.

The handwriting was even and steady and unmistakably Seneca's. Nobody, reading it, would have known that it was written in the maw of death; a final, dying plea. Two final pleas, actually.

I ask you to honour this woman as you honoured me.

It's obvious now, of course, but it wasn't then. Pantera was being asked to give to me the same loyalty he gave Seneca, to accept me as the new spymaster. *Her name will be the Poet.*

Seneca had been known to all of us as the Teacher and that name died with him. I chose the name Poet for myself and do not think it any more arrogant than his.

But for Pantera?

A woman, *this* woman: me. Not him. Spymaster.

Owner, commander, caregiver to the entire Senecan network.

He raised his head. I was trapped by his gaze. *His eyes look through you, until they don't . . .*

Outside, small birds tussled over a nest. I wrested my gaze from his. I said, 'He presumes much.' I didn't ask if it was too much.

Pantera laid the scroll down on the table, and placed his palms flat beside it. 'He wanted to believe himself loved,' he said. 'And if not loved, then hated.'

If I had misunderstood him then, I have no doubt that Pantera would have left, and there was every chance that he would have taken the network with him. I knew he had planned for this moment and that he could have done it. Whether he would have destroyed it or run it for his own ends was a different question; I'm not certain even he knew the answer.

Uncertainty lit the air between us.

I said, 'We all want that, don't we? Not to be ignored? Not to be so insignificant that we are not even worth hating?' I smoothed my stola and let him see that I carried a knife at my girdle, although in truth he had already seen it.

It's not as if I expected him to be afraid. Or unarmed. But I wanted him to understand the same of me: that I was not afraid, nor unarmed; a match for all he had become.

I said, 'It's hard not to hate the man who uses you and would throw your life away on an instant did it suit his ends.'

'Will you do the same?' Pantera asked: *will*, not *would*. He was halfway to a decision.

'Of course.' I smiled, but it felt tight, and not convincing. I had worked for years to bring us to this point, and everything balanced on the blade's edge. Control was all, for both of us. 'You would do the same if Seneca had named you, not me. And you'd hate yourself for it daily, as he did and I will.'

Looking out of a window, I bit the edge of my thumb, carelessly. I was in profile, then, with the sun behind, and there are few spring fabrics that are not at least a little translucent.

I heard the catch in his breath; he was not one to be snared, only to be reminded that snaring was possible.

When I looked back, he had dropped his eyes and was reading the letter again, where were only a dead man's words.

From Seneca to the son of his soul . . . He did say something like that once; I heard him.

I said, 'He told me that you'd be hardest. But also that I could not succeed without you. I would like to suggest that we forget any loyalty either of us might have had to our late teacher. As the new spymaster, I will ask only that you keep what promises you give. And if you can keep none, nor wish to make any, that you say so and leave. Now.'

'Did he tell you that I had sworn never to give my oath to Rome?'

'He did. He said that you had told him once that you would give the oath of your tongue, but never the oath of your heart. But he also said that you had changed since then, that there were things that mattered to you more than the sum of your dead. He said he hoped you knew that.' All this is true, I swear it now, by your gods and mine.

Pantera said nothing. He had reached the letter's second request. If anything, it was more momentous; certainly more dangerous.

If I am dead, then Nero still lives: I made him and I would have destroyed him, but I have failed in that and you are left to repair the damage I have wrought. Find a man of worth and substance: find a match for Caesar – the Caesar, Gaius Julius – and put him on the throne. Somebody has to.

Corbulo.

A victorious general, beloved of his legions; a man who could easily have become the new Caesar.

His name was not written on the page, but leapt from it none the less. None of us was going to write it down; it would have been a death sentence for the empire's best hope if it had been found. Even so much as was written had the potential to end all our lives.

Nothing in this room was there by accident, certainly not a lit candle in the good morning light. Pantera leaned over and tilted the letter to the flame's bright tip. The paper was Egyptian, thin and costly. It crisped and curled into smoke.

He held it until his fingers were scorched, then, dropping the last corner, said, 'I have to go east; there is a man in Caesarea whom I must kill. Afterwards, if I am alive, we will talk about what oaths I can and cannot give.'

CHAPTER NINE

Rome, 3 August AD 69

Jocasta

Second meeting: eighteen months later; still in Nero's reign. Pantera was alive and his enemy was dead. So was another man, one who had come to matter to him more; a king who could have saved his people. It was a year since that one had died and the hurt was still fresh in Pantera's eyes when I met him.

It was autumn, time of first frosts. Trees were cast in bronze and black; roads were etched with ice, and dangerous. I had arranged to meet Pantera in the Mariner's Rest, a tavern at the port of Ravenna, where the eastern fleet of the Roman navy waited out every winter.

Outside, two dozen warships wallowed at anchor and gulls slid on hard, salty air. Inside, the innkeeper kept a vat of hare stew against the cold. The smell of juniper berries and rich flesh was earthen in its power.

The room was packed with legionaries and marines. Pantera pushed through to where I was sitting at a table in

the corner and we waited while the stew was placed before
him. Unlike the first meeting, this one saw us both somewhat
disguised. He had the dress of a moderately successful
merchant; I was a tavern wench, hair down, coarse tunic cut
low.

The Rest wasn't a bar that entertained many women, and
so those few of us who were there caused something of a
stir. When I leaned in to kiss Pantera's cheek, the men at the
neighbouring tables glared their hatred at him, wanting to
see what he had that they lacked. He smiled at them, blandly.
They looked away.

The stew was truly excellent. After two months at sea, I
imagine anything would be good that didn't taste of fish, but
this was better than that: something to come back for.

I let him savour the first burst of flavours, then said, 'Who
has died?'

Spoon halfway to his mouth, Pantera raised a brow.
'The two sailors at the corner table, the Gaul and the Greek,
are planning the detail of how they will take you when I
leave.'

Nice try. I shook my head. 'They won't do anything while
Barnabus watches over us.'

Barnabus was the tavern's owner, barman and door guard.
I glanced across at him. He smiled at me and nodded; we
knew each other well.

'Ex-navy?' Pantera asked. The marines of Ravenna had a
reputation that made the legions seem restrained.

I said, 'He was captain of his own ship before he retired
and bought himself a wife. I caught the man who raped his
daughter and delivered him here.'

'Alive?'

Of course. I nodded. 'Nobody will touch me in here. And
out there' – I tipped my head towards the world beyond the
door – 'they won't find me. But it was a good distraction, a

worthy try.' This was neither the time nor the place for our previous long, weighted silences, so I continued without waiting for him to speak. 'You sent a message saying you were coming back to work with me to make Nero's successor. If you are in mourning, it may affect what we do. I need to know the details. Who was he?'

Menachem. The name stuck on the two sides of his tongue, closing his throat.

My informants had been effusive in their eulogies of the warrior-king on his milk-white Berber mare, his black hair flowing from his helmet, and the thin loop of his crown dazzling in the morning sun. A legionary of the XIIth killed him, they said: Demalion, with Pantera's own bow.

The story told itself anew on Pantera's face: the shock of the death, the emptiness after, the slow climb back to normality, if his life could ever be described as normal.

It was not my place to be kind to him. I said, 'I need to hear you speak his name. To know you can.'

Pantera set down his spoon. 'Menachem. His name was Menachem ben Yehuda ben Yehuda. He made himself king in Judaea.'

'He made himself king?' I asked. 'Or you made him?'

'I helped show him how it could be done, but he was the raw material that made it possible. He was born to it. I have never met his like.' He looked down; we both did. His finger, clearly unbidden, had sketched a horse in spilled wine on the tabletop.

It was not a good horse. He swept it away with the heel of his hand.

'Did you love him?' I asked.

'Not in the carnal sense. But I found in him a man worth following. I could have lived in his service and not felt my life wasted.'

'I envy you,' I said, and it was true.

Pantera raised one brow. 'I thought you had found the same in Nero?'

'Nero?' I was genuinely puzzled.

'Why else does he use Seneca's network as his plaything?'

Now, I was horrified. 'Do you seriously think I have taken all that Seneca built and handed it to *Nero*?'

'I think that Nero thinks that you have. Certainly he has made full use of all your resources this past year in Parthia and in Britain.'

If ever I was going to strike a man, it was then. Pantera saw it; his entire body grew tense. But I am not so impulsive as that, not so caught up in the chaos of my own feelings that I would have given him the satisfaction of driving me to violence.

Softly, with venom, I said, 'The *empire* has had use of our resources; it has always been so. Nero can still be guided. Until or unless we remove him, we must offer him aid in the interest of the greater whole.' I leaned back, still angry. 'Why are you here? Why did you come back when you could have stayed in Judaea?'

He shrugged. 'Last winter, in Caesarea, we heard the news of Corbulo's death.'

Well yes, that was old news; nobody in Rome thought of Corbulo by then, except with faint regret for what might have been.

Pantera said, 'I have met his replacement. Someone who can do what Corbulo could have done, but better than he could have done it.'

'Really?' If I was cynical, I had good reason. Do you know how often I had heard that?

'He's a war-hardened general and he's only the first genera-tion in the senate. His brother's a notorious sycophant, but he himself hasn't had time to become corrupt or venal and he certainly isn't weak.'

'Vespasian?' I laughed and that shocked him, but there was a look of discovery in his eyes, as if he had learned something new about me, and interesting.

Drily, I said, 'I'm the daughter of a consul and sister to a celebrated poet; of course I know Rome. I know every second son and disgraced cousin, I know their strengths and their weaknesses and how they might be bought. Certainly, I know Titus Flavius Vespasianus.'

'Then you must agree that he is all that Corbulo was, and more?'

And so I understood at last the fire in Pantera's eyes. Losing Menachem, he had lost everything, but now he had once again found his soul's dream: a man he could respect, a man he could follow, a man he could serve and not feel himself demeaned.

Seneca had always told me that Pantera was looking for this, and that when he found it no one sane would stand in his way.

But I am Jocasta, not Seneca, and I did not love Pantera; nor was I afraid of him. I did not intend to let his obsession ruin Rome.

I said, 'This is a man who didn't even want to be a senator until his elder brother shamed him into it. And you think he wants to be emperor?'

The smile he threw me was gone so fast that if I'd blinked, I'd have missed it. 'I'm sure he doesn't. Which is exactly why he'll be so good.'

'Only if he has what it takes to see it through,' I said. 'A half-cocked civil war will be worse than no war at all.'

'If he can be made to want it, he has what it takes.' Pantera leaned across the table, took my hands in his own. You know him, you know how unusual that is. The men at the neighbouring tables were one step closer to killing him for it.

Ignoring them all, he said, 'I've seen him with his men.

94

He'll sweep through Judaea and the legions will adore him. They'll follow him to Hades if he asks them. All we have to do is make sure he asks at the right time.'

This was long before Galba made his move; it was even before the Judaean war had really started. We didn't know yet what Vespasian could do. Except Pantera, obviously, who had seen enough to be sure.

He went on, 'He has eight legions he can call on. That's enough if we can put the weight of the Senecan network behind him. With them he could rule the world from Jerusalem. Or Alexandria. Or the Rhine. But he won't need to. We can give him Rome.'

This, then, was the true reason Pantera had come back to see me that autumn: to find out if I would throw the network's full weight behind Vespasian when I had only given parts of it to Nero, and then only at second hand.

Then and there, in the bar of the Rest, I still had a choice. I could have tried to turn him back and I didn't.

The decision not to was mine alone, and I take full responsibility for it. I gave him what he wanted and if you want to call that weakness on my part, you are welcome. But ask yourself this: in my place, knowing him as you do, would you have acted differently? *Could* you have?

'Does Vespasian know you want this of him?' I asked.

It was as good as saying 'yes'. The light in Pantera's face was something to see.

He shrugged, like a boy caught out in a half-truth. 'Not yet, but there are people around him who do. Hypatia, Mergus, Estaph . . . They'll help to steer him in the right direction.'

'He's a stubborn man,' I said. 'It won't be easy to change his mind.'

'But it can be done. There's a prophecy in Judaea which says a leader will arise out of the east to rule the whole world. He listens to such things.'

'Does it apply to him?'

'It can be made to.'

And it was. I have no idea how he did it, you'd have to ask Demalion for the details, but after the fall of Jotapata, Yusaf ben Matthias had emerged alive from the wreck of Hebrew hopes, and proclaimed Vespasian the inheritor of the Star Prophecy; then, later, an oracle at Mount Carmel said the same, and another at the shrine to Venus outside Alexandria.

They say Vespasian paid attention to such things, but even if he didn't, his men certainly did.

All that said, it was Lucius' assassin who tipped the balance and set Vespasian on the path to civil war. We might not be here if that one man hadn't tried and failed to kill the general, and if he hadn't said what he did to Pantera.

But he did, and that led directly to our third meeting.

CHAPTER TEN

Rome, 3 August AD **69**

Jocasta

The third meeting between Pantera and me took place on the same day that Trabo returned to Rome. I didn't know that at the time, but we found out soon enough.

Pantera had sent word ahead that he would meet me in the early evening at the Inn of the Crossed Spears. I got there before him and took a place in a corner of the courtyard, where it looked out on to the street, and waited.

He arrived near dusk, weaving drunkenly through the crowd, jeering and laughing at the girls on the tightrope, at the jugglers who flung their fire sticks up and round and tossed swords at each other.

He looked seasick. He isn't a good traveller, and while it was two days since he had hit land at Ravenna, I think he was still feeling the ground sway beneath his feet. He looked as if the smell of wine was going to make him vomit, but it may have been an act; he was playing the part of a centurion and carried papers in his belt pouch that said he was from Britain, sent with news of the latest insurrection.

It was a subterfuge he could carry easily; he'd lived in the province for long enough to be able to talk for days about the tribes and their uprisings if he had to. It was all to waste, though: nobody challenged him. Rome was full of strange centurions; another one here or there made no difference.

He reached my table, just another drunken officer greeting his wife, or more likely his mistress. That evening, I was better than a tavern slut, but rather more gaudy than a good Roman matron; more gilt on the brooches in my hair, brighter stones around my neck. If I was a bought woman, I was expensive.

We each played our parts with the ease of long practice. Anyone looking at us would have thought our attention was all for each other; a passionate, erotic delight, barely kept decent by the public place in which we met. In reality, we were both watching a bearded carter with a wide-brimmed hat who was not paying quite enough attention to the whore on his knee.

I had watched him come in and knew he was out of place, but I was impressed by how fast Pantera picked him out from the rest. He sloshed his wine on the table, hiccoughed a laugh, swept the mess away with the heel of his hand and stumbled down beside me.

Leaning in for a kiss, he said, 'Man at the far corner. The one with the girl on his knee who's watching a house in the street of the widows. He walks like a soldier.'

'I know,' I said. 'That's Trabo.'

Pantera eyed me sideways. 'Are you sure?'

It was well over a decade since anybody had questioned my skills. Tightly, I said, 'We lived next door to each other as children. My brother was in love with him. It's him.'

'So, then, what is an enemy of Vitellius doing watching the house of Vespasian's mistress? He *is* Vitellius' enemy?'

'If he wasn't, he is now. A tribune of the Guard drew his name in the lottery two days ago: Juvens.'

'That should be interesting.' Pantera whistled, softly, then glanced around the bar. Really, it was barely a look, but he said, 'I count three men that are yours, plus the boy collecting the empty beakers. Did you pay the tumblers too?'

I could have lied, I suppose, out of professional pride, but why bother?

'Yes.' I shrugged. 'I thought we might have need of them. Zois and Thaïs can provide a distraction that no man will be able to withstand.'

'And all without losing their maidenhood. Very clever.' He toasted me, lifting his beaker. He tipped it back, but he didn't drink.

Two small boys were watching us, round-eyed. For their benefit, Pantera hooked an arm around my shoulders and drew me into the shadows where it was possible to speak almost normally.

'Tell me about Juvens. I thought Nero had killed him with Seneca and the rest?'

'He did.' I rested my head on his shoulder. He held me close, pressed his lips to my head, but he didn't lose his focus as another man might have done. Did I want him to? I didn't expect it, he was too professional for that, but I expected . . . something. Some stirring of the loins or quickening of the pulse to show that I had reached him. There was none of that.

I might have thought he loved only men, but I knew about the healer-woman, Hannah, about the child they'd had, about what she'd meant to him.

What I didn't know was whether there had been another woman since the night of the fire when he had loved her. The news from the east was limited and it all came from people who knew him, and cared for him. He had that effect on those he touched: they wanted to protect him because he spent so little effort protecting himself.

So if he had his secret loves, they stayed secret, and he was not about to be seduced by his own spymaster.

I answered his question.

'Juvens the father is dead. The elder son tried for the consulship and when he failed he fled into exile. This is Juvens the younger. He escaped to the Rhine legions, and was there when they made Vitellius emperor.'

'And thence to the new Guard. Does Trabo know about the lottery?'

'If he doesn't, he deserves to die. If he does, it would explain why he's made himself into a carter.'

'But not why he's watching the home of Vespasian's mistress.'

I thought about that. 'He was Otho's man. He might have the same purpose as us. Your letter was less than explicit, but I am assuming our purpose is to visit Caenis?'

That was a guess, and only recently made. I had ordered her house watched, of course, from the moment Pantera had named Vespasian as his man; information is the currency of a spy and I needed as much as I could get, but nothing had been reported beyond the daily routines of every other woman whose man was away on extended duty, or dead.

Every day without fail, the lady Antonia Caenis rose with the dawn and walked down to the markets that line the Tiber in the company of the retained freedman who kept her accounts, served her at dinner and organized the maintenance of her cottage. She returned to the cool of her atrium before the noon sun roasted the day, and in the afternoon she visited friends, or entertained them, before an early supper and bed.

In the streets around were women whose candles burned long after the midnight hour, but there, in the Street of the Bay Trees, the widows retired at a seemly hour and their night lamps were rarely lit. There was a brief span of time just before dusk in which the daily household chores were completed, and visitors might approach the house.

Now, in fact.

Pantera said, crisply, 'My letter was designed to endanger neither you nor the person carrying it if either was stopped and searched. Yes, we are going to visit Caenis, and if Trabo has a similar plan and he's recognized and taken for questioning before they kill him, we could be finished before we start. We'd better move.'

He leaned back and lifted his beaker. It was almost empty: what little had been in it he had sloshed on the table. Theatrically, he drained the last dribbles, and stretched out his hand.

'I think it's time the centurion and his lady paid their respects to Vespasian's mistress, don't you? Do you suppose your acrobat friends could be persuaded to create a small diversion?'

They did as he asked.

At my nod, they danced out of the courtyard, across the road and into the Street of the Bay Trees. The crowd followed, as goats follow the herd boy.

Caenis' house was halfway along on the right. We staggered arm in arm towards it, laughing, carousing, waving our wine beakers with the rest.

Near the house with the oak leaves carved above the lintel, Pantera bellowed a laugh, threw a coin at Zois – he missed – and leaned in to kiss me, fumbling at his toga, as if unfamiliar with the raising of it. By happy fortune, we fell up against the door with the oak-leaf carving. It was unpainted and otherwise unembellished, but new, of strong, green timber; someone had spent gold on it, recently.

Pantera thumped the heel of his hand once above the

latch. Footsteps padded close and presently the door cracked ajar.

'Leave,' said the little Hebrew freedman. He was bald, with a small pointed beard and sad eyes. He was already closing the door.

Pantera jammed his foot in the doorway to hold it open. Through the gap, he proffered Vespasian's ring; the big, heavy one, of poor gold, with the oak leaves on it. 'Your mistress will want you to let us in.'

The little man knew that ring. The colour leached from his face. 'What news?' His voice was hoarse.

'Nothing bad,' Pantera said. 'The general is well. But in his name, we must speak to your mistress. We are only two. And you should lock the door after we enter.'

The door swung back, letting out a whisper of cool air, scented with lilies. Beyond was a small vestibule and beyond that a modest, four-pillared atrium with an angled roof open to the sky and a pool below the centre that reflected the few clouds left over after all the rain.

Plaster busts of past emperors and their women – mostly their women, when I looked more closely – were set in niches along the walls. Between them, curtained doorways led off. From one of these a melodious voice, light and true as a flute, asked, 'Matthias? Who comes?'

'Two persons, lady, with news of the master.'

Sober now, stripped of pretence, we followed him in.

We were left to wait in the atrium, where couches were set about the central pool. Behind, a small garden was alive with lilies and citrus trees. The late afternoon sun lay low in the sky. The shadows had clear-cut edges. I watched Pantera move to the place where light and shade combined to make him least visible.

As I said earlier, his instinct is to cleave to shadow, whereas I have always thought that there is an advantage to being in good light; I can learn as much from a person's reaction to me as I can from seeing them.

So we were there, him half hidden, me in the last light of the sun, and both watched a curtain slip aside from a doorway on the far wall.

How shall I describe her, Vespasian's love?

Like her freedman, Caenis was small and slightly built, and she had an easy grace. Olive-skinned, with hair the colour of autumn leaves, she was Greek, I thought, although Greeks are not often enslaved these days, so perhaps she was at least partly Dacian; that would have accounted for her oval face and green-brown eyes.

And she was sharp; already her gaze had glanced past me and found Pantera. I should have expected that: for many years she was amanuensis to Antonia Tertia, known as the Younger; the elegant, cultured woman who was daughter of Marc Antony, niece of Augustus, mother to Claudius, grandmother to Caligula.

Which means that, while still a slave, Caenis had been clerk and confidante to one of the empire's most powerful women; she was always going to look first into the shadows, and only afterwards study what was in the light.

More important, she was loved enough in her youth to have been freed by her mistress, and she was loved enough in her later years to have been installed here, in the widows' quarters, where few men's attention fell.

And her lover had sent Pantera to see her safe.

Chapter Eleven

Rome, 3 August AD 69

*Antonius Matthias, freedman of the
lady Antonia Caenis*

We had heard the tumblers in the street outside. My lady was writing a letter to the master, I think; she wrote him a great many letters through that summer. She was his eyes and ears in Rome. Did she send them? Some – not most, but enough – made their way east with messengers she could rely on.

The evening in question, the first we knew of anything amiss was the sound of the crowd surging past, raucous, crude, boorish, loud; all that my lady least liked about Romans en masse. It's true that she was born here and she had only once been outside Rome and that was to the island of Kos, lately, with her lord, but she had Greek blood in her veins and that is always more civilized, don't you agree? We both knew that Athens bore herself with a dignity that Rome could never match. That night was proof in point.

We ignored the commotion until we heard someone come

close, heard the slurred words and the splash of urine as they pissed on the side of the house, and then they knocked.

My lady would have gone to the door right then – she has the courage of a lion – but I persuaded her to step back and let me answer.

I opened to a man of no consequence and was closing it again when I saw the ring: the oak leaves in gold. I could not turn away any man who bore that. And so I invited them in and took them through to the atrium, where were the couches for visitors. My lady called out and I answered and she came to meet them.

She saw the lady Jocasta first, of course. She was breathtaking, if your mind turns that way, the kind of woman some men lose their heads for: tall, elegant, very graceful in a composed way. She had the true patrician gaze of the noble woman, the one that disdains everyone below them, although I am pleased to say she had the good breeding not to turn it on my lady Caenis.

In looks, she had a neck like a swan, a high, arched brow, and her hair . . . in years to come, men will take out the poems they wrote to her hair, and re-read them and remind themselves of their fecund youth.

It was raven black, with the blue-brilliant sheen of a perfect feather, and as she walked she pulled out the garish pins that had held it up and let it fall back and back and back past her shoulders, until it swayed halfway down to her waist. Even I, who have never looked on a woman as more than a friend, could not help but imagine her naked. Even my lady was struck by her beauty; I heard the suck of her breath.

But Jocasta was right in what she told you; my lady had been trained by the best. The lady Antonia taught her long ago that the stranger standing in the shadows is always more interesting – and far more dangerous – than whoever is in the light, and nine times out of ten she was right.

I had signalled her with my eyes, but she was already looking towards Pantera. She knew there was a man, you see; she had heard him at the door and so she was looking for him as she walked out of the side room, and, after that one striking moment of looking at Jocasta, she found your Pantera.

He was by the pool, a little back, where the reflections from the water wrought ripples in the air, making of him a shimmering shadow, an almost-not-there spirit. Their eyes locked for a moment, and he gave a small bow. Then my lady spoke.

'He is alive?' No name was mentioned. Caenis glanced meaningfully back to the blue silk curtain that blocked Domitian's doorway; the young lord, you understand, lived with the lady when his father was away.

He was safe with us, and kept himself to himself, but the one thing guaranteed to draw him out of his studies was his father's name, and I could tell she didn't want him to come out yet; not until she knew why these two had come. He's a sensitive boy, and there's no saying how he would have taken bad news of his father.

Jocasta understood at once. She said, 'My lady, he is alive and well and sends you his earnest regards. Is there some-where we may speak in more detail?'

Her necklace was gone with the hair pins and she had wiped the paint from her lips. Without them, she was a different woman. Caenis took her at her word and led them through to the garden.

Here, songbirds, tame to my lady's hand, followed her about. The small fountain, barely up to knee height, shaped like a rising carp, spilled water into the central pool, making sound enough to cover a quiet conversation from all but those engaged in it.

My lady put her back to an olive bough, seeking the security of its strength as she often did in those early days. 'Swiftly, then, what brings you here? Is he wounded?'

This time, Pantera answered. 'My lady, he was in good health when I left him. He was injured in the knee by a sling-stone while assaulting one of the minor cities of Judaea in the winter, but you know of that.'

Caenis did know of that; it didn't prove that Vespasian had sent this pair, but it was at least a step in the right direction.

'Then why has he sent you here to— *Oh!*' Her hand flew to her mouth. She is so fast; she thinks things through in a flash. I could tell that even Pantera was impressed. He tipped his head in invitation to her to continue.

She put her fingers together, as she does when she is marshalling an argument. 'For reasons that will be obvious to you,' she said, 'I cannot leave Rome, nor can Sabinus, nor Domitian. You know this: to be safe, we must continue to declare our support for the emperor Vitellius. If we are seen to run, it will be taken as a sign of disloyalty and our lives will be forfeit. This is obvious, and he for whom we care most would not ask you to take us away from Rome. Therefore, he has sent you to offer us protection: he would do that.'

Pantera smiled a little, bowed, even paid her a compliment. 'My lady, I knew you must be exceptional for your general to have loved you so long, but he did not tell me you had the sharpest mind in Rome. I came expecting to spend the entire evening discussing that which you have just laid out so clearly: you cannot safely leave Rome, but none the less your safety is my first priority. Whatever else happens, it matters most to the general that his family remains unharmed. Perhaps, now, we can discuss how that may be done?'

She saved his life with her quickness, didn't she? That may not be a good thing, with all that came afterwards, but I don't think she would have done it differently, even if she had known.

At the time, she said simply, 'It is best, I believe, to speak as we find. If you are to be our protector, it might be constructive if the general's son were to be privy to the conversation.'

And so, after all that, there was nothing to be done but to call for Domitian, and let Pantera learn how different was the second of Vespasian's sons from his brother.

CHAPTER TWELVE

Rome, 3 August AD **69**

The lady Antonia Caenis

Domitian. What can one say of him, who is son to me in all but name and blood?

I am offering no insult, I think, if I tell you that Domitian was not in a sociable frame of mind on the evening Jocasta and Pantera came to my home with their so-clever illusion.

If one were to be truthful, it would be more accurate to say he was never in a sociable frame of mind, but within the confines of our family this rarely posed undue embarrassment. I was happy to leave him to his solitary games of dice, right hand against left, to his collection of insects pinned to a board, to his early sleep and late rise and the occasional day when he could go from dawn to dusk without once noticing my existence.

The day in question was one of those. I knew it already, but if I had not I would have read it in the brittle smile fixed on Matthias' face as he held back the blue curtain that screened Domitian's private chamber from the atrium. I indulged myself in a moment's silent cursing, and then, as I must, forced a smile.

'Domitian, welcome. These people have come from your father. They have news.'

My eyes signalled him a warning. The boy – he is eighteen and I really must start thinking of him as a man, but he has the round-faced, smooth-skinned look of one who has barely begun to shave and his voice is still light, like the touch of soft rain, and it's hard to think of him as anything but a child – the boy chose once again to ignore me.

He was gazing at Jocasta, which was a surprisingly normal response. You've met her, so you know how striking she is. Any man would favour her with a second glance. Domitian, being . . . Domitian, stared straight at her for an uncomfortably long time, and then said, 'You can't have been near my father. Titus would have kept you.'

There was a moment's scandalized silence. If he would only smile as he said these things, but no, he thought it and so he said it and there was no humour anywhere in it. I shut my eyes; a coward's way out, I admit, but there are times when the solitude of darkness is one's only respite. I looked again only at the sound of Jocasta's flute-like laugh.

She said, 'You flatter me, lord, but it is true; I have not been with your father. My business kept me in Rome. Pantera, whom you see here, is the one who has journeyed by fast ship from Judaea.'

Lord. Nobody except Matthias had ever spoken thus to Domitian. Flushing, he bowed. 'Madam, you honour me. Will you come and take wine? I see you are not yet served.'

It was stiff. It was awkward – a series of phrases stolen from other mouths and stitched together without any true understanding of their import – but it was said, and it was real and it took a great effort for me to keep my hands by my sides that I might not clasp his face and kiss his brow in my joy. Both would have dismantled all the good just made.

Matthias didn't need my nod to go and fetch the wine; he backed away, bowing, and I followed Domitian back through into the garden area where the late, rich sun gilded everything in tones of amber.

We stood amid the citrus and lilacs in silence until the wine was served; it wasn't expensive, but it was white and sweet and had been cooled in the well so that beads of water formed on the outside of my best glass beakers.

Domitian studied Pantera and Jocasta, each in turn; there was nothing subtle about his inspection. At its end, he said, 'So the rumours are true? My father is mounting civil war against Vitellius and Lucius?'

I hope I didn't show my relief at that. He may be strange, but one could never call Domitian stupid. I had always suspected that, in his strange, solitary way, he was brighter than his brother; it was just that he spoke too little for us to be sure.

I saw surmise and surprise flicker across Pantera's face, gone before they took hold, replaced by a kind of interest. 'Yes.' He matched Domitian for the baldness of his speech. 'They have asked me to keep you safe; you and the lady and your uncle Sabinus.'

Domitian sneered. 'My uncle Sabinus, who is calling my father an idiot, a reprobate and a fool? My uncle Sabinus who has sworn to shed his own blood in defence of Vitellius' claim to the throne? Does he want you to keep him safe? And if he does, can you do that and still foment revolt?'

There was another pause; this time, I believe Pantera was fighting not to smile.

'As to the first: does your uncle wish to be kept safe? I have yet to ask him. To the second: can we keep him safe while fomenting revolt? We can try. We are not without resource.'

'Even though your name was in the lead lottery on the Capitoline two days ago? Geminus drew it.'

And that surprised us all.

Pantera's eyes flicked to me. 'I hadn't heard.' He made it sound like a statement when it was really a question.

Truthfully, I said, 'I hadn't either, but Domitian goes abroad in the evenings and listens to the slave-talk that I hear less than I used to. Slaves know everything.' Of Domitian, I asked, 'What did you hear?'

'That Pantera, the leopard who saved Rome from the fire, is the target of Lucius' ire. That Geminus, who knows him, was made to draw his name in the lottery. That he is to be taken alive, not killed like all the others.' Domitian's smile bore a satisfied edge. 'They think they have kept this a secret, but the man who cut the lead tablets with the names on is lover to Aponolius, who is also lover to Demetra who can be paid in small coin for small facts, particularly if she thinks them unimportant. So' – this to Pantera – 'what will you do?'

Pantera shrugged. 'First and most easily, I can change my appearance. Given half a day's work, my own mother wouldn't know me. Once changed, with my lord's permission, I can be hired as servant to the lady Caenis, that I might not arouse suspicion. As you have said, nobody notices the slaves—'

His head snapped up. From somewhere outside came the sound of a songbird; a high, trilling whistle. It sounded almost normal, but nobody in the room believed it so.

'Guards.' I crossed swiftly to the rear door. 'That's the warning the street boys give. You must go. Lucius has not yet dared to touch me, but if the Guards find you here he will have no scruples. There's a way out from the rear door, a slaves' route, that takes you into the ghetto. You will go under my protection.'

Pantera glanced a question. I said, 'We slaves protect our

own. Even those who are no longer strictly slaves. If you go straight for a hundred paces and then go left beneath the two houses that meet above the road, you can—'

'I'll take them.'

In the short time my attention had been turned the other way, Domitian had donned his good, dark cloak. He was standing by the door, ready to go out.

'I know the routes as well as anyone. I'll do this. For my father. Trust me.'

I'm ashamed to say that I *didn't* trust him. Nor, I am certain, did my guests. They exchanged a brief, wordless conversation at the end of which Jocasta, mellow-voiced and lovely, said, 'May I suggest that my lord takes me alone and permits the spy Pantera to go out of the front door to lead the Guards away? If they have seen him enter, they need to see him being sent away or your aunt's life and liberty will be forever endangered.'

Domitian gave a credible impression of a grown man whose opinion was frequently sought on matters of imminent danger. Gravely, he said, 'That is wise. I will keep you safe and escort you home. Pantera should go out now, and when he is free once more he can come to the Street of the Lame Dog which runs behind the inn where the acrobats meet. Ask one of the boys for the Fly-catcher. He'll let me know where you are.'

The Fly-catcher? I had no idea they called him that. I wanted to ask more, but there was no time; Pantera had agreed and was making preparations. The lady Jocasta was standing tight-lipped and silent. She gave Pantera a glittering smile, full of meanings I could not discern, and then followed Domitian out of the small rear door used by the servants, which led out into the slum that sprawls across the lower reaches of the Quirinal and Palatine hills.

Pantera watched them leave, then said, 'How long have we

got before the Guards are here? I assume the whistles give detail within the warning, or do we just know they are on their way?'

I didn't ask how he knew; for this, too, there was no time. 'At first whistle, they were coming down the Quirinal hill from the barracks behind. Each new whistle brings them a street closer. They are, if I have heard correctly, five streets away, up the hill. If they run, they will be here in the time it takes to lace your sandals.'

'They're running. I can hear them.' He was standing by my new front door with his ear pressed to the wood. With one hand, he was sliding back the bolts at top and bottom of the door. With the other, he was loosening a knife I had not seen he carried strapped to his forearm.

Turning, he threw me a grin that reminded me so much of Vespasian that it hurt.

'Throw me out,' he said. 'Be theatrical. I have talked my way in with news of the general and it is clear I have never been near him; and in any case, you agree with Sabinus that Vespasian is a fool. I was offending your honour, abusing your servants, threatening to steal your wine and your silver. Make it loud and make it real. Can you do that?'

'Tonight,' I said, 'I can do anything.'

'Good.' He hurled back the door. '*Now!*'

CHAPTER THIRTEEN

Rome, 3 August AD **69**

Geminus

'There! The centurion . . . Pantera . . . whoever he is. The widow's throwing him out! See? On the other side of the acrobats. Get him!'

The gods were smiling, it seemed. Lucius had sent word that the spy, Pantera, had come to Rome disguised as a centurion and had just been seen to enter the house of the oak leaves on the widows' row. Sadly, that was the limit of his information. He hadn't been able to give any suggestion as to how long our target might remain inside or where he might go when he left.

I nearly broke my fingers throwing on my sword belt, gathering my team, setting them to run down the road, but even so I feared we were going to arrive to an empty house and spend the next few days chasing shadows.

Running, I prayed to Jupiter Best and Greatest, and, miraculously, my prayer was answered, for as I turned the corner I saw Pantera himself being summarily ejected from the house with the oak leaves by a small, dark-haired woman with a voice like a harpy.

I skidded to a halt and signalled the men to spread out into the crowd. I had Juvens with me, plus Artocus and Saturninus, two solidly reliable men of the IVth Macedonica, whom, with Lucius' agreement, I had commandeered for the duration of our hunt. We had all fought together in the recent past; we knew each other's signals and likely movements as well as we knew the marching patterns of our morning parades.

Within two paces, each of us had slowed to a walk and were threading through the men, women and children who filled the street.

Juvens was nearest the door: Juvens, the least predictable of our team, who treated this entire undertaking as if it were a new and exciting adventure, which, as I frequently said, only showed how utterly he had failed to grasp the situation.

I was in command of this unit, though, not him, and so I pushed slowly through the heaving, sweating mass of humanity, and peered through a tangle of acrobatic limbs, and saw that Pantera was now out on the street.

I sound as if I was sure it was him, when in truth I hoped it was, which is different. It might have been Pantera, but then again it might not; I had no idea how accurate was Lucius' information, and in my experience, if you pay good coin for something as intangible as a sighting of a stranger few people can recognize, there will be a great many such sightings for exactly as long as it takes you to come up with some valid system of verification.

Lucius was far from gullible, but he did have an air of hurried desperation about him and desperate men often listen closest to those who tell them what they want to hear.

The man who might have been Pantera fell forward, shoved by the woman in the house. As the door slammed behind him, he tucked neatly, rolled forward and came up on his feet, like one of the acrobats.

He looked furtive, but not theatrically so, if you get my drift. He had a quick look round in case anyone had seen him doing something that wasn't the usual act of a drunken man, but when he found that the crowd was apparently still absorbed with the show he spat out a mouthful of dust, brushed himself clean and sauntered off down the street towards the Inn of the Crossed Spears.

I got a decent look at him then and became more hopeful we'd got the right man. Certainly he had the right build and height and his hair was the colour of old leaves, just as I remembered it. It had been burnished a little by the summer's sun, but then if he'd been in Judaea that made sense.

The others were looking for my lead so I signalled with the flat of my hand stretched out straight like a javelin, which means 'Follow', and we all four began to thread our way through a crowd that didn't want to move, even for Guards.

Particularly, you might think, for us, the newly made Guards, newly brought here, newly prone to pillaging the city that had become our home. The officers of our new Guard were Roman, mostly, but the men were from the provinces and to them Rome was just another city under occupation.

I'll accept that the Urban cohorts and the vigiles of the Watch were doing their best to keep order, but they were four cohorts each against four legions and, worse, they were led by Flavius Sabinus, Vespasian's brother, and he had quite enough difficulties of his own to contend with. Being brother to a traitor meant he had to spend his every waking hour proving loyalty to Vitellius, and calling his cohorts on to the streets against the emperor's new Guard was hardly going to help his cause.

The end result was that here, in Rome herself, the *pax Romana* hung by an absurdly fine thread, and this evening in particular, hot, sultry, with a crowd on the edge of a riot, there was a sense of unfocused danger that gnawed at my guts.

Around me, the acrobats were finally running to the end of their repertoire and the crowd was reaching a peak of uncontrolled rapture.

The two girls, one dark, one fair, were lifted by the two tallest men and hurled high in the air. Blazing torches followed them, spinning in the soft moth-light of dusk, and were caught, each at the apex of its arc, so that the girls hurtled down again, a torch in either hand, to be caught in their turn, lightly, by their menfolk. The applause was wild, chaotic and deafening.

What can I say? You'd have to be made of stone not to have been dazzled by such a display, not to imagine what it might be to take the girls, one or both, there on the street, or at the very least, to lift them high and carry them into one of the upstairs rooms of the tavern.

They would have been compliant; you could just see how their bodies screamed it. And the expression on their faces, alight with the joy of the throw, was so like men in the afterglow of battle, full of what they have achieved, or women in the afterglow of . . .

I bit my tongue and wrenched my gaze away – and Pantera was gone.

'*Fuck*. Where is he?'

'Vanished while we were distracted,' Juvens said, grimly. 'You might even think that last show was put on for his benefit.'

'He's not far,' Artocus grunted. He was one of the few who had paid scant attention to the acrobats. Uncharitably, I thought that if it had been a boy who had been tumbling high in the sky he would have found it less easy to keep his gaze averted.

Still, he was a reliable man on the battlefield and now he said, 'Your man turned left at the head of the street. The lane there runs back up the hill to where the senators live.'

We were moving before he'd finished the sentence.

Chapter Fourteen

Rome, 3–4 August AD 69

Trabo

So there you have it; I came to the inn to deliver a letter and what should I find but a man running from Vitellius' Guards, which was, if you'll forgive me, of more immediate interest.

I didn't know they were following Pantera and his name wouldn't have meant anything to me if I had heard it, but I knew this man had led Jocasta into that cottage and come out without her and that was interesting in itself, never mind the four Guards trying to catch him.

Jocasta? Yes, I knew her from the first moment in the inn. Even dressed like a whore, she shone like a peacock amongst sparrows. I've known her all my life: I grew up with her, played with her in my grandfather's gardens on the heights of the Quirinal, me and her against our brothers, or the other way about.

She was turbulent even then, prone to scathing verbal attacks and wild, dangerous play. That day, seeing her play-acting the whore, I realized there was a level at which she was not playing at all, that I was seeing her as she really was: wildly dangerous.

And she'd been left inside the widow's house while the fake centurion she had entered with was laying a trail away from it, in the way the hind lays a trail away from her fawn, leaving it safe in the long grass.

I did wrestle for a moment with my conscience, but Otho had said it was of utmost import that his letter be delivered discreetly and there was nothing discreet in walking up to a house the Guards were watching, so I stepped out of the courtyard and followed the stranger up the Quirinal towards the more prosperous residential area.

Here the streets were broader, and slave-carried litters drifted slowly up and down; white ships becalmed on the sea of dusk. With wider streets and no crowds to hide in, the Guards had to become more tactful, less bullish. They slid up the sides of walls, making the most of the shadows, and separated, so as not to move in bulk.

But it was the fake centurion who led the dance and I tell you, it was a masterclass in distraction. I watched that man weave round statues, duck into doorways, walk freely up the street and then pause and dive into side streets and out again before turning and retracing his steps while the odd, disjointed tail of men following him never quite caught up.

It was growing dark and each of them made the most of it. The Guard became shadows, hunting a ghost. Up ahead, halfway up the Quirinal, a brazier glowed red in the centre of a small walled courtyard set bang in the middle of the street; a shrine to the cult of Isis that stays active through the night, as you know.

The courtyard had gates at each of the four directions; Pantera could have cut straight across from the lower gate to the upper, but if he'd done that he'd have been caught in the fire's glare while everyone else remained hidden in the dark. To avoid that, he had to go round one side or other; or so we all thought.

The Guards, seeing their chance, gathered into two pairs. One duo circled sunwise, the other counter-sun, or that was the plan. Pantera let them get halfway, and then ducked through the eastern gateway and doubled back at a dead run across the courtyard.

He was getting away. There was no chance they could circle back and catch him now. I gave a silent cheer. I still had no idea who he was, but at that point in the game, as far as I was concerned, any enemy of Vitellius' Guards was a friend of mine.

Which is why I ducked down behind a crumbling wall as Pantera fled fast-footed past, and then dodged out and followed him. I took care not to be seen. I wanted to get close enough to him to ask him questions, to find out who he was and what he knew about Jocasta. I hadn't thought of her in years; but now, having seen her, I could think of little else.

The broad street that leads down the Quirinal was too open for safety; Pantera could never stay there. Almost at once, I was led in a series of tight turns left and right and left, back into the stews where alleys were narrow and rarely straight and where the populace was less law-abiding than the senatorial worthies who live on the smart part of the hill. Here the streets were poorly lit; splashes of torchlight struggled against the night. The ground was uneven and dotted with unsavoury traps for the unwary. I could smell rancid horse, dog and pig dung laced with fresh human urine.

I stepped warily, hoping for solid ground under each foot, and tried to keep my eye on the man ahead. It was this straining into the night, the sifting of one shadow from others, that let me see the bandits just before they closed on him.

These weren't Guards, quite the opposite: big fuckers with

shaved heads who could have been gladiators, except they didn't move with the grace of a gladiator but the short, sharp speed of the street thug.

There were seven or eight of them, maybe nine, and they knew whom they sought; someone, somehow, had been a step ahead of his shadow-dance down the street and made sure these men waited ahead of him. They hefted their cudgels and blades and came in slowly, all focused on Pantera.

They had no need to hurry: where could he go? They had him surrounded. In the half-light of a distant lamp, I saw him hug his arms to himself and was disappointed; after the display out on the street, I had expected more of this man.

Then a spinning knife shimmered in the muggy light and the nearest of the attackers was down before the others could react.

I've seen a lot of men throw a lot of knives, and this one was exceptional, but it wasn't enough; the odds stood now at eight to one and that's still bad numbers in anyone's book.

I saw him stoop to pick something up from the ground, and in the time it took him to stand up again his enemies had closed in, swinging their cudgels.

I am not the kind to stand by while others have all the fun, and besides, it had been five months since I was last in a proper fight; my blood ached for action.

I had no weapon – a carter does not bear a blade, and I couldn't risk being searched as I came into the city – but I had my belt, which was full of gold, heavy and solid as a brick. I had it undone and wrapped around my hand before the bandits reached their target, and then – Hades, but it was good to be fighting again! – I stepped in and swung hard at the biggest and ugliest of the attackers.

I felt his skull shatter under my fist like rotten winter ice. His knees buckled and he dropped like a rock. I sidestepped his falling body and swung again, less cleanly this time. I caught the next one on the side of his face; teeth flew free and I saw the shine die in the man's eye as it split and leaked.

I pushed this one down, sending him into the path of a third, who had seen me by now, and was turning, swinging back his own arm, raising his cudgel high—

And had that cudgel removed at the top of its swing by the light-footed dancer who was my new friend.

He flashed me a grin, a man alive with the joy of battle. I saluted him, I think, certainly he returned it; we were like brothers in the field who have known each other half a lifetime, and then we were at it again, swinging our weapons, two against six, perhaps, and then five as Pantera used his newly acquired cudgel with devastating force, and then threw himself to the ground, rolling, to avoid the blows that rained down on his shoulders, his arms, seeking his head, not yet hitting it, and then not even really aiming because by then they had all realized they were fighting two, not one, and their attention was dangerously split.

I ducked a blow that would have swept my skull from my spine and, stepping in tight to the one I had chosen, slid my left hand up to his face, clawing for his eyes, driving him back to give my gold-heavy right hand a chance to jab short, hard punches at his groin, gut, face and neck until he doubled over and dropped.

My arm ached from the weight of the gold, and my hand was crushed inside my belt. I kicked the body at my feet and stamped on the side of the head as we did in the legions. I wasn't wearing my nailed sandals, but I felt skull bones crack beneath my foot and spun away in time to hear a shout in guttural Greek and see the last three remaining bandits break off the engagement and back away.

'No!'

I was beyond reason, in that place of red-veiled madness that takes me sometimes in battle, where to end a fight is almost as bad as to lose it. I was *not* going to stop now, not going to let them leave with the fight unfinished.

Jocasta was forgotten, Pantera an irrelevance; I was Trabo and I was back in Rome and if I needed an excuse it was that I had an oath to fulfil and a blood lust to satisfy and killing the agents of Vitellius was almost as good as killing the upstart himself.

CHAPTER FIFTEEN

Rome, 3–4 August AD **69**

Caenis

'My lady. I am so sorry . . .'

I woke sharply into a night that was far warmer than my dream had been, and far less threatening. Matthias was standing over me, mortified that his courteous taps on my door had not been enough, that he had been forced to touch my person to wake me.

I sat up swiftly and pain knifed in my temples; it does that, often, if I rise too fast. I kneaded it away. 'What news? Has Domitian returned?'

'My lady, he has not. But the spy is here again.'

'Pantera?' The name made me shiver, I don't know why.

'Yes, lady. He is hurt, but not mortally. He would speak to you if you allow it.'

Of course I would allow it. He came from Vespasian; how could I not?

Matthias had brought me a new tunic to slip on over my night shift. I took my time, splashed water on my face, combed my hair, settled a loop of silver about my neck. My mirror was kind and did not show my age: the woman who looked back at me was a cool and subtle courtier, not in the least engaged by her late-night company.

Pantera was in the dark of my atrium again, losing himself in the rippling shadows that spun up from the pool. Out of courtesy he moved into the light when I appeared, and I could see that, yes, he had been hit on the head, and probably elsewhere beneath his clothing. Even so, he was sharper now, tighter, just as Vespasian used to be after a day's training.

As I would have done with Vespasian, I crossed to look at him more closely and so saw the ugly wound on his brow. His swollen hands were blotched with bruises. He favoured his left leg as he stood.

I asked, 'Are you hurt?'

'Not enough to concern you, lady.' He smiled, taking the edge off the lie. 'I am, however, gravely concerned that Lucius knew I was here with sufficient certainty to send the Guards, and that he knew there was a chance I would escape, with sufficient certainty to set a small company of bandits on to me when I did so.'

'You are sure it was Lucius?'

'If he has not access to these, who has?' He opened his palm. On it lay thirty or more silver denarii, each one newly minted. Vitellius' head was emblazoned on each, a sight which, even now, sets my teeth on edge.

In the markets, the rumours said that Vespasian was minting his own coins in the east, and that they were of gold, not silver. I yearned for the day they were in circulation in Rome.

Pantera said, 'These came from the men who attacked me: six each. Not the Guards, the bandits who came afterwards.'

Six silver denarii each? And perhaps the same again when the job was done, if they had succeeded. That's a legionary's wage for a month, and it was paid for a night's work.

127

But Pantera was there, which meant that almost certainly the men who had been sent against him were dead, or injured to the point where they no longer posed any danger.

I said, 'This isn't proof. Just because you were attacked by men all paid in the same coin doesn't mean Lucius or Vitellius or any of their men did the paying. Rome is full of these coins. Every Guard has hundreds burning holes in his purse. They are scattered like grain before chickens.'

'Not these ones,' said a voice behind me, and Domitian was at my right shoulder, flushed with the adventures of the night, his eyes burning with an inner light that was normal in his father or elder brother but was, in those days, not normal at all in him.

He reached across me and took one of the coins from Pantera's palm. 'These are new.' He flipped one over, flipped it back again. 'The first coins of Vitellius had Victory on the reverse side. Then they struck thousands with Liberty instead and gave them to the new Guard by the handful. But these have the Wheat Sheaf, sign of plenty, on their reverse and that has not been seen in Rome before today. These are newly minted. I would wager my father's chances of success that they have not been through more than two sets of hands.'

For Domitian, that was a lengthy speech. Stranger even than that, he had taken Pantera's arms, as men do after battle, and was saying, gravely, 'It's good to see you safe when the lady Jocasta and I had thought you dead. We lay on a rooftop at the edge of the street and watched you lead the Guards a dance up and down the Quirinal. The lady Jocasta said you were the best she had ever seen; breathtaking, was her word. But then we saw the bandits attack. We wanted to help, but there were so many of them and the lady Jocasta . . .'

He stumbled, tripping over the unaccustomed weight of his own words, flustered in a way that was not common for a young man who, since childhood, had known the value of each syllable and hoarded it, miser-like, against the right moment.

Gently, Pantera said, 'Is she safe, the lady Jocasta?'

'She is. I escorted her to the door of her own house. She lives high on the Aventine. Her house is . . .' Domitian made an inchoate gesture with both hands, of fullness, and wealth and care. 'She said she would visit tomorrow, in more propitious circumstances. She asks that if she comes as a lady, rather than as a centurion's whore, will the lady Caenis receive her openly? It is not known that Jocasta favours Vespasian. Rather the reverse.'

It was the hesitation in his voice that sealed it for me. That, and the fact that, for the first time in his entire life, this quiet, private boy had transformed into the image of his father.

Domitian was in love.

I bit my lip. I had not thought him lacking in love, simply that he had always been more enchanted by his flies and coins and books than by any human soul.

In a moment's inattention, I let Pantera catch my eye. The spy raised a brow that said more than I ever could. I wanted to clasp Domitian to my breast and tell him to go back to his collections of insects and his reading of Aristotle and leave the lady Jocasta to the man who had cared for her so clearly in the early evening.

I did not, of course, say any of this, and in any case the moment was lost when Pantera yawned, widely.

Matthias was scandalized: such things are not done in polite society, but Domitian, who could only have seen it from the corner of his eye, stretched his own jaw-cracking yawn, and, catching himself, flushed deeply.

'My lady, lord,' he bowed to us both, 'I fear I must take myself from your company. I am not myself after dusk and would retire at once, with your permission?'

We gave it, of course, and thus, swiftly and easily, he was gone.

In his absence, Pantera leaned back against the wall and then subsided slowly down it. He came to rest, crouching with his knees hugged to his chest. Exhaustion softened his face.

I said, 'My lord, we cannot offer you a bed in our rooms, but there is a cot in the servants' quarters . . .'

'Thank you, no. I must leave soon. I endanger you every moment I stay.' Hands flat to the wall, he pushed himself upright. 'Lucius is a dangerous enemy. I would like to believe your rank and position protects you from the inquisitors' tools, but Nero tortured Piso's wife and we have no reason to believe Lucius has greater scruples.'

Really! 'If you are suggesting there is any danger I would ever betray—'

He held up his hands. 'I am sure your courage is as great as any, but it's not a risk I am prepared to take.'

'Then what will you do? We will not leave the city and you cannot if you are to promote Vespasian's cause.'

This late at night, I was prepared to speak the general's name aloud. I would have used any weapon I had to bind Pantera close. Whatever the danger – and I had lived in the palace under other emperors; I knew exactly what the inquisitors did – I wanted to be a part of what was coming. I needed to be.

Matthias was hovering, concern written on his face. I signed him to bed and when, unwilling, he had gone, I said, harshly, 'You are to protect three of us: me, Sabinus and Domitian. In addition, you have sworn to help Vespasian ascend the throne. You can't do either if you run from Rome.'

Pantera gave me a long look. 'I wasn't planning to run anywhere. There are ways to be in Rome and be invisible. I am merely trying to protect you from—'

'From the danger of your presence; I heard you. You said earlier that you planned to stay here as a servant. Do you plan that still?'

He took a moment to reply, which seemed unusual for him. The candles were dimming. I moved them closer and saw Pantera wince against the new light. He was sweating, and it was not all down to the evening's sultry heat.

Sighing, I took his wrist, felt the sharp, hard pulses at the base of his thumb. Briskly now: 'Tomorrow we can worry about your future and mine and how they may be protected. Tonight, you need a safe bed and a physic. Go to Scopius, the dream-teller who owns the Inn of the Crossed Spears, tell him Artemis asks of him that he give a stranger a bed and lends the skills of his wife in tending to his injuries.'

'Artemis.' His eyes were river brown in the lamplight, and full of humour. 'You are, of course, a goddess.'

'And, of course, I am not.' I snapped at him; I hadn't snapped in months – years. Vespasian could drive me to it; few others. With more restraint, I said, 'I played the part in a play once, when Scopius and I were children. He was . . . attached to Antonia's household for a while, not as a slave, but as a boy servant. The empress encouraged her servants to create our own entertainment. She thought it better than that we seek it outside her household.'

His gaze didn't flinch, but still, we were both reminded that I was not a lady and never could be, even if my man became emperor.

I made light of it; I did not want to shame him. 'Once a slave, always a slave. If you need to get word to me, send it with one of the silver-tongues. For Scopius' sake they will hold their silence against any inducement.'

'Silver-tongues?' He looked at me strangely.

'The street boys who carry messages around the ghetto are called silver-tongues. The ones who sell their bodies are silver-skins and those who thieve are silver-hands. Often the three are one and we call them silver-boys.'

'But not always.' There was a depth behind his gaze that I didn't understand: I do now, of course. He said, 'I take it Scopius knows the most reliable ones?'

'Always. And they know their way here. I may be a lady in dress and style, but on the streets, I am still one of their own.'

Pantera nodded, slowly. 'Good. Then it may be . . .'

He closed his eyes, pressed his fingers splayed against them. They were broad, strong fingers, darkened by the sun, but they turned pale as he pressed them to his brow, bone on bone.

With dogged clarity, he said, 'My lady, this is a suggestion only, you are free to turn it down, but it might be useful if you were to go to the market tomorrow morning as usual, and were to be seen to fall, to injure, say, your hip or your ankle, something that is not serious enough to need a bone-setter, but serious enough for you to plausibly hire a litter to bring you back here, and thereafter take one wherever you go. Does Scopius the innkeeper hire out litter-bearers?'

'He does.'

'Then, if it suits you to do this, send Matthias to hire a team from Scopius; trust us to see to it that he gets the right ones. Spend the next few days visiting your friends, lots of your friends, particularly those who support Vitellius. Nobody expects you to stop loving Vespasian, but let it be known that you fear for his life and wish he would not pursue this cause. Be subtle, but clear. Visit Sabinus and make sure he takes the same line. If I need to send a message, I will use the silver-tongues, as you say. And when it is safe, I will come to you.'

Chapter Sixteen

Rome, 3–4 August AD 69

Julius Scopius, innkeeper and dream-teller

I am Scopius. In childhood, I was a friend of the lady Caenis before she was a lady. Now, I am innkeeper, dream-teller, husband to Gudrun, and father to the acrobats Zois and Thaïs. Amongst other things, I own the Inn of the Crossed Spears.

Your man came to us that night shyly, shamed to be asking for a bed and unwilling to ask for more. He was hurting and desperate and he wanted us to think he could simply sleep did we but give him a safe bed on which to lie.

With another man at another time, I would perhaps have given him the keys to one of our private rooms and if he was dead in the morning, who would care? But I am a dream-teller and Gudrun watches the branching futures in the smoke bowl and we both knew that this man must live.

Why? Because we would not be here, talking now, if he had died, and here is where we need to be.

So; he came from Caenis who had saved my life once and

133

for that alone we would not turn him away. We knew what he needed and we each have our specialty; me, Gudrun, Zois and Thaïs.

Between us, we bathed him and oiled his hurts, the old as well as the new, and wrapped his hands and his head in willow bark and when he was warm again, and had drunk the hot, sweetened herbs that Gudrun cooked for him, and was pliant, we laid him on a bed with a good straw mattress and sang him to sleep.

In truth, he was already sleeping. Better to say that we sang him good dreams, to sweep away the nightmares in which men hit and burned him. They were not helping him to heal.

He woke before dawn the next day with less pain than he deserved and more than he wanted and then, at his request – still shyly made, but he knew by then what we could do – we set about changing how he looked.

Gudrun mixed the paste for his skin and hair and I smoothed it on, to be sure that every part of him was covered. Some hours later, when he had endured as much of the itch and discomfort as he could, we let him wash it off at the well; his self-respect needed it by then.

I gave him sacking to dry himself and then Gudrun held up the broad, flat, silvered bowl that he might see himself.

'Will you look?' she said.

He looked at her queerly, then. I think he did not remember her speaking the night before and this was the first time he had heard her truly. Her voice is northern, far, far northern, from the ice floes where walrus lie and many-horned deer run across the plains, and she speaks her Latin as one who learned it late, and still it splits her tongue. I love the sound of it, round in my ears, but it can take some getting used to.

Or maybe it was the bowl he recognized, for she had looked in it at the smoke-futures while he lay on his mattress and he might have woken and seen her.

But she was holding it up for him to use, so he stopped looking at her and instead looked at his own face in the bowl's reflection. We saw his eyes grow wide with shock and knew we had done what he needed much better than he had expected.

He took the bowl from Gudrun, tilted it this way and that, and what he saw was the same from every angle. Truly, he had become a Berber: every part of his skin was as dark as a paste of walnut juice mixed in ewe's milk butter with the egg of a dark-feathered hen can make it. On top of that, Thaïs and Zois had worked for an hour with certain other pastes so that the wound on his head, which had been angry and swollen the night before, looked as if it had been done in childhood.

His hair, once straight to the nape of his neck and glinting amber where the sun had caught it, was now black and curled tight to his head, like lamb's fleece. Since he was become a Berber tribesman, we had fashioned on his face the spiral tattoos that those people wear. With a sharpened quill, Gudrun had applied a mix of copper rust and powdered granite and ash that gives the look of an old tattoo, but will come off again with vinegar or lemon juice.

Catching sight of them, Pantera tilted the mirror so that it caught the light and sent dazzling patches a-dance across the walls and we could see the work as if under the noonday sun.

Gudrun grasped his chin and manoeuvred his face a little to examine her craft. Her fingers worked a little around the edge of the contusion on his brow, blending it in. If I say it myself, he was a testament to a great art; the scar looked ancient and the tattoos, too, looked as if they had been done at a puberty so long ago, the world had aged in between.

Only Pantera looked young and vital; our songs and our medicaments had rejuvenated him. Then, setting down Gudrun's mirror, he wrought his own magic, and even as we watched he seemed to age before us, to shrink into himself, to grow smaller, more frail; if you had passed him on a street corner you would have thought him half dead with the weight of time laid on his shoulders.

He looked at Gudrun, and then at me. 'If I need to change back,' he said, 'can it be done?'

'I am Scopius,' I said. 'Anything can be done. Come to me with a night to spare and you can become who or what you will.'

He gave me a sharp glance, but took me at my word. 'Then all that's left to be done is that I go and lie for half an hour on the manure heap, so that I smell more like an unwashed Berber grandfather and less like a good winter stew.'

He was recovering his sense of humour, and we were coming to recognize it. Zois, above all of us, was mesmerized by him. As soon as he was awake, she had come to sit cross-legged at his feet, to ply him with questions. He, for his part, had answered them honestly and freely, treating her enough as an adult for her not to feel patronized, not so much that she was lost. I know now that he had a child who would have been around her age, had she lived; then, I thought he was just taken with Zois, as so many men were, and that I had need pay mind to her virtue.

So I was more than half concerned when she asked, 'Where will you go?'

He could have sent her away, told her it was none of her business, or that she was safer not to know if the Guards came visiting, all of which was true. He did none of these things, but rather magicked a silver coin from the tip of his nose and tossed it to her, saying, 'Into the market, first, I think, to buy a sack of nuts or dates to carry: nobody looks much at lame Berber grandfathers, but even fewer will look at one if he is balancing a sack of dates on his crown.' His eyes met mine across the top of her head. 'I may also visit the silver-boys. Unless you would caution me not to?'

That gave me pause; nobody visits the silver-boys who has not been one, and I did not know him, or thought I did not. But then Rome is a big place and the silver-boys of the Quirinal, where we were, are different from those on the Palatine who are different again from those on the Capitol, and so it goes for each of the city's seven hills.

'They will be safe for the likes of you,' I said. 'And you may give them my greeting.' Which is to say, my assurance that he, Pantera, was safe. It was the greatest gift I gave him that day, but neither of us knew so at the time.

He lifted the mirror-bowl and held it a moment in such a way that my daughters were shown in it together. Zois is like me, small and dark and stringy; she will never turn men's heads with the curve of her figure, but she has a sharpness to her features that raises the blood.

Thaïs takes after Gudrun, since you ask; they are both ice-blonde and Nordic, and while the girl has not yet grown into the stature of her mother the signs of it are there, and are what hold men's attention when she dances on the tightrope across the street or spins at the top of a pyramid of men.

Pantera took the bowl and set it down, so that the only reflection was his. 'I saw your wife watching the smoke-dreams last night, after you had put me to bed.'

'You should not ask what she saw,' I warned him.

'I don't plan to.' He gave a tight smile. 'If death is coming, I would rather not know. If it's not . . .' He shrugged. He had been close enough to death often enough to know that there are worse things than dying. 'I wouldn't want to become careless. I just wanted you to know that I had seen.' And then, briskly, shaking himself clear of the memory, he asked, 'Have you been out to market this morning? Have you heard any news?'

The question was directed at me; he must have known I'd been out.

'If you mean are they hunting you,' I said, 'yes they are. Half the Guard is out asking for you by name and description in the morning markets. They say you are an enemy of the state and offer five hundred denarii for news of you. A lot of people say they have seen you. None of them is telling the truth. Yet.'

An enemy of the state is what they called Nero, which was enough to make him kill himself when he thought they might take him alive. Enemies of the state have their necks caught in a cleft stick and are flogged to death, although not, of course, until they have revealed all they know about other enemies of the state. People who harbour them are subject to the same sanctions.

Pantera's face grew grave. Formally, he said, 'I endanger you all by my presence here. I'm sorry, I had not thought they would be so swift to act. I will leave now.' He delved into his money belt and brought out gold. 'Perhaps this, for your trouble.'

I was the shy one then. It was Gudrun who put words to it. 'We don't need your gold.'

This was true: we owned the Inn of the Crossed Spears, plus the entire acrobat troupe who played in it. At least half of the houses strewn along the Street of the Lame Dog were ours while the inhabitants of the other half, if they didn't owe us rent, at least owed us loyalty.

Pantera closed his fist over his hand. He didn't turn away. 'Every man has his price. How long before the emperor's silver outweighs a promise?'

'Long enough for what you need,' Gudrun said and then, seeing his face, said, 'We have our dreams, too, and they tell us we shall not be betrayed while you are with us.'

Zois, who has eyes of the same hot-ice green as her mother,

looked up at him and said, 'Your death is not at our hands.'

It was on the tip of his tongue to ask whose hand would kill him – we all saw that – but he must have known the ways of the dream and how it harms a man to hear too much of his future, for, with no further comment, he donned the loose white robes of the Berber, took a stick that we gave him, and leaned on it. He stooped his back, dropped his left hip as if the arthritis had crippled him, and like that, bent and old, he ventured out into the city that was hunting him.

CHAPTER SEVENTEEN

Rome, 4 August AD **69**

Marcus, silver-hand of the western Quirinal,
speaking for his brothers

The little wizened Berber didn't look like a man who had been beaten half to death, although we had seen that happen. He didn't look like a man who was hunted by Rome, either, though there were Guards throughout the forum and the markets, asking questions and spreading news of the rewards for his capture.

Did we know who he was, with all his black skin and wiry hair? Not at first. But we saw him come out of Scopius' inn, and had not seen him go in, so we followed him on the rooftops, making the whistle signals, and we knew soon enough that he wasn't what he pretended.

From the first, when he came out of the inn, he didn't leave by the front entrance into the courtyard and on to the main street that runs up the Quirinal, the one with the widows' houses off it. He went out of the back, down the Street of the Lame Dog where the Guard don't dare go, and turned deeper and deeper into the hidden ways where the sun never reaches and bandits live with thieves and neither welcome strangers.

He was lame, he walked bent over, like he was crippled, but he didn't walk as if he was afraid, and in those streets he should have been.

He came into my place then, where I owned the rooftops.

How did I get them? You think I'm too small to fight for them? Well, then, don't ask me how. They were mine. Nobody was going to take them from me.

We were whistling one to another, just following him along, and then he went and ducked into a doorway and tucked his head out twice, to see if there was anybody watching. There wasn't, not at ground level, so he waited a bit longer and then, not lame at all, hopped on to the wall that goes round the courtyard where Phenris kills his pigs and then up on to the rooftops. Fast as you like, he was here, where only the boys should be.

We all lay flat, and he didn't look at us, but ran up and over the top and down the other side and then along and along and gone!

Well, some of the boys was for backing off and leaving him alone then. I mean, it's not right, is it? The boys leave the rooftops behind when they become men – those that live to become men, which is few enough.

But he was there, heading down into a place that used to belong to the Kosian before he died of marsh fever, and before that it was Circan's, and before that it was Florian's and before that . . . anyway, it has always been someone's place; we each have our own special place, hidden away, where nobody sees and the wind don't reach too strong.

This one has brick on either side from the house walls and tiles that meet in the middle at the back and catches just enough sun in summer or winter to be warm all the time, but never too hot. It's a palace of a place, really.

Pantera leaned back against the brick and tiles, looking like this is home.

We stopped whistling, all of us. There isn't a tune for 'That bastard's just dropped into the Kosian's place'. The others were all looking at me and I had to do something, so I picked two of them, Que— that is, Marcus and Marcus, and we went over to see him. You have to, don't you? You have to face these things.

He'd got his eyes closed, all peaceful, and we just dropped in and settled down and waited for him to look back at us.

Which he did soon enough. He looked at us like we were friends, as if we didn't each have salt in our hands, ready to throw in his face in case he tried to jump us. Actually, Fe— Marcus had something worse than salt.

He nodded at us as if we'd spoken, then brought both his hands out, nice and slow, like, and turned to one side and placed his palms flat on the wall and counted along the bricks.

We thought he was addled then, but we stayed and watched and after a while he pushed on a brick with the heel of his hand.

Nothing happened. Which, actually, was scary.

But he kept pressing and then gave a huff of frustration and hit it hard and then the brick jerked in, maybe only the breadth of your thumb, but still, it shouldn't have done that, see?

Very slowly, with his eyes on us, he took his knife out from his sleeve and slid it in along the side of the brick, breaking the mud and shite that looked like mortar, and then, when he'd got it free, he worked the brick out.

It was only half a brick. So he laid it on the roof and stuck his hand back in and we all held our breath then, because whatever was in there'd been in since before we was born.

Finally, he got to what he was after: there was a kidskin pouch, tied at the top with rough twine and sealed with a blob of dark wax. The whole thing was clean and dry and untouched. He laid it on the ground between us and broke the wax with his knife and opened it, so that we could see what was inside the same time he did.

Coins. A stash of silver coins. All with the head of Tiberius on, as clean as the day they were made. No one'd cut them, no one'd marked them, no one'd tested them with his teeth. Did he let me hold one? Of course he didn't! I saw, that's all. I'm a silver-hand; I know what you're carrying, how much and where. And in that pouch were fifty silver coins. Trust me.

He tipped the pouch a little towards us.

'All yours,' he said, 'and perhaps gold besides.'

Gold? No one ever pays us in gold. There's not many as pays in silver and then only when they want us not to talk about what they've done. Or to show anyone the marks. It always goes wrong in the end.

Anyway, he offered gold and we laughed in his face; not aloud, but he saw what we thought, and that we were ready to leave.

He hadn't lifted one of the coins out, I'll swear on my life he hadn't, but suddenly he had one in his hand anyway, and he was turning it over and over, making it slide under one knuckle and across the rest, as if it was flowing in loops round his hand.

So we stayed, to see what else he could do. And he said, 'Drusus, he's at the House of the Lyre still, aye?'

He spoke like us, or like the boys used to speak back in the time of the Kosian and before. Some of it is Latin, some of it's Greek, or Dacian or Gaulish or, if you're near Drusus, it's German, and we like to be near Drusus; he is one of us, grown and survived on account of his size; he gives us money from his own earnings, and food, and gets us work at the House if we want it.

And this man was asking about Drusus and the place he worked. So we listened to what he said next. It was a kind of code, see? To prove he was one of us, really, however weird he looked.

'There is a house on the Aventine,' Pantera said, and gave us a description, where it was, what it looked like; we knew it, and who lived there, but we let him tell us anyway; no point in giving up what you know if you don't have to.

He said, 'I'm going there now. You can follow me as long as you keep out of sight. One silver now if you do, two more this night if I know who comes and goes after I am gone and more yet if I know who follows me this day.'

He picked up his pouch, laid one silver coin where it had been. The face of the emperor Tiberius stared up at us like a ghost from the past.

I nodded. I took the coin. He knew already that I was leader.

To me, he said, 'I will speak to Drusus later. He will tell you who I am and what I have been.' He rose, smoothly, not lame at all, well maybe just a bit, in his left ankle. 'It would be useful did I have a name to call you by.'

I told him Marcus. Yes, all of us. We were all called Marcus.

'Marcus.' He said it as if he'd never heard the name before. 'A fine choice. Marcus, you will know where I am.'

Which we would, of course, because we could follow him when he crossed to the Aventine hill and went to call on his friend.

So we did.

Chapter Eighteen

Rome, 4 August AD **69**

Jocasta

Where were we? Pantera's visit to my house on the
Aventine. Yes, I remember. I was reading, I imagine,
when Caliope came to find me.

Caliope was eighty-six and had had her tongue removed at
fifteen by a senator who needed discretion and believed all
women gossiped by nature. He cut off her ears at the same
time, apparently thinking to make her deaf. A deaf and dumb
servant is useful, you see; she can't tell tales.

Anyway, Priscus was an idiot and my mother, Tiberia,
bought Caliope while the wounds were still fresh, and nursed
her back to health. She was beautiful in her youth, and showed
a capacity for figures and accounting that outshone me or
either of my brothers. She had had control of the household
accounts in our family for nearly forty years and even now,
when her sight is failing and she can only see figures written
thrice their usual size, and must work the abacus by feel alone,
she is fast and accurate. She is also utterly loyal.

The day we are talking about, the day after Pantera was beaten by the bandits, she came fast to me up on the third floor and tapped a spread-fingered rhythm on my arm. Her sign language is impenetrable by anyone outside the family.

'A man?' I asked. 'The same one who came yesterday?'

No. A curt shake of the head. Caliope's hair is white as winter ice and cut short, to evade the lice. In the mid-morning sun, it shone about her head like ermine, framing the dark holes of her ears.

She mimed a small man, hunched, and her vocal hands said that his skin was black as night. He asked for you by name. He said to tell you that he was here in the name of his Teacher.

Pantera, then. Nobody else still referred to Seneca by that name. Nobody else still spoke of the old man at all, except Pantera.

I called for wine, splashed water over my face, put on a smile and let Caliope lead me downstairs to where Pantera was waiting for me in the slaves' room on the lowest floor.

The stench reached me before I saw him. I rounded the corner, saying, 'I'm sorry, I—'

'You can't invite me upstairs. It's all right; I know.'

Hades, but he looked different. I was expecting a disguise, but *this*? If he hadn't spoken, I'd have thought Caliope had finally gone mad and was inviting in the debris from the streets.

I clamped my mouth shut and studied him. He wasn't angry, and clearly he didn't wish to talk about the night before, which was fine by me.

It's possible he hadn't seen me and the almost physical struggle I'd had with Domitian on the rooftops to persuade the boy to come away from the fight.

146

It's just as possible that he hadn't spotted the small, quiet, costly man I sent to follow Domitian home, but my man had seen Pantera and everything I have ever heard about this spy suggests to me that he sees those who follow him long before he is seen.

So I was fairly sure that he'd known I was there, and known also that I'd seen him in danger and not gone to his aid. And yet there was no rancour in his gaze. He seemed only to be waiting for my impression of his appearance and how he had changed.

What can I say? It wasn't just that his skin was black and his hair curled, his whole demeanour was different; he was another man than the one I had met in the inn last night and he, again, had been different from the one who had spoken to Caenis in her house that evening. I could have said so aloud, but I thought that if he could read me at all, he would know that his guise was good.

My mother used to say that when in doubt, it's always wise to pour the wine; so I did. My hand was steady.

'How did you survive?' I asked.

'Last night? Your friend Trabo helped me.'

So he did see. 'Did he know who you were?'

'No, but he knew you in the inn and he had watched us go into Caenis' house. I assume he followed me out. He left when the last three attackers tried to run. He killed them and then spent the night hunting Guards. Five are dead if the rumours are true. Give him long enough and he'll wipe them all out.'

'If they don't get to him first.'

'Which, of course, they will.'

There was another silence. Each time we met there was silence.

Irritable, I handed him his wine. 'What brings you here?'

He rubbed the knuckle of his thumb along his brow and

I watched him change his mind about what he was going to say and that, I have to tell you, was quite easily the most disconcerting moment in the entire series of disjointed, disconcerting meetings I'd had with this man.

With a kind of slow reluctance, he said, 'Lucius knows who I am, *what* I am. We thought he did when he sent an assassin to Vespasian, but last night proves it. He knew I was going to the widows' street. The Guards couldn't have got there in time otherwise.'

Hades. I had gone cold. My palms were wet. 'Nobody knew in advance where you were going, not even me.'

'Somebody found out.'

He moved a little and I had to hold myself still not to flinch. He was armed, obviously. So was I, but I had seen how fast he could throw. It was a measure of how unsettled I was that I even thought he might attack me.

Nothing happened, naturally. We each waited for the other to make the first mistake, in the way Seneca taught us. We were his children, both of us, the product of his making, and we were never easy in each other's company, even later, with everything that happened.

I searched his face for clues, but he was a small, black, wizened monkey of a man and his eyes were the same as they had always been, which was no help at all. And he believed there was a traitor close to Vespasian's cause. I could have wept, but where would that have got us?

'Did Caenis know to expect you?' I asked. That was always possible. 'Vespasian must have written to her, surely?'

'I asked him not to, but even if he did, she loves Vespasian and he her. Many things can be bought, but not love. If we can trust anyone, we can trust her.' He waited for me to answer and when I didn't – I had nothing to say – he said, conversationally, 'Lucius came to visit you yesterday.'

Who? Who told you that? Have you spies in my household? In his? Or do the silver-tongues on the street report to you so soon, when you've been here but two days?

I had spent three hard years trying to buy the favour and trust of the silver-tongues. I thought I had bought Scopius and his wife Gudrun at the Inn of the Crossed Spears, but never the boys who lived on the rooftops.

None of this I said aloud. None, I believed – I still believe – showed on my face. I shrugged. 'He is coming back again today. Soon. I thought you were him.'

'Does he know what you are?'

'*No!* Do you think I'm insane?' No other man knocks me off balance this easily. I pressed my lips tight, turned a circle on one heel, all the things one does to regain composure. I came back to him with my temper on a tight rein. 'He has . . . difficulties with his wife. She is not the woman he wants her to be.'

'And you are?'

'He thinks I may be. I have not disabused him of that idea yet. I thought it might be useful if one of us was close to him and it can't be you or Caenis or any member of Vespasian's family, he wouldn't allow it.' I was talking too much. I stopped.

Whore.

The word hung between us. I waited for him to say it, for evidence that he was even thinking it, but there was, if anything, a new respect in his eyes that I hadn't seen before.

'Useful.' He nodded, slowly. 'Also immensely dangerous.'

'Unlike walking round the city in broad daylight with a price of seven hundred sesterces on your head. Which is, of course, entirely safe.'

His laugh was there and gone too fast to catch, like a flash of winter sun, but there was a genuine warmth that was all the more surprising for its cause. Seneca had loved him. Slowly, over many meetings and in small currencies, I was beginning to understand why.

Still amused, he said, 'Seven hundred already? I last heard six, but that was in the Palatine stews. It was five at dawn this morning. I am growing more precious by the hour.' He sobered quickly. 'So we each face danger.' He leaned back against the wall, arms folded. 'If it can be done safely, I think you should let Lucius know that the lady Caenis has invited you to dine with her. Let him know that you will report to him what you hear there. Let him know that you might be useful.'

'And if he accepts? If he asks me to spy for him, what do I tell him?'

'That you have to be free to use your own discretion, and that things will change with time. If it were me, I would tell him as much of the truth as I could without damaging me. Let him know that Caenis is intimately involved in Vespasian's bid for power; if he hasn't worked that out already, he's not the man we think he is. Tell him small things, enough to make him trust you. If we're going to defeat him, it will be by the piling on of small facts of questionable truth that hide the one big lie at the centre.'

'So you trust me not to tell him everything?'

'Truly?' His smile grew thin and hard and didn't go near his eyes. 'At this moment, I don't trust anybody. But I would like to grow to trust you.'

He was not that different, then, from every other man who ever crossed my path. Somehow, I had expected more. But I have had years of practice at hiding that kind of disappointment.

I said, 'How will I reach you? I can't be seen sending servants to Scopius; it's too dangerous.'

'With this,' he said, and opened his palm. On it lay a small and shrivelled date. 'Take it.'

I did, and discovered that it was not a date, but a simulacrum made of fired clay and painted so that it was the exact shape, size and lustre of an old winter date, the sweet kind, that breaks apart as you eat it.

My mouth watered just holding it, even when I had learned how to twist the two ends in opposite directions and open it to reveal the hollow centre where the stone would have been. Inside was a tight-rolled slip of finest paper, enough to write perhaps two dozen words, if the letters were small.

'Be brief,' he said. 'Use the oldest ciphers. Nobody else will remember them.'

It was his compliment to me that he thought I would. I didn't, but I had Seneca's papers and could work them out. Very likely, he knew that, too.

Later, after he had gone, I opened the paper rolled up in the date and read what Pantera had left there: a phrase of Seneca's reproduced in plain text, without any kind of code or cipher.

Most powerful is she who has herself in her own power.

She. Seneca wrote the lines for a man; Seneca wrote everything for his men. Pantera had reworded it for me.

She who has herself in her own power. I have always had that. I was not going to change then, or now.

I burned the note and hid the dangerous date and waited for Lucius' visit.

He came less than an hour later, and he was, as ever, suave and urbane and endlessly courteous. He brought me gifts of gold and pearls and diamonds, and a fine mind and a ready laugh.

He was, in short, everything that Pantera was not. And he

was not dangerous to me as long as he thought I was giving him what he wanted: my mind and then my body.

I planned to give him both, though I hadn't yet yielded to his touch. I gave him conversation and laughter and quick, ready answers.

Neither of us, I think, was disappointed with our intercourse. He promised to come again, and I believed him.

CHAPTER NINETEEN

Rome, 4 August AD **69**

Horus, owner-in-part of the House of the Lyre

If you speak to the Marcuses, they will tell you that Pantera came to the House of the Lyre by an indirect route, down the Aventine, across the forum and south into the ghettos and slums on the side of the Capitol – the heaving, stinking, built-up rat warren where neither fire nor Nero's building regulations have effected any serious change to the architecture for generations.

There are apartment blocks eighteen storeys high there that lean on to the side of the hill like drunken men on a bad morning, leaving dim alleys beneath where the sun never penetrates and the worst of humanity can slake its lust in eternal shade. Pantera said to me once, some years ago, that he felt less safe in the slums of the Capitol than he did in the forests of Britain and he was not safe there, not when he was a Roman, hunting Britons, nor later, when he made himself a tribesman and was hunting Romans with his warriors.

Now, with the whole of Rome offered real silver to catch

him, he hugged those unsafe places as if they were friends. And he immersed himself in his new guise.

Even the silver-boys, who can transform themselves from street thieves to boy nymphs in the twist of a smile, said that he had utterly changed himself into a Berber grandfather, a lame date-carter, making a pittance carrying his wares balanced in a sack on his head, which made his limp worse. He was afraid of dogs.

He left behind the last of the summer sunlight and moved deeper into the heart of the slum.

In this place are inns that cater only to slaves, and others that cater only to freedmen. There are fishmongers, iron-mongers, bakers, carpenters, tanners, fullers, dyers, spinners and weavers: if a trade stank or might cause a fire, or blind its crafters, or pollute the local water, it was done there, in the sink of the city.

And then there were the brothels, which at least smelled sweeter.

Their doors, on the whole, were painted in martial red, with carvings of men in full erection all around. The shutters had breasts painted on them that made pairs when closed, and strange anatomical impossibilities when pegged open. For the hard of thinking, the door knockers were shaped like engorged phalluses, if giants gave their members to madams for their premises.

With the Marcuses watching from their rooftops, the little black Berber that was Pantera passed through all these without pausing long in any one place; just enough to look back and be sure he was not being followed by other than they. He whistled occasionally when they lost him. Yes, they lost him, which is almost unimaginable, but you have to remember he was one of them once; we both were. We know how they think.

He came to the outer, southern edge of the ghetto, where

154

the brothels mixed with ordinary houses and were less indiscreet. Down one carefully unspectacular side street was a particular door painted lilac set between thrown-back shutters that showed musical instruments played by fully clothed youths of both genders. The knocker was in the shape of a lyre.

Pantera walked past once, carried on to the end of the street, turned right and right again in a circle, rested his dates on the ground and waited. The city was at its busiest and he must have known that if one of Lucius' agents was following him, this was when they would have been hardest to see.

There were no Guards in the vicinity. He must have passed a dozen or more detachments on his way here, but they wouldn't be in this particular street; the House of the Lyre has its own reputation and it would sit ill with the man who upset its management if that upset were passed to the clients, most of whom outranked any member of the Guard.

Yes, I am proud. We made this house, my sponsor and I, and it has grown in less than fifteen years to be the foremost of its kind in Rome.

But more of that presently. On the day in question, which was the fourth day of August that year, Pantera the spy made his circuit a few more times, and then, on the fourth or fifth pass, he stepped up and knocked lightly on the lilac door.

A giant German with a small head on vast shoulders and inked marks on monstrous biceps answered. He was so big that his member might well have graced the doors deeper in the slum, except that nobody would ever have been suicidal enough to try to take it. He cost a fortune, and was worth every slip of silver; nobody, however drunk or drugged or finely born, was going to offer violence in his presence.

Pantera was not intimidated; quite the reverse. He cocked his little wizened head to one side and, bright as a blackbird, said, 'The seas were stormy when I travelled here. Perhaps the House of the Lyre can offer balm to a travelling soul?'

The giant blinked down at him and stared and blinked again. He gave the impression of a man who thought slowly, and then followed with his fists. It was, as Pantera knew, and I can attest, an entirely false impression, but he played it well.

'The seas can be rough,' he said presently, in passable Latin, 'but we always have calmer waters in our house.'

He nodded his tiny head, a sight altogether like a pea bouncing on a bough; then, in rougher, easier Greek: 'It's been long enough.' He held out one massive arm.

Pantera clasped it fondly. 'Drusus, I miss you every moment I'm away. But it can't be helped. Is he in?'

'He is. And alone. I could take you up, but—'

'But you won't because we're all safer with you guarding the door. This for your time.'

A piece of silver changed hands, not enough in most circumstances to buy entry to the House, but this was Pantera; he had rates all his own.

So what can I tell you about our house? If one were to enter as Pantera did, by the front entrance, which is the only one permitted to clients, one would pass from a plain and inexpensive street into sophisticated, genteel beauty. The door gives way to a small vestibule, but that's only for show. Beyond that is a large courtyard garden, open to the skies, so that the five storeys of the house look inward over an abundance of late-flowering lilacs, olives heavy with fruit, citrus trees, cherries, balm.

Doves settle and coo in the bowers. Songbirds shower the visitor with golden notes. Doors lead off on all sides, on all floors. Those above the ground floor have rails and balconies that look down on to a garden that is laid out to be as restful seen from four storeys up as it is to walk through. Staircases lead up from the two diagonals; the northeastern and south-western corners.

Pantera took the latter, which was closest. He ran lightly up four flights of narrow, claustrophobic stairs. The frescoes were new, but nothing he hadn't seen before in one form or another.

On the lower walls are images of sexuality; not the grotesques of the inner-ghetto brothels, but subtle frescoes of silk-clad women regarding their reflections in slow-flowing rivers, young men poised in acts of bravery and strength. As he ascended, the images became more explicit and the faces more recognizably those of the men and women who worked in the House. Each had a specialty, and these were depicted in unashamed detail, so that by the time the visitor reached the top floor he or – less often – she would have had time to examine the possibilities in theory, and so would be ready to explore them in practice.

Some of those explorations were taking place as he passed, giving rise to the sounds and scents of intercourse; even now, in the mid-morning, we had clients who had paid for a full day, dusk to dusk, and were loath to waste time sleeping.

Elsewhere, the employees of the House slept off a night's work, together or alone. A few of them passed Pantera on their way to or from the baths on the lower ground floor. They slid past clad in silk, eyeing the lame, wizened Berber, deciding that he must have a great deal more money than appearances might suggest. We keep an exclusive establishment and nobody comes here who lacks the means to spend freely. Everyone who comes requires absolute privacy and will pay to preserve it.

On the top floor, the fourth, an expensive drift of frankincense underlined, strengthened, deepened, made more intimate, exotic and enticing the enduring smell of human sex that leaked up from below. Pantera took a left turn at the top of the stairs, skirted the balcony that looked over the now vertiginous drop into the courtyard garden, and entered a corridor that stretched out away from it; a spur that led away from the main building.

The floors on this level were painted in a brilliant, martial red: a man's entire body of blood could have flowed along here and been invisible until you trod in it. The walls were paler: Mars met the white light of the moon and made a delicate pastel pink. There were fourteen doors along the corridor, seven on either side, painted progressively in the colours of the rainbow, beginning with a deep cherry red at the head of the stairs and cascading through amber, sun, spring, sky and midnight to a single lilac door at the far end that stretched across the corridor's full width.

Not that Pantera inspected the rainbow hallway in any depth. You see, when he feigned his fear of dogs in his Berber guise, it was not all a sham; he had learned by sad experience to be wary of hounds and there was one in particular where, shall we say, a mutual respect had arisen.

That hound was Cerberus, a vast, black, strong-tailed, loll-tongued, prick-eared monster with great brown eyes and teeth as long as your thumb, and he was stationed outside the lilac door. A chain ran from his iron-spiked collar to a rivet in the floor, but it was coiled in loose piles and it was impossible for a visitor to estimate its length.

Cerberus wasn't howling to announce the presence of a visitor, he was too well trained for that. He wasn't straining to reach him either, but still, Pantera was not inclined to move close. Without moving his eyes, he pursed his lips and began to whistle; not a command to stay or come, but a low, rolling air that blended with the murmuring of doves nearby. It was his signal to me, to let me know who he was.

It's possible I might have known him without that; I am used to seeing the truth beneath men's subterfuge, but I heard the air before I looked, and so, squinting through the spyhole in the door's ornament, I was able to appreciate his disguise in its fullness. Still, I didn't rush to invite him in.

Pantera whistled. The hound blinked. For a long time, nothing else moved.

Pantera finished the tune and had no other and it looked to me that he was about to turn away. I couldn't let him go like that, difficult though his presence was for me.

I let the door open a fraction. 'The Guards are offering six hundred sesterces for you alive, did you know?'

'Seven.' Still Pantera did not move. 'Would you prefer that I leave?'

I said nothing, just undid the chain, let the door swing open and beckoned him in.

On the inside of the door was a silvered panel four feet by two that showed the new visitor how he looked to those around him. Women have been known to enter on occasion, but I have found that men, in particular, like to be assured that they look good.

As Pantera stepped in, we were framed together: him, a wizened Berber grandfather with tattoos like knife cuts on his cheeks and an ancient wound on his head that was not there the last time I saw him; me taller, because I was standing upright, though we are of a height when both standing the same. The mirror flattered my Alexandrian colouring, the doe-brown eyes, the blue-black hair, the olive skin; my patrons find me beautiful and I pay attention to my looks: no hair in unfortunate places, my eyes always enhanced with shading in the Egyptian style. My robes were of lilac silk and cost more than anything Vespasian or his agents could have afforded: the House of the Lyre never skimped on quality.

Pantera shut the door, slid across the three bolts and fastened the chain; he had always been careful, but that day he was doubly so.

He came fully into my domain, then. Though it was hidden away, the room was the biggest in the House, larger than most atria. A beaded curtain divided it in two and beyond was a silk bed big as a boat, and beyond that, a wide, sun-bright balcony on which doves and songbirds dozed amidst hanging vines.

The area nearest the door had no bed, but a low table carved in boxwood inlaid with coloured stones and a couch upholstered in a midnight-blue silk so deep, so lustrous that a man could have fallen asleep in its embrace and not woken for a month. On a table nearby stood a Greek vase that rose to waist height, wrought around with images of naked men. It was centuries old, from the glory days of Athens, when the world was a simpler, more beautiful place. Wherever you were in the room, that vase commanded attention.

The only other thing of note, which I must mention now, so that you know for the catastrophe that came later, is that there was a lilac-painted cupboard that served as Cerberus' kennel at the far end of the couch. It was painted to fit with the restrained beauty of the room, but it was clearly the hound's domain.

Pantera knew what it was, and, accordingly, sat at the far end of the couch. Cerberus lay down in the open kennel door and set his head on his great feet. His eyes never left Pantera's face.

Pantera stayed quite still. 'What do I call you?' he asked.

I ignored the question at first, caught his chin, tilted it to the light, studied the work that had been done on his face. The wound on his head was new, but only by close scrutiny did I discern that. At length, I said, 'Very good. I wouldn't have known you if you hadn't whistled. Clearly Cerberus did, or you would be dead.'

'You are nameless?'

I laughed, softly. 'If Lucius succeeds in taking you alive, I

160

will very much appreciate being nameless, yes. If I must have a name now, you may call me Horus.'

'You were Osiris once.'

'Then we may agree that I have refined my pretensions.'

He looked so old, then, when I know that we are within six months of the same age. We were silver-boys together, two of the very few of our generation who didn't end our lives floating face down in the Tiber.

We found our sponsors, you see. Pantera, of course, found Seneca who took his raw talent and polished it to the rough diamond he became. Seneca found me, too; I had some talents he valued, but my best and greatest sponsor was, and is, Mucianus, who was leading the armies for Vespasian.

Pantera knew this, I'm sure; we had never spoken of it openly, but he would have been a lesser man had he not. He knew that Mucianus owned the House and that he paid for its upkeep. You could have said that Mucianus owned me, if you like, but both of us would have denied it. He was generous. He is very generous, in fact. He did not consider ownership necessary and I have never been his slave.

For my part, I had my own sources of information, so I already knew that Pantera had come from Vespasian's side and that he was in Rome to protect the general's family and to promote his attempt to become emperor. The message doves had brought other messages, too, for Pantera.

I said, 'Hypatia sends you her greetings. She says to tell you that Kleopatra fulfils her promise, that Iksahra hunts with her hawks across the sands to great effect, and the general is settled and safe. I don't wish to know what any of this means.'

He relaxed a little, sat back, smiled like in the old days. 'I wasn't planning to tell you. If you are taken, I would prefer you, too, to know as little as possible. Has anything come from the east?'

'Two birds. The messages were sealed. I have not opened them.'

Cerberus guarded more than my person. I knelt by him then, and took off his collar. Pantera looked at me as if I had gone mad, but the hound leaned on my shoulder and swiped his tongue across my face and his tail hit the floor hard enough to make it shake.

There were eighteen spikes on his collar, each two inches long. I unscrewed the third along from the tie and tipped out the two small ivory cylinders from the centre.

'I don't know the ciphers,' I said, which was true, although it was also true that one of the skills Seneca found and nurtured in me was that of code-breaking. You wouldn't think it in an Alexandrian with the looks of a girl, but there were few ways of disguising a message that I could not read, given time.

My other skill? That was forgery. I can mimic any man's hand, or woman's, come to that. Which is why, obviously, I was uncertain of Pantera.

But we digress. I handed him the cylinders and told him I didn't know their contents and he gave me that sideways smile again, because he and I had spent months in our youth breaking into other men's private correspondence. I think he saw it as a testament of my respect for him that I hadn't looked at these, and truthfully, I hadn't.

He opened the heavier of the two cylinders first and, after a moment, held it out so that we could both read the contents. The sparse lines on the rolled bark inside were written in a simple letter-substitution cipher he had created himself twenty years ago, which both of us could unravel in our heads as we read it.

From Mergus to the emperor's spy, greetings.
We have met Vologases, King of Kings of Parthia, who promises peace between our empires when Vespasian

*rules. He has offered forty thousand archers to our cause.
Vespasian will not accept foreign aid, but is grateful for
the offer. Mucianus marches west with five legions. We
are for Alexandria. Men seek you with ill intent. Take
care.*

'Interesting?' I asked.

'Marginally.' He laid the missive down on the table. 'I
didn't know about the archers. It's good to know the King
of Kings is choosing Vespasian as his preferred emperor. It
could mean peace in the east.' He had been there, you see, to
Parthia, or at least close. He had spoken to the King of Kings.

The second message was from Mucianus, which was a surprise; I thought he only wrote to me. He used a more complex
cipher of his own creation so that Pantera had to ask me for
the key and then for a slate so he could transcribe it. It wasn't
impenetrable, don't think that: a competent code-breaker on
either side could have mastered it in a morning. With the key,
it was effortless. Pantera transcribed it on the first pass.

*From Mucianus, to the maker of minds. We need Ravenna.
It must come to our cause.*

Just that. Pantera stared at it, chewing his lip.

After a while, I said, '*Maker of minds?* Does he always call
you that?'

'Never before.'

I said, 'He is not one to waste a bird.' He knows the trouble
we take to get them to him. He would never do that.

'Nor to speak the obvious.' Pantera raised a brow. 'Have
you a candle?'

The candles were on the far side of the beaded curtain,
with the bed and the cooing doves. I passed through, setting
it chiming. When I returned, Pantera was holding one of the
beaded threads, studying the beads. In wonder, he said, 'I
had thought these were painted wood.'

He held in his hand a fortune threaded on a few feet of silk. The beads were of ivory, pearl, palest amber. The very lowest bead on each strand, which weighed the others down, was a nugget of raw gold.

I said, 'Mucianus sends me beads as he finds them, or things he thinks can be fashioned to be suitable. There's a trader in the city, Ostorius – you'll remember him from the rooftops? The black-haired half-Dacian with the smallest finger missing on his left hand? He's a woodsmith now. He can carve anything into a bead, given time.'

With every passing heartbeat, we were receding further into our shared childhood. We huddled together on a couch that seemed suddenly too big for what we had become. I passed him the candle in a silver stick and the kindling ember held in a small pot. He lit the wick.

Heated, the thin paper crisped at the edges, but across the width of the page grew letters, darker than the darkening bark around them.

Beware treachery. F & A not alone. One other: you his sole target. Now dead. Did not have a name to give, or a face.

'F and A?' I asked.

His face was pinched. 'Fundanius and Albinius. They were two centurions in Lucius' pay who tried to assassinate Vespasian in Judaea. Fundanius said before he died that I had been his second target.'

'And Mucianus has caught another who was sent to kill you alone.'

'Evidently.'

'How do they know who you are?'

'If I knew that, I would sleep better at night.'

Pantera burned the two messages, dropping the last fragments into the ember-bowl where they charred and curled and became fine threads of sweet smoke.

'I should go.' Pantera stood. It didn't seem likely to me that he had got all he came for, but he gave every sign of leaving. 'If anything else comes in, the silver-boys will know how to find me.'

'Are you back for good?'

'I'm back for now.' In two strides, he was at the door, and Cerberus had not moved to stop him.

He paused in the process of leaving, as if struck by a thought. 'Do you still have dealings with Tiberius Nisens at the palace?'

This, then, was why he had really come.

'The bath-master?' I had to think about that. 'What kind of dealings do you mean? He's not a client of the House; he can't afford it.'

'But you see him still?'

'Sometimes. He's a friend.' He was almost a brother, once, but that doesn't always lead to trust.

'Do you still have sufficient connection to him to suggest subtly that he take on a new masseur?' Pantera asked.

'Probably. He won't take you, though. Vitellius is a big man; he needs big hands on his body.'

'Are Drusus' hands big enough?'

'Hades!' I haven't laughed in years the way I laughed then. And then I stopped laughing, because he was serious.

'You'd have to pay gold,' I said. 'Drusus is not cheap.' He was not for sale for any money, actually, but I knew that he would do what Pantera asked; there was a love between them that I had never been part of.

Pantera said, 'I have Vespasian's writ. I have all the gold we need. But I need a man inside the palace, who hears what Lucius says when his guard is down. Drusus is one of the bravest men I know.'

'If I tell him that,' I said, drily, 'maybe you won't need gold. He worships you. I can't think why. '

It was Pantera's turn to grin like a boy. In truth he loved this place, the memories of it, the lifestyle, my company. He didn't have to say so, it showed in his eyes.

He said, 'I can't think why, either. And I will pay gold in any case. See if you can get Drusus into the palace. Leave word for me with Cavernus at the White Hare on the Esquiline.'

Cavernus. And me. And Drusus. All the relics of his far gone past. I said, 'Is there nobody newer you can call on?'

'When my life is worth seven hundred denarii and rising? Only the distant past is safe from that.'

'Then you might want to know that Julius Claudianus leads one of the gladiator schools now. He trains on the Capitol side of the Circus Maximus. Vitellius likes him. He may have access to the things Drusus can't hear. And there's—'

'Stop.' Pantera put up his hand. 'What you are doing is already enough. And what you don't know can't endanger you. Do you employ the silver-boys still? The Marcuses?'

'When they ask me to.' The fact that he knew them by name told me all I needed to know. 'I'll send them with word if anything comes in.'

Pantera gave a small salute, a lift of the finger that the street boys use to say the road ahead is clear. 'Keep safe. I'll whistle for Cerberus when I'm back.'

CHAPTER TWENTY

Rome, 4 August AD 69

Borros, freedman, formerly slave to
Cavernus of the White Hare

I was born in the White Hare tavern and, until Pantera came, had never slept a night away from it.

It was a fair-sized place, stuck halfway up the Esquiline, spreading over the whole of the corner between the carters' street and the main thoroughfare; a good, clean hostel with good wine at good prices and food to go with it and by noon on most days we had all of our regulars in place: men who preferred our benches to their own, our gossip to their memories.

They weren't soldiers, as such. If I'm honest, we were the kind of inn that attracted soldiers who had gone to seed, not so much a legionary tavern, but rather a former-legionaries' tavern, where men came to share stories of the life that they had lost.

Tiberius Cavernus was the owner and bar-tender, a tall, big-built Rhinelander who said he'd been a duplicarius in the legions in the days of Claudius and had saved his pension just for this.

He had straw-bright hair cut level with the lobes of his ears and he trimmed his nails once a week as he had done in the legions. His whores were clean and went about their work cheerfully and no thieves hung around the tables, not for long. I had always been surprised that he didn't serve a better class of client: real military men instead of the bitter has-beens who drank to forget.

That day, I discovered the reason.

I was tending to the beer stock when this little Berber trudged in and dumped his sack of dates on to the low pine table that served as a bar at the back. Cavernus was swiftly at his side.

'Leave, stranger. We have no need of—'

Cavernus' expression didn't change; I was watching him and I saw nothing, except that he had stopped speaking.

After a short, stunned pause, he jerked his head to the small door that led to the latrines, and beyond them to the kitchens. Only his voice was strained as he said, 'Dates, are they? Out the back with you, then.'

He ushered the little man through ahead of him. I was a slave, I had to go out anyway; they barely noticed me following them as they passed the latrine trenches and went through another door to a small room where the food is prepared.

The women took one look at Cavernus' face and backed out. I remained at the door, peering through the gap at the hinge. My mother always said I was overly curious, but when you're a slave you either learn things or you learn nothing; there's no in-between place.

Cavernus was looking worried. His gaze roamed the small room with an air of regret. 'That's some disguise,' he said. 'I barely knew it was you. Have you come to claim what is yours?'

The little Berber date-man shook his head. 'This is your inn; it has never been mine. I gave it to you and I will never take back a gift freely given. But I have a favour to ask.' He spoke like a Roman, not at all like a Berber.

'Of course.' Cavernus wasn't as relieved or cheerful as I'd have thought. He still looked wary. 'What can I do?'

'Tell me, has anyone been here asking for me by name?'

'Who hasn't?' Cavernus laughed, shortly. 'Before this morning, nobody spoke your name in my hearing in the past fifteen years. This morning, more men than I can count have asked for you and each with his blade sharp and ready.' My master's hands worked at the cloth at his belt. He looked ashamed. 'I haven't had time to send word to you.'

'You couldn't have done that; you didn't know where I was. I'm not blaming you. I bring my misfortunes on my own head. I just needed to know if there was anyone asking here in particular. If they knew that I knew you. It seems not. In which case . . .' Pantera opened his sack. 'Since I'm here, you'd better look at these.'

Cavernus chose one of the dates from the second layer, bit it, rolled it round his mouth before he swallowed.

'Good enough for the White Hare.' He sounded more like his usual self.

Pantera said, 'You can have half. The rest I need to take on.'

Sticky-fingered, they began to scoop the fruit out into a wooden barrel at the side.

'There must be something else,' Cavernus said as they worked. 'You didn't come here in the day's heat only to ask if anyone knows I am your man.'

'Ever wise, Cavernus.' Pantera flashed him a smile that was all yellowing teeth with gaps at the side. 'I want you to listen. To find a man, or men, who were officers, but left the legions in poor regard. Someone bitter enough to take silver to betray the current emperor. They don't have to be overly discreet; just willing.'

I began to understand, then, that this was why Cavernus had chosen to ply his trade to the has-beens when he could have aimed so much higher: because once, a long time ago, this little Berber had thought it might one day be useful. And now it was.

Cavernus said, 'There are two or three who fit that bill; the trouble will be finding one who doesn't drink from dawn to dusk. When I have the right man, do I use the old ways of sending a message?'

'Not yet. I'm not sure they're all safe. For now, send one of your men to the market to buy dates. He's to ask for the big Syrian ones he got last week. Ask all the date-sellers. I'll hear it.'

Pantera picked up his sack. He paused at the doorway, half hunched, lame again.

'Do you still own Borros?' he asked. The hairs stood up on my neck then, I can tell you. I didn't know whether to keep looking or to press my ear to the hinge to make sure I heard every word. In the event, I didn't need to do that. I could hear it easily and still see.

'That mad fuck of a Briton?' Cavernus pulled a wry face. 'He died in the fire, trying to save his wife and three of his children.' A flash passed between them of shared sorrow and memories best forgotten. We are all like that, who knew the fire.

Cavernus brightened. 'Young Borros lived, though; the son. He's grown well.'

'Is he reliable?'

'If you can call it that. He's twice the size of his father, and twice as mad. He hasn't actually killed any of us in our beds yet, but I wouldn't put it past him, if he— You're not serious?'

Three gold coins had just materialized on Pantera's palm.

They jumped and spun and when they fell they were one atop the other.

Cavernus' laugh billowed out into the bar room. 'You're as mad as he is. I'd be lucky to get half a silver for him at auction, even if I spent a month polishing him up.'

'Will you sell him to me?'

Something passed between them, some remembering I couldn't know, for nothing was said, but Cavernus rolled his eyes, wildly, the way men do to show madness. 'You're crazy. He'll cut your throat and get on the next boat home.'

But the gold was gone, the deal sealed. Cavernus shrugged, wiped his hands clean, slid the gold into the pouch he kept round his neck, sucked in a breath and bellowed out my name. '*Borros!*'

I couldn't believe it. In that moment, all I could think of was my mother, my father, the brother and sisters I'd lost in the fire – and that the White Hare was my home. I had been born there, on a bed Cavernus had provided. I'd eaten from his table, drunk his ale, been beaten by him and learned not to weep. I never thought he'd sell me. But what could I do? I waited long enough for it not to look as if I was standing just outside the door, then pulled it open and went in.

I saw Pantera properly for the first time, then; he had set down the dates and wasn't stooping any more and had run his hands through his hair so it looked less like a crow's nest and he had that look in his eye . . .

I don't know how to describe it, but I felt safe in his company. You know when a pack of hounds meets a strange dog and he just walks in and eats their food and lies in their sleeping places and they let him, because they know he'll find them food? Pantera was like that, so I didn't feel quite so broken, and then he opened his mouth and said, 'Warrior, from today you are a free man. But if you want to hunt with me, I pledge my life for yours and ask only the same oath in return.'

Only he didn't say it in Latin, or even in Greek, which was what we all spoke except on formal days, he said it in the tongue of western Britain, with the accent of the Ordovices, my mother's tribe.

A child could have pushed me over then, with one fat little hand. I gaped at Pantera like an idiot and couldn't speak. Cavernus, trying not to smile, pushed a stool up behind me and I collapsed down to sit on it and only then, seated, did I find the words to answer in kind. 'My life for yours, of course.'

It's the old oath that warriors give one to another, and while I might have been born into slavery my mother taught me the ways of our gods, the honouring of oak and stream and the north wind and the sun, and how warriors pledged to each other before battle.

Pantera took my arm, hand to elbow, and I read an honesty in his eyes that I was not used to in men. 'You are surprised now. I won't hold you to it. But if you wish to come with me, perhaps I can make it sound more attractive. If not, you may leave, a free man. I will sign your manumission papers in any case.'

It was too much, too soon. I have never been a fast thinker.

I heard Cavernus walk out muttering something about a fucking waste of good gold and Pantera, serious-faced, said, 'You can always stay here if you want. Cavernus will take you back in a flash.'

'No!' I was on my feet then, my head spinning. I saw the world open before me, in new colours, with a new feel. 'Show me what you said, and then I'll decide.'

'Good.' A small smile flickered across his face, as if I'd done well, and was being congratulated; as if I was a good man. You don't know how rare that was. 'Do you have anything to bring?'

'No, nothing.' I had small things, but I didn't want them; I was going forward into a new life.

'Let's go, then. If you could walk apart from me, as if you don't know me, but watch to see if anyone else is following me, that would be good.'

I did my best. I saw one of the small boys on a rooftop when now I know there must have been at least a dozen, but I didn't see anyone more important and I am sure that's because they didn't know yet what guise he had taken.

We criss-crossed the city twice in the day's heat. Twice we stopped and Pantera went in somewhere. Once was to a tanner's in a foul-smelling yard, once was to a scriptorium in the back of a block of small shops, a place where scribes rented out their skills.

Each time, he came out with another man behind him, and each looked as dazed as I felt, as if their world had turned over and been shown to be other than they had thought it.

The first, from the tanner, was a youth of barely twenty years, with a squint and dirty blond hair that looked as if it would shine like spun gold if only he washed it.

He was a killer, I will tell you that now. I might not have grown up a warrior, but I have had my share of street fights and bar-room brawls and I know the type: they're lean and lanky and slightly awkward and they look as if they couldn't land a clean blow on a man if he was held still by six others and then you blink and look again and you find he's got a knife in his hand and he's cut the throat of a man you'd think he could barely reach and is heading for the next one. That was Felix. He was left-handed and quiet and deadly and he tagged along behind Pantera on the far side of the street and I barely saw him again until we stopped.

Amoricus was the Egyptian scribe, from Memphis; he wasn't old either, perhaps in his mid-twenties, but he walked strangely, as if he had a pole up his arse, and it wasn't until the next morning's latrines that I realized he'd been gelded.

It turned out he'd been a priest of Isis and had committed

some heinous crime, spat on the altar or some such, and they'd cut his balls off and sold him into slavery and he'd been forced into writing because he couldn't do anything else.

But he was a good scribe. He had ink on his fingers that morning and came with his own writing kit, blinking in the sunlight as if he never usually saw it and trotting along the middle of the road behind Pantera like a faithful hound. He'd been on the bright end of that smile, too, I'd wager, and wanted to see it again.

We went down to the river, through the cattle markets, and crossed over the bridge there, to a tavern on the far side called the Retiarius. It wasn't nearly as well kept as the White Hare – when you've lived in a place for eighteen years, you learn what it takes to keep a good bar – but it was busy, which meant nobody paid us any attention and we could sit down out of the public eye.

Pantera stopped us outside and told Amoricus to pretend he was a scribe and we were his slaves, himself included. Pantera had never looked more disreputable than he did when we shuffled in after the little man from Memphis to the table in the corner where Pantera was directing him by tugs at his sleeve.

He sent me to the bar with silver and I came back with passable ale and some cheese and olives and we ate together in a kind of wonder that grew greater as he spoke to us all in the language of western Britain. And we all understood.

To this day, I don't know how he did it, but he had found three slaves who were of the right temperament and ability to do what he wanted, to *be* what he wanted, and each of us had a mother or a father or had been reared by a grandmother who had come from Britain. And he had lived there, loved there, fought there in the wars for freedom. That was what bound us in the first place, the language, and all it meant to us.

Then he told us what he wanted.

'From today, each of you is a free man. Amoricus has paper, pen and ink and will write your manumission papers when we are done. I will sign them, you will each keep your own. If you wish to go, you are welcome.'

'And if we wish to stay with you?' asked Felix. He was the quiet kind, who only spoke when necessary, but when he did it was to the point. 'You sound as if we might wish to do that. What are you offering us?'

'Gold, in the end. And a position as Vespasian's freedmen if you wish to stay. Freedom to leave if you wish to go, and land where you want it.'

Felix said, 'Vespasian is not emperor yet.'

'We shall make him so. We four, sworn as brothers, my life for yours. There will be some killing. There may be some dying. We will be hunted by Lucius, brother to the upstart Vitellius, and the one thing we must all pledge each other now, in a binding oath, is that if one of us is captured, the others will do all in their power to kill him cleanly before he is taken to Lucius' questioners.

'I will teach you to be spies. You will almost certainly have to kill men of Vitellius' army, perhaps others. You will live roughly, in many guises. You will be nameless and unrecognized, except by me. It will be dirty and hard and painful and at worst will end in a death so slow that crucifixion will seem like a blessing. Will you do it?'

Felix said, 'There are men calling your name through the whole of Rome today. For eight hundred sesterces, I could sell you to Lucius now.'

Pantera said, 'I fought at your mother's side in the battle of the Fallen Oak. She was one of the most fearless warriors I have ever met. I do not believe a son of Cunava would willingly sell out one who fought with his mother. Or you—' He looked at Amoricus. 'Your grandfather held a bridge alone against half a century of men for half a day. You are his grandson in looks as well as heart. I don't believe you would sell me either, but if I am wrong you are welcome to try.'

He was like that, full of quiet confidence. If any one of us had stood up in that bar and said who he was – we'd all worked it out by then – we would have been rich. To a slave, six, seven, eight hundred sesterces was a lifetime's silver. Pantera was offering gold, but there was no real promise we'd ever see it. What else he offered, though, was more important to each of us than gold: he offered us dignity.

We were in a tavern, so I could not stand up and grip his arm, but I laid my hand flat on the table, palm up, and waited until he laid his on top of it.

'My life for yours,' I said. 'And if you are taken, a clean death if I have to die to make it happen.'

They say that swearing to give his life is the greatest thing a man can do, but we knew, who had lived as slaves with the threat of crucifixion always hanging over us, that a clean death was the greater boon.

I gave my oath willingly, the first thing of my own I had ever given anyone, and the newness of it was like the first flush of love.

I wasn't alone. I watched the faces of the other two as they swore, saw tears prick their eyes. We were strangers and we were brothers. And we were free.

It was afternoon by then, heading to evening. Pantera drained his beaker and nudged Amoricus to stand so that we could all follow.

'We should get to work,' Pantera said. 'We're going to a hiring fair, to see if we can get ourselves taken on to carry the litter of a lady. You three go first. I'll come last and we'll see if it can be done.'

CHAPTER TWENTY-ONE

Rome, 4 August AD **69**

Trabo

I saw that hiring fair; it was the best entertainment I'd seen in months.

It was the evening after the fight in the alley, and I had returned to the Inn of the Crossed Spears after a day of getting to know the city after seven months away.

I had no real reason to go back there, but the courtyard had a clear view of the widow's house on the Street of the Bay Trees – I still had my letter to deliver – and, better, it was packed with off-duty Guards who were talking over the day's news.

Most of it was about Pantera. The better parts were about me.

'. . . four, all from the Macedonican, they say . . .'

'. . . crushed to pulp. Looked as if they'd been beaten by a bear . . .'

'. . . no claw marks. Must have been human, but Quintus Saturninus says . . .'

'. . . only the Guard, so far. Lucius says . . .'

I turned away, as if studying the lithe, dark-haired girl who carried the drinks and who I thought might sell herself to me if I bid right. Just then, though, I was more interested in the trio of Guardsmen sharing their miseries three tables along, but I couldn't appear to be listening.

'Lucius says he'll flog any man he hears spreading the rumour that it's a bear. He thinks it's one of Vitellius' Guards come to take his revenge, that he'll cut us down one by one if we aren't careful and that we ought to have caught him by now.'

'Is he making threats? Lucius, I mean, not the bear-Guard.'

'Not yet.'

'He will.'

'He always does.'

The three Guards ran out of words and sat staring into their drinks. None of them was known to me, none was substantially different from any of the thirty or forty others drinking there, but I was hunting again, and all it took to make men my targets was that I notice them, that I pick them out from the crowd.

How many had I killed the night before?

That's difficult to say. Four of them had come on me as I killed the last of the bandits. Yes, they were all dead: once men begin to run, if they can't turn and regroup and perhaps set an ambush, they are finished.

The four Guards had seen the bodies and tried to question me. Two of them died there, with the last bandit. The other two tried to run.

At the end of the alley, they separated, thinking to lose me in the winding streets of the ghetto, but I was a hunter before I became a tribune of the Guard, and in tracking the bandits I had discovered that hunting Vitellius' Guards fed my need for vengeance in ways I had never imagined. I had stood over the crushed and bleeding bodies of the dead and commended their wandering souls to Otho, to join his retinue in the lands of the dead.

Now, in daylight, bruised, exhausted, stiff in limb and fist, I knew a peace I had not known for five months, and presented with the possibility of another night's hunt . . . I can't tell you how good that felt.

I knew they would catch me eventually, of course: Lucius was right about that, but long before then I planned to have cut such a swathe through their ranks as would be spoken of in whispers for generations.

I leaned back and did not look again at these three I had marked for death. I knew their faces by then and could not safely be seen to stare.

So I turned my attention instead to the far side of the courtyard, where Scopius, the little silver-haired innkeeper, dream-teller and father, apparently, of the small dark serving girl who might therefore not have been as available as I had thought, was organizing a hiring fair with the same quiet calm he brought to everything else.

The women were hired first; eight of them, from a girl not yet at puberty, offered by her mother, to a bent crone, seeking work washing linens. The bidding was fast and quiet and everyone knew everybody else. The old woman and the girl went to a tall, brisk steward from a house on the Quirinal, which seemed to please them both.

The men came next. There were more of them, and of greater variety. None so far as I could see was selling his body for sex, but all for brute work.

The inky-fingered clerks were hired first, and then the labourers with their shovels or pickaxes on their shoulders, to show they could dig, even now, in the height of summer when the ground was like stone. The fruit-pickers followed, late in the season, having come in from nearby towns.

A dozen litter-bearers, some spectacularly unkempt, were just lining up when a wizened, black-skinned Berber ancient skipped in, sweating and loudly apologetic. He was unsound on his left leg: if he had been a horse, I would have had him poleaxed on the spot.

I watched, laughing, expecting Scopius to send him away, and certainly there were some hard words, some waving of hands, some pleading, but no summary eviction.

Everyone was watching now and we all cheered as the grandfather was admitted to the group of men at the auction, shuffling backwards to take his place in the ragged line-up.

It was only when he turned to introduce himself to the man on his left that I realized there was something about him, something in the lift of an arm, the tilt of his head . . . When you have fought back to back with a man, you come to know him as well as if you had slept with him, perhaps better.

I left my corner bench and went to stand behind the bidders. Two stewards were hiring for their separate households; one litter each, four men per team.

They were looking to match their purchases in height and bearing and basic hygiene. The bidding was swift and decisive. Truly, there were only eight men whom anyone would have wanted to hire and they were divided evenly between the two buyers. Neither wanted the half-lame, wholly mad Berber or any of the other four ill-matched men who were still standing there.

The bought teams were ushered away. Ever the optimist, Scopius raised his arms high and called out his wares once more. 'Litter teams for hire! Best on the Quirinal! Fit, strong . . .'

He was an honest man, Scopius. He ran his eye along the line and saw men either too old, too deformed or too unsavoury to carry a litter for anyone.

He let his arms drop; there was nobody left who might

have bid for them anyway, except there was, suddenly, a slim, balding steward shoving his way through the dwindling crowd. He was flustered, with the manners of a man who was used to doing everything in timely fashion and did not like to rush.

He hurried to Scopius' shoulder. 'Litter-bearers? I need four, swiftly. What have you?'

Scopius pulled a face, took his elbow, turned him aside. I only caught half a phrase, lifted on the sultry air: '. . . tomorrow. Nothing of worth . . .'

The mad little Berber heard that, too. He leapt up, an animated bundle of rags, and caught the steward's arm.

'One denarius, nothing more. Just one, and I will carry your litter on my own!'

He was pitiful; the kind of idiot you would ride past in the street and ignore, but he had his claws in the steward's arm and Scopius could not prise him off.

'One silver coin, to carry your master's litter!'

'It's for my mistress and it will need more than you.'

With wary distaste, the steward viewed the other four men. They were not particularly even, but none was as wizened, as old, as veritably mad as the Berber. He was about to take those four when the little man rushed forward and grabbed three, apparently at random. One was a tall and bulky British slave who looked as if he'd rip your head off in your sleep; another was smaller, with the look of a eunuch who had ink on his fingers and had lately been a scribe. In my experience, men who can read and write do not, on the whole, carry litters, so this one had almost certainly been dismissed for forgery or larceny or worse.

The last was the most disturbing: a lean, scruffy blond boy with a squint, who gazed vacantly at the sky with one eye and me with the other as if he were wondering how soon he could cut my throat; he made my stomach heave, I tell you.

The mad Berber dragged him forward, leaving the fifth, a Gaul who kept staring at the clouds and pointing, as a child might, and looked at them now as if he might weep.

This was first-rate entertainment. All about me, Guards were laughing, clapping the steward on the back, telling him to shout for their help when his mistress was robbed and he had need of the Guard to stop worse from happening.

It had all been so cleverly done. It was seeing it, understanding what underlay it, that first made me think this man at whose side I had fought might be the spy the Guards had spent all day hunting for across the city, raising the price on his head with every hour that went by.

There's nothing like hiding in plain sight and they'd all seen what he wanted them to see: a mad little Berber grandfather, small and wizened and lame, and none of them had thought that if he stood upright he'd have been their height or taller, and if he let his face grow smooth he'd have been half the age he looked. If he had been olive brown, not black, he'd have looked Roman enough to sit in the senate.

If you looked closely, there were signs on his body of the beating he had taken the night before; not nearly as many as there should have been, but they were there, if you knew what to look for.

Nobody did, though. That was the point. They all saw what Pantera showed them, and he let them make fun of him, and what man suspects that the object of his derision is making a fool of him in return?

I caught his eye and gave the smallest of bows. He ignored me, but I expected that, and settled back into my corner, grinning, as the steward ushered his uneven crew out of the courtyard and up the street, looking for all the world like a man who had set out to tend his herd of goats and had come home with a flock of tigers.

Chapter Twenty-Two

Rome, 4 August AD 69

Caenis

I didn't know where Matthias had gone; but I knew something was going to happen.

Earlier in the day, I had put pebbles in my shoe against the possibility that I might forget I was too lame to walk up the hill to see Sabinus. By the evening, the pain in my foot was becoming tiresome. Leaning on Matthias, I hobbled out of the front door of the cottage on the Street of the Bay Trees and out to the waiting litter. Four Guards watched me do it; they had been there from midnight to midnight without cease and there are few things more irritating than knowing that four men are watching your every move. It was tiresome, of course it was, but what could we do?

I was running a little late, and the litter was already up on the shoulders of the bearers. They lowered it for me and scooped it up again swiftly enough, for all that they looked exceedingly ill matched.

Scopius at the Crossed Spears was known to provide a

clean, swift service, with graded men. Today, though, a dust-strewn Egyptian shared the rear poles with a blond boy of not more than fifteen who had one lazy eye and a slight leer. If that were not bad enough, the boy was taller than the man so that the litter would have listed to the left had not the disparity in their heights been counter-balanced by that of the front bearers, a bulky Briton and a wizened old Berber who looked ancient enough to be his grandfather.

We progressed in our uneven way up the hill. Sabinus was waiting for us outside his big, gilt-roofed villa on the upper elbow of the Quirinal hill. No Guards openly watched him; he was prefect of the city, commander of the Urban cohorts and the Watch: his power in the city was almost as great as the emperor's and Vitellius had to treat him with a degree of respect.

Nevertheless, he was elder brother to the man who had named himself imperator and on my three previous visits I had seen the same bearded thug guarding a nearby villa where there had never before been a guard, and two others working to rebuild a wall which had not progressed so much as a hand's span in the past nine days.

Sabinus gave a fractional nod as he moved in to embrace me.

'Sister, are you well? Your leg is improving?' All solicitude, he took my arm. 'You must let me call for the bonesetter. Aescetidorus is exceptionally skilled in these things. He would have you walking sound as a horse in no time.'

'Thank you, I have no wish to walk like a horse.'

I waved a hand at Matthias and, as all the stewards do, he took the litter down the street a little way to where a neatly favoured inn served the servants of the senators who lived on the hill.

Thus, simply, did Vespasian's lady and his brother appear as we needed to appear while each knowing where the danger lay. Sabinus took me inside. Neither of us looked at the men watching his house.

Like my own, Sabinus' home was built around an atrium, but where mine had a small pond and only four columns holding up the central roof, his had a water garden with five fountains shaped like nymphs and satyrs and sixteen columns, and as many rooms linked by a covered walkway around the edge.

The walls were painted in crimson overlaid by frescoes and mosaics showing Greek tragedies and Roman victories. It was a man's house with no redeeming subtlety, a statement of ostentation; quite hateful, really.

I didn't hate Sabinus, that must be clear; he was a good, kind man and from the first, when Vespasian and I were new lovers, he treated me with utmost respect, which I have returned in kind. Even so, he was, in all ways, the opposite of his brother.

Where Vespasian was over-generous, impecunious, a hater of politics and a lover of war, Sabinus hoarded money all his life, and thrived in the backstabbing atmosphere of the senate. He was never likely to be exiled by Nero for sleeping through a recital, nor to emerge from a governorship with less money than when he entered it.

For all that, he was still the bluff country boy, one generation away from the soil, and he was kind to me in the dark years when Vespasian was married and siring two sons and a daughter on another, more suitable, woman.

His wife and daughter are both dead now, and I had care of the younger son. I was as married as I could ever be to the man who had let his legions name him emperor. Nobody was likely to forget that I was once a slave, but next to Vespasian, his brother Sabinus had always come closest to managing that particular feat of perpetual amnesia.

That evening, as soon as we stepped indoors, Sabinus held

out his arm for me to lean on while I took the pebbles out of my shoe as if it were normal to greet any visiting lady this way.

After, he walked ahead of me through the vestibule to the atrium and came to stand by a fountain shaped as Youth.

It was an unfortunate juxtaposition of images. He was sixty-nine years old and each year had cut another line of worry at the margins of his eyes. He was not as ruddy as his brother, more olive in his complexion, but his chin narrowed to the same point and his ears stuck proud of his head in the same way. He took my hand and kissed it fondly.

'What news? Or are you here simply to confound the Guard?'

'Wait.'

I held up my hand, listening. Matthias had left the litter at the tavern and returned by the servants' entrance. He walked past in one of the servants' corridors and I could tell by the singular rhythm of his feet that he was unhappy. I listened after, and heard, if not a sound, then what we might call the absence of a sound; a gap, that was more telling than anything.

Aloud, I said, 'The spy, Pantera, has perhaps more news than either of us? If he has access to the general's messengers?'

I was right: he was there! Pantera's quiet voice answered me, from somewhere nearby.

'My lady, I can tell you that the general is safe in Alexandria where he chafes against the bit and yearns for action, that Mucianus is on the march and that the King of Kings in Parthia has offered forty thousand archers, and has promised not to invade Judaea while Vespasian is emperor.'

'He can't accept the archers!' I spun to face the place whence I thought Pantera's voice had come. 'He'll be said for ever to have used foreign aid to take the throne, to have made Rome a vassal of Parthia.'

'He knows that, lady. He won't accept.' He wasn't where I thought he was. I spun again as he spoke on. 'But it's good news that Vologases won't invade either. I think they find much in common, our general and the King of Kings. It will be good for them to find this out for themselves.'

I could see him at last, and it was not only that he had found the darkest shadows in Sabinus' blood-red room to hide in that had made him hard to see, but that he was black of head and foot and hand and hair; he was, in fact, the Berber who had carried my litter and I tell you truly, had he not spoken, I would not have known him.

To give him credit, Sabinus didn't call his own steward to have this intruder ejected. He stood on the far side of the room biting down on his lower lip, which Vespasian only did when he was immensely angry.

I stepped between them, saying, 'My lord, may I introduce to you the agent sent by your brother to keep us all from harm in the coming months? Circumstances overtook him and now he must come under subterfuge.' I favoured Pantera with an acid glance. 'Sebastos Abdes Pantera, this is Titus Flavius Sabinus, prefect of Rome, commander of the Urban cohorts and the Watch and uncle to Domitian. I must tell you that the Guard are offering eight hundred in silver for you—'

'Alive. I know. And I am told that alone of Nero's people, the inquisitors have survived all three of the recent palace purges. It takes a long time to find individuals with the skill and vocation to break a man and yet leave him able to answer questions. You could enquire of your friend Scopius, sometime, as to the content of my dreams. He has been very careful not to interpret them for me.'

That was clever. I felt Sabinus' anger dissolve as he came over to join me. It would have taken a harder heart than his to feel anger for long at a man whose dreams were filled with his own long-drawn death.

I was perhaps the one feeling most aggrieved. I asked, 'Does Matthias know who you are?'

'If he doesn't,' he said, 'you really ought to find another steward. Nobody in his right mind would have taken on the men currently carrying your litter.'

That set me back. Something of my discomfort must have shown, for Pantera said, drily, 'Matthias cares for you so much that he will set aside his honour to lie for you. And he finds in himself surprising depths, I think, and a versatility that does you great service.'

'Did you come just to tell me to praise my steward, or are you here for a better reason?' I was sharp with him, I admit it, and not yet ready to think well of Matthias.

'I came to introduce myself to the senator, to bring his brother's greetings and to tell him personally that the safety of Vespasian's family is my first responsibility while in Rome. And to tell you both that you must be assiduous in your support of Vitellius and your denigration of Vespasian.'

'You tell us what we already know,' Sabinus said. 'I have pledged my oath to Vitellius more times than I can count. When he resides in Rome, I attend him when he wakes, I host dinners that will beggar me for years, I assure him of the devotion of the Urban cohorts and the Watch. I tell him how reckless is my brother and what a stain he lays on the family name. If there is more I can do, you have only to say it, but I know of nothing.'

'There is no more you can do, lord.' Pantera gave a small bow, hand on heart, after the manner of the Egyptians. 'But the lady Caenis, I think, may be able to lend other aid to our venture?'

I had no idea what he was talking about, but there was a warning in his eyes, or perhaps a plea, so I said, 'Go on,' as if this were something we had planned.

He said, 'The general wishes to ascend the throne with as

little Roman blood spilled as can be managed. To achieve that, we must find those tribunes and legates of the legions most readily persuaded to his cause. We must commend them, flatter them, bribe them, threaten them; do whatever it takes to win them to our side. To do *that*, we must have a means of communication by which we can reach them and they can reach us.'

'You need messengers,' Sabinus said. 'My brother has many.'

'He does, but everyone knows it and what Lucius knows of, he may buy.'

'We can't trust them?' Sabinus sounded genuinely perplexed. He was a politician, but he had the blind spot of all well-bred Romans who think that men who vow to their service will be loyal for ever.

Gently, Pantera said, 'When the future of Rome is at stake, we must trust very few and all of them secretly. I have a means of communicating with Vespasian and Mucianus, but I cannot reach the men of the Rhine and Balkan legions, or the navies at Ravenna and Misene, who are crucial to our cause. To connect with these, we need men with horses: honest men who can be trusted to deliver a sealed letter and return with its answer; resilient men who have good reason to be on the roads and can answer questions honestly when stopped; above all, men unknown to those who know Seneca's routes and Vespasian's. Lady—' His eyes were on me, sharp, hard, direct. 'Would I be right in thinking that the lady Antonia inherited her father's message service, and that it was greater, in its day, than that of Julius Caesar?'

I blinked, slowly, thoughtfully, to cover my shock. 'You would be correct, yes.'

'And so would I also be correct in thinking that her freedwoman, her amanuensis, inherited that service when her mistress died?'

I could feel Sabinus' gaze burn into the side of my face. He was a decent man; kind, honest in his way, but for all his scheming in the senate he didn't have the depth of deceit that was needed to stay three steps ahead of men such as Lucius. Or Pantera.

I was not sure that I had that depth of deceit either, but I knew where I was being led, if not why.

I said, 'Did Vespasian tell you?'

'No. If he knows, he would not say so to me. He will do nothing, ever, to risk your safety, and what I propose is not safe.'

'Yet still, you will do it?'

'If it can be done without risk to you.' He took a breath and I thought him uncertain, which was unusual enough to be interesting. 'I am asking that you cede control of the network into my hands. That you give me the pass-phrases, the names of the men, the means to set it all in motion. And that you trust me enough to allow me not to tell you all that I do with them.'

'For my own safety, of course,' I said, drily. 'And so that if I am arrested, I cannot be made to divulge it. You, of course, will never be taken?'

Pantera had dreams that said otherwise and had been rash enough to mention them; there was nothing he could say to that.

I said, 'I will cede you control, but only under the condition that you inform me of everything you do. If you are taken, we will find ways to leave Rome. We are not without resource, but if you don't know what we plan, then we have that much protection.'

I had bargained with merchants all my life and I knew my own bottom line and how to hold it. There was a moment's silent pressure and I saw him concede.

'As you will, lady. If you would—'

'Having messengers is only the first step,' Sabinus said. 'You need a list of officers in the legions who may come to Vespasian's side.'

'Can you provide such a list?'

'I can make a series of educated guesses. I can have them within a day, but we have the problem of how to get them to you without being seen. As you will have observed, we are closely watched. Perhaps if the lady Caenis were to be taken ill now, and was unable to dine tonight, she might recover and return again tomorrow? We can plan together what to do.'

So it seemed that Sabinus, too, wanted to join in the planning. I could tell Pantera didn't like that. It was obvious that the fewer people who knew what he was doing the safer he was, but this was Vespasian's brother, and Pantera didn't have the authority to argue.

His lips were set in a straight, hard line and I decided that I didn't want to be the focus of his anger on the day when it turned outward rather than in.

But he bowed to us both, saying, 'My lady, if you give me a time to return to the porter's inn, and then send Matthias to fetch us, we will bring the litter for you. Make your illness a good one; we shall be watched.'

CHAPTER TWENTY-THREE

Rome, 4 August AD **69**

Trabo

I had no idea what was wrong with Vespasian's mistress as her litter came back down the hill again.

She wasn't screaming in pain or anything; well-bred ladies rarely do until they're staring death in the face, and often not even then, but she was clearly unwell, in a decorous kind of way. The echoes of her anguish rippled up and down the Quirinal in a manner that seemed likely to draw her to the attention of even more cutthroats and bandits than carried her litter.

Sure enough, they turned up before she was halfway down; five or six, or eight, or possibly ten quietly shambling figures homing in on either side of the floating white cave like jackals on a new corpse.

The Guard detachments should have stopped them, but, bizarrely, I couldn't see any Guards any more. They'd shadowed Caenis all the way up the hill and kept covert watch on the house she had been in from the moment she entered.

Now, though, they'd all vanished, even on this, the second largest street up the Quirinal, which was, at the very least, a dereliction of duty. When I was employed to protect Rome, my men and I had marched the hill in tent-units of eight and, believe me, none of us was ever out of sight of those coming behind or going ahead.

The litter-bearers seemed to have noticed neither the lack of Guards nor the bandits slowly closing in on them. They trotted across the courtyard to Isis' shrine as if there was nothing amiss and continued down the hill.

I followed, a strategic distance behind. I hadn't killed any Guards yet that night and my blood still sighed for the hunt, but this was more interesting: Vespasian's mistress had been visiting Vespasian's brother and one corner of her litter was borne, if my instincts were right, by Vespasian's spy.

It may have been that the shady men following didn't know that, but they were careful, not the mindless thugs of the night before, and if I had had to bet, I would have said these were off-duty Guardsmen, sent out under cover of night to do what could not openly be done by day.

The litter came to the steepest part of the hill. The bearers leaned back, stiff-legged, taking the full weight on their shoulders in an effort to stop their burden careering down the hill. Sweat shone from them, briefly, in the light of the few lamps. Then, in three paces, they left the lucent puddles behind and entered a lampless dark where there was no sweat, no shine, only the ghosted outline of the litter and the sound of men in labour, and a woman's groaning.

'Go!'

I didn't need to hear the hissed order to know this was where the ambush must take place; I had set enough myself to see the obvious. But the command came in Latin, which confirmed all I had thought and gave me, if I needed it, the last excuse to intervene.

As the men converged on the lumbering litter, I ripped off my money belt and wound it round my right hand. No pain now; the promise of battle made me well-nigh immortal.

I was Achilles. I was Zeus. I was the bear-man the Guards feared so much that Lucius had threatened to flog anyone who mentioned it in his hearing.

The attackers were running downhill, cautiously because it was dark. This might have been the Quirinal, but that didn't mean the route was necessarily free of debris.

I caught the last man in the line before he reached the litter. Surprise was my best weapon and I needed to kill in silence. My left arm hugged my enemy's throat, crushing it tight. My gold-weighted right fist struck hard below his ribs, from the side and slightly in front. It crushed upwards, seeking the heart, the liver, the kidneys; anything soft that could be bruised and broken.

There was a moment's frantic struggle; fingers clawed at my arms, a gladius swung up and had to be blocked, a nailed heel struck down on my instep, ripping the skin; I had to step back to avoid it a second time.

The man was good, and fought well, but I had the first grip and that's what counts. I braced my right fist against my left to make a lever, pulled once, hard, and the fight was over. I lowered the body to the ground.

I had armed myself during the day with a small double-edged knife which I had strapped to my left ankle. It came free with a tug. They thought me a bear, and so I used the blade to slash once across his throat, and then thrice more across his face: no harm in keeping up the illusion.

Ahead, the litter was no longer wobbling. At a single, quiet command it had been set on the ground and the four half-lame, squint-eyed, disreputable idiots who bore it were looking less lame now, more confidently competent. They bore cudgels that were the mirror of the ones the bandits had used against the spy the evening before; they might have been the very weapons, collected and stored for later use.

For one last moment, the night was perfectly still. To the east, a star fell from the sky, leaving a long singing trail across the dark. As if on that divine signal, the remaining ambushers attacked. There were a dozen of them; a tent-unit and a half, and they came forward in a particular formation that all the Guards know, called the Goose Wing: a staggered line that curves into the enemy and can slice open a waiting block.

There was a gap at the far right-hand edge of their formation where the man I had killed should have been. I slotted myself into his place, wielding my little knife in my gold-weighted fist; once committed to a thrust, nothing short of a shield could stop it and these men weren't carrying shields.

The nearest of the attackers was to my left. Reaching him, I turned, lifted my blade in salute and was rewarded by the fleeting grin of one who thought he had a friend at his side. The illusion lasted another two paces and then, launching forward, I struck my blade across his unarmoured throat.

Too easy! And there was not time to crow over the body. Happy now, but not happy enough, I spun, found another target, swept up the fallen gladius and used it in my left hand, to balance the knife in my weighted right. Another enemy fell, his throat laid open, his blood soaring in diminishing arcs on to the empty street.

A fourth came at me, blade thrusting fast, straight for my chest. I slewed sideways, felt it skitter past, shifted the gladius to my right hand and stabbed in, ferociously fast, hard, at an angle to the man's unprotected flank.

There was a sense of resistance destroyed and I lost my fist in the blood-hot ribcage as the weight of my belt carried me through mere skin and flesh and fragile bone. The Guard choked on a gout of his own blood and toppled like a tree, dragging me with him.

I stumbled, caught in a tangle of legs. I landed on my out-flung palm, felt my wrist crack, rolled, swearing, and—

And lay very still. A blade sliced the air above me and stopped on a level with my eye. Its point was black with flesh and gore.

'If you move very slowly,' said Vespasian's spy, 'I will let you rise. If you try to move fast, I will kill you, my gratitude for your help last night notwithstanding.'

About him was silence; a dozen or more Guards were dead or dying. Not one of the attacking force had lived. The odds were three to one in their favour and they had fought as motley a group of eunuchs, barbarians and squint-eyed youths as you could never want to assemble in one place.

But it was the Guards who were dead and not one of the litter-bearers so much as scratched. What could Otho have done with these men on his side? What could Vespasian do?

I lifted my hands to show they were empty, and levered myself cautiously to my feet.

'We need to talk,' I said.

'One of us does,' said Pantera, and took my right arm and twisted it behind my back and marched me over to where they had set down the litter.

CHAPTER TWENTY-FOUR

Rome, 4 August AD **69**

Caenis

I felt like a block of carved granite, set in the flimsy surround of the litter.

Outside was a violence I had seen often at a distance, but never this close, never this personal. Matthias was armed with a cudgel – *Matthias!*

He was a stranger to me, lost in a sea of silently fighting men, holding his own, but against unspeakable odds.

Long ago, Vespasian had offered me a blade and bade me carry it, 'to protect my virtue'. I had laughed at him, poked his naked ribs, reminded him that slaves have no virtue to protect and if his name did not protect me, a blade was hardly likely to. 'I'm not going to offer an assailant a weapon he may not have.'

It had sounded good, in the safety of his bed. Now, in the darkness of a hot summer night with men fighting outside, it was an offer I would have grasped with both hands, if only to make a clean end of myself before they came for me.

I lifted the hem of my stola and considered whether I could rip it and make a noose for myself as braver women had done before me. The first, yes, the second, no; I didn't have that kind of courage. Not yet, anyway.

I made irrelevantly unfulfillable vows to myself that I would never again allow myself to be caught in a situation where I was so impossibly helpless. And then I sat still: helpless.

Outside, the grunts of exertion grew fewer and further between. A voice issued a stream of quiet orders; Pantera, I thought. He was speaking a language I had never heard before and it warped his voice from what I knew, but the tenor of command changes little from tongue to tongue and I had lived near enough to soldiers for there to be a certain security in it.

I was surprised to feel the litter twitch in that edgy, erratic way that meant four men had taken hold of the carrying poles, and lifted. A hand appeared at the flap, and after it Pantera's dye-darkened face. At his side, held in a grip that looked likely to cripple, was a bearded ruffian who smiled at me convivially, ignoring the blade angled at his jugular. In his turn, Pantera ignored him; his attention, at least outwardly, was all for me.

'Lady, I apologize for the inconvenient delay. Sadly I am unable to continue my duties as your bearer. Matthias will take my corner to deliver you home. It's not far; a few hundred paces and we'll have you safe, if such a thing exists in Rome tonight.'

The door flap dropped. He hadn't asked for my permission. Why would he when he was so effortlessly in command? And Matthias had lowered himself to carrying my litter. Truly, the day had reached an unprecedented level of strangeness.

For a brief moment, I allowed myself the luxury of hating the man who had brought us to this, and his paid henchmen, and Vespasian, who sent him in the first place. It didn't last long, but it filled me with a hot, red, savage rage, which sustained me round the corner into the Street of the Bay Trees, and on the hundred yards to the front door of my house.

Which was where I should have dismounted and dismissed the men. I had lifted the flap and was stepping out when Pantera's hand caught my arm.

'Stop,' he said, and I did. 'Someone's in there. The door's been unlocked.'

'Guards?' I asked, looking as far as I could up the empty street. 'Where are the watchers?'

Pantera nodded. 'Indeed. Where are the Guards? They may be the ones inside, but if not, they have taken themselves away. Or been ordered to leave. There are some things even paid watchers are better off not seeing.'

He gave orders again, one pitch above a whisper, and his four men – Matthias was his now, sprinting to obey – made a ring around me, facing out, cudgels hefted, while Pantera thrust his captive ahead of him as a shield and barged fast and hard in through my terrifyingly expensive, worryingly unbarred front door.

Chapter Twenty-Five

Rome, 4 August AD **69**

Caenis

'Jocasta?'

'Trabo!'

'Jocasta!'

'Pantera?'

'Domitian?'

This last, of course, was me, coming late across the threshold, hemmed about by rough men who smelled of garlic and olive oil and rich-sour battle sweat.

Domitian stood ahead of me in the atrium, holding one of my best wine glasses in his hand. The flask was on the floor by the couch on which his guest was reclining. Or she was until Pantera barged in.

I think that's the first time I saw Jocasta as she was, not acting. I had seen a woman in utter control of herself, playing the whore and the diplomat and shifting from one to the other without pausing for breath.

Now, she flung herself to her feet and up close to Pantera's prisoner. With a delicacy that was entirely surprising, she traced her exquisite fingers round the margins of the raised welt on his cheek that promised to grow into an angry bruise.

There was wonder and a real affection on her face, maybe something more; certainly a shared history that went back longer than this one night. It occurred to me that I had watched Pantera devote to her the kind of attention I didn't think he lavished on anyone else, but had seen nothing but courtesy in response. Here, with this bandit she had called Trabo, was more than courtesy.

Sharply, she said, 'Why are you holding him thus? He is Trabo. I told you.'

This to Pantera, who had not set down his knife. By way of answer, he tightened his grip and pushed his man further into the room.

I was ahead of him, lighting candles. It was one of Matthias' duties, but I thought I had lost Matthias to Pantera; certainly he took his orders from him, although he remained behind with us when the other three ruffians left at Pantera's quiet order: to guard the house from the outside, or to leave so they were not caught, I still don't know which.

So I lit candles, which gave me a measure of calm and allowed me to study the changing tensions on the faces of the four men and one other woman in my atrium.

Walking from one wall bracket to the next, I passed Domitian who had been flushed and happy, the lord holding forth in his house, and now was peevish and angry and coming to realize that his love had eyes for other men, and they for her.

Every man in the room had eyes for her, actually. Even Matthias, who until that moment had adored me and reserved his lust for one of the silver-skins on the Palatine, paying him in monthly silver for a fidelity they both knew to be fiction. But here and now he was gazing at Jocasta as if she were Aphrodite walked out of the sea.

But these two, much as I loved them both, were the bit players in this drama; the two men at the centre of the room commanded the better part of my attention.

The bearded bandit – Jocasta had called him Trabo – was grinning at Jocasta with a delight that pushed the boundaries of decency. He was not stupid; he had seen Domitian, and even as I watched, he glanced over and lifted a single raised brow and let his eyes ask the question. *This one? Him? Really?*

Jocasta had her back to both me and Domitian and neither of us could see her answer, but the ruffian's face did not fold as it might have done, only creased in a dry, knowing smile that crushed my heart.

Poor boy. He had had his hour of joy and had seen it end.

Pantera knew already of Domitian's infatuation, of course. Still, as he watched Jocasta and Trabo, I saw surprise sweep across the landscape of his face, and something else, gone too fast to identify. It might have been love. I thought it was at the time.

Jocasta had asked him a question. He answered it in the same even voice he had used since the first attack. 'He watched your house all morning. And this evening he was following me. He may be the most famous tribune of Otho's Guard, but just because Vitellius has put a price on his head doesn't make him an ally to our cause.'

'Have you asked him?'

'I am about to.'

Nobody asked how Pantera knew Trabo's movements, or Jocasta's. In her place, I would have asked that first, but the moment had gone and we have to suppose she knew his methods. In any case, Pantera had moved his knife so that it angled more steeply at Trabo's neck, which captured everyone's attention.

'It will cost me nothing to kill you,' he said. 'The lady Caenis will disapprove of blood on her tiles, but it can be washed away. So you have the length of my patience to explain what you are doing and why. It would be a mistake to assume it long.'

Trabo lifted a slow hand in salute to me. Without moving his head – to do so would have been to slice his own throat – he looked towards me.

'If the lady Caenis would care to open the secret place in the back of my belt, she will find therein a letter addressed to her.'

I didn't move. A slave's training had little to recommend it, but it taught me never to move unless required to. It stood me in good stead now.

'A letter from whom?' asked Pantera.

'The emperor Otho. It was the last thing he wrote before he killed himself.'

Trabo's cultured voice roughened at the mention of the death. If he was an actor, he was a good one, but we were in the company of two excellent actors already, that he was a third was always a possibility.

'Jocasta will take your belt,' Pantera said. 'If you move, you will die.'

Jocasta unlaced the belt. It sagged in her hand, weightier than it looked, which is always a sign that there's gold inside. The leather had a long, narrow filet along the back on the inside, which, when opened, revealed a fold of fine paper, bruised to fragility, dark with sweat. My name swept along one face of it, in fine angled script.

'Is that Otho's hand?' Pantera asked.

'It is.'

I was unexpectedly moved: I had liked the importunate boy who pushed his way to the throne. In the brief flower of his glory he had written to me often as to a sister, asking advice, sharing thoughts; and now this last letter.

There were ways to do this properly. I had a small desk in

an alcove beyond the fountain. I carried the letter there and Matthias came to his senses at last and brought me the tall soapstone lamp in the shape of a swan that was my last gift from Antonia.

He did not lay down his cudgel, even then. I wondered if he ever would; does every man live to fight, if only he has the chance to find it in himself?

The letter's seal was recognizably Otho's: on the pale yellow wax, a sheaf of grain surrounded by the sun. He was ever an optimist, right to his death. My knife sliced through it, clean and clear. I scanned the salutation and the lines, and looked up, sharply, at Pantera's prisoner.

'Have you read this?'

'No, lady.' Trabo gave the faintest shake of his head and even that scraped his skin across Pantera's knife, bringing a feather of blood. 'But I watched him write it: he wept as he wrote his name at the foot.'

Jocasta said, 'Can you read it for us?'

I read aloud, lightly, swiftly; Otho's writing was strong and angular and easy on the eye.

'To the lady Caenis, with my thanks for your help and past comforts. You will know by now that I am dead. Trust the man who brings this; he is one of my best and his heart is the truest I have known. He will do what it takes to aid you in whatsoever you desire.

To that same end, I append a list of those men who will be true to you and yours. If the freedwoman of Antonia can rouse those who need it, it may be she will be raised as high as she deserves. None deserves higher.

Know that you have my heartfelt support, and gratitude. Rome's future lies in your hands, and my good name.'

I looked up. 'Below, he has written a list of a good two dozen names. He is sending to me what he could not – dared not – send to Vespasian.' My heart was a great stone in my chest, rocking too hard, threatening my ribs. 'He is telling us who will defect from Vitellius. He wrote this in April. Vespasian wasn't hailed imperator until the first of July.'

That date had been engraved on my liver since I first heard it. You will find it at my death, if you care to cut me open and look. 'How did he know? How did he *dare*?'

My question was for all of them, but it was Trabo who, gently, said, 'We all knew, lady, who was most fit to lead the empire after Otho. Our question was only would Vespasian accept what was offered, not whether that offer should be made. As to how Otho dared – he was about to die by his own hand; nothing in life could touch him. That gives a man great freedom.'

Trabo was near to tears and wrestling with something else. I waited to hear it; we all did.

Red of eye, he said, 'My lady, forgive me. I should have brought the letter sooner, only he told me to move slowly, to stay behind Vitellius' advancing army for my own safety, and I did so, thinking he had written a signal of affection, nothing more. I'm sorry.'

Out of charity, I asked, 'He gave this to you himself? At the end?'

'At the very end, yes. I was with him when he . . .' His hands described a small and futile circle that ended near his chest. His colour was high and tears stood proud at the angles of his eyes.

There was no question that he was genuine, and if he had not forgotten Pantera's knife, he cared about it a great deal less than he did before I opened the letter.

'Tell me,' I said.

And he did.

CHAPTER TWENTY-SIX

Rome, 4 August AD 69

Trabo

It had been dawn on the sixteenth of April. Otho was in his tent. We had not yet had news of the defeat at Bedriacum, but we had had no notice of victory either, so we knew it wasn't good. He – the emperor, *my* emperor – abhorred civil war. He would not risk men's lives to save his own.

He had truly believed that Vitellius would surrender his claim on the throne when he saw that the Guard supported *him*. He had not understood, however often we told him, that Vitellius was only the mask, that the men whose faces hid behind it did not care whom the Guard followed; they wanted victory for their man, whatever the cost in lives and blood.

That morning, the sixteenth, Otho at last understood, and would not let any other man pay the blood-price but himself.

Standing in Caenis' atrium, with Pantera's knife still at my throat, I closed my eyes, and shut away those watching me. Without effort, I was in another world, a sunlit morning, with birdsong, and the sour aftertaste of a failed battle. The past was far more alive to me than the present.

Otho was dressed in his emperor's battle armour, polished and peaceful, as a man is who knows that his end has come and he controls every moment of it.

Around him lay the scattered ashes of his correspondence, burned by his own hand so that none might be called to account for aiding him. The lead lottery was not his fault; the list of those who had helped to assassinate Galba had been given to his steward after he left Rome, and was supposed to await his return. None of us had imagined he might not come back.

Thinking always of others, Otho had arranged carriages and safe conduct for all who could leave: his generals, his brother, his loyal followers. He had kissed them goodbye, one by one, and ushered them, weeping, from the tent, until only I was left.

By design, he was standing in the cut of dawn sun as it slanted through the part-open tent flap. His hair was tousled; no amount of grooming would control it. His skin was clear, his gaze steady. He held out his knife to me, hilt first.

'Lord, I cannot, *will* not—' My throat tore apart with grief. My hands tied themselves behind my back.

Otho flashed the quick, easy smile that had won me and all his men long before Galba named his unfortunate heir and so precipitated his own death. He said, 'I want you to sharpen it for me. I would trust no one else. Unless you'd rather I called back Plotius with his weeping and promises of easy victory?'

That was unthinkable. I dragged my hands from behind my back. 'You honour me, lord.'

Otho had the stone, and, although it was impossible to put a better edge on the knife, the rhythmic sound of iron stroked against the grit was a balm of sorts to my grieving soul. Also, it covered the sound of Otho's careful whisper.

'You will remain with me while I do this. You will be my witness. And before you step out to call the others in, you will take from beneath my pillow the letter that is there. When today is over, you will deliver it to Vespasian's mistress, Caenis, at her home in the Street of the Bay Trees on the Quirinal. Don't rush. Don't go into Rome too early; Vitellius' forces will not welcome you. Caution matters more than speed in this and you will be hunted, whatever Lucius and Caecina may say to the contrary.'

'Yes, lord.' I didn't know it at the time, but he saw the future more clearly than any living man should have been able to do; standing on the edge of death gave him clear sight.

'The knife, then,' Otho said, and there was a moment, standing in the burst of sunlight, when we were both alive, and had all the hopes of the world between us.

And then Otho moved, one single inward stroke that drove the blade into his heart, and all hope was gone.

I held him as he died, felt the wild, erratic rhythm of his heart leap and buck and patter to silence.

I closed his eyes against the cruel day and lowered him to the floor and then, before I went out to speak to the officers, freedmen and slaves waiting outside the tent, I reached under the pillow, still warm from his head, and transferred the letter that lay there into the breast of my tunic.

In Caenis' atrium, I opened my eyes. I saw her first; a small, bright sparrow of a woman, with a fine mind and moist eyes.

She had known Otho, and cared for him. Jocasta had known him too, she who was not small or sparrow-like at all, but burned bright as a furnace, her wild intelligence un-shielded; vital.

And behind me was Pantera, who had not yet let his blade drop. I turned my head, slowly, and felt it score round my neck. I stopped when the tip was digging into my larynx.

'I am yours,' I said. 'Accept me now, to help you in any way I can, to promote your mission, whatever it is, to expend my last tear, my last drop of blood, in the defeat of Vitellius – or kill me. The choice must be yours. I have said all I can.'

There was a time when I would have laughed at any such grand, noble gestures, but then Otho had made his one grand, noble gesture and changed my world. I laughed at different things now; dead Guards, mostly.

I thought Pantera might laugh, and, laughing, kill me. I was strangely at peace with the thought.

The tip of the knife was a focal point of pain; just enough to notice. Blood pooled in the hollow of my throat. I counted a dozen heartbeats before the pressure slackened off.

Something had gone on over my head, a silent exchange between Pantera, Jocasta and Caenis that I wish I had seen; Jocasta was like a lamp burning in my soul by then, and I couldn't think why I had ever left her in Rome, unwed.

It was Caenis, with her innate compassion, who spoke first.

'Will you renew your Guard's oath,' she asked, gravely, 'in the name of the emperor Vespasian, accepting myself and Pantera as his agents, to be obeyed in all things?'

After Otho's death, I had not expected to find joy again, certainly not so soon. But it was with joy that I turned, and knelt and placed my hands in hers and spoke again the words of my legionary oath that had been inscribed on my heart since my first day in the legions.

'I swear in the name of Jupiter, Best and Greatest, that the emperor Vespasian is my lord and master in all things, that unto death will I serve him and his and at his command. I offer my life in the protection of his demesne. And' – this was not in the oath – 'I will undertake personally to reach the men on this list, as many as I may, and tell them of our lord's endeavours, and bring them, heart and soul, to his support.'

They allowed me a small silence, a moment of dignity, and

then Jocasta said from behind my right shoulder, 'You may do that, but someone has got in ahead of you. This is the news I came to bring. Lucius heard it this morning and told me: Antonius Primus, the legate of the Seventh Galbania, has brought together the five Balkan legions and sworn them to Vespasian. He is marching at the head of thirty thousand men, straight for Rome. If nobody stops him, he'll be at the gates by Saturnalia. So now the only way to prevent all-out civil war is to identify those men who will support Vespasian and push them into doing it openly. If enough legions can be brought to his side, Vitellius' generals might abandon their cause.'

CHAPTER TWENTY-SEVEN

Rome, 4 August AD **69**

Jocasta

I'm not sure what I expected after I told them about Antonius Primus and his blatant opportunism, but it wasn't that we'd be up all night talking through strategies to turn him to our best advantage.

By dawn, when we'd run out of words, my eyes felt as if they'd been rubbed with goose grease and sand; each blink was slow and gritty. Thinking was hard.

'We should leave.' I stood, slowly, rolling my shoulders. 'The Guards will come back with the sun and they must find the lady Caenis and lord Domitian here alone. The rest of us must leave while it's still dark.'

'I could escort . . .' Domitian had been half asleep. His cheek held the scarlet imprint of his fist where he had leaned on it for the past hours. He pushed himself upright now, scrubbing away the memories of dreams with the heel of his hand.

I smiled for him; he was a good boy. Strange, yes, solitary, inward, scarred by a life lived in the shade of his perfect brother, the soldier and seducer of queens, but good all the same. Whatever else happened later, you must believe me when I say that I did not want to see him hurt.

That August morning in Caenis' atrium, with the early sun shining silver on the flat sheen of the pond, I said simply, 'Thank you. It would be good to have your company, but you must stay here with the lady Caenis. You must seem to wake if the Guards come. You must be ready to lie for your life and ours. Can you do that?'

You see? I was good to him. His smile was radiant. I squeezed his shoulder as friends do to each other. Trabo glowered, which was ridiculous, but he was as exhausted as the rest of us . . . one has to make excuses. Caenis, on the other hand, looked as if her heart might break on Domitian's behalf, which was unfortunate, but there was nothing I could do about it just then. He was the son of the man who might become emperor and I wished to remain on the right side of him, but I had no intention of relieving him of his virginity, which was what he so clearly wanted.

What did Pantera do?

Nothing. That is, I don't remember him doing anything particular, except that he grasped Caenis in a brotherly embrace and kissed her cheek and it looked to me as if he whispered something. So yes, all right, he did do something, and very probably it had a bearing on what came next.

A last moment's brisk leave-taking gripped us all and then we three who were leaving stepped out into the remains of the night, each heading in a different direction.

Trabo went along the road to the Inn of the Crossed Spears, Pantera turned uphill and I headed west, towards the Aventine, and home.

I had gone maybe three streets when a low whistle ahead

and to the right made me spin away into the shelter of a doorway, reaching for my knife.

'It's me.'

'Pantera? Are you trying to die?' If I had been less tired, or more tired . . . but he was hardly fresh himself. The strain of being constantly hunted was taking its toll. He was leaning back against a wall, as if brick and mortar were holding him up as much as willpower.

He said, 'How much of what happened tonight will you have to tell Lucius?'

'I'll tell him I went to visit Caenis. He'll flog the men for not seeing me, but that's fine. I'll tell him she is concerned for Vespasian's safety but there is remarkably little she can do besides offer succour to such men of his faction as come to Rome.'

'Trabo?'

'I won't tell him about Trabo, no. And I won't tell him you were there. I won't tell him what we planned. Particularly, I won't tell him what I must do to Valens and Caecina.'

This last was the heart and soul of our night's plan so I may as well tell it to you now.

From the start, it had been clear that it was far too late to turn around the legate Antonius Primus and his five legions. To be honest, I don't think even a direct order from Vespasian would have got him to stop; he'd just have killed the messenger and then denied the order ever reached him.

I knew him, you see, from his time in Rome. He's one of those men who is a nightmare in peacetime but you want him on your side when war starts if only to keep him from going over to the enemy. Lucius had made a big mistake in not wooing him, but the man was a legionary legate of a minor legion stationed in Pannonia; if he'd tried to woo every single commander who might have decided to win glory for himself he'd have drained the imperial coffers within days.

So; Antonius Primus was an ambitious idiot who had risked everything in a pre-emptive move, but he *was* moving, and he had to be supported. If he were beaten, many of the men who would otherwise have sided with Vespasian would turn their backs on him when he needed them most.

Vitellius' men knew this equally well, so they were bound to send some or all of their legions to try to stop him in his tracks. Pantera thought it would be useful, therefore, if only one of Lucius' two generals was able to take to the field. Furthermore, it would be doubly useful if the active general was inclined to Vespasian's cause.

That's where I came in. I offered to make sure that either Caecina or Valens was incapacitated and the other was inclined to defect. Nobody had asked me how I planned to achieve this but I thought that Pantera, who knew most about me, might have guessed.

In the early dawn light, he was a shadow leaning on a wall, radiating exhaustion.

He said, 'You don't have to do this.'

I laughed. 'You would rather Caenis tried? I'm sure she'd do her best, but do you truly think she knows how to poison a man so that he falls sick three days after the meal, and only him of a table of twenty?'

There was a silence. Presently, Pantera said, 'There are very few who know how to do that.'

I pressed my advantage. 'And could she catch Caecina's eye and hold it, and perhaps talk him into committing treason against the man he has fought so hard to bring to the throne? Caenis spends her afternoon gatherings making loud noises in Vitellius' favour, but everyone knows she is Vespasian's to the end. They tolerate her because she used to be a slave and they believe her to be powerless.'

'And you they think quite safe?'

'We have to hope so.'

214

'It won't be easy.'

'That's what Seneca said. He was right.'

Pantera laughed a little, and looked down at his feet. When he looked up, there was a compassion in him I had not expected. Softly, he said, 'When you need to stop, send me word. You know how.'

I wanted to say something brave – *I won't stop until we have what we want* – but he wouldn't have believed that and, just then, neither did I.

I said, 'You'll hear from the silver-boys when Valens is ill. I'll do what I can with Caecina. You have enough to worry about if you're going to bring the Ravenna and Misene fleets to our side, and manage Antonius Primus so he doesn't do anything else reckless. Go now.' I found his shoulder in the half-dark, leaned in, and kissed his cheek, drily, as he had kissed Caenis'. 'Get some sleep.'

He didn't. Neither did I. Because I'd seen him kiss Caenis, and watched his lips move, and I knew he was going back there.

If you have spoken to Caenis, you know what went on. Nevertheless, I must tell you that I followed him back, and when he went indoors I climbed up on to the roof and lay with my head by the opening to the atrium. I heard every word.

Chapter Twenty-Eight

Rome, 4–5 August AD 69

Caenis

'Lady!'

It was not Matthias who broke my dreams this time, but young Toma, who rises early every morning to bake the day's bread, and whose twin sister Dino cooks the rest of my meals.

'A man is here. He says you will see him. It is about the matter of Antony's horse.'

Toma, bless him, has no clue about my past, no knowledge of history, no curiosity, unless it concerns the better resting of bread dough.

I prised my eyes open, dragged myself back from the waters of Lethe. 'Show him into the atrium. I'll be with you presently.'

'Lady, he is already there.'

And so he was, but all the same, I had to look to find him. Pantera was sitting on my unswept floor with his back to the fountain, his knees drawn to his chin, his skin slick with tiredness, veins marbling his dye-darkened temples.

Without opening his eyes, he said, 'Caenis?'

'What?' I crouched beside him, and smelled from myself the staleness of sleep and late middle age. 'You'll kill yourself if you don't stop.'

'Soon. I'll sleep soon. But you and I must have . . . ways of talking that are not overheard. The other three men who carried your litter tonight, the big Briton, the boss-eyed Gaul, the gelded priest; you can trust them. And the silver-boys; the tongues, the skins, the hands. They will be true to us.'

I had thought they were only true to me. In a moment's clear sight, I said, 'You were one of them?'

'A long time ago, but they recognize their own.'

'And their loyalty is absolute.'

'When you have nothing else of value, loyalty is the greatest coin. They won't betray us. Anybody else might: Domitian, Sabinus, Jocasta, Trabo – particularly Trabo. He plays the innocent too well.'

'You really think that Domitian or Sabinus might betray us?'

'I know that they *might*. What I don't know is whether they will.'

He was so tired. His voice dragged with the need to sleep. I said, 'What is it you want to talk about?'

'Antony's messenger service, the Antonine Horse. We spoke of it earlier.'

I opened my mouth to say . . . I would like to think I was going to say all the things that are obvious now, but I didn't. Only: 'Speak, then, or ask what you need to know.' All the things we didn't talk about in Sabinus' company.

He was awake then, animated; impossible not to join in his enthusiasm.

'This must be between us only, you and me, but if we can revive the messenger service, if we can bring together the men whose grandfathers swore fealty to Antony, whose fathers gave their oaths to Antonia, who are now sworn to you, we will have a network that crosses the empire that Lucius doesn't know about and so cannot suborn. We need to be able to send messages swiftly and safely. This is our means to do it.'

He spoke crisply, with a clarity that had been missing in the small hours of the morning. Of course, I know now that Domitian was listening. And Jocasta too? Did he know that? I suppose we must assume he did. How much it cost him to speak with such clarity I will never know. A lot, I am sure.

At the time, I was still wrestling with what he was saying, and the implications for my family.

I said, 'Sabinus knows of this. We discussed it in his house up the hill.' Less than half a day before, though it felt like an age.

Pantera nodded. 'And so if Lucius finds out, it will be because Sabinus has told him.'

His eyes were still and cool and his gaze held mine and because of that I did not look towards the blue silk curtain and Domitian's room on the other side.

I said, 'You would sacrifice something so precious, to test his loyalty?'

Pantera said, 'Vespasian may be in open contest against Vitellius, but Lucius and I are engaged in our own, more private war. Each of us is trying to outwit the other, acting second hand through proxies who are themselves not always reliable. Men can be bought, and bought back and bought back again, owned by both sides or neither.

'The Antonine Horse is a pearl of highest value. For something this big even Lucius may become careless, and in this war whoever makes the first mistake will lose not only his life, but all he has fought for.

'Sabinus knows the theory, but only you know the detail. Will you write it for me now, please, the step by which I may set the roads alight once again with men who owe their absolute loyalty to you – and, through you, to Vespasian?'

PART III
DOUBLE AGENTS

Chapter Twenty-Nine

Rome, the ides of September AD 69

Borros

September brought an end to August's stifling heat and the beginning of cooler air. It wasn't cold yet, but the early leaves were turning and the clouds were thin as silk, and lofty.

By then, Pantera's little Berber cripple had gone; the Guards had got wind of that disguise and it was no longer safe. Gudrun had cleaned the tattoos from his face early in September and the wound on his head had healed enough to be invisible. He had set aside the sackcloth tunic and taken on white robes, and become younger, taller, darker, with a long, lean spring to his step.

On the ides of that month, he was a Mauretanian merchant and his three personal slaves followed him: that's to say, me, squint-eyed Felix, who was the fastest man with a cudgel I had ever met provided you let him use his left hand, and the scrawny gelding Amoricus, who had once been a priest of Isis.

I don't know how Pantera found him, I never asked, but if

Felix was a natural born killer, Amoricus was, as we swiftly discovered, as skilled a picker of locks.

You might think that we who had once been enslaved would have hated to be made slaves again, even only as a disguise, but in our month of freedom we'd found exactly how much easier it was to remain a slave for a while longer than to learn how to be a freedman in a city where the slaves envied us and the freeborn inevitably continued to despise us as mere freedmen, with no real standing.

And so we were slaves again, if only in name, and Pantera led us in a train through the markets towards the Circus Maximus. We had dressed with care: scruffy enough to look impoverished, not obviously muscled enough to look dangerous.

We made a line astern as he swept downhill to the corner tavern known as the White Hare where my old master, Cavernus, held sway over his clientele. Pantera stooped under the lintel; truly, he was not so tall that he needed to, but he was *thinking* taller, and so we all thought him taller too. He found a seat in a corner and we trailed after him and sat on the floor.

Cavernus served us himself, making much of his new client's evident wealth and showing no sign of recognizing either him or me. As he bent over the wine, Pantera murmured, 'Your man: is he here?'

'Claudius Faventinus. He's been in since the first hour after dawn.'

Cavernus' eyes flicked to his right, where a balding Roman was staring with dull inattention into his own wine beaker. He was carrying too much weight to be fit, but not so much that it couldn't be lost again. Broken veins lined his nose and were spreading on to his cheeks.

'What can you tell me of him?' Pantera asked.

'He was a centurion in the western fleet at Misene.'

'Discharged with honour?'

Cavernus shook his head. 'He says so, but nobody else agrees. Don't trust him. He'd sell his right hand for the cost of the next jug.'

'Just the man I need.' Rising, Pantera laid a silver coin on the table. 'Hold this place for me, will you?'

He gave orders to us in a language that I suppose might have sounded Mauretanian to those listening but was, in fact, the tongue of the tribes of Briton. He spoke it always with the accent of the west.

'If this man is not what he seems,' he said, 'we will need to kill him. Listen, but not obviously. And watch for how he moves.'

He swept across the floor, his white robes whispering behind, and approached the table of a man who was too lost in his own self-pity to notice that he was coming.

'Claudius Faventinus,' he said, leaning over, making much of his imagined height. 'May I join you? I hear the navy lost a good man when you left . . .'

Pantera left the bar-room shortly after noon, with the three of us following behind.

Out of sight of the inn, he stopped. 'Follow Faventinus,' he said to Amoricus. 'I need to know where he goes, who he speaks to, what he eats, what he drinks, whose bed he shares and what he dreams of while he sleeps. I need to hear everything of his life. Is that clear?'

'Very.' Amoricus was a straightforward boy in many respects. He had wanted to be an actor in his youth and we had discovered early that he had a memory better than a Hebrew's, and a facility for extempore speech-giving that would have left half the city's actors raw with envy. With better looks and a richer voice, and his balls still hanging on his body . . .

All that might have been, but was not, was written on his face, but nearest the surface was a delight that Pantera had trusted him with this new task.

With two of us left in his train, Pantera set off on what had become a daily tour of the city. He stopped at a shrine to Bacchus and threw a coin into a fountain, leaning over as the god dictated to look at his reflection in the rippled surface.

In doing so, he reached underneath the rim and retrieved from beneath it a long, thin flake of birch bark, carved along its inner surface in Etruscan script. *There are those among the gladiators who will dance to your tune. Gladius.*

Pantera dropped the wood into the burning fire of a small shrine to Aphrodite on the next street corner and we watched it bloom with bright flames, so that the letters briefly stood out white against the charcoaled wood before it all fell to ash.

Moving on, he bought a barrel of wine stamped with an oak leaf and a lyre. Some distance away, he emptied it into a gutter, cracked open the barrel and read what was written beneath a coating of clear wax on the inner surface of one of the staves.

Antonius Primus leads three legions towards Rome. He has met no resistance. Six centurions who stood against him from within his own ranks are dead. The rest favoured Otho, and so hate Vitellius. They will stand firm.

The stave was broken into pieces and that, too, was burned before we moved into the more expensive parts of the Capitol hill, above the vast shrine to Isis that housed her principal priests.

There, a message spoken in low tones, through shrouding smoke, by a veiled woman told us that the sun in Egypt seared the sand and that those who wished for water must wait for the end of winter. As an afterthought, she reported that the lily continued to bloom through the summer and probably into next year.

'Hypatia is in contact with Vespasian, who has the legions of Egypt ready to sail in the spring if we need them,' Pantera said as we walked away. 'We'll need to secure the Misene fleet if they're to land safely. And Titus is still in love with Berenice, who was a queen in Judaea.'

We absorbed this, Felix and I, and stored it for future reference. It came from you, didn't it? You are Hypatia? We didn't understand half of it and told none of it to anybody.

At the foot of the hill Pantera received from a particular date-seller a pebble of fired clay the exact shape, size and colour of a date, which, when either end was twisted, opened to show a hollow core containing a brief message in a cipher that took him nearly an hour to translate.

Written out, it said, *The marines at Misene are ripe for the picking. Speak to these men.* A list of ten names was added.

At an ostler, he paid for the keep of a horse that did not exist and received a message in a sealed pack.

Three streets away from the stables, Pantera examined the packaging. The heart of the wax seal contained a single black horse hair which proved, on close examination, to be unbroken. On the seal's surface was the imprint of a galley under full sail: Marc Antony's sign. Within was a simple uncoded note.

Antonius Primus has stopped at Verona and is making camp. The people of the countryside fear the coming war.

Returning to the market, Pantera bought paper, wrote a reply, folded the paper across and across and slid his knife blade along the folds to divide it into four pieces. Each was bound into a new package, identical to the original.

Back at the ostler, one package was handed back as if it were the first one, unopened, to be sent back to the sender; the seal was the same, but with a new hair set in the centre.

It was from Felix, who had the finest, palest hair of us all; only if you knew what to look for would you have seen the difference.

Later, at the big, busy livestock market by the Tiber, an ox-cart drover, a muleteer and a travelling bladesmith each accepted a silver coin to deliver their packages unbroken. With the silver coin went a phrase: 'It is many years since Antony lost at Actium. May there be many more before such a battle comes again.'

Thus, simply, was Pantera's reincarnation of the Antonine messenger service ordered. The men were dour, closed-faced individuals; I wouldn't have picked them out of a crowd, but Pantera had talked to them all in the course of the past month and they all worked for him with a devotion as great as any of us.

Felix and I held back when he spoke to them; it wasn't that he didn't trust us, but we all knew that Lucius was becoming more desperate by the day and that if one of us was taken alive, it was better for everyone if whoever was taken didn't know the details of the men Pantera had sought out.

What that means is that while I could describe them for you, and where he met them, I couldn't tell you their names, or what they were paid, or whom they delivered to.

Were we watched? Of course we were. The silver-boys followed us everywhere and Pantera did nothing to lose them, at least not while we went about our daily message round. If one of them had chosen to betray him, they could have done so. But he wasn't arrested, which means they didn't, right?

In the mid-afternoon, after one such conversation, Pantera said to Felix, 'It might be that there is no bear hunting the streets tonight.'

'Trabo is taken?' We knew he was the bear, you see.

Pantera shook his head. 'No, but he may be occupied else-where. Still, it would be unfortunate if the Guard were to be spared, don't you think? If two or three of them were to die, marked by the bear, it would keep them on their toes. Make sure you are not seen.'

'Of course not.' Felix, who lived to kill, grinned like a child who had expected hard labour and instead had been sent to play in the fields. He left us, quietly, unobtrusively, cheerfully.

Pantera sent me back to the Inn of the Crossed Spears with orders to keep an eye out for Trabo and to protect him if he needed it. I did as I was bid, but Trabo didn't come there that night, and, for all that there were so many Guards obviously waiting for him, there was no violence to speak of.

They hadn't laid a finger on him since July and they showed no sign of getting any closer.

Chapter Thirty

Rome, the ides of September AD 69

Geminus

Yes, well, that wasn't for want of trying, was it?

You have to understand that the best part of July and all of August passed in what felt like a flurry of activity during which, in fact, we achieved precisely nothing.

After that first day's near misses, we were back to relying on informers, and, as I said before, if you offer a fortune for a sighting of someone who can change his appearance more or less at will, a lot of people will discover they have seen someone who must be him.

For the first four or five days after that first street fight, Juvens and I spent half of each day interviewing men, women and children who charged us handsomely for their dross, then rushing about the city following their lies. Eventually, Lucius lost his temper, and had the latest two beaten until they confessed that they'd fabricated their evidence. Then he had their hands cut off, saying they had attempted to rob the treasury which was a tenuous extension of the truth if ever we heard one.

One of them died as the executioners tried to cauterize the stumps. The other one was sent home with his hands in a sack about his neck and word soon got round that making things up was unwise. After that, the flow of information dried to a dribble, but it was coming in then from Lucius' sources in the city. He spent a lot of his time studying the papers Nero had left that described Seneca's network.

You wouldn't have thought Nero was a fastidious man, or prone to extensive record-keeping, but his notes were surprisingly full and Seneca had clearly been something of a personal obsession. There was more detail of his agents, his network, his ciphers and codes than any one man should have possessed and Lucius was like a pig in an acorn field; he could barely believe his luck. He thought if he read it all he'd be able to build his own network in a far shorter time, and pretty soon he set about doing exactly that.

He found men he could trust and paid them good silver and it began to yield results. Near the end of August, we heard that Pantera was using the guise of a Berber cripple. We scoured the city for Berber cripples and found a few but none of them was him. I think we might have got close once or twice, but always the news we received was that little bit too late, or was mildly ambiguous, or sometimes turned out to be just plain wrong, and on those occasions the fact that we'd rushed halfway up the Esquiline to a particular tavern at a particular time of day probably helped Pantera to work out who it was that was feeding us the information. It didn't make any material difference, anyway; we still wasted weeks chasing down cold trails with no sign of that changing.

Added to that, whoever was slaughtering the Guard carried on whittling away at our men until they wouldn't leave the barracks after dark unless we ordered them and then never in groups of less than eight. We had to hire in whores and then ration them and then deal with the resulting fights. The whole summer was a nightmare, really.

September fell on us like a winter tree.

One day it was August, and my worst problem was the nightly predations on the Guard and the frantic rumours that arose from them, and the next it was the first of September, which was the emperor's birthday with all the havoc that entailed.

It brought Vitellius back from the southern hills whither he had gone to escape the heat and smells of the city in summer. That much was good: if the people had not quite forgotten they had an emperor, they were forgetting that his name was Aulus Vitellius, not Lucius. So he came back for a day of processions and fanfares and pomp and majesty . . . and feasting. So much feasting.

Afterwards, the rumour was that Vitellius spent his life feasting at other men's expense when in truth it was only this one birthday, which spread out over the ensuing days like a fat man on a bath bench, so great was the number of senators desperate to show their loyalty to their emperor.

There were over a dozen of them, each anxious to put on a greater show of wealth and extravagance than his predecessor, each eager to find a new dish that might delight the tongue of so fine a connoisseur as this man who had fallen on to the throne and did not quite know how to hold it.

Thus Vitellius, who actually preferred plain fare but had not the strength to say so, was subjected to goose liver and lark's tongue pâté, to stuffed dormice, to whole roasted ostriches, bathed in many-flavoured sauces.

Quinctillius Atticus paid a fortune for a pool to be built in his dining room within which live carp swam, so the emperor could choose the best for himself as it passed under his nose: his steward practised catching the things for half a month beforehand and still failed on the day, the fish having become more adept at hiding than he had at netting them.

Suetonius Mellos went one better and brought in a dolphin from the sea, while Titus Calpurnius bought a black and white striped kind of wild horse from Africa that killed three of his men before they could kill it, and when the survivors had done so they found it a rickle of bones, so that the cook had to kill a mule and substitute its flesh for the other. Everybody was agreed, thereafter, that neither mule nor zebra, however finely roasted, was fit food for an emperor, but the striped hide was worth its weight in gold.

The grim marathon of eating, vomiting and eating again came to an end, and with it, to our great relief, the flood of Guards that had been required to man the streets to ensure the emperor's safety. Every Guard in the newly made cohorts who was fit to stand had been ordered out during those three days. Nineteen of them had not come back alive.

The bodies had been left openly displayed around the city, rarely in the place where they had been killed. All bore the now familiar marks of the bear-man who was supposed to be ravaging them.

But – finally! – their killer had made a mistake, a series of mistakes, really, and we were on to him.

Over the course of the past half-month, three men had escaped his attacks. Each of them had provided us with a description of a bearded man with sandy hair and light eyes.

And one of them had said, 'If you shaved his beard off, it was Trabo. I'm sure of it.'

Trabo? *Trabo!* Of course, it made complete sense, and asked the same question the other two had agreed: yes, it could have been Trabo. Yes, if pushed, they would be sure. Juvens was beside himself with joy. A pale-bearded, big-built man is not that hard to find, even in a city the size of Rome.

It had taken us a few days, but by the ides of September we knew his routines. A dozen men of the Guard were watching the Inn of the Crossed Spears, with orders to send a runner to me and Juvens as soon as Trabo appeared. We weren't expecting him to head for the inn until late in the evening, and so at dawn I was in the main parade ground, where Clodius Icelus, a Guard in my cohort, was being flogged for repeating one of the many rumours about the killer.

He had ceased to scream, but the wet-iron taste of blood stained the air and the sound of his breathing was a ragged nightmare. I couldn't walk away from it, any more than I could have walked away yesterday, the day before or any of the other days in the last two months when men had been flogged for rumour-mongering.

There were no bears in Rome, even before the recent revelations, I had been certain of that; no shapeshifting men hunting abroad as beasts at night; no deathly ghûls called forth from the deserts of the east by Vespasian's necromancers. Vespasian was a man like any other, and I knew he could be beaten like any other; but not if the men who might have been doing the beating were talking themselves into defeat before ever they set foot on the battlefield.

They were scared, I accept that; they drew lots for what had once been routine night patrols of the city and had become instead a venture into a threat-filled nightmare, with strong odds that if you came back alive it was only because someone else you knew had died, messily.

Men gossiped under these circumstances; it was only natural. And it was equally natural that the officers ordered them to be flogged, hoping for silence, knowing it wouldn't come.

I watched the sun burn the morning's haze off the city, let the slow silent blue of the sky still my wandering thoughts, and waited for it to end.

And then it was over. The unconscious Clodius was carried to the physicians who had the skills to keep him asleep for three days with serum of poppy and nightshade and then send him back to his unit. Unless he caught blood fever and died, there was every chance he'd be on duty again before the next full moon, but he'd be left behind when the rest of his unit marched out to meet Vespasian's legions.

They were due to leave at noon, and they weren't any happier about that than they had been about the night patrols of a city that had become so exceptionally dangerous. Because this was the truth we all faced: Antonius Primus' armies had stepped on to Italian soil earlier in the month after a string of martial victories over pro-Vitellian forces.

At forty-nine, Primus was nearly twice Caecina's age, and could not have hoped to inherit the empire from his chosen lord: if nothing else, we all knew that Vespasian had two sons to inherit after him. But you could smell the raw stench of ambition even down the full length of Italy, and Antonius Primus, legate of the VIIth Galbania, self-appointed leader of Balkan legions, reeked of it.

In Vespasian's name, he was leading five legions toward Rome, plus their auxiliaries, cavalry and anyone else who had tagged along hoping to profit from the carnage. Against them, Vitellius was sending detachments from eight legions, plus cavalry and auxiliary. Over half of the forty thousand men who had marched into Rome in the late spring were marching out again and the Roman people had lined the routes to cheer them on their way with a patriotic fervour that was only partly feigned: their daily prayers were that Rome might not remain a military garrison for the rest of their lives, and the news that men were soon to march out in large numbers had sparked something close to holiday fervour.

Vitellius was proving surprisingly popular. The people liked him, although whether that was simply because he wasn't Lucius was hard to say. Whatever the reason, he had gone out amongst them after his birthday celebrations and, one smile at a time, was winning his city back from his brother, from his generals, from the torpor and muttered disquiet of his people.

Sending his two leading generals north with the army was part of his strategy.

It was a good idea, ruined by the fact that only Caecina had turned up at the barracks that morning, and in a foul temper.

He it was who had ordered Icelus flogged. He it was who had stood close enough to be coated in a light spray of blood, so that his skin, ordinarily healthy, was mottled with raised spots from which men naturally recoiled.

He was screaming orders now, harassing Guards who were already running to their duty. Disgusted, I had turned away when the light, unmistakable tread caught up with me.

'If this lot meet Antonius Primus and his legions, they'll lose. They are sheep with no sense, and they fear the thought of real battle.'

I had been at Cremona with exactly these men when they had fought Otho's forces through the night and half of the following day. Never in my life do I want to see a battle more real than that one – and we won it.

I was concerned, briefly, that my brows might rise and betray me, but no, my face had schooled itself to the tepid acceptance I most despised and had most frequently used of late.

I said, 'With luck, Antonius Primus will turn tail when he

sees the size of your army and you'll be back in Rome before the start of winter.'

Mentioning the season was a guess, but it struck the target. Caecina's eyes closed a moment and opened again only slowly.

'Winter,' said my commanding officer, 'is too fucking close. We shouldn't be marching anywhere now. We should be training these lazy bastards until they have forgotten their own names and their mothers' names and the name of the girl they fucked last night if they ever knew it at all and remember nothing but their place in the formation and how badly they want to kill the man opposite them. We should be blocking the passes into Italy and securing the navies. We should be . . .' He cupped his hands to his face in despair. 'We should have left by now and we're not ready. Most obviously, we don't have Valens and Valens is supposed to be leading half of this fucking army. Find him. Bring him here. Remind him of his duties, however pleasant you have to be. You can be pleasant, I'm sure.'

Caecina wasn't Lucius, he didn't freeze a man's blood in his veins with one look, but he wasn't a happy sight when he was angry and he was beyond angry now. With the thought of that as my spur, I set off for the big double gate that let out on to the Quirinal and from there to the Capitol.

That day, the gateway was far more crowded than it had been, but that was to be expected; the half of Rome that wasn't lining the streets to cheer the legions' departure was here trying to make some last-minute sales to men with too much silver in their pouches and little hope of spending it on anything approaching luxury in the days ahead.

At the gates, I had to shoulder my way past boys selling luck charms (Long life and good health to you!) and women selling finches in small cages (Bright songs for bright spirits! Joy on your march and good health to you!), and I was contemplating what kind of chaos it would cause if I set about the citizens with my staff when Juvens appeared at my shoulder.

'Going somewhere interesting?'

Until recently, Juvens had been despondent. Failing to find Trabo had buffed the shine off his reputation and he'd been sullen and sour for over a month. But since discovering that his nemesis was the bear-man he'd never looked more cheerful: however fearsome your quarry, hunting a living thing was preferable to hunting a shadow. I should know; I was still hunting Pantera.

The men at the Inn of the Crossed Spears were Juvens', and they had clear orders to follow their man but not spook him. Still, I would have been with them, were it my target and my men.

'Why are you not at Scopius' inn?'

'Because Trabo knows what I look like and we'd lose him for ever if he saw me.' Juvens' smile was irritatingly indulgent. 'You're looking cross. Did I see the blessed Caecina venting his wrath on you?'

'No, you saw him vent it on Icelus. I merely caught the backlash.'

'Which is why you are veritably running across the city.'

'I'm not running.'

'Of course not, just walking at a speed that would put a bolting horse to shame. May I trot alongside?' Juvens was panting. I slowed my pace and found the veins were pulsing in my neck.

I shoved past a tall Mauretanian curse-vendor (Honoured lords! Lay low your foes, whosoever they may be!) and wondered if I could buy one of his tabs for Caecina, and what it might cost to pay for his silence afterwards. I was safely past before the thought had taken root.

'Are we going to collect Valens?' Juvens asked, at my shoulder.

'I am going to find General Valens, yes. You, meanwhile, are waiting for a report from your men and are instantly ready to act on it. If not, you'd better have a good excuse.' Turning, I found I could walk backwards almost as fast as I could forwards. 'Unless you've been ordered to follow me?'

I didn't want to think that likely, but it wasn't impossible. Lucius was ten times more frightening than Caecina and Lucius delighted in turning a man's family against him; or if not his family, then his closest friends. Squeezing through the crowds, I studied Juvens, searching his open, playboy face for signs of subterfuge.

Ten paces on, I gave up; I wouldn't have known what to look for anyway and I wasn't going to treat my closest friend as an enemy. If I did that, Lucius would have won, and while I might have given my oath to the emperor, and had every intention of holding to it until death, I had given nothing at all beyond necessary obedience to the emperor's brother, nor did I ever intend to give more.

Quite what we thought would happen when Lucius ascended the throne – because he was obviously aiming for that and part of the reason Caecina was so unwilling to leave Rome was that it meant leaving Lucius behind with his brother – was anyone's guess and too far away to contemplate. Thus did I keep myself sane.

With Juvens easy at my shoulder, I came to the Aventine, strewn with big houses with gilt-tiled roofs and fountains that had flowed with wine instead of water on the occasion of the emperor's birthday.

Here was the real wealth, the vast, overstated, too-much-money-and-no-sense wealth that buys fripperies because they are today's fashion; British slaves this month, Thessalian next; pâté of larks' tongues today, caviar tomorrow; wine yesterday, a different wine today, a different one again tomorrow. Always wine. And gold; there was so much gold here, a man could have died blinded by its shine. Valens lived on the crest of the hill, with a view north in the direction his legions were due shortly to march.

The front door to his house was locked and barred as if he had already left and sent the slaves away, but a door at the side gave on to a walled garden aburst with colour and scent; many dozens of fruit trees bowed under the bounty of their harvest, while late-flowering roses climbed the walls, assaulting the air with their perfume. A small river flowed cheerily down the slope, though I would have bet it was not natural, and that Valens was not paying his due to the water commissioners for diverting their aqueduct to this small patch of glory.

This was my first impression, taken in a single sweeping glance, which ended at the gardener's hut. There, a group of slaves was huddled round a prone figure, headed by Hermonius, physician to the wealthy, and, in my opinion, one of the most morbidly dangerous men in Rome.

'Valens?'

I was running now, if not fast enough to put a bolting horse to shame, then at least fast enough to leave Juvens behind. At the hut, I skidded to a stop: it was Valens, prone, perhaps breathing, with a splattering of vomit near his head and clumps of foul, bloody diarrhoea clotted about his buttocks and the ground around.

The stench was enough to throw a man back. I gagged, covered my mouth with my hand, and knelt, feeling for a pulse. The slaves had backed away; they had no authority and could exert none. I grabbed the closest, a youth of perhaps eighteen. 'Run to the Quirinal hill. Find Scopius who tends the Inn of the Crossed Spears. Tell him we need his wife, to tend your master who has both vomiting and loose bowels. If you can't find him, ask the silver-boys. Tell them there's gold in it and no harm to their master. Don't gawp at me, child; I was born here, I know how the streets run. *Go!*'

He ran. I turned back in time to grab Hermonius, the physician, and bodily prevent him from taking a lancet to the general's veins. 'You can leave. We don't need you.'

'You, sir, have no authority, while I— *Ah!*'

I had drawn my blade and slammed the flat of it back-handed across the physician's chest, sending the man flying into a pile of mule manure.

I stood over him, with the point at his face. 'My blade is all the authority I need. You will leave. I will send for you should we have need of your particular lack of skill.'

I watched the physician scuttle away, and then rolled my general gently on to his back, sent for sponges and water and waited for the slave to reach Scopius and Gudrun, praying all the while that at least one of them would come.

CHAPTER THIRTY-ONE

Rome, the ides of September AD 69

Geminus

'Valens is ill. If he hasn't got the bloody flux, then he's been poisoned. Either way, he may not live to see the next new moon. He certainly won't be riding out today or tomorrow.'

Hard though it was to believe, Caecina was in a blacker mood now, at ten o'clock in the morning, than he had been at daybreak. He heard out my report in silence, pacing back and forth a dozen strides each way, hands caught behind his back, shoulders concave.

At the end, he spun on his heel to face me. 'Then we need another general. I cannot possibly be expected to lead detachments from eight different legions, four of them loyal only to Valens. If I am to . . .'

He drifted to a halt. His eyes grew wide and his scowl swept through a startling spectrum from fury to surprise to self-examination to a slick-hair, straighten-belt smile of sunny delight that I had never before seen on his face and would have had real trouble imagining.

'*Jocasta!*'

He was past me, veritably leaping across the parade ground to the gate, where stood a tall dark-haired woman dressed in a stola of deep, deep red, almost black, fashioned from a silk that radiated a quality, a richness, a raw, demanding sensuality that was a forgotten thing on a parade ground, and often in a fighting man's life.

Caecina was a comet, a blazing ball of light, so complete was his transformation. Long before I could have reached him – I didn't try – he had bowed, made his excuses for the state of his barracks, his hair, his dress, and swept the lady forward into his office. They entered it, unchaperoned.

Without undue effort, I managed to find duties that allowed me to keep an eye on the door. Nobody entered and nobody left until shortly before noon.

Caecina came out first. He had combed his hair, but otherwise he looked much as he did any time he walked out of his office; he was never the kind of man to let his belt hang awry, or to have stains on his tunic. He was a monument to perfection in the legions, and he knew it.

The lady Jocasta emerged on his heels and she, too, had not a hair disarrayed. She was as cool as any Roman matron going about her business in Rome. This did not necessarily mean, of course, that their intercourse in the office had been entirely cerebral.

In my experience, the men and women of the senatorial class are trained from birth in how to look outwardly cool while their inner lives are in turmoil. They could have been rutting like rats on the far side of the door, and nobody would necessarily have known anything about it.

Whatever they had done, Caecina was manifestly in a better mood. He escorted the lady to the gate and assigned eight Guards to escort her wherever she might choose to go next. There was a spring in his step as he marched back to me so that I had to fight not to grin at him as he approached.

'All well?' he asked as he came within hailing distance.

'All is well, lord. The detachments of the First, Third, Fourth, Fifth, Fifteenth, Sixteenth and Twenty-first legions are ready. The Twenty-second has had an outbreak of thrush in their stables; eight mules have gone lame. Replacements are being sent for and they'll be ready by nightfall. They can march to join you with tomorrow's dawn.'

'Excellent! Excellent.' Caecina rubbed his hands down his arms. 'They are the best Rome has to offer. Get them gathered so that I can tell them so. We're going to march out of here today shining – *shining!* – so that Antonius Primus and all the rest of Vespasian's men know exactly what's coming against them, and tremble at the sight.'

It was such a spectacular change of tone, delivered with such enthusiasm, that it was only many days later, when the disaster had happened, that I looked back and saw the seeds of catastrophe sown in that moment when Caecina's talk was all about how well his men looked, and not at all about the strength of their fighting capacity.

At the time, I did as I was told: gathered the men, ordered them into tidy lines and stepped back to let Caecina take his rightful position on the podium, ready to address them—

And found I had trodden on Lucius' foot, and must move aside, awkwardly, and fall into apologies; I was most sorry, I had no idea that the emperor's brother had graced us with his presence. I absolutely did not intend—

'Of course you didn't.' Lucius' whisper was more deafening than most men's shout. 'Stop grovelling and listen to me. I hear you are on the verge of capturing Trabo?'

'Juvens is, yes.'

It was Juvens' job. Juvens drew his name. Lucius should have been speaking to him.

'Don't.'

'I beg your pardon?'

'Don't take him. Watch him, yes. Approach him, definitely. Find a place he can't escape from and corner him. But don't arrest him, and certainly don't kill him.'

'May I ask why?'

Lucius' smile was quenched in snake blood. 'We have word that Trabo is working with Pantera. The two have made an alliance. Since July, I have been trying to place someone on the inside of Pantera's network and now we have someone handed to us on a plate.'

'I'm sorry, do I understand you rightly? You think Trabo, who held Otho as he died, who has given pledges on the altar of the legions' god that he will see Vitellius removed from power, you really believe he can be turned to our cause?'

'I know he can. The man is an incurable romantic, prone to grand gestures. Corner him, and offer him a deal in exchange for his life: he will spy against Pantera for us, or we will kill those for whom he cares most before we kill him. Let him know that the lady Jocasta is vulnerable if he refuses. If you need to sweeten it, tell him the price will be removed from his head the day Vespasian is dead and the insurrection dies. If he serves us well, he can be a tribune of the Guard again.'

'And if he accepts, what do you want him to do?'

'You will arrange a means by which he can contact you. Keep it simple. Keep it foolproof. I want details of everything Pantera does, of who helps him, who doesn't, what they offer. And particularly I want to know how he gets his messages to and from the generals. He has reawakened the old Antonine messenger service from the days of Caesar and Octavian and he's using it to keep in touch with the legions. When Pantera dies, that service will be mine. It's more important than he is.'

'Then why don't we take Trabo and question him? He could tell us where Pantera is and then we could question Pantera. However committed he is to his cause, there is no man who can withstand the inquisitors for long.'

Lucius pulled a face. 'He lasted three days in Britain and told them nothing of value. I would like to think we have greater skill, but we can't be sure of it. If he dies and we have learned nothing, we will be in more danger than if we had left him alive. The enemy you know is a dozen times easier to fight than the one you don't.'

There was a light in Lucius' face I had not seen before; he thrived on the hunt and, like Juvens in the morning, had seen his way clear to a kill. Except in his case, he wanted to prolong the chase as long as possible.

He clapped my shoulder. 'Geminus, you're a natural diplomat. Use all your skills on Trabo and get me what I need. There's a generalship in it for you if you succeed in this.'

There was a time when I would have given my right arm for the chance to serve as a general. But only emperors can make or unmake senior officers and the very fact that Lucius felt safe in making the offer without first asking his brother left me profoundly despondent.

I saluted, and went to find Juvens, to tell him the news that he wasn't going to get to kill Trabo and I wasn't to be allowed to arrest Pantera, and what we had to do instead. I knew he wasn't going to be happy. I wasn't quite ready for the explosive fury that followed.

'Fuck that! I gave my oath in the temple of Jupiter that I'd hunt Trabo down and kill him and now you want me to call him a friend? Are you completely out of your fucking mind?'

I shrugged. 'Lucius ordered it. If you want to tell him he's an imbecile, feel free. I'll wait here.'

'Fuck you.'

'Right, then . . .'

We spent most of the afternoon setting up what we needed. When we had done, I have to say, it went with satisfying smoothness.

Chapter Thirty-Two

Rome, the ides of September AD 69

Trabo

I was repairing a wheel that afternoon, as I remember; but then, I spent a lot of those days repairing wheels. It would have been surprising had I not been.

I'm not a wheelwright by trade, but in my guise as a carter men expected me to be able to at least repair the spokes and set the rim true and I had found I could do that readily enough; after twelve years in the legions, I can turn my hand to most things.

It was a satisfying occupation. I liked the smooth feel of wood under my fingers, the smell of the shavings as I whittled a new spoke to fit its socket. I liked the satisfaction in a job well done at the end, as I set the wheel spinning down the hill. That kept the children happy, and impressed some of the less world-weary customers.

More important, it allowed me to sit at the side of any street in Rome without anybody paying me too much attention.

Which, in turn, allowed me to watch the people who mattered most to me.

The first of these, of course, was Jocasta, who was endlessly fascinating. I could have followed her all day and not grown tired of her. And she was easy to follow; far too easy. It may be that she knew I was there, and so was going out of her way to smooth my new mission as her self-appointed protector, but it was also possible that she was just distressingly easy to follow.

Take, for instance, her visit to Caecina that morning: she had made no effort to hide where she was going and none to hide that she had been there afterwards.

Given the nature of her mission as defined in Caenis' rooms, this seemed to me at first to be the height of folly: she had successfully poisoned Valens and pretty much immediately after, she walked straight into Caecina's office.

I know she'd said she'd do it, but fuck, I hadn't thought she'd be so *open* about it. With the grace of a few hours' thinking, though, I had realized it was little short of genius: what woman – what man, even – would walk into the heart of the enemy and seduce a general away from his chosen lord? In a city that thrived on subterfuge, there was something brilliant about hiding in the open.

She had done the same when she had invited Caecina, Valens and Lucius to a grand and busy dinner three nights before: she was a widow of high means and part of the social hub around which Rome's elite revolved. The fact that of the eighteen guests only Valens fell ill, and that three days later, was an impressive – and deeply disturbing – testament to her skills with poisoning.

If she was my first target, then after that evening Caecina was my second. The general had clearly evolved an infatuation, for he called on the lady Jocasta the day after and stayed longer than propriety allowed, and, frankly, I hated him for it, but I couldn't kill him.

Caecina never went anywhere without a cluster of Guards around him and these were not randomly selected men, drawn from the lottery pool, but the best of the best, chosen for their competence: men like Juvens, Geminus, Marcus Sulius Constans. I might have considered taking on any one of these in a matched fight, but not eight of the bastards at once.

And so I had watched Caecina for the next two days until noon on the ides, when he had emerged from the garrison gates on his high-stepping bay gelding, dazzling in white, with a gilded breastplate and helm and a tall white plume of ostrich feathers piercing the high blue sky, so that he had looked more like an emperor than a general; certainly more like an emperor than Vitellius, who had made the occasional foray into the forum recently, to read speeches clearly written for him by someone else.

Vitellius had had the sense to send Caecina out of Rome, though; sent him north with his legions to assault Antonius Primus and secure victory for his emperor.

Which meant there was nobody left to watch and I thought I might as well go home to the Inn of the Crossed Spears, to eat and drink and sleep awhile before night fell and I could begin to hunt Guards again. I had spent my nights hunting all this time and was becoming adept at finding and killing the men foolish enough to step on to the streets in Vitellius' name.

The last wheel was nearly finished. A brazier at my side kept a pot of pitch on a low boil. I dipped my brush into it and drizzled hot, black tar into the sockets I'd cut, ramming the spokes home swiftly, so that rubbery pitch oozed up on to the inner surfaces of the rim and the hub. I painted more pitch along the outer rim, enough to make a good waterproof seal, and spun the whole thing a few times on the flat of my palm to let it dry.

There were silver-boys watching: silver-skins or silver-tongues or silver-hands, I didn't know which, and didn't really care; they were all one to me, but they liked playing with my wheels and so I stood up, swung my arm right back and hurled the new one down the road, setting it bouncing over summer ruts, gathering speed as it went.

It was the boys' job to catch it before it shattered to tinder at the foot of the hill. The slower ones raced after it in a racket of high-pitched squeals, more like young pigs than boys. The brighter ones had already stationed themselves halfway down the hill. There were three of these and they stepped out as the squealing reached its peak, and set themselves in the wheel's path.

The smallest was the leader; even from here, I could see that. Pinch-faced, with dirty blond hair, he ordered the other two and they stepped aside, angling up from him, so that when the wheel came down they were in V-formation, and could catch it effortlessly. They didn't even bring it back to me for the copper coin I had promised, but passed it to the squealing toe-rags who had skidded to a halt around them.

That's a lot of trust – or authority – for one small boy and it wasn't the first time he'd done it, either. I wanted to learn his name, to find out where he lived, perhaps to recruit him to more interesting tasks than catching spun wheels.

I turned to the watching crowd, singing out, 'All done here! I'll be back tomorrow, or at least tomorrow's tomorrow. Bring your wheels and I will mend them. Best repairs in the city!'

I had the patter off by heart now, so I could speak while I packed my gear and my eyes roamed the shadows where the muddy-blond silver-boy had been – and found he had gone. That's the habit of these boys: they know how to vanish and they'll only reappear when they want to.

I slung my pack over one shoulder and lifted the container of hot pitch carefully, one-handed, by a loop of iron wire

with a wooden grip for a handle. Every inch the wheelwright,
I trudged down the hill from the garrison, heading for my
corner bench at the Inn of the Crossed Spears where a flagon
of wine had my name on it, or at least the wheel mark of a
carter, which was as much of a name as I used in those days.

I turned left again and eased my way through the slum,
heading towards the Street of the Lame Dog and the inn where
Gudrun's cooking awaited me: lamb stew, with rosemary and
thyme.

Amidst all the scents of cooking that assailed the streets,
this one stretched out. I built a solid image of it, the smell, the
sight, the taste of the first spoonful—

'Psst! Carter!'

It was the silver-boy from the hill, the one who had controlled all the others while they caught my wheel.

He was half my height, with his dirty blond hair and
grubby nails, and he was beckoning me with an imperious
wave of his hand. I could have tried to evade him, perhaps,
but I doubt I'd have managed it: there may be places in Rome
where a man can escape the Guards, but there is nowhere out
of sight of the silver-boys.

With a shrug, I turned sharply right and followed the
flag of his old-straw hair as he disappeared into this latest
twisting alley. We ran along it at a swift trot, the boy light
as thistledown, me hampered by my pack and my half-can
of cooling pitch. When the boy turned right and right again,
into ever-narrower going, I lost sight of him, speeded up,
hurtled round the corner, and—

'You!'

'Me. Indeed, so,' said Pantera.

He was sitting on a barrel, playing finger games with some
twine. Around him huddled a dozen filthy, entranced boys.
Not one of them had dirty blond hair.

'Where's he gone?' I asked. 'The boy who rules them?'

'Marcus?' Pantera looked around, as if searching. 'I have no idea. He does what he's paid to do and then he leaves. He was paid to bring you here. He's done that; there's no need for him to stay. He isn't interested in the shadows made by string.'

For the rest, who were manifestly fascinated by what was nothing more than sleight of hand, slickly done, Pantera called the string into a delicate, angled shape that sent the shadow of a hare and then a wolf on to the patch of wall which caught the only light. The boys sighed in awe, and then again in frustration as Pantera palmed the string and stood up.

'Time to go,' he said, shooing them away. 'Later, we can make more.'

I watched them disappear, effortlessly swallowed up by the city. 'Are they all called Marcus?'

'So they say.' Pantera smiled; a flash of warmth swiftly gone. 'They know who you are.'

'The boys?'

'No. I mean, yes, of course, they always have, but they're not your enemies. I mean Geminus and Juvens. And Lucius. Three of your victims lived. One saw your face. They have a dozen men waiting for you at the Inn of the Crossed Spears. You can't go back.'

'Fuck.' I leaned back against a wall. Gudrun's stew was a dream on my tongue, but there were compensations and the thought of all-out war against the Guards wasn't a bad one.

I closed my eyes. My hands flexed over and over on my pack and my pitch. My mind swam with plans, but within them was a kernel of doubt. I didn't trust Pantera; since that first evening at Caenis' house, I never had. He was too tricksy, too much the spy, and there was something about him here and now that was not quite honest.

'You've seen them?' I asked.

'Of course. They think they're being subtle, but they're Guards . . .'

'And Guards think subtlety means wearing a plain belt, without legionary markings.' I forced a smile. 'So I need to find somewhere else to live. I can move from the inn, go down the hill to—'

'Trabo, you need to leave Rome.'

'*What?*'

'We need someone to go to Ravenna, to bear a message to Lucillius Bassus who leads the eastern fleet. He's halfway to our side but he needs some final persuasion. I have a letter in Vespasian's hand, bearing Vespasian's seal, offering Bassus land and gold and a commission in the legions if he'll come to our side. You can deliver it, and stay with him, and talk him round. You've been in the Guard. You can talk tactics where even the best messenger can only relay what he's told.'

The letter lay on Pantera's open palm: a scroll, pale in the dusk light. It was a forgery, of course; no letter from Vespasian could have got here so quickly. He wanted to make me into a messenger boy.

Screw that.

I laughed and heard it bounce off the walls. 'I'm a free man. I don't take orders from anyone. Go fuck your mother.'

I turned and would have walked away, but the not-vanished silver-boys had shifted piles of debris into my path. Nothing much, just a couple of barrels, a sack full of evil-smelling food waste, a dozen smoothed planks that were too good to be there and must have been stolen from a building site. They had done it with such quiet care that I hadn't heard them move, but I was trapped as efficiently as if they stood there with spears to hold me still.

I spun on my heel and threw out the only weapon I had to hand. 'If you're trying to get rid of me so you can have a clear run at Jocasta, you can forget it!'

'A clear run?' This time, it was Pantera who laughed, and it wasn't a pleasant sound. 'I rather think Caecina is ahead of me in that queue, don't you? And then Domitian. And very likely Juvens and Geminus. At the very least, they have men following her who are far more subtle than you. And she knows about them, too.'

'You think I'm an idiot?' His tone . . . I could have hit him, but there was too much junk between us and I'd seen how fast he could throw his bloody little knife.

He knew it, obviously. With exaggerated calm, he said, 'You're far from an idiot, but you've spent too many nights hunting Guards and too many days tracking a woman across the city and the sum of these has made you careless. I think you'll be safer in Ravenna, and also useful.'

'I'm not—'

Pantera cut across me. 'Listen to me. If I wanted you dead, you would be lying cold on the street, so just this once, do what you're told and think it through later. Deliver my message to Bassus and the navy. It's sealed in a way that will show if you've opened it, so obviously you won't. Can you write?'

'What? Of course I can write.'

'So then I ask only that you write a report of everything you see and hear and send it to me.'

'But . . .'

Pantera pushed himself off his self-made throne. In two steps, he was in shadow, barely visible. His voice trailed back to me. 'Trabo, don't make this more difficult than it has to be. Your life hangs by a particularly fine thread. I am doing everything I can not to have to cut it. You will be safer outside Rome, trust me on that. And you will be just as useful to all of us. I will need to send messages to the fleet, to Antonius Primus, to whoever else defects from the Vitellian side. You can be my go-between to all these and you can fulfil your oath to Caenis while you're at it. Go now. Find yourself a bed for the night somewhere small and quiet and in the morning there'll be a horse waiting for you at a tavern called the Retiarius on the western edge of the cattle market. It is being held in the name of Hormus, which is the guise you will use; a freedman of Alexandria. You should ride out with the dawn. The silver-boys will see you safe.'

He was gone. I was left alone, furious, to work my way out of the alley with Gudrun's stew a dry memory in my mouth. I didn't trust Pantera, but there was a chance he'd been telling the truth about the Guards at the Inn of the Crossed Spears and I couldn't take that risk.

I turned back into the winding alleys of the slums, turned left and left and left, heading towards the Quirinal, not entirely sure where I was and simmering on the injustice of all Pantera had said while at the same time striving to think where else I might go, what I might eat, how I might plan a night's hunting and still get to see Joc—

Juvens.

And Geminus.

And Marcus Sulius Constans, and five other Guards of similar calibre, strung out across the alley ahead and behind in an ambush as fair and square as any that might infest your nightmares.

When they come for you like that, you have to move fast, right?

'Ha!'

I swung my pot of half-congealed pitch in a fast, looping arc. Hot tar spewed out, spraying the nearest men. They fell back, cursing viciously, but quietly; someone had commanded them to keep at least a modicum of silence.

I didn't care about quiet; the more noise the better, especially if the bastards were keen on hush, that was my theory. My pack was my shield, my stave-knife my sword. I was on the first of them – Constans – ready to kill and then to die.

I was already angry after Pantera's petty jibes, and now I dropped all pretence of civilization. I was free and wild and reckoned I could kill at least three more of the bastards before they sent me to join Otho in whatever afterlife he was in.

I slashed my blade back-handed at Juvens' beautiful, much-admired face, then flicked and slashed forward at a man I knew by sight but not by name. Blood sprayed back to the alley walls.

Three men hurled themselves at me, cursing, clearly aiming to kill.

I turned, howling. 'Come on then, motherfuckers! See if you're hard enough!'

Geminus got in between us, his sword arm outstretched. 'Stop! Stop it, damn you! The first man to draw blood on Trabo will be flogged to death at tomorrow's dawn!'

He stopped them all right, but he didn't stop me. I had no idea what game they were playing, only that I didn't plan to be a part of it.

I slammed my shoulder into Constans' chest, thrust my blade in under his kidneys, pulled it out, readied for a second strike to make sure he was dead – and could not move my arm.

My right wrist was clamped in Geminus' two hands. Moments later, someone caught my left hand, planted a nailed foot in the small of my back and cranked my arms back.

In a sudden, shearing agony, I heard my shoulders pop, and wondered if the ligaments were tearing. Then I felt both wrists roped and knew they had me alive, and could kill me as slowly as they wanted to; which would be very slowly indeed.

Unless I could make them kill me swiftly, now. I kicked out, hard, and caught a man in the balls; to this day I have no idea who it was, but he was gone, anyway, doubled over and whining.

I grinned and kicked again and again, until my tied arms were hoisted up behind me, high, fast, hard.

I couldn't move. My feet were barely touching the floor, all my weight was hanging on my arms, my shoulders exploded with a kind of pain I'd never known. I was retching with it, weeping, desperate.

I stopped trying to kick; there was no point and I needed to conserve my strength. I refused to give up hope until they nailed me to a plank and hoisted me higher than this, but I had to be clever about it. I was trying to see what was happening when someone wrenched my head up by my hair and Geminus came to stand in front of me.

Usually, in circumstances like this, the leader of the group would kick the life half out of the poor bugger they'd just caught, to teach him a lesson for having killed one of their people. But not this time.

Nothing happened. Nobody touched me.

Geminus, ever-steady, never-rash Geminus, said quietly, 'You are working with Pantera. No – don't start; we know everything and we don't have time to listen to your denials. You are the bear-man who has been killing our Guards and you are also in league with Pantera. On both counts, you are an enemy of the state, and should be flogged to death. This will happen if we have to take you into custody now, although I imagine Lucius will want to question you in detail first.'

Of course he fucking would. I spat in Geminus' face; you have to at times like that.

He didn't flinch. Instead, as if we were taking wine together, or sharing a lazy bench in the baths, he said, 'I am empowered to make you an offer. Work with us. Tell us everything we need to know about Pantera: what he is doing, who his messengers are, whom he trusts and who trusts him. In return, we will give you your life. And that of the lady Jocasta. Refuse us, and you can watch her die before you do. It will not be swift.'

Jocasta? I was bent so far over I could see my knees and my arms were screaming pain from wrist to shoulder, but even so, at the sound of her name, I felt the colour flood from my face.

In a voice that was far from my own I said, 'What do you mean, you will give me Jocasta's life?'

'If you work with us, she will not be touched.'

My guts were in turmoil. In the red mist in my mind, I could still see Pantera's smile, hear his clear, acid voice, and the laughter in it. 'I rather think Juvens and Geminus are before me in that queue, don't you?'

Jocasta. Held by these men?

I must have said her name aloud.

Geminus smiled, amiably. 'She is not in custody yet. Nor will she be if you walk away from here as our man. Moreover, the price will be removed from your head the day Vespasian dies, or otherwise relinquishes his claim to the throne. On that day, you will be free to live in Rome, and your lady with you. Naturally, if you refuse our offer, I cannot guarantee her safety. Lucius, as you know, is somewhat . . . impatient.'

I did know, and more than that, I knew the ways of the Guard. Lucius, Caecina, Valens . . . all of them were two-faced double-dealers you wouldn't trust to sell a lame mule without lying, but they had sent Geminus to talk to me because everyone who was anyone knew that Geminus never lied. And so this was the truth; I had to treat it at face value.

I said, 'Pantera has ordered me out of Rome. He came to me . . . earlier and told me to take a message to Ravenna. He thinks he can bring the marines on to Vespasian's side. I am to send him written reports of everything I do there. If I refuse, he'll want a good reason.'

They weren't expecting that. Geminus rolled the tip of his tongue round his teeth. He looked across at Juvens, who said nothing; I couldn't see his face.

Geminus said, 'You can write?'

'Of course!'

'Then you will go to Ravenna as Pantera has instructed. You will do everything he asks. But you will report to us every order he sends, every bribe he issues, every approach he makes. You will give us the names of his men and those who might become his men; above all, you will report all the detail of Antonius Primus as and when he reaches the port. If you do this, Jocasta will be permitted to walk free in Rome. Fail, and you will watch her die over many days. Lucius will do this. He has no pity.'

'I know.'

'Then you agree?'

'For Jocasta's sake.'

'Good.' He didn't laugh; none of them did. He gave a small, tight smile, as at some inner jest. 'It goes without saying,' he said, 'that this conversation never happened.' And then to the men on either side: 'Cut him loose.'

None too gently, they slit away the cords from my wrists, dropped me to the ground, and watched while I massaged the pain from my arms.

I said, 'We'll need to set up a route for my messages to you. We can't use the silver-boys; they're all in Pantera's pay.'

'All of them?' Geminus swept a hand through his hair. 'Hades . . . how much gold has he got?'

'He doesn't need gold. He used to be one of them. They'd sell their own mothers for him if they had them, and not charge him a penny.'

It turned out that Geminus already had a plan for exchanging messages, and it didn't involve the silver-boys. He laid it out in its elegant simplicity, and I added one small refinement of my own and that was it, we were done.

The men lined up ready to go. Geminus stood before me and saluted, officer to officer. 'We feared you,' he said. 'There can be no greater respect. Do whatever Pantera asks of you, and report the results to us. Go safely.'

It hurt as much to return the salute as it had done when they hauled me up, but I managed it and the strange thing was that it felt good, and real and right, as if the unruly anarchy of all those nights spent hunting had been the illusion, not the other way round.

When I was young, they used to say that a man may run from the legions, but if he is truly a legionary, he will find that he cannot leave the army life behind. I thought I had escaped and now I found that I hadn't, I couldn't and I didn't want to.

Otho's shade gazed at me mournfully as I walked away. I renewed my oath to him, to honour his memory and see Vitellius dead, just that I had found a new way of doing it.

He shook his head. *Later,* I promised him, *All will be as you wanted it. Later.*

CHAPTER THIRTY-THREE

Rome, the ides of September AD **69**

Horus

It was a challenge by then for the silver-boys to try to follow Pantera. Sometimes, he let them, and that night was one of those times; they followed him easily all the way from the Quirinal, where he'd accosted Trabo, across town to the House of the Lyre.

At the House, the door was guarded by Segoventos, a gigantic, much-scarred Belgic tribesman who could have been Drusus' cousin but was, in fact, a failed gladiator I had bought for a good price only half a month before.

He wasn't Drusus, by any means, but in the short time he had been with us he had learned how to be our doorman and he eyed this particular visitor with a cultivated air of suspicion.

Pantera bowed, hands to heart.

'My name is Osiris. I have a meeting arranged with the gentleman Horus.'

'Osiris. To see the gentleman Horus.' Segoventos ran his

tongue around his teeth, found a gap, sucked at it. Presently, he rang a small silver bell and repeated this same to the silk-clad boy who appeared, listened and sprinted back into the incense-laden interior of the House.

Time passed, during which, as if manifest by the gods, a gold coin appeared on Pantera's palm; evidence, perhaps, of his wealth, his discretion, his suitability for audience. Nevertheless, Sego was good to his training; he allowed a seemly length of time to pass before he took it, to show that he was the one doing the favour, not receiving it.

Presently, the boy returned, flushed and panting, and nodded to the Belgian, and then again, startled, to the white-robed stranger who had just handed him a silver coin.

'Top floor,' Sego said. 'Last door in the corridor. Don't go near the hound.'

'There's a hound?' Pantera conveyed a degree of concern above the average. 'Perhaps the boy could escort me . . . ?'

Segoventos rolled his eyes. But there had been gold, and might yet be more.

'Marcus will escort you,' he said, with false grace. 'And he will not charge for it.'

This Marcus had darker hair than his namesake who owned the rooftops, but was otherwise cast from the same mould: fleet of foot, sly of hand, swift of mind and tongue – and the very soul of discretion. He led Pantera not up the nearer, easy stairs at the south-western corner of the atrium, but through the courtyard towards the set of more hidden stairs opposite, which, amongst other things, afforded his visitor an opportunity to study the garden on the way past; a garden much changed from the mornings. The House of the Lyre came to life at night, and now, in the mid-evening, that life was beginning to flourish.

The sun was going down, lancing long, lazy beams through open shutters, lighting the garden to amber green, wrapping soft shadows around the dozen or so masked men and women who gathered amid the citrus boughs.

At this stage in the soirée, by deliberate design, it was impossible to tell who was client and who whore; all were impeccably dressed, jewelled and coiffed; all wore masks that offered anonymity; all talked in low tones, taking wine served by boys named Marcus to the tune of lyres played by girls named Julia.

There was gentle laughter, touching of hands, first hints of nipples that hardened to a look, first glimpse of calf, first meeting of eyes and minds.

Marcus led Pantera up the stairs to the first floor, where four fragrant young women in diaphanous silk gathered round a man who sported senatorial robes, tented out, just then, by his erection. Above the mask his greying hair grew thickly, with no hint of baldness.

Pantera, passing, barely gave him a glance. On the way to the second floor, he murmured to the boy, 'Quinctillius Atticus?'

'If you say so. He comes every night and never has less than three and never the same ones. He pays for each of them in gold.'

'Amazing he has any left after the carp pool he made for the emperor.'

The open areas of the upper floors were empty, although the rhythmic thrust and murmur of intercourse spread from behind the walls where early clients – those with wives who insisted they attend dinner – were making the most of the cheaper rates.

On the top floor was silence. They reached the spur. Ahead was the corridor, and at the end of it the lilac door with the great hound outside.

Marcus stopped almost out of earshot of the door. Swiftly, he said, 'Lucius never comes, but Domitian has been once,

264

Vespasian's son. He wanted an older woman, tall, with raven hair, and got her to show him all the ways a man might pleasure a woman. He took no pleasure himself, but paid in gold when he left. They say he's in love with the lady Jocasta.'

'Who's "they"?'

Marcus shrugged. 'The slaves in the baths. The women who cut hair. The boys from the Palatine.'

'Do they say where he gets his gold?'

'From his father's mistress.'

Pantera considered a moment, then more silver appeared on his palm. 'And our friend? Has he had any visitors?'

I was 'our friend', yes. He must have known that Marcus was as loyal to me as he was to him, but he asked anyway, and Marcus answered with the truth as he knew it.

'Three or four. One of them is a Guard. Tall with dark hair and sharp eyes. I don't know his name.'

'Find it before I come again.'

The boy skittered off down the stairs. Pantera cautiously advanced to where Cerberus awaited him. He stayed back out of reach and whistled until I opened the door and invited him in. For his sake, I left Cerberus outside.

I began to speak even before the door shut.

'Drusus is close to Vitellius now; a personal guard as well as masseur. The emperor and his brother have begun to use him for those executions they dare not entrust to the Guard.'

'You mean other Guards?'

'Those, and highborn men who may be married into Guard families. He has killed two such in the last days. One was an instructor at a gladiator school. Fabius Longinus. The other was a merchant who ran a date-selling business on the Palatine. I don't know his name. Lucius thought both of them were your men.'

'And now he knows they weren't.'

'I hope so.'

I was nervous, and trying not to show it. I led Pantera through to the farthest part of the room, beyond the curtain of pearl and ivory, beyond the vast, oceanic bed, on to the balcony. I had a garden there, smaller and more discreet than the one downstairs, where the clients paid a thousand sesterces a night to have their senses drawn to the tightest, finest pitch.

I said, 'Lucius is obsessed with you. He talks incessantly to Vitellius about how he will outsmart you, outflank you, catch you and kill you slowly. He has prepared . . . you don't want to know what he has prepared, truly, you don't. He has men who are sending him messages from within both the fleets; Claudius Faventinus claims he has your trust, and hands over your messages as they arrive. Other men report from within the gladiator schools, and from close to you on the Quirinal.

'Lucius thinks you poisoned Valens, but he doesn't know how. He knows for a fact that you are sending out forged letters that purport to come from Vespasian. He believes you were in the guise of a date-seller, and that you are endeavouring to seduce the gladiators to treachery. He thinks he is blocking you at every path.'

Pantera leaned on the balcony's iron railing and looked out and to the side and down. Any other man might have been taking in the view. Pantera, if he had not changed, was planning eight different routes of escape in case he were ever cornered here.

He said, 'He may be right. We have to wait and see. In the meantime, I need to send a message to Vespasian.'

Why else had he come? I indicated a cage on the left, big enough for perhaps eight birds, if they lived closely. 'I have three birds remaining that will fly to him. No more after that and no chance of getting any before the spring. You can only send three messages between now and then; is this one so important that it must be one of them?'

'If you had only one bird left, this is the message it would carry.'

'You have it ready?'

'Not encrypted. I need your day codes for that.'

'Wait.'

In a shimmer of beads and roses I was gone, and swiftly back with the tools of our trade: a sheaf of message paper, fine as onion skin, bought from Egypt at a price far beyond its weight in gold; a slate with what looked to the careless eye like a shopping list written on it, but was in fact the day codes that I had set with the dove-keepers in Alexandria; and a wax tablet on which to make the transitions that turned a sentence into gibberish for those who did not have the means to turn it back again.

'Your message?' I held out my hand, so different from his. Mine are manicured three times in a month; his, never.

'I didn't write it down.'

'Of course not. Here.'

The wax was perfect; just warm enough to take the mark readily, not so warm that his words smeared out of recognition before he was done.

Pantera wrote, *To the emperor Vespasian, from his servant, greetings. Your kin are well. Caecina leads Vitellius' forces against Antonius Primus who marches five legions in your name. Both naval fleets will soon be ours: Ravenna within days, Misene within a month if all that we attempt bears fruit. Rome will be yours by Saturnalia.*

Discretion personified, I fed the birds, holding out my cupped palms with handfuls of crumbled nuts. Doves and finches clung to my fingers and pecked freely. I didn't look up until the transcription was done and the upper half of the wax tablet wiped clean of the original message.

'Will you write it for me?' Pantera handed him the tablet. 'My script is not small enough.'

To be carried by a dove, the script must be tiny or the message short. I can write letters so small they look like ant tracks across a page, and only the best-eyed scribes can read them. I can make and break these straightforward ciphers as fast as normal men can write and I can write in any hand; if I see it once, I can mimic it to perfection the way some men can speak in voices not their own, or alter their appearance.

I had, for instance, penned every one of the letters 'from Vespasian' that were circulating amongst Antonius Primus' troops, and, by dint of double agents, had also reached Caecina's legions, to let the troops know what was on offer should they choose to defect.

Here and now, I wrote in my own hand and finished with a salutation in plain, unencoded text that Pantera had not written.

Blessings upon you, Emperor of Rome.

'For decency,' I said. 'If he will truly be emperor by the year's end, you need to begin to treat him as such.'

'I have always treated him as such,' Pantera said, flatly. 'When can you send it?'

'Now is as good a time as any. The bird can still fly some way at dusk and there are places to rest in the forests of the south. If you wait, you can see it go.'

The chosen dove was one of the slate greys pacing the breadth of the wicker cage. It crouched at the sound of my voice, and it was the work of moments for me to fold the fine paper to exactly the breadth of my thumbnail, roll it into a cylinder and slide it into the tube fixed to the bird's leg.

Done, I lifted my hands and opened them. The bird stood tall, took in its surroundings, bobbed its head at its fellows and then launched skyward on a racket of wings that sent the pair left behind into a clattering alarum.

Pantera watched the bird until it was a pinprick in the un-stained blue of the sky. He left then, with little more said.

On the way down, the stairs were busier, not so much with traffic ascending or descending as with men and women who had moved away from the rest for the semblance of privacy while not yet abandoning the party.

Downstairs, the bower garden was busily full. The serving boys were now naked to the waist, the girls' tunics were kilted shorter, and opened to show the first curves of their breasts.

The music was pitched to a different note; it wove through the vines, the citrus branches, the standing and lying couples, drawing the sexual tension to breaking point, and holding it there. The masks were gone now, and the pretence; and those who preferred to display in public were making the most of the wide couches set at angles to the great many-stemmed candlesticks.

A woman sat astride a man, head thrown back, her nipples clamped between his rigid fingers, their tight-locked hips moving with increasing urgency. Nearby a man stood with a woman held in front of him, her back to his chest, his fingers working at her groin. She pulled his head to hers, and bit on his ear. Elsewhere, a boy knelt, a girl lay naked on a couch, a trio of young, lithe bodies made a triangle of lust.

Pantera noted the names of those he could identify, and the figures of those he couldn't.

At the door, the giant Belgian accepted another gold coin and waved him away, smiling.

CHAPTER THIRTY-FOUR

Rome, the ides of September AD 69

Jocasta

I went to Trabo in the evening, a little before dusk.

He was in the Retiarius, one of those foul little taverns where men gather after the circus to dissect the fight. There hadn't been many of those lately; Vitellius' first and only love was for the chariots. He had no interest in watching men gut each other publicly, so the tavern supplied its own battles: slaves or hired men who wrapped themselves in boiled bull's hide and hacked at each other with blunted blades, or sharp ones if the watching men paid enough.

It smelled of piss and that metallic sweaty stench of too many men locked in too small a space on too hot an evening. The fight that night was between an albino Thracian and an ebony-black slave brought in from the hinterlands behind Egypt.

Trabo wasn't watching the fight, although it took me some time to discover that. I was dressed as a tavern whore and working the room was necessarily a slow business; men to fend off, men to let down gently. I couldn't afford to cause a riot and while I have no qualms about protecting my virtue by force if I have to, on that particular night I had to make sure it didn't come to that.

When I had been through the entire room and failed to find him, I headed upstairs to the third floor, where were the better-smelling rooms with clean straw on the floor and fewer lice. The one in which I found him was surprisingly wholesome. The blanket on the bed was clean, after a fashion, and the walls had been newly whitewashed in the spring.

Trabo had eaten of their stew and had a flask of wine to hand. He was seated on the bed, writing a letter, when I entered.

'Jocasta!'

His sword met me, face-high, as I stepped in through the door. He lowered it, but did not sheathe it. He was gaining wisdom, I think, or just so unsettled that he didn't know whom he could trust any more. 'What brings you here?'

'I came to apologize.' I pushed the door shut behind me, slid the bolts across. 'May I sit?'

'What? Yes, of course.' He swept away the writing from the bed, set it neatly on the floor. That was Trabo all through; impetuous, but neat-minded. The combination had a lot to recommend it. 'And wine? Would you like wine? I only have one beaker, but . . .'

'We could share it?'

I sat on the edge of the bed. I had dressed in a rough tunic without adornment, and pinned my hair up with cheap bronze pins. I pulled them out and leaned forward to set them atop his letter, which let me scan the first lines.

To Geminus from Trabo, Greetings. I leave at first light on a horse Pantera has provided. He

I straightened, sat on the bed. Trabo looked as if I had just slapped him across the face. He was standing there with his sword in one hand and his beaker of wine in the other and didn't know which to thrust forward first.

'Geminus got to you through me,' I said. 'I'm so terribly sorry.'

'You know about that?' He was so relieved, it was heart-breaking. He leaned back against the wall – he almost fell on to it, really – and slid down until he was sitting on his heels with his hands laced around his knees. He looked more haggard than I'd ever seen him. More than when Pantera had a knife to his throat and he was within three breaths of dying.

Do I believe Pantera would have killed him back in Caenis' cottage? Without question or hesitation, yes. Do you think Pantera doesn't kill? He's ruthless; he kills whoever gets in his way.

But now he had a use for Trabo, and Lucius had a use for him too, and poor Trabo was caught between, not knowing whether to serve both or neither, and terrified that one side or other was going to gouge out my eyes and rip out my tongue with hot irons in front of him if he made a mistake.

Wretchedness etched his every feature; it hung from his bones, it melted his features in the evening light. Hesitantly, he laid down the sword, and held out the beaker.

I took it, and set it on the floor. Then, standing, I crossed the small space between us and took his poor, misery-ridden face between my hands.

'My dear man . . .' I kissed the side of his cheek. 'You are not made for this kind of despair. When we were children, you were a handful of sunshine, scattered among us. Where has it gone?'

'They threatened to . . . harm you.' He would not be more specific.

'I know.'

'You do?' He pulled my hands from his face, held me at arm's length. 'How?'

Perhaps I could have told him that I'd had men following him who had listened to every word and brought the news straight to me, but I didn't want to add to his paranoia. Maybe if I had things would have been different later, but they might have been differently worse, not better. Trabo is a soldier, he's not built for subterfuge. We all used him and it was like using a spoon to cut meat; it might work after a fashion, and if it's all you've got you make the best of it, but everything is damaged in the process.

So I let him hold me. We were close enough for me to see the fine veins threaded across the whites of his eyes, the lips that the beard didn't quite hide, the arc of his brows. He had always been a handsome youth (my brother always fell for good-looking men) but for all my protestations of his sunny disposition there had ever been a rash, adolescent side to him that made him heady, prone to outbursts of righteous temper.

There, in that room in a seedy inn on the wrong side of the Tiber, what I held in my hands was a grown man in trouble, but a good one, and Rome was pitifully in want of good, grown men.

His eyes were locked on mine. I could feel the first stirrings of interest beneath his tunic, but he was too troubled, at first, to pay them heed. He said, 'What can I do? Pantera told me to leave Rome and I'd barely walked three streets when Geminus was telling me to report to him. I can't serve them both.'

'Why not?' I leaned my head on his shoulder. 'You are offering Lucius an ear in the heart of Vespasian's front line, or at least where the front line will be when Antonius Primus reaches Italy. Believe me, he'll be glad enough of that.'

'But if Pantera finds out, he'll—'

'Pantera understands.' I took his hand, turned it over, kissed his palm. 'You are too good a man to lose. That's why he did what he did. He is doing his best to protect you, although I think we can do better.' I folded his hand closed. 'Do you want to leave Rome?'

'What do you think?' He was listening to his body now. For the first time that evening, I saw him smile. Sweat stood proud on his brow. I smoothed it away with my thumb. 'Do I want to leave you? Am I crazy?'

'I hope not.' I pressed more tightly against him and turned my face up for his kiss.

He slid his arms round my waist, carefully, as if I were made of some fragile glass that might be easily crushed. I felt the weight of his elbows on my hips, the skin of his palms on the back of my neck, rough and ridged were he'd held a sword for days on end, and killed with it.

He was not killing now. For all his evident strength, there was a surprising delicacy to his touch as he lifted me up and laid me back on the bed. I drew him down on top of me, but later, when we had paused to slither out of our tunics, I pushed him down and lay on top of him and explored his body fully with my lips and hands before I let him enter me.

We slowed when dark came, and lit a candle and gentled each other by its light, as new lovers do, tracing the fall of shadows, the new curves and crannies that it created. 'I've always wanted you,' he said. 'How did I not know it?'

'The time wasn't right.' I traced round his nipple with the edge of one fingernail and watched it stiffen in response. 'You don't have to leave Rome, you know.'

'I do. They'll take you and—'

'No, listen. You have to go out; they have to see you go, but if a bearded carter in the name of Hormus arrives with sealed messages for Lucillius Bassus at the naval base in Ravenna and that same man writes back detailed reports to both Pantera and Geminus, who is going to know they aren't from you?'

He swallowed, tightly. His skin felt cold, suddenly, under my palms. 'Where would I be instead?' he asked.

'You would be without your beard and with your hair less dark,' I said. 'If Gudrun at the Inn of the Crossed Spears can make Pantera into a Berber, I think we can find someone to turn you into a northman. You couldn't be a carter any more, you couldn't go back to the inn. You couldn't risk being seen in Pantera's company or mine. But Rome is a city of millions. There are places a man can hide if he chooses.'

I had been kissing his chest, nipping the hairs that grew there between my lips as I spoke. Then I looked up. His eyes shone rich with hope.

'If I stayed, could I see you?'

'I would like it if you did.' I kissed him. It felt good. I corrected myself. 'I would be heartbroken if you didn't.'

We slept soon after that, and made love again when we woke, and by the time he went to find the horse that had been booked for him in the name of Hormus, we had a workable strategy planned.

Trabo had finished his letter to Geminus and had pressed on to the closing wax a small circle of wheel-binding wire that he had woven into his own makeshift seal, to prove that the letter was his. Geminus had its twin, to match against it in a rough but effective scheme dreamed up in the alley.

The seal was now in my possession, to give to a man loyal to me who would be well paid to take Trabo's place on the trip up to Ravenna. I didn't find it necessary to tell Trabo that the group would be ambushed and all the others killed and only Hormus would 'escape'; as I said before, Trabo is a soldier, not made for subterfuge, and there are things we had to do to ensure his safety that he was better off not knowing.

That apart, we had a good result. Lucius thought he owned Trabo and Pantera thought that Lucius thought it while Pantera was the true owner. And I knew that Pantera thought so and was wrong: if anyone had rights over Trabo that September, it was me, and me alone.

Everyone thinks that it was Pantera's actions that changed the course of this war and brought about what happened, and while on the larger scale that might be true it is also true that here in Rome, Trabo was the hub about which we all turned; his loyalty was the one thing we had all bought and none of us owned and in the end it was that – his loyalty – that we all needed.

PART IV

DOOMED SPIES

Chapter Thirty-Five

Rome, October, AD 69

Geminus

October brought us cold and rain and Lucius began to arrest anyone he even suspected of knowing Pantera and question them under duress.

Some of them, it turned out, did know him. There was a date-seller who, after two days of close attention, had revealed details of a hollow date that could be used to transmit messages. He had been too disfigured by then to send out on the streets to act as a decoy, and although we tried it with a substitute that trail ran cold.

There was an ostler who gave us little more, a slave who carried water; small people who told us small things and from those we learned that Pantera had been a small, wizened Berber, and then a tall Mauretanian merchant and was now neither.

He might well also have been an Ionian poet, a Dacian tanner, a British freedman – or perhaps he kept a Briton as a freedman, we were never clear – and a failed priest of Isis. The temples of Isis throughout the city maintained no knowledge of him and there were limits to even Lucius' powers; none of the priests was brought in for questioning.

Lucius, therefore, was in a foul mood while I read him the steadily lengthening reports sent by Trabo from Ravenna and concluded that the hero of the legions was as fond of the pen as he was of the sword, which surprised me quite a bit.

'Antonius Primus, legate in charge of the rebel legions, keeps to his camp in Verona. He has ordered that all the statues of Galba that were overturned be reinstated. The men of the VIIth Galbiana are pleased.'

'Pantera sent a message to Lucillius Bassus yesterday telling him that Caecina was within a day's march of Ravenna.'

'Lucillius Bassus believes that Caecina may attack him in passing, and has put his men in readiness to fend off an assault. He has ten thousand marines at his beck, it being the winter season and the sea lanes closed.'

This last came early in the month and caused Lucius to send messengers on fast horses to warn Caecina so that he marched his men along a curving route away from the port to avoid any confrontation with the marines.

And then there was a gap of half a month with no reports at all and I feared that Trabo had been exposed and was even now in some small and bloodied room, being subjected to the same knives and hot irons and crushing devices as Lucius was using against Pantera's suspected allies.

When, one day at the end of the month, a letter did finally arrive, it was twenty-six pages long, and even the first page tore the world apart.

'Caecina has defected!'

I exploded into Lucius' office, uninvited, unwelcome. I didn't even stop to salute. 'Of all the two-faced, insane, treacherous bastards . . . This is the man who got us through the mountains when everyone said it was impossible. He held us together after the mess at Cremona. He practically took the empire single-handed. What the fuck is he playing at?'

I looked up. Lucius was alone, which was a blessing, but only barely. He blinked and I came to my senses. I saw a crocodile once, when I was posted to Alexandria as a young man. They threw it a slave who had dropped a dinner plate in his master's presence. I remember the screams sometimes, in my dreams. The crocodile had blinked as it watched them drag the wretch to the pool's edge. Lucius' blink was just like that.

He said, 'Did his men defect with him?'

'What? I mean, I don't know. I didn't read that far.' I looked down at the letter.

To Geminus, centurion of the Guard, and to Juvens, greetings, from Quintus Aurelius Trabo, centurion of . . . et cetera, et cetera, et cetera. The salutations took up a third of a page. For the rest . . .

'Yes,' I said, and then, 'Actually, no. He tried to take them. He nearly succeeded, but they resisted and arrested him. Listen.'

I read aloud from the second page of the letter.

'. . . *the day before the full moon in October. The weather was cold, but dry thus far although there had been some distant thunder. Our enemy, Antonius Primus, was camped with his legions at Verona, having had word from Pantera ordering him to wait in Vespasian's name.*

'*Caecina, meanwhile, had stationed his thirty thousand men in an open space between the town of Hostilia and the river Po, his flanks defended by marshes. He was unassailable, but he was thirty miles from Verona, too far to reach it with any semblance of surprise. He had planned instead for defence in strength.*

'*Soon after this, he received the unwelcome news that*

the Ravenna fleet had finally defected to Vespasian's side. This was on the thirteenth of October. Caecina used this news as a reason to negotiate with Antonius Primus over the surrender of his men.'

I stopped, too angry to continue. But Lucius, he of the famous temper that could order a man's limbs broken and his face held into a fire if he was in the right kind of filthy mood, said only, 'What were his terms?'

And that's when I realized it wasn't news to him; he had sent Caecina out knowing that he was planning this, perhaps had even told him to. I just didn't know why and I couldn't ask. Sometimes, a sensible man doesn't pry.

I read from the letter.

'Caecina's terms were poor. He stressed the folly of civil war and pointed out the strength of the men he planned to bring to Vespasian's cause. He asked for nothing and offered everything. His letters were read out to the rebel troops by Antonius Primus, who jeered him. He did not once mention Vitellius, nor suggest our cause was just.

'Antonius accepted the terms, and, on the morning of the eighteenth of October, when the men were out of camp on foraging duties, Caecina summoned the officers left in camp and proposed to them that they join him in taking their men to Vespasian's side. By the morning's end, they had all sworn their oaths anew to Vespasian and the portraits of Vitellius had been removed from the standards. The legions no longer owed him allegiance.

'That situation prevailed until the men came back for the evening meal, and noticed that all sign of their emperor had gone. They quickly gathered, forced the details out of their officers and set about reversing the deal. These were the same men who had been victorious in the spring and they intended to be victorious now. They were certainly not going to give themselves to their enemy without a fight. They

arrested Caecina and put him in chains— Ha! That'll teach the motherfucking, goat-buggering bastard . . .'

I faltered. Lucius was beginning to look annoyed. I read on.

'*The loyal troops restored the images of Vitellius. All was well until the following night, when the heavens displayed their wrath at Caecina's treachery, for the moon became bloody, dripping red to the earth, and was swallowed by the night sky, so that the men fell to their knees and prayed that the power of the omen be on Caecina's head and not theirs.*'

'That was the night of the eclipse,' Lucius said. 'The eighteenth of October. Nearly half a month has passed since then. Why has it taken so long for us to hear of this?'

'I think Trabo followed the army, and was caught up in the fighting. Do you want me to keep reading?'

'No. If I wanted someone to read me a book, I would call a clerk. Just tell me what it says.'

So I gave him the gist: that the new commanders of Caecina's legions, seeing the eclipse as an omen – or, at least, telling the men that's what it was – had struck camp before dawn, crossed the river Po and cut the bridge behind them to hinder any following force, then fast-marched their men to Cremona, where the rest of Caecina's legions had been sent.

They had covered a hundred miles in five days, which may be nothing if you're on horseback but when you're moving a line of men two miles long it's five days of hard marching with little rest in between.

They got there in time, but only just.

In the interim, Antonius Primus had heard of Caecina's attempted defection and was rejoicing that he'd won the war without bloodshed as Vespasian wanted: he didn't know that the defection had failed. It was two days before he learned that Caecina was under arrest and his men were still loyal to Vitellius.

At around the same time, Antonius heard that General Valens had finally left Rome and was intending to catch up with the men, take command and drive them in a wedge straight at Antonius Primus' five legions.

What could any general do but respond swiftly? Antonius Primus gathered his men and marched them quickly along the Postumian Way towards Cremona.

Yes, Cremona. Before the legions destroyed it last spring, Cremona was a small town of small wealth and small satisfactions; of wooden houses barely gilded, ragged children playing games in the street, town councillors puffed up by their own importance; of quiet people, who did not understand that the legion which came to camp outside their walls was bringing ruin. They fêted them and fed them and took them into their homes and offered them every hospitality, as good citizens should.

Then the other legions arrived and the fighting started and the men inside would not let the town's councillors surrender, and even if they had the men outside wanted to take the town by force, because then the rules of war meant every spoil within it became theirs by right.

And so by summer Cremona was a small town burned to charred roofbeams and the stubs of walls with a great banner of smoke lying heavy across it, holding in the stench of burned flesh and hair and bone, and the sounds of women, screaming.

And then this autumn, after the eclipse on the night of the eighteenth of October, it all happened again.

They shouldn't have gone there. Really. Anywhere but Cremona. It didn't deserve that.

Antonius Primus' advance forces got there first, but the bulk of his men were eighteen miles behind. He sent for them and they ran the whole way and then insisted on fighting. Caecina's forces, meanwhile, arrived at the end of their hundred-mile march and they, too, insisted on fighting a battle that stretched into the night, where Roman fought Roman and men were able to switch sides to sabotage the enemy simply by picking up the shields of fallen men and listening to others speak the watchword.

You know by now how Antonius Primus himself was in the front line and when his men were routed by an early attack he killed a retreating standard-bearer with his own sword and picked up the banner and carried it to the front and shamed his men into standing and fighting back.

Maybe that's why they won. Who knows? In battle, one brave man can turn a whole field; they teach us that as we train, and it's true.

So maybe Antonius Primus really did win single-handedly. Or maybe our men had lost heart when they lost Caecina. Or the terrain was against them, or perhaps it is true that at dawn, after a night's hard fighting, when the men of Antonius' eastern legions turned to raise a shout to the rising sun in Mithras' name, our men thought they hailed reinforcements and lost all heart.

But in the end the reason doesn't matter. It's the facts that count and the fact was that in this, the biggest and most important battle between Vitellius and Vespasian, we had lost.

CHAPTER THIRTY-SIX

Rome, October, AD 69

Jocasta

'We won!'

Domitian, who had never seen war, punched the air, dancing. Around him on the couches or standing by the pool in my atrium were Sabinus, Caenis, Pantera and me. We had all lived through too many wars to contemplate another with anything but horror.

'What?'

Domitian rounded on us, his eyes alive with scorn. He had become more animated, more mobile, more expressive these past months. It's possible, I agree, that I might have had something to do with that. I was kind to him. I didn't reject him. I also did not sleep with him, ever.

Now, when his gaze fell on me, his scorn became uncertainty. 'Would you rather we had lost?'

I said nothing. Caenis was the one who answered, and she did it gently.

'We would prefer there to have been no battle at all,' she

said. 'For every victorious man there is another dead, with his wife a widow, his children fatherless, his life gone, and all to satisfy the pride of legionaries who would rather fight than yield to the inevitable.'

'But it wasn't inevitable.'

'No, it wasn't.' Pantera pushed himself to his feet. He was shaggily blond now, not the shimmering, almost-silver gold of Felix, the boss-eyed assassin who padded after him, but more like aspen leaves at early autumn; it gave him a more youthful look.

Cleverly woven leather made a neckpiece and silver rings set with small, glittering gems adorned nine of his ten fingers so that, did you look at him unclosely, you'd have said he was someone's ageing catamite, not older than twenty-five; fading, but not yet having lost all his beauty.

Of course, this wasn't true, but even I had to stare at him hard to remember who he really was, so you can understand why Lucius hadn't taken him yet.

He had been sitting on the floor by my feet until then, close enough for his shoulder to press against my knee. We were becoming easier in each other's company; not yet friends, but allies, at least.

Standing now, he said, 'Nothing in war is inevitable. If Caecina's legions had reached Cremona sooner, they would have swung the balance. We were lucky, and a good war doesn't depend on luck. So . . .' He stepped half a pace to his left and was no longer in shadow. 'We must make sure we don't rely on luck next time.'

The change in Pantera had not all come from Gudrun's dye pots; the strains of all that Lucius planned to do to him weighed on his cheekbones, hollowing the flesh beneath them. He was leaner, fitter, sharper. The set of his mouth did not allow for compromise, if it ever had.

'To that end, perhaps it would be useful if we surveyed the

terrain and the positions of the legions and looked at what may be coming between now and the year's end. Caenis? Can it be done now?'

It could, evidently, whatever 'it' was.

With a small and secret smile, Caenis nodded to Matthias who rang a silver bell, and in moments her Spartan atrium had sprung to life with servants carrying things in from a side room, setting them down, and shifting them around until everything fitted together. Matthias fussed over the end result for a moment, then stood back and clapped his hands.

The room emptied again, leaving behind only those of us at the heart of the conspiracy: Pantera, Sabinus, Caenis, Domitian, and me.

On the marble floor, in the clear space by the pool where Caenis' writing desk had lately stood, was a new waist-high table, and on it was something I had heard of from the old days, but never seen: a scaled model of Italy, about the length of a man lying down.

Mountains stood proud, the indented seas dipped deep, painted pale blue across their floors so that when Matthias poured water into them from a copper jug, they seemed truly to be minor oceans, shimmering with promise.

Caenis stood beside it. She was a small woman, but she dominated any room she was in. Her eyes were bright and thoughtful and never rested anywhere long enough to be impolite, but always long enough to see what was there to be seen.

Her hair shone and was modestly kept, with few pins and no veil. Her skin was perfect. Her hands were steady and not yet knotted with the arthritis that affects so many who have once been slaves; she had been a clerk, well trained and well kept, and it showed.

She said, 'It is good, at last, to be able to offer something concrete to our endeavour. This map is over one hundred years old. It was a gift to the lady Antonia from Marc Antony, her father. Sadly, the old symbols and figurines that showed Antony, Caesar and Octavian, with their legions and fleets, are long gone. In their place, I have had more made.'

So saying, she opened a silk bag, and lifted out on to the edge of the table three dozen lifelike models of mounted horsemen, carved in wood.

They were all identical, or as close as human hand could carve, but as she set them out on the terrain she laid across each shoulder a cloak of blue for Vespasian or green for Vitellius, these being the colours each was known to favour in the chariot races. Those legions whose affiliation was not yet known she coloured white.

Thus did she bring the map to life: a river of blue-clad men surged towards Rome with streaks of green standing thinly in their way. The greatest mass of green was in Rome, of course, where the Guard remained, but most striking of all was the vast mass of twenty-five thousand blue-clad men led by Mucianus making their inexorable progress towards us from Syria.

When Caenis stepped back to let the rest of us come forward, she was rewarded by our growing delight. There was a childlike pleasure in moving models on a map, and one as beautiful as this made it an art form. We could plan campaigns and move the men to suit our whim, and test feints and mock retreats and see where the terrain would hamper us.

Domitian was first to start arranging the men differently. He said, 'Antonius Primus can't be down here at Cremona any longer. He won't wait at a battle site, in case Valens manages to raise an army and falls on him. He must be coming up Italy by now.'

He had hold of a figure in a blue cloak and was moving it up the roads that were marked as deep lines on the map.

'He is,' Pantera said. 'He has joined Lucillius Bassus, who has pledged his oath to your father. That was at Ravenna, here, on the eastern coast. The marines have moved out of the port to provide support on his flank.'

He placed a number of blue cloaked-pieces inland from the port where a ship wrought in the bronze showed the navy to be resting.

He went on, 'Antonius Primus is coming on towards Rome now, with an advance army of perhaps ten thousand men, mostly fast-moving auxiliaries and cavalry. The infantry are coming on more slowly behind. All the early estimates still stand: he'll be with us by Saturnalia.'

Saturnalia. Less than a month away. A winter war.

This shocked us all to momentary silence. Sabinus broke it, saying, 'Vitellius is hiding in the palace as if nothing were happening. Surely now he must act.'

'But what can he do?' I pointed to the map, where Pantera was setting blue-coated horsemen in a line pointing straight for the heart of Rome. 'Caecina has defected to our side and Valens is still in the depths of Italy. The emperor's two best generals are absent. He has nothing left but leaderless men.'

'He has his brother,' Pantera said.

'Lucius will never leave Rome,' I said. 'He's the core of the administration. It will fall apart without him.'

'Which is exactly why we need to lure him out,' Pantera said. 'And we have to do it before things become complicated at Misene. See what happens if we can persuade them to join us.'

His hands swept across the map. The flowing blue river of Antonius' forces advanced in a great curving line towards Rome. But behind the city lay a mass of green-clad men: the marines at the western naval port Misene, who, we had to assume, were as able as their counterparts at Ravenna. Before our eyes, Pantera changed their cloaks from green to blue.

Now, when we looked, the green cloaks in the city were effectively surrounded; there were blue men advancing along the Flaminian and Appian ways, north and south, and no escape routes remained for those who would flee the city.

There, graphically outlined before us, was a stark truth: if the marines at Misene went over to Vespasian, then Vitellius and Lucius were effectively trapped in Rome.

'Clearly, the marines are our key,' Pantera said. 'I'm working on bringing them to our cause but we need to lure Lucius north. If he's still in Rome when the marines defect, he'll be down on them like a hammer on a naked hand and we'll lose the west coast. And if we lose the west coast' – he pointed away from the dog's head of Italy to where Egypt lay – 'Vespasian will not be able to reach here in the spring if he is needed.'

'How can you make this happen?' Domitian asked bluntly. 'You don't command Lucius.'

'No, but if he thinks I really don't want him to go north, he'll do it.' Pantera gave a dry smile. 'Trabo was made an offer he couldn't refuse. Since July, he has been with the fleet at Ravenna passing to Lucius every letter I have sent to Antonius Primus. Shortly, he will pass on one I sent three days ago, which said that I was doing everything in my power to prevent Lucius from leading the legions north on the grounds that he could do us serious damage and interrupt the assault on Rome. The battle between us has become intensely personal. If he thinks I want him to do something, he will do its opposite. I have no doubt of that.'

We left soon after. The last thing I remember is the sight of Caenis looking hard at Pantera, as if she had caught him out in a lie, but I thought it had something to do with Domitian.

Pantera and I collided in the doorway. I was waiting for my litter-bearers, he was heading out into a city where death waited for him round every corner. Already he looked smaller, more exhausted.

'Come back with me,' I said. 'I can offer a clean bed and hot food and safety, at least for one night.'

'No you can't. You'd be endangering yourself and not help-ing me. I couldn't let you risk that.' We were close, and I could feel the warmth of his body, taste his breath. This was not the faked slobberings of a pretend-drunken centurion and his pretend-whore. I could smell him, that scent of slightly scorched linen that hovers over some men and makes the air sweeter. I caught his wrist.

'Come. You will be safe.'

I felt his hesitation. He did want to; I truly believe that. But he shook his head. 'I can't. One woman, caught between two men. It never ends well.'

'Two men?' I stared at him. 'You surely don't think Lucius . . .'

'I wouldn't so insult you. But without question Trabo is in love with you and has reason, I would say from the frequency of your meetings, to think his passion is returned.'

Shocked, I took a step back; he had just lied to the entire group about Trabo's being at Ravenna. And I had believed that he believed it. How did he know? And how long had he known? 'Are you following me?' I asked.

'No.' He gave a small, rueful smile. 'But I am most certainly following Trabo. You've done well, both of you. And the reports from Ravenna are exceptional in their detail and literacy. Whoever you sent there is far more competent than Trabo would have been. I commend your choice of agent.'

He lifted my hand and kissed the back; just a touch of dry lips, no passion in it at all, but it carried more intimacy than anything we'd ever done.

'Good night, Jocasta. This war will be different next time we meet.'

CHAPTER THIRTY-SEVEN

Rome, October, AD 69

Trabo

Jocasta came to me late in the night and I could tell she was upset.

I wasn't at the Retiarius any more; I had my own lodgings on the edge of the Capitol, by the gladiator school, a brisk but easy walk from the Circus Maximus.

Pantera had got me that job. Don't ask me how or why, because I don't know. I had thought my staying in Rome was a secret, known only to Jocasta and me, but it became clear that Pantera was in on the deal when, sometime in the first month, Borros, the big lumbering Briton who served him like a dog, found me at the Retiarius.

He made me buy him a drink, sympathized with my lack of work and then told me that Pantera thought it would be 'useful' if I were to offer my services to one Julius Claudianus, formerly a leader of the marines at Misene, now senior tutor at Courage, one of the foremost gladiatorial schools in Rome.

He said that I should offer myself as an undercook, and

make no approaches, but that I should befriend Claudianus if I could. My story, if I needed it, was that I was one of the former Guardsmen returned incognito to find work in Rome because I couldn't bear the exile. All I had to do was find another name and so, for a while, I became Julius Demonstratus, which aroused nobody's interest.

I'm not the empire's best cook, but I can soak beans and boil them and make sauces to pour over them; a gladiator school is not that different from the legions except that we were forced to eat more meat – I spent a winter eating hare and boiled beef once, and never want to see either again. The gladiators feast on more wholesome fare.

So I trimmed my nails tight and rolled up my sleeves and spent my days cloaked in broth-flavoured steam, washing pots and scrubbing vegetables and boiling beans and my hands have never been cleaner, my shit has never been so regular and I have never seen so many men so tired of fighting.

I didn't talk about the legions much at first, but I found myself in the neighbouring tavern one evening with some of the other cooks and weapon-cleaners and general facto-tums and Julius Claudianus came over and took me aside and asked me a couple of pointed questions and I admitted that I had been in Otho's Guard and that I was in Rome because I couldn't bear to be away. I swore him fealty and said I wasn't any threat and I wouldn't cause trouble, all of which was more or less true.

He was a decent man: he eyed me up and down and said a good soldier deserved more and three days later I was the second cook and living in my own apartment room with a girl, Tertia, available if I wanted her. I didn't want her; I wanted nobody but Jocasta, but it would have looked strange if I hadn't taken her, so I did.

Tertia was easy and compliant and I grew to like her. She was intelligent enough to keep away when I had company, though that wasn't often. Jocasta came to see me when she could, but there were days on end when I didn't hear from her, then she'd turn up out of nowhere and we'd be together like a married couple for three days in a row. I told her about the job, naturally, but I never said that Pantera had got it for me. I thought she knew.

My room was on the eighth floor of the adjacent building, with one window that looked out over the main street and another that looked north, towards the Tiber. If you leaned out of that one and looked to the right, you could just see the temple on the Capitol's peak, hidden behind the high rise apartment blocks that forested the hill's flanks.

Inside, I had room for a bed and a chamber pot and a wooden cupboard with a lock on the door where I kept my spare clothes and a knife. I had a good mattress on the bed and linen over it. I thought it homely, and dreamed of somewhere like it, but bigger, where I could live with Jocasta when the war was over.

We talked of it sometimes, but not on that night when she'd seen Caenis' bronze map and Pantera had told her his plans. I didn't find out about that until later; when she came, she wasn't in the mood to talk.

She wasn't in the mood to do anything but fuck, hard; harder than anything we'd done before. I'd always held back until then, although now I can't think why. I was afraid she might despise me, I think. There was something untouchable about her, even after we'd spent so many nights in bed and barely slept through any of them. I knew every inch of her body and I didn't know her at all.

She pushed through the door that night with a look on her face that would have stopped any man in his tracks. I was halfway through undressing and she finished it for me in moments, then kind of punched me down on to the bed and slid over me without taking her clothes off.

I felt bruised all over when she'd done, exhausted, as if we'd just run through the night and then fought a battle. My back was shredded and bloody from the rip of her nails.

Afterwards, when she had mellowed a bit, I risked saying, 'It's Pantera, isn't it?'

She wouldn't speak at first. In the end, she said, 'He's trying to force Lucius into going north by saying he wants him to stay in Rome. He thinks Vitellius will be more pliable without his brother at his side.'

I knew she was close with Lucius. I didn't know how close and I didn't ask. She came to me of her own free will and that was enough. If she knew the danger I posed to her, she didn't speak of it.

I asked, 'Is he right? Will Vitellius be weaker?'

'Probably.' She was nibbling at the side of her nail, looking up at the ceiling. Wherever her mind was, it wasn't on the eighth floor of an apartment building on the Capitol.

'How is he going to make Lucius go? It's not as if he can give him orders.'

'But he can, you see. That's the point. He's going to let him find a letter saying that the last thing he wants is for Lucius to go north.'

'So he'll go.'

'Of course he will. He's an idiot.' She rolled over and buried her face in the pillow. She had a bruise or two of her own on her back, near the wings of her shoulders, where I had held her too tightly. I traced the outline with the knuckle of my thumb, gently.

She gave a long, hard sigh. 'I hate them both.'

And in that, I believe she was telling nothing but the truth.

CHAPTER THIRTY-EIGHT

Rome, October, AD 69

Geminus

'One thing's certain, then. Wherever I go, it will not be north to meet Antonius Primus!'

Lucius was in buoyant mood. He had spent the past four months torturing men to death for news of Pantera, but this was the day I realized that all the while he had had someone inside Pantera's innermost circle who was feeding him information.

There must have been a point, surely, when this individual could have handed Pantera to Lucius on a plate with a ribbon tied round his mouth, but Lucius didn't want that. Instead, he had let the spy continue with Pantera's plans, had listened to them and learned from them, and now he had an opportunity to thwart them.

Which meant he had killed a dozen men slowly as a ruse to make Pantera believe he was being hunted by a man who had no chance of catching him, which was exactly the kind of soulless, ruthless, inescapable logic that left me slick with sweat.

But you couldn't deny that it had all come to fruition when Trabo sent us a copy of Pantera's latest letter to Antonius Primus, and Lucius, forewarned, knew enough to outwit his opponent.

Pantera was running a bluff, trying to trick Lucius into going north by saying he didn't want him there. And so the last thing Lucius planned to do was to leave Rome. If he hadn't been warned, that letter would have set him off like a hound after a running hind, I'm sure of it, but as it was he dug in his heels and began shaping plans for the defence of the city. And all because Pantera didn't want him to do that.

I, who had delivered Trabo's letter into Lucius' hand, found myself the object of congratulations I didn't deserve and rewards I didn't want.

Twice now, Lucius had patted me on the shoulder, which was entirely disconcerting and could only bode ill for later when his mood wore off. I wished Juvens were there to share the accolades; he weathered Lucius' rare moments of joy far better than I ever did.

'We have to tell the emperor.' Lucius was jittery, fizzing with uncontainable energy, pacing back and forth across the full breadth of his small office. 'He refuses to believe that Caecina has defected and Valens has gone.' We'd heard nothing of Valens for nearly a month by then; he could have been anywhere. 'My brother thinks the war is already won and that I am simply making difficulties to embarrass him. This will make him believe otherwise, if anything can. Come on!' He flung open the door. The dreg ends of October battered him with rain-sodden wind. Miserable Guards stood rigidly to attention, praying, if they were anything like me, not to catch Lucius' eye. 'Bring that letter! We'll find him now.'

Vitellius' favoured palace was on the Palatine, on the far

side of the city from the barracks. Sixteen Guards flanked Lucius and me as we made our way across the city, the minimum that was needed to feel safe these days.

Nobody was popular any more; the toxic pall of war had reached Rome and death haunted the streets. Everyone wanted someone else to die; *anybody but me.*

I was no different. On Caecina's defection, when men he had favoured were removed from their posts, I had been promoted to first centurion of the first cohort of the Guard and given permission to move out of the barracks and buy a house in the city, but I hadn't so much as looked for one yet, for all that I would have been given preferential rates by men desperate to curry favour with Lucius. I preferred to sleep at the barracks and to travel, when I had to, with Guards about me. It occurred to me more than once that if Lucius could have done something to make Rome feel safe again, I would have reconsidered my assessment of him as a dangerous lunatic given too much power without any controls.

We reached the palace unassaulted. This was not Nero's vast gilded pleasure palace, but a smaller, more functional house that had survived from the reign of Octavian, who became Augustus Caesar.

It was painted white, like the other houses around it, and only the full detachment of Guard on duty outside set it apart from its neighbours. That, and Vitellius' crest of the four-horse chariot, newly wrought in gold and bronze, on the columns at either side of the entrance.

Lucius was one of the few men in Rome who could enter without the emperor's permission. He did so, slamming the door open before the Guard on duty could get to it, sweeping through the marbled rooms, calling to slaves and freedmen alike, 'My brother? Where is he? Where's Aulus? Where's the emperor of Rome when I need him?'

The emperor was in the baths; a small private suite set near the back of the house, with hot and cold pools big enough for perhaps half a dozen men, and a massage room adjacent.

Today, I had to stand inside the door, not to let the heat out, breathing in a fog of warm, damp steam, while Lucius laid out for his brother the reality of the armies that were ranged against him, the specifics of Pantera's plotting, the cleverness of his own strategies.

It was hard to know if the emperor Vitellius was interested in the parlous state of his empire. He lay face down on a slatted wooden massage table, pillowing his brow on his crossed forearms. When he spoke, his voice crawled out from under his armpit, wreathed in oils and petal scents.

The masseur who worked on him was vast, with biceps as big as my thighs and inked marks rippling there that spoke of unspeakable rites done in forests that very likely involved the eating of human flesh. His neck-breaking fingers worked delicately on his master's calves as Lucius finished his narration.

Vitellius' muffled voice said, 'You told me you were going to kill this spy. Or at least render him safe.'

With strained patience, Lucius replied, 'If we kill this one man, others will take his place and we don't have time to find out who they are. Pantera was trusted by Vespasian to ensure the safety of his family in Rome. It is better by far to know what he plans, and thereby neutralize it, than to blunder around in the dark. This is what we are doing.'

'Then why come to me?'

'Because Antonius Primus is still marching on Rome. I may not go out to meet him, but someone must.'

'No. Caecina will return to us. I know that man. I have dined with him. I trust him.'

Vitellius waved the masseur away, pushed himself upright. He was a tall man, once lean, but the months of high living had wreathed him in fat. It lay in folds about his belly, sagged on to his thighs and hung from his arms. His hair was straight and fine, the colour of grey sand, vanishing in a circle on the crown where he rubbed it, to help himself think.

His face had the look of a bust sculpted in wax that had been left too near a fire, so that everything above flowed down into everything below. When he smiled, the effort it took to lift everything upward was vast.

He made that effort now. 'I sent a centurion, Julius Agrestis, to spy on the enemy lines. He returned this morning. I have word that he would speak to me. Let him be summoned now, and you can hear from his own mouth that you have been duped by this Pantera; things are not as dire as you have been led to believe.'

Julius Agrestis was a small, sturdy man with peg-like teeth and fuzzed brows. He was third centurion of the fifth cohort; not a particularly notable position, but one from which it was possible to climb. I remembered him as ambitious but untalented.

He was also terrified of Lucius, which was only common sense but didn't help when it came to giving his report. Everyone knew what the emperor thought; almost everyone knew the truth was different, and to a man the Guard knew that Lucius would skin them alive if they told the emperor anything Lucius didn't want him to hear.

The problem was in finding out precisely what Lucius didn't want his brother to hear when there was nobody to ask and you were called to speak in front of them both. The risk of saying something unfortunate was large and real and terrifying.

So Agrestis gave his report from kneeling, with his gaze fixed on the blue-ocean floor tiles and his parade-ground voice reduced to a whisper.

'Antonius Primus is three days' hard ride away. He is a

Roman and must be respected as such, so rather than scout in secrecy I entered his camp, introduced myself and told him I was there to assess his strengths on your behalf. He was polite and accommodating, showed me round his camp, introduced me to his centurions, and gave me dinner in the evening before setting me back on my way the following morning.'

'And?' Vitellius was draped in towels that hid his fat. He looked like a pink-skinned merchant, sly-eyed, thoughtful, striking the best deal he could to offload a troop of lame mules on to an unsuspecting buyer. 'How is his camp? How many men has he? Where is Caecina?'

It was his tone that was so desperately depressing; the hidden supplication, the hints of weakness that any fighting man would despise. He wanted to hear that Caecina was held against his will and even now was making plans to escape and lead his men to glorious victory in Vitellius' name.

Julius Agrestis was not stupid; he must have known this, but he had his own integrity and held to it.

He lifted his head and with a commendable courage said, 'My lord, the traitor Caecina is in fine health. He dines nightly with Antonius. Together they consider the strategies that will defeat my lord's Guards and his legions. His men, by contrast, are utterly loyal to you, their true emperor. They are in good heart and will fight for you if given the right command. It would be a pleasure to lead them.'

He dropped his gaze at the end, and so did not see Lucius catch the eye of the giant masseur and share a nod. I saw it, but did not understand it at first. I was too concerned with Vitellius, who was rocking back and forth, with his fingers jammed under his armpits, chewing on his bottom lip.

'Caecina? Dining with Antonius Primus? He must plan some strategy, surely? He must be going to bring all of the enemy's men to our side. He cannot have sold himself to

Vespasian. What coin would purchase such a man when he fought so hard to make us emperor?'

Nobody answered. Lucius was lost in a rage that threatened to break the walls of his skull, or at the very least to rupture a blood vessel.

I was silent because only a particularly stupid man – or an elder brother – would have dared to speak when the veins were knotted purple on Lucius' temples.

Being his brother, Vitellius spoke.

'I could resign. Sabinus is our friend. He will take our abdication. He will smooth—'

'*No!* Brother, forgive me, but this war is far from over. Centurion Agrestis is a loyal man, but he tells us nothing we do not already know. Antonius Primus is not yet at the gates of Rome. Let one of your loyal, stalwart, competent – always competent – commanders lead the bulk of the Praetorian Guard out to block the routes to Rome.

'We have fifteen thousand men who will march in your name: they can reach the Apennines in days and hold their passes for the rest of the winter if they have to; and we can provision them from Rome while Antonius Primus is forced to rely on the marines at Ravenna to ferry him supplies.

'And meanwhile let me lead the remainder of the Guard south to secure the western port at Misene, where Vespasian imagines he will land with his Egyptian legions in the spring. Let these things be put in place and you shall come into the spring ruler of an empire once again at peace with itself.'

'Do you think so?'

Vitellius' hand had risen to his bald spot and he was rubbing it, round and round and round, stirring up the hair at its edges. He stopped in mid-circuit, and brought the hand back to his lap, staring at it, puzzled, as if it defied his control. 'What if Antonius were to win? What then, if you have taken all the Guards out of Rome?'

'Lord, you underrate your Guards.' I spoke before my good sense could stop me. 'We will fight to the last blood of the last man for you. We can hold those passes for years if we need to, and if your brother can hold the western port, then we can supply Rome and the men indefinitely from our loyal provinces.

'Other loyal legions can be brought in, too, from Gaul or Britain or Hibernia. They can attack the Flavian forces from the rear or sail into the port at Misene and strengthen Rome. None of this is impossible. Let us only do it and you shall see how you are loved.'

The silence ached. The big masseur was looking at me thoughtfully; I knew that look, and that blood followed it. In that moment, I realized that Julius Agrestis was as good as dead and there was every chance I was going to follow him to the underworld. Even together, I don't think we could have overpowered the giant German.

I didn't care any more. I was sick of the plotting and the double speaking. I wanted to get out into the fresh air and fight.

I said, 'Let me lead the men north to face Antonius. I guarantee you they will not yield while I remain alive.'

'No.' Lucius answered before Vitellius could draw breath to speak. 'Juvens will lead them; he has the same vitality as you do, he can hold a line with the same skill, he is as loved by his men. And you are needed in Rome. In my absence, you will organize the defence of the city, the provisioning of the troops, the control of the streets. We need a man we can depend on.' He turned to the centurion. 'Julius Agrestis, you are dismissed. Drusus will escort you out. Geminus, you will accompany me back to the barracks and we shall set in train the means by which you will provision two armies and keep Rome fed.'

So I wasn't about to die. I could have said something to

win a reprieve for Agrestis, I suppose. Perhaps I should have done, but Lucius was never inclined to revoke his commands for execution and so I stepped back and let the condemned man walk out past me.

He looked relieved, as if the threat had passed; he barely noticed that the giant masseur had followed him. I counted thirteen slow heartbeats before I heard the crack of bone and flesh and the sudden exhalation that comes with a death. I have never been one to see the spirits of men as they depart, but I felt the iced fingers of a ghost passing down my back as Agrestis died.

'Why?' I asked, as Lucius and I left. 'He told the truth.'

'There is truth, and there is too much truth. He crossed that line. It will be put about that in his desperate desire to prove to my brother the nature of the danger we face he threw himself on his own sword, saying that if my brother did not believe his tale of being ready to die in his imperial cause, then he was of no further use in this life. A fitting epitaph, I think?'

I didn't answer; Lucius was prone to rhetorical questions and could presume agreement where he chose.

The sad thing is, there are men who will believe what they are told. And then those same men will be inclined to repeat what they believe to be a noble act. Thus does insanity infect the legions.

CHAPTER THIRTY-NINE

Rome, October, AD 69

Trabo

October was the month when everything changed. At the start of the month, when Geminus and Lucius thought I was sending reports from Ravenna, I was, in fact, one of three senior cooks in Julius Claudianus' gladiator school.

I still saw Jocasta sporadically, but not as often as I would have liked. I saw Julius Claudianus far more often; any time he wasn't actually driving the men through their exercises, he was in the kitchens.

He said he came in to watch over us, to ensure that his men were fed only on the best, but he had picked up the sweating sickness somewhere in his travelling youth and I think he liked being in the heat and the steam. And he held meetings in our presence; we became his second office, a place where he could hold private meetings without the risk of being overheard.

Which was necessary when his visitor was the emperor's brother Lucius, come to ask if the gladiators of Courage would form a cohort to fight in support of the emperor.

Julius Claudianus was a big, loose-limbed, shambling man, but there and then he drew himself upright and sucked in his stomach and almost wept with the devotion he could promise from himself and his men.

As a former legionary commander, he knew, he said, exactly what qualities were required in a fighting man, which were not always the qualities of a gladiator, and he might not have enough at his own school, but if the emperor's brother could offer gold then Julius Claudianus could bring together a century or more of the best fighting men in Rome.

Lucius offered an unlimited amount of gold. The deal was struck.

They clapped each other on the shoulder like sworn brothers and Lucius came over to taste the goat's cream and chicory sauce I was cooking. He deemed it fit for an emperor and ordered some for his brother for that night.

Later, in the tavern, Julius Claudianus bought me a drink, sat me down in a corner, took a pair of dice out of his pocket and asked me for a game. When we finished, one of his dice had become mine. It was about the size of my thumbnail, beautiful, and well weighted.

Julius rose, and patted my arm. 'Give it to Pantera,' he said, although neither of us had spoken his name before then. 'To him and nobody else.'

I did. It took me about eight days to set up a meeting; I had to find Borros and tell him and then we had to take care that it wasn't just a way to trap both of us in incriminating circumstances.

We met in a tavern on the far side of town with Felix and Borros standing guard. I gave Pantera the die and watched him slide his knife under the six face and lift it free. There was a note inside. Opened, it read, *The gladiators will be raised for Lucius.*

It wasn't news, I had already told him that, but what it told me was that Julius Claudianus was Pantera's man.

I didn't mention any of this to Jocasta when next I saw her. Pantera told me to put it out of my head and I did. If I'm honest, I thought she knew and it would have seemed like gossiping.

CHAPTER FORTY

Rome, November, AD 69

Geminus

I had heard about the gladiators in October when Lucius first commissioned them, but hadn't paid them much attention. We were busy planning for Juvens' triumphal exit from Rome and I didn't have time to think about anything else.

On the ides of November, I watched him leave just as I had watched Caecina leave two months before; in fact they looked much the same. Juvens had had his usual mount taken away and had been forced on to a grey parade gelding all done up with white plumes, and he wasn't happy about it. His men had been polished till they shone and they marched after him, looking almost as unhappy.

Fourteen cohorts of the Guard plus all the cavalry wings at our disposal went with him. The city cheered much as it had cheered Caecina, which didn't feel like a good omen. Realizing this, Vitellius issued an edict to the effect that Caecina's name was no longer to be mentioned, and that all talk of treachery was to be met with the greatest severity.

Given that there were only two cohorts of the Guard left behind, plus the Urban cohorts and the Watch, both of whom were loyal to Sabinus, who was looking increasingly like brother to next year's emperor, that kind of order was always going to be difficult to enforce.

I had been left in charge of the Guard, with responsibility for discipline and order, and so found myself arranging the men into groups big enough to take care of themselves and sending them to those parts of the city least likely to harbour dissent. The problem, of course, was working out which those areas might be from an ever-dwindling pool of possible options.

We managed like this for half a month, and then we had word from Juvens that he required the emperor's presence.

It was late November by then and Juvens had marched his cohorts a mere seventy-two miles up the Flaminian Way; he should have made that in half the time. He had dug in at Mevania, a small and insignificant town on the western edge of a flat plain, opposite the Apennines.

It was a good, defensible place with hills at his back and open country around and if all he had had to worry about was the enemy army that was currently marching through steep mountain passes in foul winter weather to get to him, he would have been fine.

But it wasn't all. Far more damaging was the constant flow of letters sent to his men from their friends in the opposing army, letters that spent pages telling of the wonders of Antonius Primus, how Vespasian was by far the better emperor, and how good was life on their side of the line, where the men feasted on exotic food sent by shipload from the east, revelling in the endless supply of women, enjoying the fruits of their victories.

Juvens could, and did, intercept and destroy letters to the ordinary serving men, but he couldn't stop the officers from reading letters that came in the wood piles, in secret compartments in the bottoms of wine barrels, in the hats of the men who treated the horses, in any of the dozen different ways that men used to communicate from one side of this civil war to the other. In the days since his army had come to a halt, he had lost a dozen senior officers to the enemy and the leak threatened to become a flood. And so he called for the emperor Vitellius to visit them to stiffen their resolve.

And Vitellius went.

And the flood became a deluge.

Truly, Vitellius was his own worst enemy. To put heart into his men a man must have heart himself, and as anyone who had known him closely could tell you, Vitellius hovered daily on the brink of abdication.

Lucius was the one who kept him steady, but Lucius was not prepared to go north himself, not when he had evidence that Pantera was busy trying to force him there.

And so Vitellius went alone, if by 'alone' you mean only in the company of every senator who wanted to make an impression on him, plus their mistresses, plus his tyrant of a mother. And yes, I went too: I was told to.

We knew Vitellius was not a natural orator, but it went far beyond that.

On his first day, he was giving an adequate enough address to the assembled troops, raising his voice at least sufficiently to be heard by the front ranks, when a flock of vultures flew overhead, so vast and so dark as to blot out the sun. Three of them came down low and knocked our emperor from his podium. Either that or he fell, recoiling in his terrified belief that they had come to lift him up to the heavens. Either way, it didn't look good; the men held their silence, but it had a dull, flat feel to it.

The next day, a bull being led to the altar for sacrifice was spooked by a runaway mule, gored its handlers and joined the mule in an orgy of escape. The gods, quite clearly, had rejected the offering. That's when the muttering started.

We might have survived both of these; it was the wine that sealed his fate. Vitellius was weak, and he looked it. He was uncertain, and it showed. He knew nothing of strategy and now, thanks to his idiocy in asking questions in public that should only ever have been asked in the privacy of his tent, if at all, his entire garrison had experienced his ignorance first-hand. And he drank from first light to last and was rarely seen sober among men who prided themselves on their ability to drink hard and fight hard and march on an aching head.

Any one of these three they could have tolerated, two perhaps; all three together, they most assuredly could not. A dozen officers were gone by the end of the first day and more each day after that.

When news came from Lucius that the Misene fleet had, in fact, defected to Vespasian, Juvens took the opportunity to suggest to the emperor that perhaps he was needed urgently in Rome. He was better gone, but when he – and I – left, we took seven of Juvens' fourteen Praetorian cohorts with us, and virtually all of the officers followed us back to Rome.

The only good thing about being away was that Lucius had stayed behind in Rome and for eight days I had been free of him. The worst thing about coming back was that Lucius was there to greet us.

He was hopping mad – quite literally springing from one foot to the other, although whether in rage or delight was impossible to tell.

He didn't seem overly moved by the desperate news from the front, and as soon as he could get me away from the emperor he virtually dragged me into a corner and gave me a lecture about his bloody gladiators.

So it was delight, not rage, that was moving him. The gladiators, by his account, were his secret weapon in his personal war against Pantera: one thousand hand-picked, hard-trained men who were going to carve through the marines at Misene like a knife through soft leather and restore the good name of Vitellius while simultaneously blocking the western port to Vespasian's incoming ships.

He dragged me down into the city to see them: one thousand men crammed into an arena barely big enough for half that number, oiled, semi-naked, a landscape of rigid muscles and shaved cheeks. If I hadn't known him always to favour women, I would have suspected Lucius of setting up a male harem on a grand scale.

While we were there, their leader, Julius Claudianus, took us to one side and said that Pantera had been seen heading for a particular brothel on the side of the Capitoline.

Actually, he said he had heard a half-baked rumour that the spy might have been there, but Lucius treated it as golden fact. I have never seen him move so fast.

He spat orders like a fishwife and within moments we had horses to ride – I was on an ugly chestnut beast that showed the white of its eye and resisted the bit – and two dozen men fully armed to go with us.

We rode as hard then as anyone has ever ridden in Rome's streets, heading flat out towards the Capitoline. Nearing the slums, I leaned over to Lucius. 'May I ask where we're going?'

'To a brothel. We were going anyway, but this just con-firms— Oh, for fuck's sake, man, don't be such a prude! Wipe that scowl off your face and listen! Pantera's been there seven times in the past two months but I've never had word in time to take him. Now there's a chance, if we move fast enough. Bring those men and come *on*!'

CHAPTER FORTY-ONE

Rome, November, AD 69

Trabo

I didn't much like Pantera, and I certainly didn't trust him, but he had courage, you have to give him that. He led Lucius a merry dance into the ghetto, using himself as bait, and given what Lucius had planned for him, I'm not sure I could have done that.

It happened the day the emperor rode back into the city. Pantera came to us in the middle of the morning, out of the blue, dressed as a slave-buyer with his three personal 'slaves' in tow. The story was that he had bought Borros and wanted to see if he could become a gladiator. You know what he's like; everyone was right for their part.

Borros himself could easily have been a fighter. He was washed and oiled and had some bull's-leather armour of a kind that went out of use in Rome when I was about three years old, but was probably still worn in the provinces. He had a great-sword that looked as if it might have genuinely been British, and a small round shield.

Julius fussed around the big oaf like a bear round a cub, insisted he wrapped his blade in thick, soft leather and his fists likewise, that he wear greaves to protect his shins, that kind of rubbish. He had pitted him against the Drake, a little Thessalyan with blue-black hair who was wickedly fast with a trident and a net, a retiarius who had survived the tendency for all of his kind to die fast in the arena.

Years ago, Claudius passed a law that any retiarius who was beaten in his bout should be slaughtered on the spot and never given a second chance, but then Claudius, more than any other emperor, liked the sight of other men's pain. Nero, who was easily the most squeamish of his family, revoked the ruling, but still, the retiarii had a noticeably short lifespan and the Drake was one of the few who had beaten the odds.

We had a good crowd for the audience: all one thousand of Lucius' fighting men, sworn to the emperor; men who had seen the chance to escape from the arena and get into the legions. They couldn't believe their luck, I tell you. Claudianus had had a dozen volunteers trying for every place. He'd had the luxury of weeding out the weak, the soft, the unintelligent, or the too-intelligent, and by the time he'd finished he had a thousand near-fanatics who would follow his commands to the letter.

They had all gathered to watch the bout between Borros and the Drake, which was fine, until a runner came panting from the palace and it turned out that the new 'cohort' was required to put on a parade for Lucius.

Pantera made his excuses and left, but not before he'd had a quiet word with Claudianus. He couldn't afford to be seen, of course; Geminus was one of the few men in the tight little clique around Lucius who could actually identify him, but I watched him leave and he didn't go far, just ducked into the ironsmith's down the road where they made the weapons for the arena. I doubt very much if he'd gone in to order a sword.

I was called inside to make a midday meal for Lucius, but he didn't eat it. I didn't see what made him leave, but he was gone as if a thousand harpies were on his tail, dragging an unhappy Geminus along for the ride: I hadn't let Geminus see me, you needn't think that. I'm not stupid.

What exactly happened to Pantera? I've no idea. You'd have to ask one of the others.

I do know that when Julius' cohort of gladiators marched out a few days later, I marched with them. Nobody asked me, but nobody told me not to. Jocasta hadn't been to see me in half a month and I was sick of wondering what she was doing. I thought it would be easier to live without her if I was away from Rome.

Of course it wasn't, but a man can dream, can't he?

CHAPTER FORTY-TWO

Rome, November, AD 69

Horus

Pantera arrived breathless at the House of the Lyre, and was ushered swiftly to the room on the top floor by Marcus-on-the-door. Mounting the stairs, Pantera took time to ask, 'Has Domitian been again?'

'Three times. Always to the same woman. He pays one gold coin to her and another to whoever is on the door. He watches her. He touches her. He has not yet taken her.' For this information: silver.

They arrived outside my door. A brazier warmed the landing against November's chill.

Marcus melted away. Cerberus greeted Pantera with a slow-thumping tail; the spy had come eight times in all, and the last seven, he had brought meat for the dog. Now he had only a handful of dates, but the hound slobbered them out of his hand and lay with a lazy grin on his great-jowled face.

I was not as easily charmed. It wasn't a good time for Pantera to visit. My eyes were patched by last night's kohl, my silk tunic creased. There had been no time to change. I opened the door fast, flustered, and let him think that the change in the weather had left me thus; I never did like winters.

'What are you doing here? I thought we had protocols. Arrangements. You're meant to send word before you come.'

Pantera still hadn't caught his breath. He spoke between gasps that came from more than just climbing the stairs. 'I couldn't. There wasn't time. Lucius is too close and the negotiations with the marines at Misene in the south are too delicate; I need to be there. I'll be away from Rome for some time and you need to know enough to keep going. May I come in?'

He didn't wait, but pushed past me into the room. Cerberus, well bribed, let him do it.

Inside, I paced the length of the bead curtain, brushing it with my shoulder, drawing out soft discordant music. There was a new vase on a stand by the far wall; tall as one of the silver-boys, and as wide. All around its belly were depictions of men in various acts of sex. It looked Greek. And very old. And very, very expensive. It was; I should have hidden it.

'You can't stay.' I stopped beneath the frieze of Dionysus on the near wall. In my nervous state, my fingers picked at the plaster. I wound them together to make them stop.

Pantera smiled. 'I don't need to stay. I need to send a message to Vespasian, telling him that the fleet at Misene will be his by December, but that I have urgent need of more gold to secure it. You have two birds left?'

'One.'

'I thought—'

'You are not the only one sending messages to Vespasian. How do you think Caecina was able to ensure that his defection would be accepted?'

'Then have you the coding sheets and we can send—'

Sharply: 'No.'

Our eyes met. With evident care, Pantera said, 'If you need me to stop coming . . .'

'If I need anything from you, I'll tell you. And just now, I need you to get out of— Oh, *fuck*!'

Down at the door, where the giant Belgian controlled the entrance, the silver bell rang, twice.

My nerves! I spun on the spot. 'You have to go. No, there isn't time. You have to hide. Out on to the balcony. *Now!*'

I grabbed Pantera's shoulders and shoved him through a shatter of pearls, past the vast, satined bed, and on to the balcony. Grey November cloud draped spider-like about the city, muting all the colours. The balcony garden was still beautiful, though. No flowers bloomed now, but many-shaded leaves gave it colour.

The opposite balcony was a good fifteen feet away and the iron railing was much the same as ours, not a safe place to leave from, or to land on. I watched Pantera judge the distance.

'You want me to jump?'

'If I thought you wouldn't die, I'd say yes. But you would, and he'd hear you.'

'Who, Horus? *Who is coming?*'

I couldn't meet his eye, and just from that, it was obvious: Lucius was coming, and not for the first time.

Pantera looked stricken. I hadn't told him. Marcus hadn't told him. The Belgian on the door hadn't told him. All his careful arrangements had fallen apart. I could have wept.

Dully, he said, 'How long?' but we were beyond that. My hands were on his shoulders, my fingers digging tight.

Urgently: 'If he catches you here, we're both dead. There isn't time to get you out, you have to hide. Get over the balcony.'

He knew me well enough to act without asking. I talked as he clambered gingerly over the iron railings. 'Go down –

there, on the left, underneath. Can you see the ledge? It's like a second floor, hidden under the first. There's room for a man to lie in there. You'll be safe. Nobody can see you from above or below.'

I had tried this out; I knew it was true. The climb was terrifying with four storeys offering certain death on the pavings below if you lost your grip and fell, but if you used the wall to hold your feet, and eased your hands down the iron rails, you could find a second platform below the first, with just enough space between for a man to slide in, feet first. The result, of course, was that the same man, if discovered, was trapped.

'Pantera?' I knelt on the balcony, head thrust between the uprights. 'If you speak, if you call out, if you fart, you will be heard and found, and if you are found, we will both face Lucius' inquisitors. I say this not as a threat, but as the truth. Believe me, he is not one to cross.'

'I know.'

'So you need to stay silent.'

'I know.'

'But will you?'

He gave an exasperated sigh, quite a feat given the evident fear on his face. 'Yes, Horus, I will. Go now, let them in. I will stay silent here all day and all night if need be. Just go! And thank you.'

'Don't thank me yet.' With one last nervous nod, I went back to open the door to my room.

I had no time to change, to wash. I dragged a comb through my hair, and checked myself in the mirror. My eyes were rimmed in black and it had smeared; I must have shed a tear without knowing it. I picked a scrap of linen from a pouch in my sleeve and scrubbed it away before I opened the door.

Two men stood on the threshold: Lucius, whom I had been

expecting, but also another man, with a broader, more open face, and kinder eyes, whom I know now to be Geminus, but then did not know at all.

I bowed, anyway. 'Gentlemen, come in. Lord Lucius, be welcome. Let me move Cerberus first. He does know you mean me no harm, but . . .'

My voice was a hoarse rasp. I thought of saying I had a throat fever, but Lucius could smell falsehood the way Cerberus could smell meat.

I unhooked the hound's collar and led him in to chain him at his kennel, but Lucius, brave, or foolhardy, did not wait; he was already in the room, sweeping back the beaded curtain and straight through to the balcony. I had been right; if Pantera had tried to escape . . .

'We nearly had him. He was seen coming in here. Where is he?'

Lucius: brusque, brisk, abrupt, was running to the end of his temper. I did not know him before his rush to power, but what I saw in him then was a man overhorsed by the glory fate had handed him, riding by sheer force of will, knowing he must be thrown sometime, and that it would hurt.

In my experience, men who find themselves in receipt of unasked-for luck become either benign, believing themselves unworthy, or dangerous, believing everyone else sees them as unfit. Vitellius, by all accounts, leaned towards the former. Lucius, quite evidently, was the latter.

I said, 'My lord, Pantera has gone. He heard you downstairs and he fled.'

'Fled? How? Where to? We have men at front and back.'

'Down two flights of stairs and out on to the rooftops of the Street of the Tanners. He never comes into any house without at least two exits.'

'And you never thought to tell us about that?'

'Lord, you never asked. You said you would never come

while he was here. I thought you wanted to know what he knew, not to catch him.'

'Nevertheless . . .' There was a pause, some pacing. 'No matter. He was here. What did he want?'

'To send a dove to Vespasian. He – that is Pantera – is going south to the marines at Misene. The message was to tell the gen— the usurper that the base will be his by the end of December as long as he sends gold enough to cover the next month. The dove didn't go. We had not the time to send it.'

'South?' He stared at me as if I had spoken Mauretanian, or impugned the chastity of his mother. '*South?*'

'So he said, lord.'

'South. South. *South!*' He was pacing, speaking the word on every step. His face split in a wide grin. 'And he tried to send me north. But I have him now . . . When will he leave?'

'Soon. He seemed in a hurry. He may be going there now.'

'When will he next come back here?'

I thought, not ever; he will never come here again, but I said, 'I have no idea. He said I would need to know enough to manage in his absence, but he left before he could say more.' I let the silent reproach on my face show: *see, lord, how much more useful I would have been had you not barged in here?*

Lucius ignored me. He was pacing, thinking, frantic. 'Could you summon him?'

'Possibly.'

'Certainly! You told us of the ways you have of reaching him if you need to: a message left with the date-seller; a mark made on the base of a fountain; a stone weighting down cloths of a particular colour in the Tiber. We have men watching them, and yet he has not been to check them in three months. Why?'

'Perhaps because you have men watching them?'

'*Fool!*'

He struck me! Granted it was open-handed, and not a fist,

but he hit me, hard, across the left cheek. I had been too waspish. And Lucius, too impatient, had hit me.

He really, really shouldn't have done that.

There was a scrabble of claws on wood and Cerberus was on his feet. He was silent in his fury, which was, I promise you, a deal more frightening than if he had snarled.

Lucius grew very still.

'How long is that chain?'

'It reaches the length of the room, lord. He is here for my safety. It would be foolish were he not able to defend me in my need.'

The moment crystallized around the understanding that Cerberus could reach Lucius in one bound. And Lucius had bolted the door behind him as he entered; it had seemed a wise precaution at the time.

A question hung between us. *Do you want to be found dead in a brothel, Lucius? In* this *brothel?*

You could have anchored a ship off the weight of the silence.

Swiftly, I said, 'My lord, I tell only the truth. Pantera was a silver-hand until his skill was seen by Seneca and he was trained beyond anything the gutter could allow. Who trained your men? Are they invisible? Do they blend with the landscape so that you don't see them even if you are looking? Can they step into a doorway as one man and emerge moments later as another? If not, he will have seen them.'

'Fuck.' A pace. Two. Three. Lucius came to a halt by the tall Greek vase. Have I mentioned how much it cost? 'And yet he still comes? Does he know you have betrayed him?'

'If he did, he gave no sign. He will know now, though.'

'But if he were to believe you a victim, rather than a willing traitor, he might continue to believe you loyal. Would you agree?'

'Possibly. I have never known how his mind works.'

'Still . . .' The gap was shorter this time, a single pace, and then all peace was lost in the explosive splinter of the vase, crashing to the floor. Afterwards, very softly, Lucius said, 'Geminus, you will kill that hound.'

He was a good man, Geminus; he didn't want to do it and it wasn't all fear for his own safety; he didn't want to kill in cold blood, even a hound.

But the order came from Lucius, who could have had him flogged to death in an instant, and so the moment's hesitation was no longer than that before Geminus drew his blade.

'Cerberus!' I hurled myself across the room, thinking to throw myself in front of my friend, to save him with my own person, but Geminus was fast and I was too far away and all that I achieved was that my hound, my beloved great black monstrous friend, was looking at me, puzzled, as he was struck.

I reached him before he died. The brute of a soldier had slashed his blade across his throat, and the blood! So much blood. More than at a pig killing, and you know how much that is. It drenched my floors, sprayed up my walls, soaked into my tunic as I cradled his poor, dear head in my arms. I wept like a child; I was broken.

I heard Lucius walk to me and if he had cut my throat then, and sent me to be with Cerberus, it would have been a mercy.

All I heard was his voice by my ear. 'You are mine. You will remain mine. If Pantera returns, you will let me know as soon as he walks in the door. If you fail, I will make your death last so many days it will be longer than your life was before it. Do I make myself clear?'

'Yes, lord.'

'How will you get word to me?'

'Tell your men to watch the front of the house. When he comes here, I will have Marcus open the blinds to let in the sun. Your men will notice that, I imagine?'

I was angry, but there was nothing left he could do to me

and I was one of the few who might have led him to Pantera. He was desperate, but he could not, yet, afford to kill me.

He left then, without another word, taking his swordsman with him.

A long time later, I looked up, and Pantera was standing in front of me, holding a beaker of water and a strip of linen.

'You have to let him go sometime.' He knelt, held the cup to my lips, supported my head as if I were a child. He said, 'Horus, I'm so sorry. I know what Cerberus meant to you.'

He was my friend. My only true friend. I could not believe that he was gone.

Pantera prised my fingers free from his poor ruined body, drew me up to standing. At my stuttered direction, he found me wine and I drank it. I wanted to die. I could think of no reason not to and a great many reasons why it would be a good idea. I still could not meet Pantera's eye.

He tried to clean up, but the room was beyond cleaning. He gathered the shards of the pot that had cost half a talent of gold and laid Cerberus out decently, with his chin tucked in, closing the wound, so that it looked as if he was sleeping, if you didn't breathe in the blood and see the mess.

Eventually, he came to sit opposite me. 'I did know,' he said.

'Did you?' I couldn't focus on him properly for tears. 'How?'

'I watched here for three days after the first time I came. I saw you go to him.' I believed him at the time. Now, I think the Marcuses told him; that from the first they were his, and not mine.

He said, 'Can I know why?'

'Oh, Hades, do you need to ask? He was torturing men to death for word of you! It was only a matter of time before he found out we'd been close as children. If I hadn't gone to him, he'd have come to me and . . . I couldn't have held silent for long when the knives came out. You know that.' I can't take pain. We both learned that a long time ago, when we were children. He can, you see. It's one of those things that makes us so different.

'I know.' He took the wine, set it down, dipped a cloth in it and cleaned my face. 'Horus, I'm not angry.'

'You should be. Or at least you should be afraid.' I was weeping big, bitter tears for more than the loss of Cerberus now. 'He will break you. He has sworn it by everything he holds sacred. It's all he thinks about. Why do you not leave Rome?'

'You don't think I can break him? Or at least, best him?'

'Best the emperor's brother? The man who is emperor in all but name? I think you're insane to even consider it.'

'And yet you protected me. One glance on your part and he'd have sent Geminus over the balcony to get me.'

'And then? Do you think the likes of Lucius would pat me on the head and pay me in gold? I'd be in chains with you and the men with hot irons would draw my soul from my living body to find out how much more I knew. Trust me, if it were different, I'd have sold you. I am only safe while you are free. Which is why I wish you would get out of Rome. Are you really going south?'

'I am really going south.'

'Lucius will come after you.'

'Yes. And we'll finish this away from Rome, where fewer people will be hurt. But only if I can get out of here. I take it that there is a route out on the third storey, but it's no longer safe to use. So there must be a different way. If you'll show me, I'll go.'

He was hoping for something he didn't know about, I could see that in his eyes: a back door on the ground floor, or in the cellars, a tunnel, a secret passage; anything, but not what he knew in his heart to be true.

'There.' I nodded towards the balcony opposite.

His eyes flew wide. 'Horus, I can't jump that.'

'Of course you can't; no man could. That's the point. Watch.'

At the back of the balcony, set against the wall, was a stand on which bird cages sat. It was made of bricks with planks laid across; roughshod, but fitting with the rest of the balcony's decor. And, because it was fitting, it was not immediately obvious that the second shelf up was made of two planks.

'Help me.'

Together, Pantera and I lifted the songbirds down, and set them on the floor, muttering and shuffling in their cages. Together we lifted the spare plank down. Alone, I eased it out across the gap until the far edge rested on the balcony opposite. It slipped snugly between two heavy vases, each holding a small, wind-shorn shrub.

I turned to the man who had once been a brother to me. 'Just don't look down.' He has never been good with heights.

'And if I don't? If I make it across alive, when I step on to the balcony on the other side who is going to scream?'

'Nobody,' I said. 'Callius and Clytemnestra are silk tailors; they never look up from their work. Should they chance to, they will say nothing. Their son's name was in the lead lottery when Geminus picked yours. They know Lucius ordered it. They hate him more than he hates you, which is saying something.

'From their house, doors lead through two more to a final door that exits on to the Street of the Weavers. Nobody will ask your name. Nobody will ever remember you have been there. Nobody will talk about it afterwards.'

'Until Lucius offers them gold for information?'

'No. I'm not stupid and this has been coming for a long

327

time. Each of these families has lost husbands, brothers, sons, who followed Otho and died for it when Vitellius took power. They won't sell you to Lucius. To Vespasian they might, but he has to win first.' I set my foot on the plank's end, steadying it. 'Don't come back unless you must. If any messages come, I will leave them with Cavernus at the White Hare. They don't know of him yet.'

'Not from you, anyway.'

My stomach turned over. 'Has he—'

'No. But tread carefully. I have never known Rome so dangerous as it is now. Only make contact if you absolutely have to, and make sure any message can be read in at least three different ways.'

We didn't embrace; we never had done. But our parting felt more permanent than any that had gone before it.

CHAPTER FORTY-THREE

Rome, November, AD 69

Borros

'Come. Fast!'

Pantera was running when he got to us. We'd been waiting where he left us, within sight of the entrance to the brothel where his friend worked.

We'd never been that close to the House before – it was always somewhere he went alone – but this time, because we knew Lucius was coming, he left us close. It was a trap, of sorts, but he was using himself as the bait and there was always a chance they might have out-trapped him, in which case our orders were clear: we were to kill him, and get out of there. I was going to Britain; I knew the ship, I knew the master's name, I had a berth booked: he was that unsure he'd get out alive.

Then he came out alone, and ran to us where we hid in the salt-grinder's hut with the air making our noses itch and he had a look on his face I'd never seen before. Wild. Not quite in control. Not like him at all. 'Where's Lucius?'

He asked this of Felix, our scout. Felix could go places a shadow would not slip through, hear conversations meant for no one, kill a man in a crowd and walk away. He had been closest to the House while we were in a room three doors away, armed and ready. I had a shortened spear stolen from a dead guard that looked like a carrying-pole if I reversed it and hung a pack over the butt end.

Amoricus, we had discovered, was a dead shot with a sling. He could split a hair held out between two hands at twenty paces and a man's head at fifty.

Felix was our knife man. He held one now, idly picking the dirt from under his nails. He said, 'Lucius hasn't come out yet. His three men are still watching the front door and five others at the street's end.'

'He left before I did.' Pantera closed his eyes, seemed to marshal himself, then took Felix's knife – which in itself was an achievement; that he could do it for one, and that he did it without thinking – and drew a swift map on the dirt floor.

'There's a route out of the House on the second floor that gives on to the tanners' street. The street bends round and makes a junction with the Street of the Lilacs about three hundred paces east of where we are. If they've gone that way, then all our easterly routes are blocked. A dozen men at the junction here – and a handful at the far end of the Lilacs, here' – he marked crosses on the rough rectangle he'd drawn on the ground – 'could block off all escape. Our only safe route is to cross over the Lilacs and into one of the alleys that lead back into the depths of the hill. If they know about that, if they've blocked it, we'll have to fight our way out.'

'They'll see us.' Amoricus sat back on his heels. Already he had three small pieces of lead shot in his hand, ready for the sling. He wasn't Felix, who lived to kill, but there was a part of him that relished the promise of combat. Funny, that. I'd have thought if you cut the balls off a man, he'd give up wanting to fight, but Amoricus was living proof to the contrary.

He said, 'The Lilacs is one of the widest streets on the Capitol. You could drive three chariots abreast and they wouldn't rub wheels.' He rose, more fluidly than I'd seen him move all summer; no sign he was sore from his scars then. 'You'll need a diversion. Wait until you hear the shouting and then just wander over as if you're coming to see what the fuss is about.' He threw a shy grin at Pantera. 'I've been wanting to do this for months.'

On another day, Pantera would have stopped him. But there was blood on his tunic and that wild look in his eye that I couldn't read and when he might have come up with a better plan, this time, he just cocked his head and said, 'Have fun,' and it made us feel like boys on a thieving trip, not men on the run.

We waved Amoricus off without much more said, then gathered our weapons and listened to the scrabbling rats, to the whistles of the silver-boys, to the burbling doves somewhere in another street, high up on the rooftops.

And then it came; the shout of angry Guards and the scuff-hammer of nailed feet running on a dry road and 'Halt! Halt, damn you!' and the snap of a lead shot smacking on armour and the tumble of a body and then they stopped shouting and drew their swords.

The sound of iron whipping out of leather is one you'll never forget, or the appalling realization that this is for real; that what they'll do to you if they catch you is beyond your darkest nightmare. That's when your bowels feel loose and your throat dries up.

'Move.' Pantera shoved his flat hand on the small of my back, thrusting me bodily forward. 'If we stay, we waste his risk.' He caught my belt and slowed me. 'Not too fast. Walk with me. Look curious, not worried.'

It was the hardest thing I'd ever done; just walk to the open street, head swinging like a bruised bear wondering where all the noise was coming from.

Amoricus was putting on a one-man show of how to commit suicide. He was capering about in front of seven Guardsmen with one lying flat on the ground behind them. Even as we watched, he loaded up another shot and, whizzing it at the nearest, felled him like a tree.

We weren't the only people in the street. Almost everyone sane was staying behind their shutters, but there were half a dozen still stupid enough, or curious enough, to come out.

Pantera slung his arm round Felix' neck like they were lovers, pointed at Amoricus and said something obscene. Felix laughed and slapped his shoulder and they tussled their way out into the middle of the road, two young men coming out to see the fun.

I couldn't have done that. I was shitting myself, or close to it. I shambled along behind them and it was all I could do to keep my spear haft over my shoulder and not bring it down and poke the sharp end at the nearest Guards.

We so nearly made it. They were all watching Amoricus, who was keeping them off him with his sling; they could have rushed him, but he'd dropped two out of eight and none of the six who were left wanted to be the next body cooling on the street.

We ambled idly across, with Felix and Pantera play-wrestling, which meant that their heads were under each other's arms and neither was readily seen, and we were within site of the alleyway Pantera had drawn for us when—

'Stop! Stop that man! On the emperor's order! A talent in gold to the man who stops him!'

A talent? *A talent?* You could have bought half of Rome with a talent of gold and this wasn't from the Guards that Amoricus was taunting, but from behind and to our left and it was Lucius, on horseback, hurtling down the road like a man possessed, screaming out what he'd give to the man who caught Pantera, and what he'd do to those who stopped him.

Of course we bloody ran. Would I be here if we hadn't?

The alley was in sight and we sprinted for it, heads down, feet pumping. Three of the onlookers came at us from the sides, their eyes alight with the promise of gold. Felix killed one with a slash of his knife that opened up the man's throat and sent blood in a wide arc across the street. Pantera stabbed another neatly in the eye, so that he staggered back, screaming.

I came to my senses in time to hurl my pack at the next, and follow through with the wicked iron end of my foreshortened spear. His wasn't a fast death; I hadn't had the practice of the other two.

We were out of the road and into shadow. Above us, the silver-boys twittered and Pantera stopped long enough to put his fingers to his lips and tweet out a response; three notes, rising then falling. To this day, I don't know what it meant.

There were horses behind us, crashing into a space made only for men. A spear burned past my right shoulder, missed Pantera by a hand's breadth. He jinked left and right, fast as a hare, then in British shouted, 'Left ahead, but veer right just before it,' and we did exactly that, slewing right, then barrelling left at the last moment, into an alley so narrow, so dark, it was nothing more than a goat track between tall houses.

The sun had never shone here; the air was dank with mould and death and debris. We couldn't run; we couldn't see where we were going, but then neither could Lucius. He had to dismount from his sweating, bloodied horse and scream for torches.

That bought us time. Pantera caught both our hands and eased us forward, step by tremulous step, deeper into a dark we knew nothing about. It wasn't like night in there, it was thicker than that, as if people waited just an arm's reach away, and were watching us. It was the late afternoon and the rest of Rome lay soaked in sun and here we were in our own private underworld.

'Go right.' Pantera's voice in my ear.

I fumbled to the right and found an opening, a doorway, and beyond it a room with a single lit lamp in one corner; a blessing of light, or a curse if it was seen outside, but it was tucked in an alcove and the door was shut behind us and nobody followed, so it can't have been.

I was wet with thick, greasy sweat. My palms were soft with it. My bowels ached with the need to empty. There was more light in there, more like early dawn than midnight.

In the grey gloom, I saw Pantera lean his shoulders against the door, with his head turned to the side, listening. He held up one hand when I might have spoken and then, with a finger to his lips for silence, pointed to a shuttered window opposite.

It opened without sound and we wriggled through it, eel-like, and out into another shaded alley, and then another opposite and another and we were halfway up the side of the Capitol and into the slums where Lucius could hunt for a year and never find us.

Felix got us watered wine, I don't know where from. I fell back against a wall and drank until I could drink no more. I still felt parched when I was done. Pantera had sunk down with his elbows on his knees and his head in his hands. He took one drink and looked up. He had aged ten years and his eyes were hollow spaces of no light.

Presently, the silver-boys' whistling caught up with us; they had lost us for a while as we dodged between alleys in places even they didn't know.

Pantera tilted his head and listened and gave an answering call. One small boy with tousled blond hair jumped down from a rooftop and spoke to him in a language that made no sense to me, gave a brief nod of his head and then vanished.

'Amoricus,' Pantera said. 'They've got him.'

'Hades.' I felt sick. 'We have to . . .'

Pantera was on his feet. 'They're taking him to the barracks. This way.'

We stood no chance of getting him, that much was clear. There were two tent-units of Guards around him, and Lucius at the front. They knew we'd try to free him. They didn't know we had an oath that said a clean death was better than what Lucius would have made of his life. And he knew too much; it wasn't all altruism. He could have destroyed us.

We took to the heights, to the apartment blocks, and one room in particular which was owned by a cook at Julius' gladiator school and overlooked the street from the front.

Amoricus came along it soon, hobbled with iron chains at his ankles and others at his wrists, with a rope tied about his neck like an ox; they hauled him along like that. Sixteen men ringed him, with their swords out and their shields raised and barely a gap between them.

Pantera took that gap. He was white as salt, but his hand was steady. I'd never seen a man throw a knife more than the breadth of a room. He threw it from a distance of fifty paces at an angle down and back, from an upstairs window overlooking the street.

Before he threw, he gave a particular whistle, like the silver-boys' talking-whistles, but also like a temple flute, and Amoricus looked up.

He saw us, I'm sure of it. And he smiled.

Chapter Forty-Four

Rome, November, AD 69

Caenis

I woke to the comfort-sounds of the house: Toma and his sister Dino in the kitchens, Matthias filling the lamps, young Katos sweeping the floors.

In the normal course of things, one of them would have come to rouse me shortly. I knew I could have risen early and surprised them, but that morning for the first time I was warmer under the covers than out, and didn't want to move.

I dozed, thinking of Vespasian, wondering what he was doing. Outside, murmuring voices mingled with the sounds of doves and the waking street. Somewhere nearby, a question was asked and answered, but I couldn't hear the words. Naked feet padded on my marble floors. *My* marble floors. Mine. To own a house still felt daily like a miracle. To have one with floors built to one's own design . . . the wonder of that would have silenced me if I had let it.

I let it instead lift me out of bed and dressed in the simple tunic I kept for days when I was not planning to see anyone.

I slipped my feet into the sandals that had once caused me so much pain; there were no pebbles in the soles by then. Pantera had long since given up bearing my litter and so I was walking normally again.

I heard Matthias come to rouse me, his careful shuffle as distinctive as his face, and swept my fingers through my hair in lieu of a comb and splashed rosewater on my face. I was patting my cheeks dry with a linen cloth when he tapped, and, at my call, entered.

'Matthias, I—' I caught sight of the face in the silver plate that was my mirror. It wasn't Matthias. 'Pantera? Is Matthias all right?'

'Exceptionally so, I would say. A life lived half in stealth suits him.'

He was right about that: Matthias had discovered in himself previously unknown skills. He could lie with a straight face, could hold a Guard in lengthy conversation for the time it took me to hide away incriminating documents and have the Guard think that he – the Guard – was the one prolonging the conversation.

He had skills in sleight of hand that impressed me greatly and I had hoped would impress Pantera. The thought that he might have seen them without my being there was unexpectedly irritating. I spun round, ready to tell him so.

And then I caught sight of his face, the grey-white exhaustion, the near-defeat, the haunted, aching eyes.

'Oh, my dear, who has died? Is it Jocasta?'

He shook his head. 'Amoricus,' he said, and when I didn't react, 'The gelded priest of Isis. Lucius has him.'

'Alive?'

'Dead.' He didn't say 'I killed him', but it was written across his brow and in the lines about his eyes. He said, 'Lucius is too close. I have to leave Rome. I'm going south tonight. I came to tell you.'

I closed my eyes, so that he might not see tears shine in them. Of course he had to go, but I didn't have to like it, any more than I had liked Vespasian going to war when we were in Greece.

Even to me, it was a surprise how much I had come to rely on his certainties, his half-spoken thoughts, his elisions and allusions and secrecy. I felt safe when he was close. With him leaving . . .

He said, 'I gave my word to Vespasian that I would protect you. Just at this moment, the best I can do is not to know what your plans are. But you must have them.'

'Plans for what?'

'For how you will escape from Rome if I make a mistake. If I am taken, there will be a limited amount of time before I start to give them the truth. You must be gone before then.'

The thought made me ill. I said, 'Sabinus and Domitian and I can all—'

'Not them. Just you. You must make your plans alone.'

I snapped my mouth shut. From the beginning, it had been clear that Pantera didn't fully trust Sabinus and Domitian, but he had never said it so openly. What could I say? I nodded.

He gave a short, dry smile. 'Thank you. I would suggest you talk to the vintners who take empty barrels out of the city. They are large enough for a small woman, and rarely searched.'

'Oh, Hades.' I pressed my hands to my eyes. In the dark behind my closed lids, I was a small girl, hiding in a tiny store cupboard, savagely beaten when found. I had always promised myself I would not do anything like that again.

A thought crept in from the darker parts of my nightmares. I said, 'I can't do that, because you know about it.'

'No. So you must pick something similar, but different.'

'How will I know when I have to go? Lucius is hardly likely to send a slave round with a warning.'

'Marcus will come to you, one of the silver-boys. He will say that the mule has foundered, and ask you to help him move it. You will leave with him at that moment, and he will get you safely to wherever you ask to go. After that, the less I know, the better.'

He gripped my shoulder, briefly, a quick squeeze and away. From the doorway, he said, 'Be safe, Caenis. In the end, it's what really matters.'

I stood in my room a long time after he had gone, and then went to find Matthias and asked him to take me to the market by the Tiber, where I remade the acquaintance of a Greek reed-seller with whom I had once had dealings and who had had a passing crush on me.

The years had treated us both well, and he was as glad to see me as I was him. He was still moving great carts of reeds from the riverbank out of the city for the limers to catch birds. They were big loads, but light, and a small woman hidden amongst them could hope to escape detection.

His name was Philiskos. I bought him pastries and agreed to visit again soon.

CHAPTER FORTY-FIVE

Rome, November, AD 69

Borros

A mile away from Caenis' house, on the far side of the market that hemmed the Tiber, Pantera met up again with Felix and me.

He was a mess, really; he was clearly grieving for Amoricus, feeling himself to blame, which was fair, but he had spelled out the risks to us all when we started and neither of us who were left thought any less of him for it, or wanted to leave.

We couldn't say this, though, because Pantera had brought a newcomer with him: a tall man with a scar running from the corner of his right eye almost to his chin. His skin was so browned by the sun that it looked like shoe leather. His hair was a fine iron grey. His nose was the eagle beak of Roman nobility and belied the peasant's rough tunic and poor belt he was wearing. He looked like a nobleman dressed up as a slave for a particularly expensive party.

Pantera introduced this walking contradiction as Petilius Cerialis, once legate of the IXth legion, who had saved its standard in Britain when the Boudica's tribal warriors slaughtered the rest of his men.

He was the kind of man we thought of as an enemy, we who spoke the British tongue, but Pantera said he had known him in Britain and he was a decent man and, at this time, he was on our side.

To him, Pantera said, 'I apologize for my late arrival at our meeting. I was unavoidably detained.'

'Not permanently, though, which is good for us, eh?' Cerialis barked the man-amongst-friends laugh that made it all the clearer that he was not one of us. 'But we're here now, at your direction, and if you can truly conduct me north to the army of Antonius Primus as you have said, I will pay for it in gold.'

'We can do it,' Pantera said. 'And as I told you when first we met, you need pay us nothing. But before we can go, we must make you look like a peasant woodcutter, a man for whom a silver coin is a fortune beyond imagining, not a legionary legate who has dressed on a whim in his slave's best tunic. May I make a few suggestions? For your safety, of course.'

PART V
SURVIVING SPIES

CHAPTER FORTY-SIX

Rome, 16 December AD 69

Geminus

Lucius was gone!

It was the sixteenth of December, the rain was relentless and Lucius had gone, taking six of Rome's nine Guard cohorts with him, leaving me to man the entire city with the remaining three, but still, I felt a lightness of heart that I'd forgotten was possible.

He had gone south, ostensibly to put down the calamitous rebellion of the Misene fleet, but in truth, as everyone knew, he had gone to hunt Pantera; by now, he cared about nothing else.

You need to know something of what brought us here. It went like this.

We didn't catch Pantera after he left the House of the Lyre. We came excruciatingly close and Lucius had all sixteen of the men who had let him kill his little gelded priest flogged. If we'd got that one home alive, I truly believe we'd have had Pantera by the nightfall.

The next few days, we all walked gently round Lucius, even Vitellius, but he was already planning his moves.

Clearly, Pantera had gone south. Clearly, Lucius needed to follow him. He just needed a good excuse, and within a double handful of days he had it.

We were taking wine in the emperor's quarters when a dissolute ex-marine by the name of Claudius Faventinus arrived with the news that, after a brief show of fighting, the thousand hand-picked, hand-trained gladiators *and* the entire cohort of the Urban cohort who had accompanied them on their march south had all sworn an oath to Vespasian.

They had been ordered so to do by their officers, led by Julius Claudianus.

I thought Lucius might explode then, but fast on the heels of the first messenger came a second, with news that the newly treacherous gladiators had joined forces with the marines at Misene and marched on to capture a small town called Tarracina, nestled on the Appian Way about sixty-five miles south of Rome. There they dug in and partied, celebrating their victory.

So Lucius had the best excuse possible to head after Pantera. He slammed his way into the emperor's presence, and found that Vitellius had already heard the news. A fraternal spat took place, along familiar lines.

Vitellius, mournfully: 'We have lost! We face a winter of no supplies and in spring Vespasian will land with his legions from Egypt, men well fed and in good heart who will fall on us like locusts and destroy the very fabric of our city!'

Lucius: 'No, brother, they will not, for I will not let them. Give me six of the seven cohorts you brought back from the north and I will uproot these vermin and make safe the port of Misene.'

Vitellius: 'I thought you were needed here, in Rome?'

Lucius, at the end of his tether: 'And I thought the gladiators were true to us. I was wrong. Geminus can hold Rome while I'm gone. I have no choice now but to go south.'

V: 'To thwart your enemy, the spy Pantera? Is that it?'

L: 'Pantera has nothing to do with it.'

Lucius was lying, obviously. I knew it, and one can only suppose that the emperor, being his brother, knew it too, but Vitellius had never yet stood his ground in any familial confrontation and so, on the ninth day of December, Lucius marched out of Rome, at the head of six cohorts of the Guard. He left an order behind for his brother to implement in his absence.

'Instruct Juvens to withdraw to Narnia; it's not far back up the Flaminian Way and it is far more defensible. Have him sit there and prepare to hold the road against Antonius.'

This, then, was the position by the sixteenth of December: Juvens was in a hilltop town which commanded the only bridge over the river Nar, an easily defended position that his men could hold for months if they had to. The officers might have melted away like sealing wax in a forge, but the men were holding firm.

Lucius had taken six cohorts of the Guard south to crush the rebels – and to find and kill Pantera. He was camped in the Volscian hills, trying to work out how to take back the town of Tarracina. I had stayed behind to hold Rome with the last three cohorts of the Guard and the notional help of Sabinus' three remaining Urban cohorts plus the fire-fighters of the Watch.

Vitellius, meanwhile, had been making an idiot of himself, offering daily inducements to knights and senators in an effort to hold them to his cause. He had gold, and he gave it away. He had property, and he gave that away, too. He offered entire provinces freedom from tribute in exchange for loyalty that could change in a moment on the back of promises that no incoming emperor was ever going to honour. Men laughed in his face.

At the last, when nothing you have has value, there is nothing to give but yourself. And so he gave it, in tears and praise and blandishments; and men despised him more every day.

None of this kept me from rising in the mornings with a song in my heart. Lucius was gone!

If I had known how to contact Pantera, I might have been tempted to tell him where Lucius was, just to make sure they met and fought it out, but actually there was no need; the emperor's brother was riding a chestnut stallion with gold braided into its mane and peacock feathers on its brow and he had led six thousand men down the Appian Way. Even if you weren't a spy with ears in every household, you'd know exactly how to find him.

In the darkest, most hidden corner of my heart, I wished Pantera the best of luck.

CHAPTER FORTY-SEVEN

Rome, 16 December AD 69

Caenis

It was midway through the morning of the sixteenth, the day before Saturnalia. I was with Sabinus, sitting at a table in his big red room, composing a letter to Vespasian. It was the fourth letter I had written this month, and none of them yet dispatched, because Pantera had gone south to force a confrontation with Lucius, and without him there was no way to send anything to my love with any real hope that it would reach him.

Still, I wrote regularly; not a great deal and most of it domestic, but hidden within the lines was news of the campaign set in phrases only Vespasian would understand.

Out of courtesy, I did not write of Sabinus, who was becoming increasingly nervous. He had never wanted to be elder brother to an emperor, and as it came closer he wanted it less and less. He was used to the power plays of the senate where each man knew his place, and he was most uncomfortable with the almost-power being thrust upon him daily by the changing events. He paced now, pointlessly, between the overdone fountains and the ugly red wall and back again.

His steward entered, coughed, but had no time to announce either the lady Jocasta or Domitian, who came with her, for the boy pushed past him at a run and came careering to a halt at my desk, where he grabbed my hands in his.

'I've signed up!'

'What?' My words to his father lay clear on the table.

My dear, your son grows daily more confident in his manner and his bearing. He walks amongst the city in the company of the silver-boys, much as did Nero, but he has more intelligence than the emperor ever had, and, I believe, more compassion. Only yesterday, he rescued an injured dove from boys who were throwing stones at it, and brought it here to nurse. He wakes earlier, stays up later, and

I looked up at him, sharply. 'What do you mean, "signed up"? For what?'

'Vitellius is down in the forum himself – *himself!* – asking the citizens of Rome to sign up to a militia to protect the city. He says he has only three cohorts of the Guard left, and that is not enough and he needs the men of the city to fight for him. So I signed up.'

'You're surely not going to fight against your father's men?'

'Of course I'm not!' He let go of my hand, described a small pirouette on the marble floor. His smile was positively mischievous and it was directed at the woman who followed him in: Jocasta. If not his shadow, she had been his frequent companion these past months.

He threw her a complicated smile, full of triumph, that I did not understand. 'I gave a false name.'

'Then why—'

'Because if Vitellius is stupid enough to give me a sword and a helmet, that's one less he can give to someone else. And if I wear them, I can fight . . .' Slowly, his smile collapsed. 'You don't want me to fight?'

I stood; he was more easily faced these days standing.

'Domitian, you're not trained for it. And you're the second son of the man who is emperor of everything except the city of Rome itself and he might have that, too, by the end of this month. Your elder brother is in Judaea and has yet to assault Jerusalem, in the course of which, if he leads from the front in the family tradition, he could easily be killed. Of course I don't want you to fight. Your father would have a fit.'

'My father has time only for men who are useful. Do you think he will look at me any differently if I stay at home counting the wings on dead flies?'

'Your father is proud of you.'

'Caenis, if you think that, you're more—' There was a familiar sound in the servants' quarters, although at that moment I couldn't quite place it. I heard Matthias and Sabinus' steward talking, then a curtain was pushed quietly across the doorway.

And then the impossible; a man was there whom I had thought – feared is better, yes – that I might never see again.

'Pantera!' I took a slow step forward and was swept sideways by a furious Domitian.

'What on earth are *you* doing here? You're in Misene!'

'Except that I'm not,' Pantera said reasonably. 'I'm here.'

'Does that mean Lucius has lost? That he's dead?' Jocasta was nearer Pantera than Domitian. Her gaze raked his features, his clothes, striving to take meaning from the peasant garb he wore; it might have been near to Saturnalia, when men and women changed places with their slaves, but he looked too much like the real thing.

He said, 'Sadly Lucius remains alive and well, but he's too deeply caught up in the fighting at Tarracina to come back when he finds out I was never there.'

Everyone gaped at him now, even Jocasta.

'*Never there?*' she said. 'You never went south at all?' It was hard to tell if she was as furious as Domitian or simply shocked.

'Sorry.' Pantera lifted one shoulder in a loose, wry shrug. 'But it was safer for everyone if you all thought that's where I was going. In reality, I went north to study the placements of Juvens' defences at Narnia in case Antonius needed to know them in detail.'

'North?' There was a brittle edge to Jocasta's laugh. 'You went to *Juvens*? And you think that was safer?'

Everyone was standing now, and Pantera walked through us, as through statuary. He glanced down at the letter on my desk, idly moved my ink stand to cover the writing so nobody else could read it.

'It was safe enough. I carried wood for the braziers, and nobody looks at wood-carriers. Besides, I was in good company. Petilius Cerialis came with me – he was the legate of the Ninth during the revolt in Britain. He wanted to offer his services to Antonius Primus, so it seemed useful if he could take with him a general's view of Juvens' troop placements and their morale. We stayed with Juvens' men for eight days and now Petilius has gone to Antonius with all the necessary details and I've come back here. It was . . . restful.'

He looked better than he had done; less haunted, less starved of food and sleep. I could only imagine the relief of not being hunted day and night by the monster that was Lucius.

Still, the fact remained that nobody was looking for him in the north because everyone believed he had gone south to stir up trouble with the marines at Misene, me included.

Do you trust no one, not even me?

I said, 'Why have you come back now?'

'First, because I can. But mainly because Vitellius is about to get a shock and it would be immensely useful to Vespasian's cause if Sabinus were to be with him when it happens. My lord Sabinus, if it please you, there's a litter waiting—'

'What kind of a shock?' Domitian asked. He had become obdurate, of late, and importunate, and rude.

I thought how I could phrase this in my letter. *In certain ways, and primarily when he feels himself slighted, our young charge has begun to emulate some of the more interesting features of the man whose singing you so admired.*

Pantera answered, 'The kind of shock that will push him finally to abdicate.'

It was Sabinus, surprisingly, who was most upset by this. 'This is intolerable! Are we under attack? Have my brother's forces slaughtered the seven cohorts at the Nar? You told me this war would be bloodless. You *said*—'

Pantera lost patience. He didn't shout, but the texture of the air became noticeably crisper.

Sabinus stepped back; we all did. With precision, Pantera said, 'I said we would do our best to spill as little Roman blood as we can and that is exactly what we are doing. I believe Juvens' cohorts on the Nar are suing for surrender as we speak; they, too, have had their shock, and now it's coming here; something personal and visceral that will make the point to Vitellius that clinging on to power will help nobody.

'Accordingly, he may wish to begin negotiations for his abdication. You need to be on hand to see that nobody can talk him out of it. Watch Geminus, he's the one with the fastest wit and trusted most by Vitellius as well as his brother. If you need to order him out of the room, do so. Do whatever it takes, but walk away with some kind of deal. Your brother's future – and your own life – hinge on it. There's a letter here' – he held it out – 'with details of all that you may offer him: safety, gold, his slaves and freedmen to accompany him. Don't go beyond this remit, but I don't think you'll have to. Your trouble will be in convincing him that it's genuine.'

'Is it?'

'Your brother will honour all of it. On my life, I swear that.' Pantera gave a brief, bleak smile. 'My lord, there is some need for haste. My men have a litter waiting. Will it please you to go promptly? And my lord Domitian, too, if he so wishes. It will be instructive for him to be present. A future emperor must know how he reached his position.'

'Are you going with them?' I asked.

He favoured me with a dry smile. 'I thought perhaps I could stay here. If it please you? If you don't consider me too much of a danger.'

I nodded. I could not have turned away a request like that. He sat on a couch nearby, a weathered man in peasant's garb, and together we watched Sabinus and Domitian leave.

Jocasta, too, remained, staring down at him thoughtfully. 'Have you had food? No? Would you like some? Perhaps Matthias can arrange it? And then while we wait for it, Pantera can tell us what it is that is going to make Vitellius abdicate.'

CHAPTER FORTY-EIGHT

Rome, 16 December AD **69**

Geminus

Juvens came to us in the mid-morning of the sixteenth of December.

I had made a habit of meeting with Vitellius twice a day to 'confirm his orders for the defence of the city', under which fiction I told him what I had done, and why, and the emperor duly issued retrospective orders that gave me the cover of authority.

That morning, a letter had arrived from Trabo telling us of the latest calamities in the north. Yes, I know now that it wasn't from Trabo, it was some agent of Pantera's leading us a dance, but then we believed it was him and took everything he wrote at face value.

My consolation is that he was telling us the truth. They had no need to tell us anything false; the gods were against us anyway.

I read the letter aloud to Vitellius, and also to his mother, Augusta Sextilia, who had taken on the role of backbone for

Vitellius. From the moment Lucius left, she had been in the audience room, reclining on a couch, listening, asking questions, making sharp, acerbic observations that left Vitellius wilting.

I hated her as much as I did Lucius. She was slight and thin, with her hair pulled tight and high on the top of her head, so that it stretched the skin of her face around her skull and gave her the air of one long dead, who walked under the light of a bloody moon.

Her unpainted eyes were Lucius' eyes and her mind was Lucius' mind. I never met her husband, but a son doesn't grow to be a vicious bastard or a kindly, self-indulgent bumbler without moulding himself on someone and the obvious conclusion is that Lucius took after their mother while Vitellius took after the father. It was hard to know whom to pity the more and safest to show it to neither.

At my most formal, I read aloud from Trabo's letter.

'The advanced detachment of Antonius Primus' force is camped at Carsulae, ten miles north of Juvens' entrenchments. Already there have been some victories. The general Petilius Cerialis arrived recently and wished to show his devotion. He was tasked with clearing the town of Interamna, five miles to our west, and closer, therefore, to Juvens. He took a company of horse and routed the men loyal to your majesty.

'*I regret to inform you that most of the men capitulated when he offered them terms, and that of those who did not, some were soundly beaten while a small number were allowed to escape and sent in panicked flight to Narnia, where their tales of massed assault reduced morale further amongst their brethren. Interamna is now held in Vespasian's name.*

'*Following this success, Antonius' forces caught the scent of victory, and, knowing how close their enemy lay, they demanded the right to assault them forthwith; after all, they were the best, the fittest, the hardest, and what worked in Cremona must work for them again now. On my oath, I believe they would have marched out under their centurions, so fixed were they on victory, so fired by the promise of unrestricted looting, of hostages taken and fat ransoms paid.*

'Only Antonius Primus himself had the authority to stop them. He gave the speech of his life, saying that no sane man could ever impugn their courage or capability, but they were the future Praetorian Guard, and it fell on them to protect Rome now, as much as they would do later.

'The men argued, saying that the enemy had not shown any sign of surrender, but he answered that Juvens' men were holding out only in the belief that Valens had escaped and was, even now, bringing up legions loyal to Vitellius from Gaul and Britain.

'Some of the men asked if this was true: had Valens truly escaped? Antonius Primus said it was not, and that he would prove it, on which Valens himself was brought before them in full command dress, and made to speak aloud his name, and to answer whatever questions they might have, to prove that he was who they claimed.

'Thus did Antonius Primus disperse his men and avert calamity. They settled, and waited for the main body of the legions to catch up with them. How he plans similarly to convince Juvens' men that Valens is in custody without giving them the opportunity to free him and use him as a figurehead for counter-rebellion is not yet clear. But the men are alert, ready for war, and are contemplating the coming Saturnalia with great inventiveness. I am, as ever, the emperor's servant in all things. Trabo.

'That's all.' I re-rolled the paper. 'Juvens' men will hold out. They don't need Valens to know their duty.'

'Of course.'

Rising, the emperor reached for the letter and paced the

room, reading it inwardly. He was a good reader; his mouth barely moved as he spoke the words to himself. Here, in his chosen audience room, he looked grander than anywhere else.

He was dressed in white, with the imperial purple over his shoulder. The circle of baldness on the crown of his head had expanded from three to four fingers across and the hair at the edges was spread through with white, like a roan horse, with the result that, in certain light, it seemed as if his head was glowing.

By chance, he was standing in this light now, a picture of regal solemnity, haloed in sunlight, when, unheralded, the vast German masseur appeared in the doorway.

Since Lucius' departure, Drusus had become Vitellius' de facto steward and personal guard. I suspected he was also Lucius' personal spy, but dared not say so.

'Lord?' He looked agitated. He carried another man's sword. In his hand, it looked like a toy.

Vitellius regarded him fondly. Who would not feel safer with someone of Drusus' proportions at his shoulder? 'Yes?'

'Lord.' Drusus bowed. His voice was a deep, chest-churning growl. 'General Juvens wishes to be admitted with all haste.'

'*Juvens?* Here? Why?' Even Vitellius, with his infantile understanding of strategy, knew that Juvens would not have been there if his men had won; not, at least, without sending word back to Rome first. 'What's happened?'

Behind us, I felt the lady empress Sextilia rise from her couch. It seemed likely she was about to speak. Swiftly, I said, 'Perhaps we may have Juvens admitted, and ask him ourselves?'

Vitellius flashed me a look of undiluted gratitude. 'Of course. Send him in.'

Drusus bowed himself out.

And so we saw him, in all his misery. My friend, the bright, cheerful, playboy Juvens, was gone. In his place was this grey-faced officer, who fell to his knees at the emperor's feet.

'Juvens, rise, man. You don't need to kneel here.'

The emperor was a kind man; nobody has ever said otherwise. With his own hand, he raised Juvens up, which was when we all noticed the bag, more of a sack, really, he was holding. A faint sweet-vomit stench of decay hung about it that made my skin crawl.

I said, 'Tell us quickly. It won't get better by stepping around it.'

'Have you a plate? A bowl?'

With no forethought, I swept the olives from a silver dish on the nearby table and thrust it at him.

'Here.'

A month ago, Juvens would have raised his brow just barely and we'd have shared a private joke about the emperor's silver olive bowls. The Juvens of now took it without looking, knelt once more, and solemnly opened the neck of his sack.

'Antonius Primus ordered him killed,' he said, 'to prove to my men that he was dead, that he wasn't coming with legions from Gaul to save them. That was when we lost.'

'Killed whom?'

For a dizzying moment, I thought Lucius was dead, but Lucius wasn't in Gaul and nobody had ever thought he might be. Valens, though . . . Valens, whom Antonius Primus had paraded before his own troops, but couldn't parade before the enemy, in case they mounted an attack and freed him . . .

Juvens nodded, as if I had said the name aloud. 'They sent us his head while it was still warm. His eyes were still open. We thought he might speak to us.'

His voice was breaking. He rolled the contents of his sack on to the platter, where, by obliging chance, the neck sat in the depths of the bowl and the face stared up at us: Valens. Dead these three days, by the look of him.

Vitellius was sick.

Drusus, the giant German, whipped a vessel of sorts – a vase? I don't know – in front of his emperor just as Vitellius heaved out a great, rancid arc of vomit. Drusus caught it deftly, and handed his lord a dampened, rose-scented towel with which to wipe his lips, his sweating brow, his hands.

Valens stared up at us, gape-mouthed, his eyelids sewn shut by an unsteady hand with black silk: a row of unstable exclamations that signalled the end of his life.

It signalled more than that for the emperor: last January, Valens was the man who had persuaded him that he could be more than simply a legionary legate in Germany.

'This is barbaric!' Vitellius was still faintly green around the mouth. The rest of him was grey. 'We are Roman! We don't butcher our officers.'

'We do if it prevents further bloodshed,' Juvens said. 'The men had convinced themselves that Valens had escaped capture and was bringing up the legions from Gaul, to assault the Vitellian forces from behind. Antonius Primus swore it wasn't true. He had the living Valens paraded in front of us but he could not bring him close enough for the men to see him clearly in case they tried to free him. And so our men shouted that he was an impostor and they would kill him, too, when they advanced. When he had no other way to convince them, Antonius Primus had his head struck from his shoulders and carried to us on a pole. Then the men believed him.'

'Did they surrender?'

'They were permitted to exit the town with their weapons, and not forced under the yoke. They have been sent north, to the German border. Technically, they are not defeated, they merely changed allegiance. But yes, they surrendered.'

'You swore you would die with them.'

The empress Sextilia Augusta's voice would have skewered a lesser man, but Juvens was bred for this kind of encounter.

He dipped his most formal bow. 'My lady Augusta, Antonius Primus gave me that option. He said my head could join Valens' in the sack, or I could bring it to you, with his message. I thought of someone else bringing both heads into your royal presence and it seemed . . . more honourable to come myself. If you wish me to die now, I will do so, with great pleasure. I will find it hard to live longer with the disgrace of this.'

With no great drama, Juvens stepped apart from us and addressed Drusus. 'I would fall on my sword, but you have taken it from me. If I may have it back?'

'No!'

Vitellius' balled fist slammed on the wall. Now, too late, he was finding his strength as a man.

'Drusus, I forbid it. No man will die needlessly on my behalf. Too many have done so already. Otho understood, didn't he, when he killed himself, that too many good men die, and it is not possible to go on in the pretence of ruling?'

A taken breath behind me was silenced by a peremptory sweep of the imperial hand. 'No, Mother, you will not speak. I am your emperor and I command it. And don't wail at me, either. If you wish to leave the room, you may do so.'

She went! By Jupiter, Minerva and Juno, the empress snapped a finger to summon her ladies to follow, and was gone.

With a short, sharp, satisfied smile, gone before it was truly there, Vitellius turned back to Juvens. 'Antonius Primus sent you with a message. Give it to me now, and then you may go with Geminus and plan for the defence of the city.'

Juvens paled, but he was a man of astonishing courage. With his gaze focused on the far wall, he said, clearly, 'Antonius Primus, commander of the forces loyal to Vespasian, offers his respectful request that you enter into immediate negotiations with Titus Flavius Sabinus, brother to the future emperor, with respect to the details of your abdication.'

'What details? What abdication?'

'Perhaps the one I am empowered to discuss?' said Titus Flavius Sabinus, prefect of the city, quietly from the doorway. 'If I may be permitted to enter?'

CHAPTER FORTY-NINE

Caenis

A day was lost in the discussions between Vitellius and Sabinus without their reaching any satisfactory conclusion.

On the morning of the seventeenth, Sabinus went to meet the emperor once again. On this occasion, the designated place was the temple of Apollo next to the palace and the whole of Rome knew they were there to discuss Vitellius' abdication. Present were two men of good character to ensure that the agreements reached were fair and reasonable.

Jocasta and I remained in my house together. We talked of small things; of good wine, of the ways to make a pastry with spiced raisins at its heart; of our plans for Saturnalia, nearly upon us, when masters traded places with their slaves, and mistresses served the servants.

Matthias would not hear of such a thing. Jocasta had an old serving woman who felt the same. For both of them, the holiday was no different from any other day. We talked of how things had been in our childhoods. We talked of nothing at all.

On hearing a knock at the door, we both rose, swiftly.

Matthias, answering, padded white-faced from the door.

'My lady, it is the lady empress Sextilia Augusta, mother to—'

'She knows to whom I am mother. The entire world knows to whom I am mother. The entire world shares my shame.'

The empress's voice was sharp and hard; fingernails dragged over fractured glass. The face was sharp and hard to go with it, although less ostentatious than one might have imagined.

I must have seen the lady Sextilia at some point when she was merely mother to two middle-ranking generals, but I cannot recall the event. I had seen her more recently, of course, but only ever entering her litter, and then only from a distance, when she was draped in porphyry silk, with a diadem on her high, tight headpiece.

Here and now, she was dressed in sober white, as if for mourning, with only a silver ring around her perfect, brush-stiff silver hair. She looked haggard and old and tired.

She said, 'Lady Caenis, forgive my intrusion, but I have come to buy the services of the lady Jocasta.'

'Buy them?'

I didn't understand. And then I did, or thought so.

'What services?' Jocasta asked, more slowly.

'Those you used with such effect against Valens. Do I look a complete idiot? Men don't listen to the bathing-room rumours, or if they do, their talk is all of battles and whores and children got out of wedlock on hidden mistresses. Ours is of each other, and our skills. You are a poisoner. I would buy from you some poison.'

'Why?' Jocasta looked suddenly guilty, like a young Vestal

caught in the act of fornication, for which the penalty was death.

She had not denied the old woman's accusations, if they were accusations. They sounded more like compliments; in the upturned world Rome had become, nothing was impossible.

'Because of my two sons, the wrong one inherited the throne. Or perhaps neither son was worthy. Lucius has allowed himself to be lured south on a fool's errand, taking with him more men than Rome can afford to lose. And he has left behind the spineless fool I gave birth to first, may the gods curse the day of his creation.'

'My lady, Vitellius is a good man. He—'

'He is a weak and vacillating idiot. If he were not reminded moment by moment by his men that he is emperor, he would forget. And he thinks he will be allowed to abdicate!'

I said, 'My lady, he will. Of that I am certain.'

'By Sabinus, yes, but Sabinus is as weak as he is. You should see them, two weak men together, each trying not to damage the pride of the other by stating clearly what must be said. My son is finished. He can go now on the pretext of abdication and await Antonius Primus' mercy, or he can cling on a few days longer, and die at the hands of the Guards.'

'Antonius Primus will not be emperor, lady. Vespasian will honour any agreement made in his name.'

'Ha!' The old crow's laugh was hoarse and full of acid. 'Vespasian is in Egypt. He will be here when? Next September? July if he hurries? And in the time before that, who will rule Rome? Antonius Primus or Mucianus and his train of catamites. I do not expect mercy from either man; each knows his duty. They will do what must be done so Vespasian can rule in benevolence. I choose to make my own fate. I have had a long life and a good one and it is time for it to end. And so I ask of the lady Jocasta that she sell me that which will bring about my demise most swiftly. I have gold.' The skin was fine as paper on her hands, bare covering to the knotted old-blue veins. She wrested two gold coins from her purse. Neither showed her son on the face.

'No, lady.' Jocasta's hand on hers was white, with the knuckles green. 'I will take no money. But I will ask that you are sure of what you do, and that you tell no one else. My reputation may not rely on much, but it relies on not being known as the poisoner of an empress. Mucianus would know how to deal with that, too.'

'That is your price?'

'Your word that you will tell no one that this is your choice, not the hand of fate. Yes, that is my price. I trust your honour.'

'Which is more than my son does.' She was smiling, archly and with anger in her eyes, but it was more of a smile than I could have summoned in like circumstances. 'You have it here? What I need?'

'No, lady, but I will bring it to you tonight, if I have your word that I may safely do so.'

'Oh, you have my word,' said the lady empress of Rome, with hollow emphasis. 'Nothing will keep me in my shame and you are my clear exit. I will leave now.'

She gave a bow of her head, such as the men do. 'Don't escort me. I can find the door, and it is best if few see us together. Sabinus is returning even as we speak. You will find him in choleric mood, I fear. But he will get his way. Vitellius has never learned how to say no to anyone.'

Later: Sabinus home in foul mood.

'He says he'll go tomorrow as long as the Guard does not dissuade him tonight. I offered him a hundred million sesterces, a villa in Campania, all his slaves and freedmen with him, if he will only renounce any claim to the throne, and he wants to ask the permission of his Guardsmen!'

Sabinus had come to my house, and not alone. The two consuls suffect were with him: Quinctillius Atticus, who looked severely distracted: a man in love, or in lust, with the object of his desire too far away; and Caecilius Simplex, a man blighted with rat-like features who never looked anything other than avaricious.

Rome was buzzing. News of the emperor's maybe-abdication had taken to the streets and run amok in the market places, the baths, the forum, the houses of the matrons and the equestrians, the inns and taverns of the freedmen and slaves; there was not a man, woman or silver-boy who did not know that by tomorrow they might well be ruled by a new emperor.

If the current emperor chose to leave them.

The men of power thought that he would. You could tell that by the fact that the two consuls, together with a delegation of twenty other senior senators, had openly walked past the Guards on watch outside my house, saluted them and instructed them to leave.

The Guards had duly walked away and now twenty-two of Rome's civic leaders were cramped around the statues and four unadorned columns of my only public room. The place reeked of nervous sweat and wine-soured breath.

Fortified by their presence, Sabinus was at his most frustratedly choleric.

'A hundred million sesterces! A man could drown in that much money. How much does he need, when nobody is ever going to visit him?'

'None at all,' I said. 'Which is his problem. He wants to be liked, and if he abdicates his authority, he will be universally despised.'

Not least by his mother, although I didn't say that. Her scent still hung in the room, not quite lost in the crush of sweating, middle-aged men with their paunches hidden in the folds of their togas and their nerves not hidden at all, or their excitement.

'Vitellius is universally despised already,' Quinctillius Atticus, the man famed for the carp pool he had had built in his dining room for the emperor's birthday, dragged his mind back from the faraway landscape it had been enjoying for long enough to comment.

He was a solid man of middling height and he wore his senatorial dignity as armed men wear their weapons. This was not the first time he had made advances to Sabinus, but never before openly, in the face of the Guard.

If anyone was looking for a testament as to how fast Vitellius' support was falling away, it was there, in the fact that this man, second in authority to the emperor, had chosen to be here with Sabinus, and not at the palace with Vitellius.

Atticus said, 'We are on the brink of Saturnalia. If Antonius Primus continues to make progress, he could be on us before the festival's end. Vitellius is no longer emperor in anything but name, and if my lord Sabinus, prefect of this city, cannot persuade him to leave by words alone, then he should rouse the Urban cohorts and the Watch, both of which are under his command, and assault the palace.'

'Ha!'

Sabinus' laugh chimed with Domitian's. The boy had been out on one of his jaunts and, arriving to a full house, had slid in at the back of the group. I sent him warning glances: *be careful; think before you speak.*

He ignored me.

His voice, being higher, carried more clearly than his uncle's. 'The Urban cohorts were staffed by Vitellius when he took power; the men are from the same legions as the Guard. They may nominally give their oath to my uncle, but in practice they will be loyal to Vitellius.

'The Watch, meanwhile, is a hopeless gaggle of retired men

who train annually in fire-fighting and dream of long, lazy nights without work. It is worse to stage an assault that won't work than to wait and let the threat of Antonius Primus and his legions do it for you.'

Speaking, he had moved to the centre of the room: younger son of the man they all now considered their emperor; the only one of the emperor's sons resident in Rome.

After due pause, when he was sure he had the full attention of all those present, he said, 'Uncle Sabinus, when did Vitellius say he would give his answer?'

'Tonight. He will speak to the Guard on duty in the palace and tell them of his intention. If they agree – I say it again: he is asking their permission! The emperor is asking the permission of his Guards! – he will send me word of his intent.

'Assuming he gains their agreement, he will walk to the forum in the morning, and tell the assembly of his decision to stand down. He will give his dagger to the consul Caecilius Simplex' – Sabinus bowed to the rat-faced consul – 'who will take it in the name of Vespasian. At the same time, those of us who are loyal to our new emperor shall gather at my house on the Quirinal, administer the oath to the Urban cohorts and the Watch, and then go together to the forum and thence to the palace, which we shall occupy in my brother's name.'

'If the Guard doesn't stop you,' said Quinctillius Atticus. 'We still have no idea what they will do, and they could stop everything.'

'They must not be allowed to. Where is—' Surrounded by men he did not yet trust, Sabinus cut himself off. His gaze met mine and then Jocasta's. 'Our friend? The one who is recently returned to Rome? He will know how to contain the Guard.'

'He might, if we knew where he was,' Jocasta said. 'But if he's not with you, then we have no idea at all where he is.'

CHAPTER FIFTY

Rome, 17–18 December AD 69

Horus

Saturnalia only really begins each year on the night of the seventeenth of December.

Throughout the empire, but nowhere more than in Rome itself, it is the time when the nobility plays at being ignoble: servants become the served, slaves become temporarily freed and may command their masters. In the legions, officers are treated as serving men and the lower ranks give the orders. There are limits to the licence, of course, but the principle of freedom and revelry is universal.

At the House of the Lyre, the traditional transfer of relationship between master and slave has a slightly different flavour. Every year, a select group of favoured clients is invited to attend a private evening of wine and food after which they must prostitute themselves for the delight of those whose services they normally buy. Men and women are invited in equal numbers and all have to swear a binding oath beforehand that no request, however outlandish, will be turned down.

There is, naturally, a lengthy list of those who would give very large amounts of gold to be invited to such an event, and so different names grace the guest list on each of the seven nights of Saturnalia. The clients are not charged, but it is observed by those who take an interest that the men and women who have invested most in the House of the Lyre during the preceding year are the ones most likely to be on the guest lists in December. November is a particularly lucrative month.

This year, the first night of Saturnalia was everything the House and its friends had dreamed of. Rome was under threat, very nearly under siege, and in the uncertainty men and women of status sought the amnesiac qualities of lust with a passion heretofore unknown.

Offered the opportunity to immerse themselves in un-diluted hedonism, to explore new ways to sate themselves, they fell on it with single-minded dedication, leaving the gardens strewn with clothing, the stairs, the corridors and the landings littered with discarded wine jugs, and the doors of the bedchambers hanging open.

Because that's the other rule: at the Saturnalia, nothing must be done in secrecy; everything must be open to view.

By midnight, the peak had passed. It had been, we all agreed, a resounding success. The wine was gone, the candles had burned to softened stubs – those that had not been taken from their candlesticks and put to other use. The couches in the garden must be recovered before the morrow; nothing would remove the stains of wine and bodily secretions, but that wasn't uncommon and they had more than paid for themselves. We had craftsmen on hand ready to make them new again.

Of rather more concern was the fact that a senator had been carried out to his litter blue-lipped and barely breathing, but he was still alive when he left, and even if he had died in the night we knew that his heirs would never press charges: the disgrace of their paterfamilias having failed to sustain his ardour through the notorious Night of Free Exchange at the House of the Lyre would have finished them.

And so the last steward and servant – there were, of course, several still sober who were not engaged in the entertainment – had gone to bed. All through the house, men and women were sleepy, full of wine and good food, their stamina temporarily defeated.

I was abed, but my door was not open. Alone of all the guests or servants, I was not governed by the rules of the Night and the House. My door was locked and bolted as was my nightly habit, but this once, unusually, I was not alone.

I, too, had explored the detail of another's body, and let mine be similarly explored. We had sated ourselves more than once and we had both found unexpected pleasure in it.

I slept lightly in the aftermath; the inheritance of my childhood. We silver-skins in the gutter never allowed ourselves to be drugged or plied with drink: our longevity often depended on rising before our clients and stealing out into the night.

That early instinct, perhaps, is what woke me a moment or two before strong fingers clasped my right ankle and tightened. I opened my eyes silently, waiting; only one person in the world knew to wake me thus.

I did not see a face to prove me right, just the faint glimmer of distant starlight on the blade that hung close to my eyes.

The hand left my ankle and Pantera's voice, warm in my ear, said, 'Rise.'

I did so. The youth curved in the bed beside me shifted slightly, but did not wake; he had experienced new things and was sleeping deeply on the other side.

My tunic was pressed into my hands, still creased from the night; my sandals; an outdoor cloak I did not own and had never seen before.

I wanted to wash, to remove the distaste of body fluids and sweat that coated my skin, but there was no time. I was led to the balcony where the shutter eased open in total silence; my fault that it was so well greased that it made no sound to arouse the guards.

I looked out into the ink-black night, and the outlines of things that wait there.

'Oh, Hades, not the plank,' but yes, it was the plank, and there was a knife at my back and I must go first with Pantera behind me, step by dizzying step into the nauseating dark where the void that gaped on either side of the wood was as solid in its blackness as the next place for my foot, and the next, and the next.

I shook, and, shaking, became less stable. Pantera's hands gripped my hips, at once intimate and threatening. Softly, he said, 'You can't turn back.'

'I know. I've seen what happens to those who try.'

I shuffled on over the aching drop. Time flowed slow as syrup.

I aged ten years before I reached the opposite railing and clambered over it with legs that refused to hold me steadily upright. Inside, the tailors were asleep, and even if they hadn't been they would have taken pains to appear so.

Down in the street we were met by two men. The first was as large and brutal as Drusus, but without the Germanic tilt to his chin: a Briton, maybe. The other was a boss-eyed youth with a lopsided grin, whose good eye feasted on my face in a way that made me sweat.

Pantera said, 'How far to the horses?'

The big maybe-Briton held up three fingers.

Pantera caught my wrist. 'Three blocks. Run.'

'Horses?' I had heard his question. I held back. 'What are we going to do with horses at this time of night?'

'Ride them. Hard. We are going south after all. And we shall need your services when we get there.'

I knew better than to argue with Pantera when he was in this kind of mood, so we ran and we mounted and we rode.

We passed with extreme care through the streets of Rome on horses with muffled hooves, changing direction often, on the instruction of the big, red-headed Briton who roamed ahead like a hunting hound.

Outside the city, we stripped the soft leather from our mounts' feet and rode down the Appian Way as fast as a horse may go in the dark, which was unnervingly fast for me; I have never been a good rider.

The horses clearly knew the route and loped along with a relish that suggested Rome was not their home, but that warm bran mash and oats awaited at our destination somewhere in the south. Lucius was south. I tried not to think about that.

I was such a bad rider that we paused along the route and Pantera and Felix, the boss-eyed blond boy, bound me into the saddle like a child, and I spent the next two hours wishing myself back in the warm silk bed with the youth who had not known what he wanted until it was shown him.

We stopped at an inn some significant time after my thighs had begun to scream in agony and my fingers had cramped immovably tight on the mane for support. I had to be helped down by the innkeeper's boy, a briskly efficient child of less than ten years who had no concern for the time of night, but unsaddled the horses while his father lit the torches in their brackets and roused the fire high in the hearth, making light enough for us to sit and eat, and shadows enough for Pantera to meet whomever it was he had come to see.

374

That meeting took place shortly, when another hard-ridden horse arrived, this time from the south. The rider wore the porphyry livery of the imperial messengers, but he clearly knew Pantera by sight. They met in a horse stall and I was with them, though I would rather have been in the warmth, eating and drinking with the rest.

By way of greeting, the messenger said, 'The moon is fine and full tonight,' which was a transparent untruth.

Deadpan, Pantera answered, 'We may have luck then, on the night's fishing. Thank you. May I?' He held out his hand and was given a package which he set on an upturned barrel with a single candle for his light.

The package was of folded linen sewn in a particular pattern. Pantera cut the thread with a razor-fine knife and slid the blade under the imperial seal. This was Lucius' personal mark; like his brother's, it showed a chariot. Unlike his brother's, Lucius' horses were racing across the winning line.

Opened, the letter was short and in a laughably easy code. I read it over Pantera's shoulder.

Brother: a slave belonging to Vergilius Capito, former governor of Egypt, escaped from Tarracina and is presently guiding us on a safe route up the largest of the Volscian hills that lie above the city. We are gaining the heights and will attack with tomorrow's dawn. Victory shall be ours and we will return to you by the evening of the day after. We shall celebrate the remainder of the festival together as victors.

'Is the slave yours?' I asked. 'Are you helping Lucius?'

Pantera laughed, hollowly. 'Definitely not. But I bet he didn't "escape" on his own. There are people who want Lucius to win just as badly as we want him to lose.'

I said, 'If Vitellius thinks Lucius is about to win, and will march back into Rome at the head of seven thousand victorious Guards by morning, he'll abandon all thought of abdicating. You can't let him see that letter.'

'I wasn't planning to. But another must go in its place: Vitellius and Lucius send messages to each other four times a day and they'll notice if one is missing. Can you replicate this hand?'

I arched my brow. I can replicate any hand and he knew it, although he didn't know that he himself had been taken in by at least one of my forgeries. 'Tell me what you want to say.'

I was given pen and ink and a stool to sit on, but the upturned barrel was my only table. Nevertheless, I am a craftsman who takes a pride in his work and, after a few test sentences, I was ready.

I wrote to Pantera's dictation, transposing the letters in my head, A to C, B to D and so on, through the alphabet. One can only suppose that Lucius and Vitellius believed their messenger service to be entirely secure or they would never have risked using such an infantile cipher.

In plain text, before transposition, what I wrote was this: *The rebels have attained the heights above the Volscian hills and are currently unassailable. We have them under siege, and victory will be ours before the month's end.*

Writing, I said, 'Isn't this still too optimistic? Will Vitellius give up his throne in the morning if he thinks Lucius will be back in January?'

Pantera was sitting on the floor with his knees drawn up and his cheek pillowed on his folded arms. Sleepily, he said, 'For the emperor, January is a lifetime away. He might waver if he thought Lucius could be home tomorrow's tomorrow, but any longer than that and he'll fold. Lucius, for his part, would never write anything that did not predict his own ultimate victory; we can't put words on to paper that he would never send. This will do what we need. But we need another, to send to Lucius, in case he is victorious. We can't take the risk that he might head back to Rome of his own accord. Felix has a sample of Vitellius' hand for you to copy. Take a clean sheet of paper and write this . . .'

At his dictation, I wrote a second letter to be sent to Lucius, and then watched with professional interest and not a little envy as Pantera sanded, folded and sealed the fresh paper to look exactly like the original, and sutured it closed with an identical, much practised, pattern of stitches.

Returning to the inn, I found that we had been in the barn for less than the time it took for Borros and Felix to eat their stew. The messenger ate standing up and departed swiftly.

Pantera, too, ate standing up, reading reports from a small man with no teeth who appeared to have been roused from deep sleep. At the end, he said to me, 'If you want to sleep, you can stay here with Diodemus, or you can come with us. It's your choice. Either way, you cannot return to Rome until Vitellius has abdicated.'

'Or been killed.'

'Or that, yes.'

Diodemus was the little toothless ruffian. He looked as venal as any of Rome's bandits. He might well have *been* one of Rome's bandits, come south for a change of pace. I felt the promise of sleep slipping away.

'Where are you going?' I asked, although I already knew; in some things, Pantera was entirely predictable and his sense of duty outweighed any normal regard for his own safety.

'To Tarracina,' he said, confirming the inevitable. 'We have men there who must be brought out before Lucius attacks at dawn.'

I was desperate to sleep, but even so, when Pantera and his men rode out soon after, I rode with them. I rode against the screaming ache of my thighs and an urgent desire for a warm bed and a decent night's sleep.

But my world was far more dangerous than it had been just before midnight when I took an almost-emperor's younger son to my bed, and I was betting my life on the belief that the safest place in the empire for the next few days would be standing right next to Pantera.

CHAPTER FIFTY-ONE

Rome, 18 December AD **69**

Trabo

I had been with Julius Claudianus and the gladiators in Tarracina for nine days when Pantera came banging on the gates.

It was a heady, exhilarating time. In theory, we had marched down the Appian Way with the cohort of the Urban Guard to put down the revolt at Misene, but I don't know of a single man who believed that was our true task; certainly none did by the time we'd reached the outskirts of the city.

I don't know if he'd been coached by Pantera or was simply using his natural leadership, but Julius Claudianus had a deft touch with the men.

He moved from fireside to fireside in the evenings after we'd camped and gradually turned the conversation to Vespasian and how good his campaign had been in the east, and what had Vitellius ever done and wasn't Lucius a complete nightmare?

Imagine Rome if he ever became emperor, which he was

clearly angling to do. He never said any of this, he just steered others to say it, and so yet more to think it.

And he never answered those questions, just left the men to talk them over amongst themselves so that by the time we got to Misene they were practically begging him on bended knee to change sides. So he had to: what else could a good commander do than yield to the wishes of his men? Particularly if they were his wishes in the first place.

Thus two thousand highly trained, loyal and dedicated fighting men became, overnight, two thousand highly trained and dedicated rebels who had no trouble at all in taking Tarracina. It had a stout outer wall, but Julius had paid men on the inside to open the gates for them and there wasn't even a token resistance.

The drinking and whoring and feasting had started that night and hadn't stopped. Saturnalia gave them the excuse, but it would have happened anyway. It was still going on the night Pantera came to us, with his rag-tag of followers.

He knocked on the door of the tavern we'd made our headquarters and the first thing I knew of his presence was the sound of his voice asking, 'Julius Claudianus, is he here?'

Julius was asleep, actually. He shuffled out of his room barely dressed, all farts and sleepy scratchings, cursing at having been woken until he saw who it was, whereupon he became warily alert.

Lit by a single smoking excuse for a candle, we all gathered round while Pantera showed us a dispatch to Vitellius he had stolen en route.

'This is real,' he said. 'Lucius is on the hill above the town. He'll be on you by dawn like a starving hound on a rats' nest. You need to move your men out of here before daylight. Get to the boats and scupper any you don't use in your escape. Lucius has no navy, he won't be able to follow you.'

There was a long moment's silence. Julius Claudianus was

a big man, solid, with no flab, and now that he was awake you could easily see him at the head of a column, marching hard and fast for battle. He had been a legate once, and led the Misene fleet. It's what made him perfect for Lucius, and for Pantera. But he was always his own man.

He snapped his fingers and servants began to dress him in front of us: linen undertunic, woollen overtunic, belt with many silver medallions, greaves, sandals . . .

He said, 'We can't run now. We have trained for this for the past three months. The men are desperate to fight.'

'Your men are singing in poor harmony on the beach. They are not in any fit state to fight.'

Julius Claudianus wrapped his sword belt around his body, slipped the baldric loop over his head. Armed, he was as dangerous to look at as any man I'd met, and I'd been living amongst trained killers for months by then.

Other men were running in, gathering behind him, and they, too, were more stalwart than the off-key singing might have suggested. He ran his glance across them. They straightened under his stare. They were bristling with the anger of men whose pride had been threatened.

He said, 'Gladiators can fight in any state, believe me. And they won't run from a battle, even if I ask them to. They'd stab me in the back if they thought I was trying.' He looked at Pantera down the vast crag of his nose. 'You didn't really send us all this way to run at the first flash of a blade?'

Pantera was furious, although it was only because I'd seen it before that I could tell. The clipped consonants and strained patience might have sounded merely weary to any other man.

He said, 'I didn't send you all here to die. And you will. Lucius has seven thousand men up that hill and every one of them has something to prove. They are sober, rested and have the advantage of height. There's no disgrace in leaving now to regroup and attack some other time.'

'When? After Vitellius has abdicated and we have lost our chance of glory?' And then, at Pantera's hard stare, 'Do you think we don't hear of such things down here, out of sight of the city?'

Pantera closed his eyes, sought patience, found something close enough.

'I sent you word of that myself, and Trabo wrote back to me so I know you got it. But someone else must also have sent an order and now a slave is showing Lucius the best routes into the city. We are not the only ones using Tarracina as a proxy for battles being fought over the throne in Rome.'

'Who betrayed us?'

'A slave, but I don't know who sent him. I will find out, but just now my first priority is your safety.'

'No it isn't.' Julius Claudianus smiled, put his great meaty hand on Pantera's back and turned him round. 'That's my worry and I'll deal with it as I see fit. You are free to go back to Rome and your not-proxy battles.'

It occurred to me rather later than it should have done that the stoutly defiant Julius Claudianus was neither entirely sober nor entirely undrugged. The pinprick of his pupils should have been a clue, but the candle was shining in his eyes and it wasn't immediately obvious. Poppy, likely. Or one of the mixtures the curse-women make that crumble on to hot coals and sweeten the air. I knew the men had been taking it. I hadn't realized their commander had been, too.

I said, 'Perhaps now is not the time—'

'This is the only time.' Pantera's lips were a tight, white line in the candlelight. 'Lucius isn't going to give you time to negotiate, or to build defences. He hasn't that kind of patience.'

He spun, looking round. A hundred men faced him, and more were coming, and none of them was sober, and each of them was fired by pride and drink and poppy. He'd have had to kill them himself to get them to stand down now.

His capitulation showed in a short shake of his head. He turned back to Julius Claudianus. 'Gather every one of your men. The slave guiding Lucius knows the ways in better than we ever will, so there's no point in trying to block the gates. We can choose the pinch points to hold and make life difficult, so that anyone who is prepared to go can make it to the ships. We just need to be sure that any that aren't used are broken: Lucius must not gain a navy by this.'

'We?' Julius Claudianus' laugh was big and bold. 'You're not thinking to stay?'

'I sent you here. I can't leave you.'

'Lucius sent us, not you.'

'Only because I manoeuvred him into it. He was supposed to spend half a month laying siege to a city that could resist for half a year, not find a quick way in and slaughter you all by morning. I won't have your deaths on my hands.'

'You don't. You think you've been manipulating us, but we were happy to go where you pushed us. This is our war too, don't forget. We switched to Vespasian because we believe he will make a better emperor than Lucius. We're all grown men. We know what we're doing. Just go.'

'Julius, you can't—'

'Pantera, for fuck's sake. My men follow me, they don't follow you, and never will. And we don't run from trouble.'

'Then I'll stay with you.'

'And let Vitellius win in Rome? Are you mad? The emperor is supposed to abdicate tomorrow. If you think that's going to go smoothly, you're a lot less clever than you pretend. The Guard will never let their man stand down. They made him, they'll keep him. You have to be in Rome to make it happen if you want to see Vitellius gone.'

Julius' hands were vast, with scars across the backs of old sword wounds, and knuckles crushed repeatedly into hard surfaces. He laid one of them heavily on Pantera's shoulder.

'You don't have to make everything right, just the thing that matters most. Get on your horse. Ride like the wind for Rome. And be ready, whatever happens tomorrow, to fight. Take Trabo with you. He was yours from the start. We'll miss his cooking, but we'll manage without it.'

Do you think I should have argued? A part of me wanted to, or at least thought that honour required that I did. But the rest of me knew that to stay was suicide. Leaving with Pantera might be the same, but it felt a little safer.

We rode out soon after: me, Pantera, his two men and the catamite. We slipped on bound feet from the town gates, and even as we mounted we heard the first rhythmic mumble of armed men marching from the hill above the town. Behind us, Tarracina might still have been asleep for all the evidence there was of life.

We stopped at the coaching inn to leave Felix behind for some purpose to which I was not privy. I was standing with the horses when I saw the flames of Tarracina's destruction begin to unfurl across the horizon, spreading outwards, to meet the first bright light of dawn.

So broke the eighteenth day of December in the first year of the reign of the emperor Vitellius; the day of his promised abdication.

CHAPTER FIFTY-TWO

Rome, 18 December AD 69

Geminus

It was the eighteenth of December in the eight hundred and twenty-first year of Rome's existence. Not once, in any of those years, had an emperor, a king, a ruler of any kind, stepped away from his reign.

At the Guard barracks at the back of the Quirinal hill, the air was dense with the iron stench of distress. To breathe was hard. To think was harder. To order the men was nearly impossible.

I stood in Lucius' office with my back pressed tight against the closed door. Outside, the murmur of three thousand men was thunder, rolling out of the gates and down the hill.

Inside, Juvens was sitting on the floor with his knees hooked up and his head in his hands and what he said in here was the same as the men were saying outside, only that his accent was more polished, his choice of words crisper, free of the profanities . . . well, mostly free.

'We're finished. He'll walk down there at first light, read out his pathetic little speech telling the world he didn't want to be emperor anyway and only the overweening ambition of Valens and Caecina made him do it and now one of them's had his head stuck on a pole and the other is helping the man who did the sticking, so he rather thinks he'd like to go back to being an ex-general, thank you very much.

'Oh, and of course he'll disband the Guard he created because obviously Vespasian will want to make his own out of the men who have just won him Rome. Welcome, Antonius Primus and the bastards who lost to us at Cremona last spring and got lucky a month ago. Remember the lottery? Draw out a name, find your man and kill him? It'll be the same again only our names will be the ones written on the folded lead. We may as well fall on our own swords now.'

'Be my guest.' I was angry. Not the fast, furious anger that comes in a rush of blood to the head and is easily dissipated by a brief flash of violence, but a slow-burning, steadily rising fury that had brought me to a point of terrible clarity.

'Is it treason,' I asked, 'if your emperor wants to abdicate and you stop him? Or is it treason if you let him set down his claim to the throne and walk away? Is the office in the man or does the man own the office?'

Juvens lifted his head slowly. He peered at me as if I had fallen out of focus. 'You're not serious?'

'Completely so. We made the emperor. We choose when to unmake him. And today is not that day.'

I stepped away from the door and wrenched it open. Breakfast fires danced and flickered in the dark. Dawn was a faint blue line on the eastern horizon; night still held the city. 'You can come or you can stay here and fall on your sword.'

A thousand men stood within earshot. They were armed,

and cloaked against the cold; their helmets were a dully undulant sea, glimmering here and there, touched by torches that guttered and flamed at their margins.

A signaller waited nearby, summoned an hour ago. I grabbed his horn, strode to the podium and sounded the summons to war.

The air was short: three rising notes and three falling, repeated three times. By the end of the second phrase, every Guard in the barracks was in parade order, waiting.

Two and a half thousand impatient men stood in front of me, and the battle rage rose from them thick as fog from a winter river, harsh as salt in a wound, pliable, malleable, mine to mould to my intent.

I sucked it in with the air I needed to speak. Never in my life had I addressed so many in one place at one time. I had to guess the pitch, the strength of voice that would make it carry.

'Men of the Imperial Guard . . .' Perhaps too loud, but it made the point. 'Today of all days, you choose your own destiny. Will you go craven into the night? Or will you stand up for all you have fought for? Will you fight one more day, and another, and the one after that, until you see—'

I had to stop; I could not shout over their noise. Antonius Primus must have heard them, and Lucius, a day's march to the south.

The holler was ragged at first, but resolved, slowly, into a single sound: my name.

'Gem-in-us! Gem-in-*us! Gem-in-us!*'

This, too, was an entirely new experience. My own rage grew, blossomed, tempered by a pride I had never imagined, and the power of it transported me beyond myself.

I raised my hands to call for quiet and the men hushed in a moment. I looked down across two and a half thousand faces and they beamed at me as if the sun rose only in my eyes. I had never loved anyone as I now loved these, my men. I took a breath, knew exactly how to pitch my voice to best effect.

'Men of the Guard. Our emperor needs our help. This is what we shall do . . .'

CHAPTER FIFTY-THREE

Rome, 18 December AD **69**

Horus

I was living through a waking nightmare. I had ridden harder, for longer, on less sleep in the past night than the cumulative total of my life.

Daylight saw me back in Rome, with the blazing hell of Tarracina seared on the backs of my eyes.

I had no idea if Julius Claudianus and his gladiators had any chance of beating Lucius' Guardsmen, but I knew they would try and that the trying would be vicious, bloody and terrible for those who didn't die swiftly.

The belief that, for the foreseeable future, the safest place in the empire was at Pantera's right hand had sustained me through the night and it sustained me now, as we passed through the gates at the head of the Appian Way and into the southern suburbs of Rome.

The horses were left with an innkeeper who seemed, if not to expect us, then at least not to be overly surprised at our hasty arrival and similarly hasty departure. He had an urn of soup ready, full of thick, floating things best not explored; we took the bowls he gave us and drank from them as we moved swiftly through the waking city. Slaves were up and about, cloaked against the winter's cold, but few others.

In some dark, unnamed alley we stopped to urinate against a wall: a line of four men – Pantera, Trabo, Borros and me – darkly dressed, not recently shaved, pissing in arcs on to the bricks. A sudden wall of noise rose from below, where the forum awaited the day's gathering.

Pantera's head snapped up. 'That's Vitellius. He's early. Run!'

We ran. It was mostly downhill, but still, I was spitting blood from my lungs on to the dirt by the time we reached our destination.

The Forum Romanum: once a market place, now the centre of civic life in Rome; a plaza, surrounded by ancient temples and newer civic buildings; a place of constant building since the days of Rome's republic.

The temple of Vesta and the circular House of the Vestal Virgins lie on the eastern edge, settled between the regia, where once kings lived, and the Palatine hill. Pantera scrambled up on to a broken wall alongside the regia.

Borros and Trabo scrambled up the sheer surface in an act of magic that I couldn't possibly repeat, but I was lifted up one-handed by Borros, so that I could see at least as far as the place where the emperor stood, surrounded by grim-faced – one might even say murderous – Guards.

A very large number of Guards.

In fact, looking through the ranks of those gathered, there were easily as many Guards as there were citizens and they were not listening to Vitellius read from his prepared script: they were watching the men around them.

Nobody, particularly, was listening to the emperor. It was humiliating enough that he read to us when any man of worth should have been able to speak extempore in times of need. Worse was the fact that he made no effort to send his voice to the crowd. He seemed to be speaking mainly to the Guard officer next to him, and that without conviction.

His son was there, poor stammering waif who no sane man had ever believed would live long enough to take the throne, and might now not live long enough to see so much as the new year. The boy was dressed in funereal grey, and now that I looked at him in the poor winter light I saw that his father was the same.

It's true: amazing as it may sound, Vitellius had come in mourning to his own abdication. And he was weeping!

Emperors of Rome are proud men. Of course Augustus wept when his Varus lost three legions in the forests of the Rhine, but that was a proud weeping, as of a father for the loss of a beloved son.

No emperor, not even Nero, wept for pity at his own misfortune. If he hadn't been surrounded by stone-faced Guards, there was a fighting chance that Vitellius would have been booed out on to the streets, bundled into a sack and thrown into the Tiber. As it was, he snivelled on to the end of his speech; short, perfunctory and inadequate.

I hadn't heard a word of it, because by then I was fixated on the Guard officer who stood so menacingly at his side. It was Geminus.

This was a new Geminus, prouder, more erect, more savage even than when he had slaughtered my beloved Cerberus, more driven; a Geminus who bore in the chiselled angles of his face all the authority that Vitellius lacked.

A Geminus whose gaze roamed the crowd, who caught the eye of every third or fourth man and gave a nod that was more of a flicker of the eyelids that I knew so well from my years in the House of the Lyre.

There, it meant 'Yes, loosen your ties now', or 'Take her

upstairs soon, before the wine becomes too much', or 'Yes, he likes to be hurt, but go carefully, he could have us all crucified in the morning.'

Here, it meant 'Yes, keep the crowd chanting the emperor's name', or 'Move a little to your left, fill that gap, don't let anyone through', or 'If the senator to your right shows any inclination to support the emperor's abdication, you have my permission to kill him.' Or her. There were women here, listening in the forum. I swear this is true. Truly, the world has changed.

At the end of his speech, Vitellius took out his dress dagger and tried to hand it to the consul, Caecilius Simplex. The weasel-faced little man was there to confer some kind of authority on the event, but had ruined it by looking at everyone except the emperor throughout the speech.

Now, with no sense of spectacle at all, he reached for the dagger's hilt. And found himself staring at the slick, clean iron of Geminus' blade.

He froze: it would have been comical if the whole situation had not already been immersed beyond redemption in pathos.

It may be shared between two men, but the office of consul is the second highest in the land. Simplex outranked a Guard officer in the way the emperor outranks a slave.

With much gesticulation, he explained this, but Geminus had gone beyond social niceties and iron carries its own authority: Vitellius had been made emperor by the sword, and by the sword he was not going to be allowed to abdicate easily.

On Geminus' orders, Caecilius Simplex stepped back. Confused, Vitellius turned a tight circle, offering his dagger to whomsoever might be stupid enough to take it.

Not a man lifted his hand: he was not, after all, offering to give away the throne of Rome, but rather desiring that someone – anyone – take from him the symbol of its office.

Vitellius found himself blocked on all sides by a solid mass of men standing shoulder to shoulder, and by then it was nearly impossible to tell which were Guards and which were citizens: everyone was united in wanting him to stay: Geminus made that happen.

In the end, the emperor took the only route left open to him and turned up the hill back towards the palace. The men closed behind him, shepherding him forward. As Tiberius warned, and every emperor since has found, you take the wolf of the empire by the ears, it is yours unto death. Rome was still his. Vespasian and those who supported him must needs fight to take it. Or wait to see what happened.

Pantera jumped down from the wall. It was daylight now; his face was easily seen, but not yet readable.

'Borros, take Horus home. Trabo, come with me.'

I was affronted. Leave me and take his tame thug with him? I said, 'I don't want to go home.'

'You have a party to host.' In theory, that was true. It was still Saturnalia; another Night of Free Exchange was due to take place at the House of the Lyre – with a different guest list, obviously.

I shook my head. 'Not tonight. Not if war is on our door-step.'

'Even so, we are going to meet the prefect of the city, Titus Flavius Sabinus, and very likely his nephew. Do you really want to meet Domitian in the cold light of day? Do you think he wants to meet you?'

It had been too much to hope that in the dark Pantera had not recognized the youth who had shared my bed last night. Yes, I had invited Domitian to the House of the Lyre and yes, it was his first time at the Night. He hadn't been old enough last year, too lost in his collections of pressed butterflies and bluebottles pinned to boards. In any case, he had been the impoverished son of a minor general who had been banished to Greece and faced almost certain death: we had never had any reason to invite him.

By this year, he was the son of the man who looked certain to become emperor. Even if he'd still been penniless, we'd have invited him. But he wasn't. He had come to us five or six times in the preceding months and paid in gold each time. So our invitation to the First Night at the Lyre was legitimate by all our usual standards.

And anyway, I had no intention of letting Pantera browbeat me into going away, not when leaving him was so manifestly dangerous.

Attack has always been my best form of defence. Brows raised, at my most acid, I set my fists on my hips and stared him straight in the eye.

'Do you really think that the emperor's son— Hades! Who is that?'

It was impossible to continue an argument in the face of what had just arrived: a litter extraordinary for its vast size and the weight of the fabric that draped it.

In my head, I was performing the additions of cost upon cost. Sixteen men carried it, four at each corner, and as a result it moved swift as a sail ship with a following wind. Until it was set down in front of us, trapping us in the alley, but also blocking us from the view of the forum.

From within, a melodious voice said, 'You may join me.'

It was Jocasta, of course, the Poet who had taken all that Seneca had built and moulded it to her own use. I helped her to do it, since she is neither a natural forger nor a good reader of ciphers. She needed me to help her understand her Teacher's encoded notes, written over decades, and then to write to those who needed letters.

But here, now, in the midst of Saturnalia, she looked neither at me nor at the fool Trabo who mooned after her so; her gaze was all for Pantera, and his for her.

I had not seen them in the same place before, but you could feel the air warp around them. They were rivals, of course. It was like seeing two gladiators who, after beating all others sent against them, finally meet their match and don't know whether to fight to the death or to clasp arms and walk together out of the arena.

Pantera solved his immediate dilemma by bowing extravagantly low, 'My lady, we are at your service.'

'I know.'

The flap was thrown back on the litter and I saw her, Jocasta, a woman whose beauty was only surpassed by the sense of power that flowed from her.

Her hair was black as polished slate, with the blue-black hue of a newly preened raven's wing. Her brows were the same, small wings that only served to accent her eyes. I had taught her, once, how to paint them to best effect and I am pleased to say she had used my tuition to great effect. Her eyes were like a panther's, glowing. Her skin was flawless, her neck slim and erect, like a swan's.

The interior of her litter – and I have slept in bedrooms that were smaller – was draped with lemony silk that transformed the weak winter sunlight into the sunburst bright of a summer's noon. Then I caught the scent of freshly baked oatcakes, of warm cheeses, hams and olives, and my mouth ached with wanting.

But I was not invited within. To Pantera alone, Jocasta said, 'Get in. Sabinus is taking the oath from the Urban cohorts and the Watch, after which, I strongly suspect, he will dismiss them. You will travel faster with me, and you can bathe and change into clothes that smell less of horse and sweat. The emperor's brother will expect you at least to be clean.'

Pantera wanted to refuse, every line of his body said so, but she had presented unassailable arguments and so, in tones of deepest irony, he said, 'My lady,' and then, to me, 'Not you.

395

You may be happy to see the emperor's son, but he may need some time before he sees you, and then not in the company of men who may one day take his orders. Gudrun and Scopius will provide a safe place until you can return to the House. Borros, take Horus to the Inn of the Crossed Spears. Meet us at the prefect's house, or at the Capitol if we've already got there.'

He was lying, and I knew it. He didn't think Domitian was ashamed of me or me of him; this was Pantera's punishment for my treachery with Lucius. He didn't know, or didn't care, what they had threatened me with: the long death, the destruction of all I cared for, the letters they would have sent to Mucianus telling of infidelities that were never important. He just knew that I had sold him, and was taking his revenge.

Chapter Fifty-Four

Rome, 18 December AD 69

Caenis

I rose early on the eighteenth of December: this day was like none other.

Pantera and his men had not carried my litter for some time by then, but Matthias had hired me another team for the day and I was transported to Sabinus' house before the first dunghill cocks announced the dawn. Matthias himself I left behind in case Domitian came; I wish now that I hadn't.

At the top of the hill, men were already gathering, stamping their feet, blowing into their hands against the December frosts, watching Sabinus' door in the torchlight, just as they would have watched the emperor's, wanting to be among the first to hail him as he emerged.

It was still dark when Sabinus walked out amongst them. He didn't yet accept their homage, but progressed through the growing crowd, greeting each by name. All eighteen senators who had attended the meeting at my house the day before were there, and each had brought along a dozen friends at least.

In their hundreds, therefore, they filled the street, a slow river of white togas and greying heads. Of the two consuls, one had gone to be with Vitellius to take his abdication, while the other – Quinctillius Atticus, famed for his fish-pool – remained here, and moved through the crowd, distributing pamphlets.

He pressed one into my hand. It bore an image of Vespasian that underdid his nose and overstated his chin, with, beneath:

THE SUPERIORITY OF VESPASIAN AS EMPEROR

There followed a rambling list of reasons why Vespasian was the only rational choice for emperor. I'm sure they were perfectly valid, but I couldn't bring myself to read them. In any case, Sabinus was there.

'Caenis!' He embraced me, his gaze sliding over my face as he glanced over my shoulder at more important men. He pulled himself back and looked me in the eye. 'Where's Domitian?'

'I don't know. He didn't come home last night.'

'Is that unusual?'

'Not really. He's free to do what he wants.' It was immensely unusual, actually, and on the first night of Saturnalia doubly so, but it was not out of character for how he had been behaving recently, and in any case I didn't feel that Sabinus needed to know all the boy's secrets.

I said, 'He'll be home by noon. He won't miss Dino's poppy-seed cakes.' I believed this to be true, and had no way of knowing that by noon I would have no home for him to return to.

Sabinus was still looking at me, frowning. I pointed behind him, saying, 'The Watch is here,' and Sabinus strode off to meet the commanders of the Watch and the Urban cohorts who had brought their men in their entirety to offer their oath of fealty to Vespasian. Within moments, their standard-bearers lined the street and Sabinus was standing at their head in his brother's place.

He needed no written copy of the oath: he had been enough of a soldier to know it by heart and to know that he must be seen to be competent for his brother's sake.

'Men of the empire: in the name of Jupiter, Best and Greatest, do you now take the oath to honour and to serve, as long as you may live, Titus Flavius Vespasianus, to give your lives in his defence and that of the empire?'

They did. All of them. Unanimously and with enthusiasm.

It was done swiftly enough and the men were sent back to their barracks to await orders: Sabinus did not wish to be seen to have taken Rome by force.

That, at least, was what he told Pantera some short while later, when the spy turned up, clean, calm, damp-haired, with the rosemary scent of a man who had recently bathed, or at least seen the attentions of a sponge.

'You let them go?' Pantera clearly thought Sabinus insane.

Sabinus, for his part, was brother to the man just named emperor by three Urban cohorts and the entire city Watch. He had no interest in Pantera's opinion.

'Vitellius has abdicated. What need have I of the cohorts?'

'Nothing, if that were true, but it is not. Vitellius has *not* abdicated. The Guard refused to let him. He has returned to the palace, and has sent his wife and son to safety. These are not the actions of a man planning to leave office in the immediate future.'

'But he gave his word!' Sabinus flushed an unmanly purple. 'He swore before the altar in the temple of Apollo . . .'

'He has reneged on that oath.'

It's amazing how fast a single sentence can spread. Within

four breaths, the crowd was buzzing like a kicked hive.

Pantera took Sabinus' elbow. 'Geminus and his Guards know exactly how much they have to lose when Vitellius goes. Having put him on the throne, they are not inclined to let him give it up. You need to call back the cohorts and march on the palace.'

'And begin a war of my own? I think not!'

Sabinus drew himself up to his tallest; he was not impressive, but he was the centre of attention and that conferred its own authority.

'We shall walk to the forum ourselves and explain to the people of this city how matters stand. The Guard are only three thousand. In a city of a million souls, they do not make the majority.'

CHAPTER FIFTY-FIVE

Rome, 18 December AD 69

Trabo

I didn't expect to see Jocasta in that gigantic litter; truth be told, I hadn't thought of her since we got back to Rome. When your friends are dying, thoughts of women fade away like morning mist and Julius Claudianus and the rest had become friends, that summer.

Anyway, her appearing out of the blue like that was a shock. I was so happy, just for a moment, until she cut me dead. The flat edge of her gaze hit me in the guts as if she'd jabbed me with the dull end of a spear.

Then she invited Pantera to join her inside, and I was left with the choice of following the painted catamite back to the inn or following behind the litter like a whipped hound. I followed the litter and heard the sounds of Pantera's ablutions as he transformed himself from renegade into respectable citizen. I learned nothing of Jocasta's motives, or her plans.

At Sabinus' house, I stood back while she and Pantera paid their respects and joined the slow-moving avalanche of nobility that was making ready to slide down the hill towards the forum.

It was a stratified crowd, each layer determined by class and station: every Roman knows where his place is, or hers, and they segregate by instinct, the way great flocks of birds mesh in flight.

Jocasta was somewhere in the middle while Sabinus and Caenis were the almost-royal almost-couple at the fore, although I knew by then that all was not well with them. Right at the start, just before they set off, Caenis had signalled to Pantera, calling him over.

'Domitian is gone.' She was small amongst all these big, overweight men. Her nose was blue with cold, her hands white about the fingers. She pushed them up her sleeves as much to hide them from view as to keep them warm. For all that, she looked proud until he asked her where she thought the boy was. She looked worried, then. 'I don't know. He went out last night and didn't come home.'

Pantera, of course, couldn't tell her what he knew; she was worldly wise, but Domitian was as a son to her, and nobody wants to learn that their son has spent the night with Mucianus' catamite.

I could see now why Pantera had sent Horus away. If the boy had been there, you'd have known, wouldn't you, what they'd done? A boy doesn't know how to hide these things. And this was Caenis' big day. You wouldn't want some filthy Alexandrian whore spoiling it.

So Pantera bit his lip and said, 'We'll find him. Stay with Sabinus. There's no point in hiding now and you're as safe with him as anywhere.'

He caught Borros' eye and nodded and the big Briton vanished into the shadows. As far as I could tell, he'd spent half the summer following Domitian and knew his habits. If he hadn't had to go south the previous night, he would have been waiting outside the House of the Lyre and would have seen to it that the boy returned home in the morning.

Pantera fell back beside me, the only one left of the small band he had led out of Tarracina in the night. We walked along near the back of the group.

'How many, do you think?' Pantera asked.

I had been doing a head count while he was speaking to Caenis. 'More than four hundred,' I said. 'Most of them old men, beyond fighting age.'

'That's what I thought. If we meet trouble, they'll have to head to the Capitol. Be ready.'

It was that kind of morning: nothing was certain. We kept to the back of the group that surged down the Quirinal hill towards the Basilica Julia and the forum. They were not all men: I had counted a number of women besides Caenis and Jocasta, perhaps one tenth of the whole.

Neither Pantera nor I had any status and we could not be seen anywhere near the front of this column, but nor could we safely let Sabinus out of our sight: Pantera's word to Vespasian still held, and in any case Sabinus was now the key to the bloodless coup we had always planned.

He wasn't hard to follow: we stayed to one side and kept parallel to the group, ranging along alleyways, rooftops, walls, scaffolding, anything to give a clear view of the route ahead.

We saw the smoke as we came over the brow of the hill on to the long incline; a thin thread, dark against the morning's haze, rising from the foot of the hill.

'*Fuck!*'

Pantera leapt into a run and I was with him. No one who had lived through the fire in Rome could have done anything different: the memories will be with us for life, vivid and appalling. Without effort, I imagined Jocasta roasted, burning, dying slowly. It gave speed to my feet.

We turned a corner and saw a small, stilted figure running up the hill towards us. It was Matthias from Caenis' house, with Toma and Dino close on his heels.

He fell at Caenis' feet, bringing the whole great mass of men and women and senators to a halt.

In front of them all, he panted out the news that an entire century of the Guard had been to the Street of the Bay Trees and assaulted Caenis' house, battering down the door with a ram.

They had not found whom they sought, but they had torched it anyway and now they were moving on to every place in the city where Pantera had been seen: to the White Hare, to the House of the Lyre, to—

'To the Crossed Spears?' Pantera's very bad at hiding his worry when he thinks he's been responsible for someone else's death.

It was then that I realized how close he was with the dream-teller and his Nordic wife, how much they meant to him. Or, perhaps, how much their welfare weighed on him. He had already caused the bad deaths of his little gelded priest and then the men in Tarracina; he wasn't the kind who could bear much more of that.

Matthias shook his head. 'Not there, not yet. Maybe not ever. It wasn't mentioned and they did a lot of talking. I think Gudrun and Scopius will be safe for now; the silver-boys will tell them if the Guards come close.'

Pantera wasn't listening. He had seen something and the look on his face made me turn so fast I nearly fell over.

Four hundred men turned with me, and saw, flowing up the hill from the forum, far faster than winter snow, a column of the Guard.

The day was soft with the promise of rain, but their naked blades were shafts of brilliant light, bouncing to the rhythm of their feet.

Sabinus raised his hand for the halt, which was entirely unnecessary given that not one of the men behind him was armed. Even if they had been, none was of the mettle to give fight to a century or more of angry Praetorian Guards.

'To the Capitol!' Pantera vaulted on to a nearby wall so they could see better where he pointed. 'Turn right and get up on to the Capitol now! If you can reach the Asylum, you'll be safe.'

This last was something of an exaggeration but the heart of Sabinus' crowd was easily swayed and the thought of safety drew the mass of men and women up the steep slopes of the Capitol as fast as their indignation had previously swept them down toward the forum. Watery sunlight seeped through the heavy sky as they ran, sending their shadows as long, lean fingers ahead.

If the Palatine was palatial, the Capitol was holy, at least at its heights, which is to say the houses on it were far older and in greater need of repair; and that the temples commanded all the best positions, set higher than the towering tenement slums which leaned against each other at such alarming angles on the slopes leading up to them.

We passed many of those. Standing amongst the small, much-patched dwellings were crumbling temples of minor deities and flat, paved areas used for the reading of augurs and auspices. A smell of fear and old blood clung to the damp December air. A light rain began to fall. If it was a comment from the gods, nobody knew what it said.

Climbing ever upward, the procession, or perhaps by now it was a scrum of refugees, slowed as it reached the steepest part of the hill. Pantera and I moved back among them, selecting men from the throng, choosing those with hair not yet silvered, who looked as if they might have seen at least some recent military service.

'Block the path,' we told them. 'Don't let the Guards past. They'll put a cordon at the foot of the hill, but we need to hold the heights until Antonius Primus gets here. It won't be more than two days.'

They didn't listen; they didn't know who we were, and they weren't the kind of men to take orders from strangers: I would have been the same.

Eventually, exasperated, Jocasta seized planks from a nearby scaffold and, helped by three other women, began to erect a barricade across the route. My heart exploded with pride, but still she wouldn't look at me. She achieved more than we had done, though. Shamed, the men we had picked out formed into groups and the single barricade soon became a wall, blocking the way up.

The greater mass of Sabinus' refugees forged on past the head of the Gemonian steps, across the saddle of the Asylum and past the teetering row of priest's houses to the temple proper.

This was the beating heart of Rome. In ancient times, when the Gauls assaulted the city and nearly took it, Marcus Manlius had held out on the Capitol for months, acquiring as he did so the name Capitolinus. From our point of view, the old tale was a reminder that he who holds the heights holds the city. We were there now, but we had to get into the temple and then hold it and neither of those was a trivial task.

Seen close up, the building itself was like a fortress, with huge walls and thick gates; assaulting it would have taken a proper military force, which we didn't have. To be blunt, if the priests inside were inclined to close the gates against us, we knew we had no means of opening them.

But gongs and cymbals had attended our march, much as the silver-boys' whistles would have attended something similar down in the city, and now, as Sabinus approached the main gate, a small postern door opened in the wall some distance to his right. A middle-aged priest emerged, robed in scarlet, hesitant and unhappy in the ever-increasing rain.

'Who seeks entry?'

It was a rote question, asked of all who came there, and this much Sabinus could manage. His voice carried across the two hills.

'Sabinus, brother to Vespasian, your emperor. We come in his name and seek sanctuary against the forces of rebellion.'

The priest blinked. He might have spent his days in an ageing stone edifice on a hill, but rumour reached the gods as fast as it did anyone else and he must by then have known the details of Vitellius' failed abdication.

But he bowed, hands on his chest, in the Persian fashion, and said, 'Be welcome, brother of the emperor. And all those who seek sanctuary with you.'

The relief? You could have cut it up and served it on a plate to the emperor; to either of the emperors. When the priests opened the temple gates the entire group piled inside, leaving behind only the stalwart few manning the barricades and even they set up a rotation and went in for a while each.

There was food in there, and water, rest and shelter from the downpour; we'd run up the hill in rain but it had become a thunderstorm by the time we reached the temple. Sabinus said, and nobody disagreed, that it had been arranged by the gods to protect us.

Certainly, it was better to sit inside and listen to the rain batter the roof tiles than to stand out in all that weather, holding a cordon around the foot of the hill, which was, we were told, what Geminus' Guards were doing. Pantera said as much to Sabinus when he was able to get him away from his throng of sycophants.

'If the rain stays like this, the Guards won't be able to hold their cordon on the hill. There will be gaps you could drive a ten-horse chariot through. We can get you out then, and away to Antonius.'

That made perfect sense to me, but Sabinus was a politician, not a military man; his strategies were all for the look of things, not the practical necessities of survival.

He smiled at Pantera the way you might smile at a slave you pitied, and shook his head. 'To abandon the Capitol now would be to abandon Rome, and I am my brother's representative: I can't do that. Use your powers to keep us safe, and I'll use mine to make sure that we have an empire to come out to when the rain lifts.'

He had practised that speech, I think. It came out sounding rehearsed, but that didn't mean he wasn't sincere.

We left soon after and went out to check the first line of defences just past the brow of the Arx.

Jocasta was still there, overseeing the creation of a second layer of barricades formed from old timbers and carefully balanced masses of old masonry that could be sent flying down the hill by five men heaving on a lever. She was striding up and down the line with her tunic belted like a man's and her dark hair flying free in the rain. She was filthy and bedraggled and she looked as beautiful as I had ever known her; and happy.

It was heart-breaking, and all the more because she didn't so much as look my way and there's a limit to how much of a fool I'm prepared to make of myself, even for her. I smiled once, and then pretended to study the battlements she had made.

Pantera, watching her, said mildly, 'You should be in Britain. There, the women lead the armies.'

She threw him a cheerful glance that knotted my stomach. 'I'm told it is cold and wet and the children are born with webbing between their fingers and toes, like ducks.'

I learned later that Pantera had had a daughter once, to a

woman of the Dumnonii. It perhaps explained the strange look on his face, the longing and sorrow and yearning mixed.

'Not true,' he said. 'It's no wetter than here. You would thrive there. When this is over, I'll take you—'

'Someone's coming!' a man shouted up from further below. Every inch the military leader, Jocasta spun on her heel and ordered the defenders to the levers, ready to send rocks hurtling downhill. They were actually leaning on the first lever when a new call came: 'He seeks the Leopard.'

'Expecting someone?' Jocasta pushed a hank of hair out of her eyes.

'Possibly.' Pantera put his hands to his mouth and shouted, 'Ask for a name!'

'Borros!' shouted Borros, and pushed up to the barricade, and was shown the only safe place where he could clamber over without risking damage to his manhood from a series of sacrifice-knives set upright in the planking.

Reaching us, he said, 'The Guard has set a cordon about the foot of the hill, but they can't hear anything over the rain and you can walk ten feet from them and they see nothing. If Sabinus wants to leave now, we could have him down the hill and out of the city to be with Antonius Primus by morning.'

'He won't leave,' Pantera said, and stepped away from the barricade. 'I'm sorry to have sent you on a fool's errand. Come away from the rain and have something to eat.'

I couldn't wait to be free of Jocasta's blank stare. I followed Pantera back up the hill and into a priest's quarters in one of the small, ramshackle houses in the row that led up to the temple. It was little more than an alcove with a bed and a brazier, but as private as any we had found when the greater mass of the refugees was clustered in the main rooms of the temple.

'Have you located Domitian?' The question had been burning Pantera's tongue since he saw Borros, but he couldn't ask it with everyone around because nobody else knew the boy was missing.

Borros shrugged expressively. 'He was still in the House of the Lyre when the Guards went to burn it.' He held up a hand. 'Be calm, they didn't succeed. They didn't even try. The Belgian doorkeeper dropped the names of several people who would be mightily upset if that place was not fit for their parties and the officers thought better of it and went on their way. But Domitian left by a back route while that discussion was happening and I didn't see where he went. One of the Marcuses might know where he is, but they won't tell me.'

Water was dripping steadily from the crag of Borros' brow on to the bedding. Pantera handed him a cloth to dry himself, and a warm cloak, filched from a priest, before dragging on another cloak. It wasn't his and it stank of incense, which is less than useful if you're trying to hide, but he needed something to shield him against the rain.

'I'll try to find him. If Caenis and Sabinus ask, tell them. If you can manage not to mention the House, it will probably save your life when the boy becomes emperor.'

Borros grinned. He sat on the edge of the bed and warmed the flats of his hands on the underside of the platter. 'I'll be in Britain long before that. And you too, if you've any sense. Don't get lost in the rain. And don't get caught.'

I followed Pantera out. He didn't turn me away, so I was there when he found Domitian and Mucianus' catamite together in a hut owned by Scopius of the Crossed Spears.

Chapter Fifty-Six

Rome, 18 December AD 69

Horus

The silver-boys told him where we were, and directed him to us with their whistles.

The first thing I knew, there was a scuffle outside and a knock on the door frame of our hut; the door itself was goat-hide, you understand. I was inside with Domitian, Gudrun, Zois and Thaïs in as cheerful a cluster of vivacity as you could ask for, all of us bunched in a ring round a hot brazier, eating flat bread and goat's cheese and playing dice for copper coins. Domitian was losing.

Pantera ducked inside with his thug Trabo close behind. I despised him, and the feeling was returned in kind. But neither of us was able to take the edge off the joyful greeting that met Pantera as he walked in.

'You're alive!' Zois, Scopius' small dark daughter, who had so entranced everyone with her acrobatics in the summer, threw her arms round him.

Thaïs, her taller, fairer, more shapely sister wasn't far behind. 'When we heard about the Guard and the burning houses, we were so afraid for you.'

It was like a family, when the favoured brother returns home, or a particularly indulgent uncle. The girls clustered round, fussing over Pantera's wet tunic, bringing dry cloths to scrub at his hair.

Trabo eyed him sourly. 'You're a popular man.'

I could have hit him for that. Pantera stiffened; the warm, easy joy was lost. Sliding behind the irony that is his shield, he said, 'I let them dye my hair. You should try it sometime.'

But his eyes rested on my face and there was still a kind of peace in them as if everything I had done had been forgiven. Or perhaps he was just lost in memories, for he said, 'I had a daughter once, in Britain. She would have been their age by now, had she lived.'

Even Trabo had the decency to look discomfited by that.

Pantera took the bread they offered him, and the cheese, and shared it with Trabo, who ate as if he'd been starved for a week. Over the girls' heads, the Leopard caught my eye. 'The House is safe,' he said. 'But the Guards may be back. If they destroy it because of me, I will see that it is rebuilt.' Turning to Domitian, he gave a bow, saying, 'Your uncle is on the Capitol, in the temple of the three gods, with all but five men of the senate. If you wish to join him, it must be done under cover of darkness; we can't slip past the Guards in daylight.'

'But we can at night?' Domitian's glance flickered up to meet mine. 'Would it not be safer if we left Rome now, and joined Antonius Primus?'

I was included in that 'we', I could feel it. So could Pantera. Domitian may have been deliberately losing at dice, but not because of me; he was relaxed in my presence, unashamed, but discreet. Nobody looking would have known we had shared a night, and planned to share more.

With a shrug, Pantera said, 'There's no doubt that leaving would be far safer. But your uncle Sabinus has said he will not leave the hill, and that means that if Vitellius chooses to abdicate in the morning Sabinus will take the throne in his stead. The first hour after a change of emperor counts for more than the next ten years. If you want to be the one to hold the throne for your father, you will need to be on hand when it becomes vacant.'

There was a flicker in Domitian's eyes, of choices weighed, of facts balanced. He was clever. I had found that out early in our brief time together; a swift mind and a quick study and a passion for getting things right.

'What of Lucius?' he asked. 'Is there any danger that he will return with his cohorts from the south?'

'I don't know. Felix has been sent—'

Gudrun interrupted him. 'Felix was here, looking for you. He left moments before you arrived. He had news from the south. We sent him out, because you weren't here, but he won't be far. Marcus can find him for you.'

A flurry of whistles and a damp walk later and we were with Felix in a smaller hut with a less well-stoked brazier, but it was warm enough and proof against the rain. Domitian came, and Trabo. Gudrun and the girls stayed safely where they were.

'Pantera!' Relief bloomed on Felix' face. Overnight, I had revised my first opinion of him. He was an interesting boy with a lot of potential in the right hands, and just then, far more than Domitian, he had the look of a man who had spent the night sating his lust.

He stood awkwardly, with his two hands hidden behind his back, and gave his report.

'Lucius sent two messengers. The first came at noon and

413

I killed him, but the second came at the fourth hour after and rode straight past the inn. I followed him, but he had an escort. I couldn't kill him. I'm sorry.'

I hadn't known him for a killer, but it was clear now. The power of it shone from him, overshadowing the shame at the second missed kill.

Pantera held out a hand. 'The message from the first?' Felix passed him the package.

There was no need to take any particular care in opening this letter; it wasn't going to be sent on. Pantera slit the threads and broke the seal.

The message it carried was uncoded. He and I read it together, in all its horror.

Brother, Tarracina is once more held in your name. Julius Claudianus, leader of the rebels, has died a traitor's death, his men with him. Three boats were destroyed and two sailed away, but we have blocked the harbour and none will sail in while we are here. We wait only on your word to return to Rome.

A traitor's death. That's what they offered Nero and he cut his own throat rather than face having his head wedged in a cleft stick to be flogged to death.

Pantera closed his eyes against the truth. Presently, he crunched the thin paper into a ball and threw it viciously on to the brazier. Together, we watched orange flames curl the fine parchment to smoke.

'So Vitellius knows Tarracina has fallen,' Pantera said, eventually. 'How long is it since the second messenger arrived at the palace?'

'Less than an hour,' said Felix. 'His horse foundered and he had to change for a new one ten miles south of Rome. I was close enough to see him, but I dared not risk an attack

414

when so many of the Guard hemmed him in. If I had been caught . . .'

'There was no one to give you a fast death. Well done. You did the right thing.'

In many ways, Felix was still a child. He drank in his hero's praise like a starving hound whelp, and repaid it with that same hound's devotion.

Pantera's gaze sought me out. 'Felix can speak his message to Vitellius, but he'll need a written reply for Lucius. Can you write for us again?'

At other times I might have bridled at the brusqueness of that, but Domitian was watching me and he needed to know I was more than a whore, however costly.

I shrugged easily. 'Have you pen and ink and a seal?'

'They're in the place I last slept. Marcus can get them.'

One of the many Marcuses retrieved from their hidden place paper of imperial weight and ink of imperial standard, a pen, a knife, thread, wax and a seal that was identical in all ways to the imperial seal but that it was wrought on an iron thumb-ring, and not a cylinder of gold.

To Pantera's dictation, therefore, I wrote, *Brother, please accept our congratulations on your outstanding victory. We expected nothing less. We have word that Mucianus plans to make use of the mild weather to attempt an assault on the south using the port at Misene to gain entry and so encircle Rome. It is imperative that he is stopped. We require you to hold that port against any possible landings until we send word to return. Aulus Vitellius.*

The paper was sanded, sealed and stitched. I said, 'Don't we need one to replace the one you've just opened? If Vitellius is expecting two . . .'

'But Felix has the ring, don't you, Felix?'

The boy flushed with joy and chagrin mixed. 'How did you—'

'You've been keeping your left hand behind your back since you walked in. So it holds something of value that fits only in a hand. And you are intelligent enough to have thought ahead. May we see?'

Shyly, Felix opened the hand that he had held shut all along. On it lay a ring of a wealth and ornament such as only an emperor might wear. Or his brother.

'Your story?'

Felix might have been a youth who delighted in killing, but he was far from stupid. Promptly, he said, 'I came upon the messenger after he had been left for dead by armed men in Vespasian's colours. He begged me to bring his message to the emperor. I am to say that Tarracina is taken, and that now Lucius has heard of a pocket of resistance at Misene and, counting on his brother's permission, has taken his victorious army to deal with it.'

'Good. Do you have the pass-phrase?'

'A brother's love is unsurpassed.'

'How many others did he give you before that?' Pantera asked.

Domitian's eyes flew wide. He had understood that Felix was a killer, but had imagined a cut throat, done swiftly, not the length of a death that would have drawn from a loyal man this kind of secret.

Felix said, 'He tried two others, but this one is real. I will bet my life on it.'

'You're about to. You know where the horses are.' Pantera slid the message I had written into Felix' pack. 'They may send you south with a reply to your message; if they do, be sure to give this one of ours to Lucius in its place. If they send someone else, he must be stopped. Can you handle a bow?'

'Well enough.'

'Good. Diogenes, who feeds the horses, has one in safe keeping. Tell him the Leopard asks that his weapon be liberated. He will give it to you then. Stay safe.'

Felix grinned. 'Trust me, life is too interesting. I don't intend to throw it away.'

CHAPTER FIFTY-SEVEN

Rome, 18 December AD 69

Geminus

On rising that morning, I had made an oath to myself that I would remain by Vitellius' side for as long as it took to secure his right to the throne.

I had no part in the fiasco at the forum that saw Sabinus besieged; that was a group of men who were entirely out of control of any officers, but once it had happened we had to make the best of it.

I sent orders to keep the hill only lightly secured (there was no harm in finding out who would commit to Vespasian, and allowing out those who were having second thoughts), while at the same time locking down the gates so that nobody might leave the city without our knowing it. Above all, I didn't want either Sabinus or Domitian to reach Antonius' troops and give them a figurehead to fight for.

I could have gone out to arrange this myself, but I was, as I've said, not happy to leave Vitellius' side and he wanted to keep me close as much as I wanted to be there; Juvens, too. The pair of us flanked him wherever he went, to eat, to drink, to the latrines: we were with him at every step, every squat, every arcing stream of urine.

When, in mid-afternoon, the messenger came with details confirming Lucius' victory over the rebels at Tarracina, we shared a moment's celebration: a jug of wine, some small pastries warm from the oven that melted away on my tongue and left lingering bursts of anchovies and citrus. The emperor might have sent his wife and son to safety elsewhere in the city, but his cooks had stayed in the palace and were keen to prove their undying loyalty.

My Guardsmen, too, were enthusiastic in their devotion. In spite of truly filthy weather, they kept Sabinus neatly penned on the top of the Capitol. The fact that nine tenths of the senate had remained with him throughout the day was unfortunate, but not irredeemable.

Vespasian had been naming new senators month on month from his safe perch in Alexandria: in my opinion, Vitellius could just as easily do the same. In fact, he should have done so in the summer, and saved all the anguish now.

I said as much, as our celebration became our evening meal and the anchovy tarts were replaced by others tasting of syrupy peaches with a dusting of powdered almonds.

'Lord, we must prepare for a long siege of the Capitol. Rome requires that men of valour and loyalty serve her. It might be that you list the names of men whom you trust, who could take on the burden of the senate, and—'

'Lord!' Drusus dragged in some bedraggled wretch by the wrist and looked likely to snap the arm to which it was attached. Actually, he looked as if he'd like to rip the boy's head off and eat it.

Whatever instructions Lucius had left with the giant

German, the events of the past days had seen this man cleave ever closer to Vitellius; his loyalty outshone the rest of the household combined.

He stopped just inside the doorway. 'This one demands to see you. He brings this.'

He thrust his hand forward. Gold glimmered on the heft of his palm and it looked like Lucius' ring, which wasn't an auspicious start.

I caught Juvens' eye, and we stepped close to Vitellius, one on either side, ready to support him if this heralded news of his brother's death.

Given what he had brought us, I took a closer look at Drusus' victim, who was, in fact, rather older than he had at first appeared, if not yet old enough to carry the responsibility of such a message.

Tousled blond hair framed a filthy face and eyes that didn't quite see in the same line. His lopsided gaze fixed as best it could on Vitellius' face and then swivelled from Juvens to me, in evident confusion. Here, where the emperor eschewed the obvious trappings of state, it was not immediately obvious who ranked over whom.

Sighing, I said, 'Speak your business. If it is to our benefit, the emperor will hear you.' I nodded to my left and Vitellius, reading his cue, took half a step forward. Good man. That settled the question of identity.

The youth was pressed to his knees, his head forced down. Muffled, his voice reached us. 'I was coming north up the Appian Way when I came upon a man who had been set upon and left for dead. He begged me to bring his lord a message.'

'Let him up.' In the back of my mind, I had been expecting this. 'What, exactly, did the messenger tell you to say?'

The youth rose. His face was blotched white and red with pain, his breathing fast as he rubbed his wrist. Drusus' fingers had left bruises all round it that would be purple by nightfall.

'I am first to show you the ring and say that a brother's love is unsurpassed. Then I am to wait to see if you will hear the rest.'

The ring passed from the youth to Drusus to me. Beneath a patina of dried blood, it was authentic: there was no question but that this was Lucius' ring, down to the notch in the setting that held the largest of the emeralds. I knew its weight, its look on a hand, the wounds it left on a man's face when he was struck by it, hard, back-handed.

And the watchword was correct; Vitellius acknowledged that with a brief nod.

I caught Juvens' eye again and we stepped away, leaving our emperor to speak to the youth with the greater authority of a man who stands alone.

Vitellius said, mildly, 'We will hear the rest of what our brother sent to us.'

The boy closed his eyes, the better to remember his message, and like that, with his face screwed tight, said, 'I am to tell you that, following his resounding victory at dawn in Tarracina, the lord Lucius has heard news of rebels massing at the port of Misene who wish harm upon your reign. With your permission and blessing, he goes there now, to suppress this fresh revolt.'

It had the ring of Lucius, the ostentation, the arrogance, the overly flowery language.

With a sigh, Vitellius asked, 'Does my brother seek my permission? Or is he going anyway?'

'My lord . . . ?' The youth's eyes snapped open. One of them looked at me, one at Juvens. It was really most distracting.

He was at a loss. 'I can say only what I was told, and that from the mouth of a dying man. He could barely speak. I heard what I could, but if it is wrong I can only—'

'Don't gabble, man. You did well, and shall be rewarded.'

Vitellius pulled one of his own rings from the thumb of his

left hand. With that, even now, a man could have bought a fast horse, a sword, put down rent on a house and live without further work for a year.

'Take this in gratitude . . . What is your name?'

'Felix, lord. A freedman of Ostorius who owns the Inn of Five Hands.'

I had never heard of that inn, but made a mental note to track it down and talk to the landlord.

Vitellius, who was not prone to suspicion, and liked to be kind, nodded gravely, as if he knew it well. 'Then, Felix, you are now a freedman of the emperor. If you will fight for us in the coming days, we may bring you into our service. We have use for loyal men. Or—' A thought came to him. 'Have you a good horse?'

Warily: 'He is not bad, lord. He carried me here with all speed, but he belongs to—'

'Your master. Of course. And he will be tired. Then you must apply to the stables for a fresh mount in our name. We have need of a royal messenger and you have proved yourself already. You will carry our reply to our brother at Misene in the stead of the man who died in your arms. We shall summon a scribe and have it written. In that time, Drusus will find you a new tunic in our colours, and ensure you have the best horse.'

CHAPTER FIFTY-EIGHT

Rome, 18 December AD 69

Trabo

The night of the eighteenth was dark and wet and cold: a bad combination for any man standing sentry duty.

It was no surprise, therefore, that the ring of iron around the foot of the Capitol hill became more of a sieve as soon as night fell.

Pantera took us all through together, Domitian and the catamite and me, and brought us past the barrier Jocasta had made with all its upward pointing knives.

'Hooks on ropes would pull those down,' Domitian said, as we passed. 'Germanicus used such things to overcome the enemy warriors in the forests of the Rhine. The Guard will know of them.'

So the boy had been reading military texts. His father would have been happy to hear it, which was probably the point.

We discussed tactics for a while, in the process of which we learned that, while Domitian and Sabinus were unable to leave the city, Pantera was sending a steady stream of men out with messages to Antonius. Their lot was harder, we gathered: the Guard around the hill might have been notably lax, but the sentry points at Rome's gates were triply manned and everyone leaving was searched.

One man had left in a coffin, wrapped in shrouds and lying beneath the leaking, stiff, stinking body. Another had gone in a cart-load of rotten fruit. Only those things impossible to imagine were safe, and soon not even those.

If Domitian had any doubts about being here, that was enough to stop them. He participated more fully, after that, in the planning of tactics for when the Guard came upon us.

When, not if. We had no doubt they would attack, the only question was when – and how much we could rely on Sabinus and those around him to fight back.

The only time I saw Domitian in doubt was when Pantera mentioned that Jocasta was there, and that she had organized the barricades. Whatever it was that flashed across Domitian's face then – fear? shame? shyness? – was gone too fast for me to read it, but there was no doubt that he hadn't expected her to be here, and wasn't pleased to hear of it. I thought he had been her lover, and was ashamed to have her see him in the company of the painted catamite from the House of the Lyre.

I hated both of them for that.

Domitian didn't see my face, or if he did he didn't care. He moved briskly on, as if her name had not come up, saying, 'The temple is ahead. Will they open the doors to us or do we need a password?'

'The password is Vespasian,' Pantera said. 'We're not seeking prizes for originality. Speak it aloud and they'll let you in.'

'Are you not coming too?'

Pantera had already turned away, and was heading back down the hill.

'I have to be sure that Felix is alive, and that he has been sent with his message to Lucius. If he hasn't, we may have to change a number of things very fast. If I'm not back before dawn, Trabo will organize the defences. Take your orders from him as you would from me.'

That, as you can imagine, pleased nobody.

CHAPTER FIFTY-NINE

Rome, 18–19 December AD 69

Geminus

Sleep was hard to come by that night. I lay in the dark on a thin mattress laid across the doorway of Vitellius' small, stateless bedroom and counted again the number of men I had at my disposal, their dispositions, their morale.

The blockade of the hill was for show only, but Rome itself was effectively under military rule: my rule. Every road coming in had at least a half-century of men holding it secure, with trumpet signals arranged to call more at need and roaming units making sure the plebeians of the city were loudly on Vitellius' side, and that the roads were kept clear where we needed them to be and blocked everywhere else.

Antonius Primus and his men were coming closer. I had no idea how fast or in what numbers, but besieging Vespasian's brother had been an extravagant mistake that was only ever likely to bring him to us faster and in greater fury. I had known that since I had heard of it, but if the fates had dealt me a poor hand, it didn't mean I had to play it badly. As far as I was concerned, as long as Lucius returned soon from Tarracina with his cohorts largely intact, we would be able to repulse the coming assault, and perhaps break Antonius Primus for ever.

Looking to the longer term, I had already sent men to Gaul, to Iberia, to Britain, where there were legions that would support our cause, asking for their aid, but in the short term all we had to do was hold out until Lucius came back.

All this I turned over in the half-sleep before waking. Dawn bled into the half-empty palace, building mountains of the shadows, filling them with enemy faces. I saw Pantera, Trabo, Vespasian, Sabinus, Lucius, the emperor's dead mother. This last was by far the most frightening. The old harpy had died by her own hand the night before; the emperor had not wept at her death, but he had not been the same since.

The emperor was still asleep: I could hear the melodic snores that marked his peace.

In the half-dark, I rose, stepped past Drusus' sleeping bulk and went to empty myself in the latrines. A sleepy slave stood in attendance, holding the sponge on a stick for me to wipe myself clean when at length I was done. I crossed the corridor to the baths and washed, quickly.

My clothes were ready folded as I stepped out of the hot pool. In the kitchens, the cooks had stoked the ovens and already the scents of honeyed wine and early baking filtered through the palace. Filching an anchovy-flavoured pastry on the way past I decided I could become used to living with this kind of luxury.

My footsteps echoed down the halls, announcing my presence to whoever chose to listen; there was no secrecy here. I reached the throne room and was surprised to find Vitellius there ahead of me. He had never been an early riser.

He was still dressed in his ash-strewn toga from the day before. Someone needed to tell him to change, that he was not about to have his throne removed and could dress normally, but I was not yet that man.

In any case, he was grey with fatigue and lack of sleep, and he had news, it was written on his face.

'Sabinus sent a centurion. He was here, at the palace.'

'What? Who?' I had been in the baths for less than the time it took to finish a jug of wine and a man had been and gone?

'Cornelius Martialis.'

The name was familiar. He was a primus pilus in Juvens' legion, as far as I remembered. It was not a surprise that these men were beginning to congregate around Sabinus; depressing, but not surprising.

'What did he want?'

'That I honour my word and abdicate. What else?'

My throat had gone dry. 'Is he dead, this centurion? Did Drusus kill him?'

'No. We are civilized still. But he has left. I sent him out by the back route, so that the Guards might not kill him for his part in a concept they loathe.'

Vitellius had a dry, cool sense of humour, but once in a while it sparked, softly, like a pearl seen on the seabed. 'I instructed him to take back to Sabinus my deepest regrets, and the news that I am no longer in control of the Guard. He left swiftly, as you might imagine. Which is just as well.' Vitellius fell sombre again. 'Because Antonius' forces have attacked in the northeast of the city.'

'*What?*'

'Petilius Cerialis is attacking in the northeast with a thousand cavalry. They've come in just to the north of the barracks.'

'Hades. I need to go—'

'Juvens has gone already. He said to tell you that he can hold the route without difficulty. His men know every house, every alleyway, every small manor of the suburbs while

Cerialis' forces are from the Danube and may as well be attacking Parthia as Rome for all they know of it. They're bogged down, confused, and half of them were loyal to us until ten days ago when he defeated them; these ones are not fighting hard. Juvens thinks this is a feint and Antonius Primus may stage a main assault up the Flaminian Way. He says if you go anywhere, go there.'

At least there was something concrete to be done. I looked around the throne room. Drusus was a solid, silent presence standing just inside the door. 'Don't let anyone in except me or Juvens. Not slaves, not the cook—'

'No.' Vitellius stepped into my path. 'Don't go. Juvens can manage this one small incursion. We need you here, to organize the defences. You're a commander now. You don't need to be in the front line.'

He couldn't have ordered me; we both knew where lay the balance of power, but he was my emperor, and, more important, he was right.

To Drusus, I said, 'Make sure any messages are brought straight to me. And send water to mix with the wine. We need clear heads.'

I sat on the emperor's couch and tried to picture the entirety of Rome, and what forces we could muster to defend her.

And so the day started.

CHAPTER SIXTY

Rome, 19 December AD **69**

Jocasta

Night plunged into the western sea and sucked the rain with it. The next day, the nineteenth of December, dawned fresh and clear and seemed as if it might be kind to those of us besieged on the Capitol hill.

Pantera came back before dawn, and seemed cheerful, and then Cornelius Martialis returned before the first watch was called with news that Vitellius had turned down the offer to abdicate – again – but that he believed his brother to be caught up in Misene and unlikely to return.

Pantera was responsible for that; I read it in the quiet confidence of the nods exchanged between Trabo and Horus. Pantera himself is too used to hiding the truth to let such things slip. But whoever had set it up, the truth was that Lucius was trapped well away from Rome and, barring miracles, there was no chance of his riding in to offer Vitellius a last-minute reprieve.

Mind you, on the morning of the nineteenth, there was

no certainty that Vitellius was going to need that. We were stuck on the hill with a cordon of Guards around and no sign that Antonius Primus was close to rescuing us. We were like a family, four hundred strong, caught in close proximity when we were better apart. Trabo couldn't look at me, and Domitian didn't know where to look when he was in my presence, except that he must not, ever, glance at Horus, which of course told its own story.

Only Pantera was equally at ease with us all. We discovered that he could play dice with distressing skill and he taught us a board game common among the tribes of Britain where coloured pieces move from square to square across and must try to surround the king of the opposite side. He didn't seem to be interested in trying to find an escape route from the hill. I had found cellars with an almost-hidden entrance below the clerks' room which I thought might have caught his attention, but he just took his winnings and carried on playing.

Soon, noises of a skirmish reached us, of horses in anger, of iron smashed on iron, on stone, on wood, on flesh. I ushered my small force of men and women down the hill a short distance and stationed them along the barricades we had built in the night. We had brought whetstones to sharpen the knives that were set upright in the barricades and goose grease to ease the levers we had set in place to roll the larger lumps of masonry down on to the heads of those coming up, but none of us expected the line to hold for long.

Domitian came too, bringing the sons of senators, who numbered a rather larger force than mine, and they climbed up ladders on to the row of dwellings that lined the long, slow route to the temple. There was a festive atmosphere amongst the dozens on the rooftops, with food and drink passed up from below and many salutations, most of them scurrilous, as befitted the third day of Saturnalia. The sun shone. We waited.

Chapter Sixty-One

Rome, 19 December AD **69**

Geminus

The desperate frustration of being stuck in the palace while men were dying in battle in the city was ameliorated only by the constant stream of reports that came to us through the morning.

They detailed, first, the battle between Juvens and Petilius Cerialis, and then what came after it. I can't vouch for their accuracy, but they seemed plausible to me. I will tell you what we heard.

'Push on! Kill the horses and push on!'

Juvens stood on the wall of a kitchen garden. On one side, winter beds stood empty, carefully weeded, cleared for the cleansing frost. On the other was mayhem: men fighting hand to hand, horses rearing, striking, kicking, falling, dying.

This was what he lived for, not the craven surrender of Narnia. Here, he could expunge the shame of that.

He swept off his helmet, ran his fingers through his hair

and shouted again, 'Vinius! Go left. Left, man! *Left!* Curve round behind!'

His voice was hoarse, had lost all its music. His hand described great arcs and at last Vinius, never the brightest of his centurions, understood and led his half-century out down the street to his left, which curved round and came out again on the main thoroughfare, the Barracks Road. This brought him in at Cerialis' diminishing force from the rear.

With that manoeuvre complete, Juvens had him trapped. The rebels were few now, and fewer with every killing stroke.

Half of Cerialis' men had been ours less than a month before and had defected at the battle's start, while Juvens' own men were solid, true and fired with the blood lust of battle. All they needed was an officer to direct them and Juvens was the right man in the right place.

'Sextus! Right!'

Juvens leapt from the wall. His blade was wet with blood, the grip sweat-roiled and unsafe in his hand. He drove it hard into the throat of the man who had just threatened Sextus' unshielded right side, grabbed his enemy's weapon arm at the elbow, smashed it back into the wall and again and again until he felt the bones shatter.

'He's dead. Juvens, he's dead.'

He dropped the still-warm body. Sextus, alive, was fighting forward. It was Gaius Publius, one of the junior centurions, who had Juvens' shoulder, and was pulling him away.

'They're retreating. Cerialis has gone. Should we follow him?'

'No. It might be a trap. Sound the gather. Hold the men where they are.'

There was time for a dozen more deaths before the horns sounded and both sides briskly disengaged. There are advantages to fighting men who have served in your own army: everyone understands the signals.

Here and now, Petilius and his handful of men glanced at each other in grateful amazement, and ran.

Vinius came back, grumbling. 'We could have won.'

'You did win,' Juvens said. 'And now we have bigger fish to catch.'

He jumped back up on the wall and raised his hands, bringing the men closer. He was a natural orator; his fine intelligence was brought to bear on his playboy wildness and the result was an intoxicating mix of leadership and showmanship.

'Is there any man who thinks this was not an attempt to liberate Sabinus?'

'No!'

'Is there anybody here who wants Sabinus to remain safe on his hilltop for another day?'

'No!'

'Will anybody come with me to "liberate" him into death?'

'*Yes!*'

The shout became a great, grating roar, a clashing of swords on helmets, on the walls behind.

Juvens stood there, letting the waves of it wash over him. The moment was god-touched, perfect. Just as I had done at the barracks the day before, he had found his destiny and it was not to stand idly by while Rome slipped away from his grasp.

He lifted his voice to carry to the outer fringes of the gathered men.

'It's time we hammered the heart out of this rebellion. Sabinus brought this on us and he has no complaint if we take the fight to him. We're going to the Capitol and we're going to kick that rebellious bastard down the steps!'

CHAPTER SIXTY-TWO

Rome, 19 December AD 69

Jocasta

They came just after noon, a wave of silent, grim-faced Guards in dull-polished helms with their swords held tight to their sides; no histrionics, no waving of weapons, but a sense of duty and drive that coursed ahead of them and brought silence to the roofs of the priests' houses, where Domitian was holding what seemed to be a raucous Saturnalia party where the rules were what you wanted them to be as long as they involved singing and throwing things.

Pantera was up there with them, at the highest point, a hundred yards in front of the temple. He leapt down, landed in dirt, skidded, made his way down through muddy slurry to the barricades where I was rallying my small band of defenders.

I was filthy, I am sure. My hair was stiff with grime; I could feel it sticking up from my head in hedgehog spines, falling away at the back in tumbling, rat-knotted tails. My shift was in rags, my nails were torn.

I was enjoying myself more than any time I can remember.

'Did Felix make it safely out of the city?' I asked.

Pantera raised a brow. He hadn't told me about Felix; I had overheard Trabo talking about it to Sabinus. 'We can only hope so.'

The Guards came on up the hill. The first of Domitian's missiles rained down on them and they slowed. We pulled on our levers and sent our rocks tumbling down at them and they slowed more. It was tremendously satisfying when we hit a man and rolled him over, but it wasn't stopping the rest from coming on.

'Is Antonius Primus likely to rescue us?' I asked.

'I have sent a message in Sabinus' name requesting that he does exactly that. If we're lucky he may choose to make a hero of himself.'

'Or he may choose to be just too late.' Someone had to say aloud what was so plainly coursing through his mind. 'He may find it easier to let us fight the Guard until we or they are dead, possibly both, then he can overrun their positions and claim victory for himself.' I raised my voice. 'To the levers. Second wave: *now!*'

Pantera looked at me queerly for a moment. 'There was a woman in Britain,' he said, after a while, 'named Aerthen. Translated, her name meant "at the battle's end". Just then, you looked exactly as she did when the fighting was about to start. You were born to be a warrior. Did you know that?'

Ahh, what could I have said? He had that power to strike where it hurt and I don't think he knew it, or meant it; it was just that he cut through to what mattered so much more keenly than anyone else.

I studied his face, seeking the weak points; found none.

But I knew some things from Seneca's notes, enough to ask, 'What happened to Aerthen when the battle ended?'

'All times but the last one, we found somewhere apart from the rest and made love.'

'And the last battle? What happened after that?'

'I killed her. I cut her throat so that no man of Rome might make her a slave.' He could not meet my eyes. His gaze stretched over the barricade to where Domitian's rooftop army was in full swing, raining rocks on the Guards.

He said, thoughtfully, 'It's the real difficulty of being a spy. You come to believe that you are what you say you are. I said I was the enemy of Rome, and I became it.'

'And now?'

'Now I want to see Vespasian on the throne as much as I have ever wanted anything.' He gave a bleak smile. 'The same could not necessarily be said for everyone on this side of the barrier. Remember that, when the fighting starts. There is at least one un-friend here who wants to see our downfall.'

There was no time to ask him what he meant, for, although the silent mass of Guards had slowed to a standstill, the smell of new fire spiked the air, sharply.

'*Fuck.*'

'Fuck,' I said, in agreement. 'The Guards have set fire the priests' houses. Are you all right?'

I wasn't in Rome when the fire took it; my memories of that night don't run so deep, nor with such horror. But Pantera had been there, and from the look on his face I'd say his ears were ringing with old memories, the snap and bustle of fire, the screams of burning women, growing higher, harder, more desperate, more impossible to forget.

He wrenched his eyes away to look at me. I said, 'Shouldn't we . . .'

437

'Run? Yes. Swiftly. The barricades won't hold against fire. Get back into the temple and tell Sabinus he needs to block the gates. After that, find Caenis and make sure she is safe.'

'Where are you going?'

'Up on to the rooftops, where else? Domitian is up there and it won't be easy to talk him down.'

CHAPTER SIXTY-THREE

Rome, 19 December AD 69

Trabo

Domitian was on the roof and I was there with him, babysitting after a fashion, or at least keeping an eye on him to be sure he wasn't captured.

Losing Domitian now would have meant the end; everyone knew that Vespasian adored his children and the boy would have been a bargaining counter beyond price, with or without the woman Caenis.

So I watched him, and while he may have spent a night with a catamite, in daylight he had courage, of a kind; he was certainly fit to be a Caesar's son.

With flames playing over his face and crisping his hair, he was a dancing, leaping, manic satyr with a startlingly accurate aim for one who had spent the greater part of his life studying insects and collecting coins.

Bending, he ripped tile after tile from the roof beneath his feet, and flung them after the manner of a discus thrower so that they spun blade-wise through the air and sliced edge-first into the men below. Around him, a band of senators' sons were throwing their missiles likewise into the faces, raised arms, hands and chests of the under-defended Guards.

By tradition, the Guard never carry shields; honour says that these men need only a blade to defend the emperor, and while this might be accurate after a fashion there are times – now – when a shield wall would have made all the difference between success and ignominious defeat.

Domitian had been winning. Supported by the youth of Rome, he had been at least holding the Guard at bay for longer than they would have wanted; they were men bent on a mission and didn't want to be stopped by a boy.

Which is, presumably, why they lit the fire. It was a clever move; everyone knows that fire is the opposite of water and runs up hills, and besides, the wind was behind the Guards; they could safely torch the priests' houses and perhaps burn the temple and run no risk that the rest of Rome would fall to ash around them.

The flames were small and faltering at first, but they grew quickly into a roaring wall that fed fast on the old, old houses with their oak beams and wattle walls. Soon there was a level of heat that even the son of an emperor could not withstand. Already Domitian's face was scarlet, sweat swimming off him. His brows had been scorched away, leaving his face naked of hair.

Pantera came up round about then.

He reached us just as Domitian staggered back from the fire's leading edge. The Guards were level with Jocasta's abandoned barricades by now. With nobody left there to man them, the planks and sacrifice-knives were of little more than nuisance value; just enough to slow the oncoming men for the time it took to lift the knives away without slicing their fingers.

'My lord.' Pantera heaved himself up beside Domitian as he wrenched a fresh tile from the disintegrating roof. 'Please, you've done all a man could do. The women are safe in the temple. But if you remain out here, you will be caught between the fire and the Guard and the one will eat you while the other will hold you to ransom against your father's claim to the throne.'

Domitian laughed, drily. 'My father would not abandon his ambition on my behalf.'

'I think you would be surprised by what your father would do for you.'

The round, bulging eyes met his. Domitian's naked brows slid upwards. 'It might be interesting to test it.'

Fire was scorching the left side of Pantera's face. With studied calm, he said, 'If you find death a source of fascination then yes, it might be interesting. Those of us who live in its shadow tend to believe we will see the Styx soon enough and we are best served by avoiding too early a crossing. If you wish to die, lord, now is your opportunity. If you wish to live to serve Rome, the temple awaits. We can barricade the gates when you're in.'

'To serve Rome . . .' Domitian looked down, chewed his lips. When he looked up again, the wild light was there again in his eyes. I truly had no idea which future he would choose, and was mightily relieved when he spun, and raised his arms to his followers. 'To the temple!'

The rest were glad to leave. They lobbed their last few missiles and didn't stop to see who they hit, or where. With Domitian in the lead, we all ran together over the tiles, and down at the end to spring for the small postern gate.

Jocasta hauled it open and threw it shut behind us. She was filthy, and thin and scratched and smoke-stained and radiant.

Caenis was there with her. Vespasian's little Greek sparrow of a mistress dropped the bar on the big main gate. Others had already begun to stack tables and wooden beams against the gates, but they must have known that they were nothing more than imaginary boundaries.

I looked round for Pantera and lost him momentarily in the crush of huddled refugees that filled this old, dry, dusty place to capacity. More had joined through yesterday and there were over a thousand now, men, women and children. The gods of the temple had not received so many visitors since the ceremony of the lottery at which Geminus picked out Pantera's name from the bag, and Juvens had picked mine.

Sabinus was moving through the crowds, making sure the women and children had water, that the men were keeping their courage.

'Pantera!'

Quinctillius Atticus, the suffect consul, came striding from the libraries. He had made an office there, amidst the three thousand bronze tablets that held the senate's decrees going back to the start of Rome. Having spent the morning distributing leaflets castigating the emperor who had elevated him to consul, he sought safety now in the constancy and reliability of law.

He drew Pantera back under cover of the porch to a place between the columns, where they could talk. There, Jupiter stood ten feet tall in bronze, a perfect image of all that was good in Roman manhood. Juno stood a dozen paces away, only a little smaller; a matron with the face of a goddess. Minerva cast her arms wide, drawing in the congregated masses to her breast. Within the sacred triangle of these three, Atticus talked in stately whispers that echoed up to the roofbeams and were heard by us all.

'We need to get out of here. We're trapped and every man and woman here is named as a follower of Vespasian. If there are reprisals, their families will suffer.'

If there was ever a man who was likely to have drawn

reprisals on his family, it was Atticus. But hundreds of men heard him, and feared for their kin.

'Lucius is not here,' Pantera said. 'And Vitellius has more sense than to start purging the families of Rome. We need to block the temple gates and hold firm until Antonius Primus reaches us.'

Atticus' hands worked each other, knuckle on knuckle, a knot of anguish. He said, 'Lucius may return. And Vitellius takes his orders now from the Guard. The priests have shown us a hidden door in the southern wall that leads down to the Hundred Steps. If we leave now, we could be clear of here by noon.'

'And where would we go, consul?' Domitian had found us; it wasn't hard when every one of the thousand men and women was listening in on the conversation.

Vespasian's son leaned against a wall, his round face still scarlet, babyish without its brows. His gaze, though, was of a man who had tasted blood and found it to his liking. His voice carried easily to the edge of the crowd.

'The Guard has Rome locked down. The gates are manned; not a rotting corpse can get through but that they search the coffin for men hiding underneath. Antonius will come to our aid. We are as safe here as anywhere. I say we block the gates and wait.'

'And do it swiftly,' Pantera said. 'The Guards are nearly on us.'

The balance hung a moment longer; if the consul had been a leader of men, he could have gathered the crowd and made a run for the south gates and freedom. But the fates do not wait for the faint-hearted and there was a roar and thunder at the front gate that spun everyone round to face it.

'The statues!' Protocol was gone. Pantera was already shouting orders, and to hang with those who outranked him. 'Pull down the statues and set them across the gate.'

'The statues of the gods?' Domitian's eyes flew wide. 'The statues of Jupiter? Of Juno? Minerva?' Hoarse, disbelieving. 'They're *sacred*.'

'And they're made of bronze: they'll withstand rams and fire, perhaps for long enough to let Antonius reach us. Unless you can dismantle the temple and use the stone from the columns in time, there's nothing else to hand.'

The light was dying; evening slid in across the sky and the fires burning out on the hill were brighter now than the sun. Domitian was level with Pantera and me. The shifting shadows blurred his face; he was a child again, briefly, and then a man. He nodded. 'The gods have brought us this far. If they wished to stop us, they would have done it by now.'

He raised his head. He was not the bull-voiced warrior that was his father, nor even his brother Titus, who was a golden Ares, but his voice was strong enough, and the gods allowed that it did not break back to the high notes of childhood.

'Jupiter in his wisdom sent the rainstorm yesterday that kept us safe. Now he offers us his body, to use in our defence. In his name, we shall take the bronze statues and set them across the gates. Later, when Rome is ours, we shall offer sacrifices on this day every year, to thank him!'

He was Vespasian's son; his word was enough to get the huddled refugees to make a stand, but it took Pantera and me and, surprisingly, Horus to arrange them into coherent groups, ten to wrap ropes around each statue to topple it, with another three dozen strong men ready to take it as soon as it lay flat and carry it to the gates.

There, Jocasta directed the laying out, as in state, of each vast figure: Jupiter lay on his back, then Juno was set across him, head to toe, to prevent any uncivil, possibly sacrilegious suggestions of fornication.

These two blocked the main gates. Minerva blocked the smaller postern gate at the side, all alone.

There was a vantage point on the temple roof where it reared high enough to give a good view out across the hill; already two or three ragged ladders leaned against the walls leading up to it. With nothing left to do at the gates but pray to the gods who held us, we three climbed up and were in time to see Juvens lead his men from the barricades and across the Asylum from the Arx to the final hill.

They came as a storm-pushed wave; dark shadows of men in the darkening night, with fire all along their right side, casting their helmets in red, their faces in amber, their raised blades in gold.

Locked together, arm in arm, shoulder on shoulder, they ran at the smoke-blackened gates.

The force of their impact was a thunderclap loud enough to wake the dead, or the slumbering gods. Their shouts ripped through the throats of us who watched, leaving our chests shaking, our hands bunched tight.

The gods held. Under Juvens' shouted commands, the Guards took thirty good paces back and came again. And again. And again.

They were demons, dragged from the underworld, come to assault the citadel of the gods; and they failed.

CHAPTER SIXTY-FOUR

Rome, 19 December AD 69

Geminus

'Stop,' Juvens shouted, and then again, because nobody was listening, '*Stop!* Fall back. This is pointless. We could run at those gates all night; they're not going to fall.'

'We could burn them?'

The voice came from the dark and could have been anybody's. Already the priests' houses had fallen in on themselves, the flames dancing to nothing. The glowing embers were bright, but not bright enough to identify a man in a crowd.

It didn't matter who had spoken; it wasn't a good idea.

Irritably, Juvens shook his head. 'Can you not smell the damp? They've soaked the wood. It won't burn unless we pile half the city in front of it and I'm not going to destroy Rome just to get to an ageing fool and an adolescent boy. We're going back down the hill. There are other ways up to that temple.'

Juvens had time to plan his new strategy on the long run

down the north face of the Capitol. At the foot, he divided his men into three groups.

'Right, Sextilius, you're leading a feint back up the hill. Go up by the Gemonian steps so it looks as if you're trying to sneak up. At the top, start gathering wood to burn down the front gates. I don't think you'll succeed, but no harm in trying. Let them see you, but make it look as if you're trying to hide. Got that?

'Priscus, you'll take thirty men and go round to the Hundred Steps on the south side. See if you can emulate the Gauls, but if they start pouring down hot oil or sand, pull away. This is not about getting through, it's about splitting their attention.'

'Where are you going?' Priscus was young and ardent and too curious for his own good.

'We're going up through the tenement towers on the north-west face. There are one or two that stretch nearly to the height of the walls and they're in complete darkness, shaded by the temple walls. If we can get up there with a few ropes and some planks, we can build a bridge across to the temple and get over the wall in force. All we need to do is open the gates from the inside and Sextilius will be there, ready to run in.'

Sextilius was a year from retiring; Juvens and I both knew he had bought an inn and a girl and was looking forward to a long and profitable old age, which was why he had spent all summer avoiding the lotteries that sent men out to die on the streets, and we had let him. He owed both of us now and Juvens was calling in the favour.

Sextilius gave a sour smile. 'I and my men will be there.'

If there was ever a place Nero's building programme should have reached, the northwest foot of the Capitoline was it. Here, the tenements sprouted up along crooked alleys that smelled sourly of pig ordure and human urine; row upon row of unstable, old-wood, up to eighteen-storey blocks that leaned and leaked and loomed up into the night in a fire-fighter's nightmare of brisk inflammability.

Juvens had marked in his mind the tallest of the blocks, but standing at the foot, peering up, it was impossible to tell which one had the pale roof that had shown so clearly from the level top of the hill. He made a guess and prayed aloud to Jupiter that it might be right, and changed his prayer half made and sent it instead to Mars, who was more likely to listen than the god whose temple he was assaulting.

He kicked in a door and found an entrance hall where the smell of urine was so strong it made his eyes water. His men piled in behind him, coughing. It was the third night of Saturnalia; the only souls left in the tenements were the very young, the very old, or the very pregnant.

'Who are you?'

Standing in the nearest doorway was a dark-haired, wide-faced woman with a belly so ripe it looked ready to split apart. She stood with her hands on her hips, her spine arched back, her face fierce.

Juvens bowed. 'My lady . . .' She was almost certainly a whore, but he had been trained in manners from infancy and would not lower his standards now. 'We are Guards in the service of the emperor. We need to ascend to the roof of this building, that we might prevent the enemies of the empire from bringing their war to Rome.'

'Real Guards? Not bandits?' She didn't believe him, and why should she have done when the Guard had never penetrated that deep into the slums? She nodded over her shoulder. 'The roof's that way.'

The stairs were narrow and uneven. In places rats or rot had taken away a tread entirely and Juvens, running up, had to lengthen his stride mid-leap to avoid the gap. His men followed in train behind and the instructions filtered back down, level by level, to those still waiting to ascend. 'Mind out! That one! Jump!'

Juvens counted seventeen landings before the last. Breathless, he stepped into darkness. He carried no torch, but Gaius Halotus, three men behind, was carrying a smoking pitch-pine torch that sweetened the air and shed just enough light to see how tiny was this place, how close the walls, how fragile.

'No windows?' Halotus was a big man, huge on this claustrophobic landing. Doors led off, but were locked; Juvens tried them as soon as there was light enough to negotiate the old, dried turds and smears of vomit. He shook his head. Halotus pulled a face, looked around at the walls, picked a place where the mortar looked most rotten, leaned back and kicked.

Three bone-jarring, teeth-rattling strikes later the wall had a window, or a door, or whatever you might like to term the jagged opening that let in the clean night air and showed that they were two blocks too far north.

'Fuck.' Juvens leaned out. The temple was tantalizingly close, a wall not more than a few feet higher than where they stood, but just too far to reach.

The adjacent building was a bare five feet away, but the slope of its roof was tilted towards them, and without the ability to take a run there was a real risk of falling eighteen storeys to the ground below. His stomach swooned at the thought.

'Do we have planks?'

'Not enough, but we can make some.' Halotus had only a passing relationship with his civic duty of care for the city. Before Juvens could stop him, he had ripped a door from its hinges and was thrusting it through the newly made hole in the wall. It bridged the gap with a hand's span on either side; still terrifying, but workable.

Juvens, of course, had to lead the way across. Someone in

the early ranks up on the landing had a rope. They tied it round Halotus to act as an anchor and Juvens crawled across the rough wood, feeling paint flake off under his hands; he had no idea what colour it was, only that it was leaving raw wood that drove splinters into his knees.

But he made it across and stood and set his foot on the edge to hold it better for the next man, who took his place, and the third, who had brought a torch, but covered it at Juvens' whispered oath. 'If Sabinus sees us, we're finished.'

Unwilling to leave themselves lightless, the men clustered round it so that the light could not leak up to the temple on the Capitol. And they prayed that neither Sabinus nor any of his men looked their way.

They had reason to hope that they wouldn't; from the fires glowing bright again on the Asylum, it seemed that Sextilius was making good progress with his feint from that direction. What Priscus was doing round the south side was anybody's guess, but there were no screams coming from there, so Juvens allowed himself a measure of optimism.

His men were all across on to the middle tenement. Halotus came last, picked up the door and carried it under his arm to the far edge of the roof.

Here, the gods smiled on them; the adjacent tenement had leaned in towards the one they were on, cosily, like a gossiping neighbour. The gap between was a mere three feet and the men had room to take a run at it. Like boys winning a dare, they ran and jumped and tumbled and soon they were betting on it as a long jump that threatened to send some men out across the other side into oblivion.

'*Steady!*' Juvens' voice was a whip cracked across them. They gathered in the centre, laughing, and the moment was swiftly forgotten. They stood on the roof and gazed into the temple compound and then it was only a matter of readying themselves to cross the gap.

They were waiting for Halotus to bring the door when they saw the barrel of burning pitch fly out over the temple walls.

I still have no idea why that happened. You'd have to ask those who were inside if you want to know that, but there's no doubt it contributed to the disaster that came afterwards.

CHAPTER SIXTY-FIVE

Rome, 19 December AD 69

Caenis

Inside the temple, relief at the day's early success had dissolved in the dark. Braziers had been lit, casting everything in a feral, ruddy glow, but they brought no cheer; there was not enough food, few blankets and no wine.

Sabinus was a bent shape, moving amongst the comfortless groups, offering words of encouragement to the fearful, exchanging memories or words of hope with the stalwart.

I saw the best in him that night. The politician who was used to the back-stabbing, double-dealing, word-twisting of the senate became another man here, offering true comfort to those who needed it. He should have been a priest; it would have suited him.

Domitian was more erratic. For a while, he had been elated by his first taste of battle. When the Guards left, he stood on the wall and screamed invective at them. Later, when they were obviously returning in greater numbers, he turned his fury on Antonius Primus, who had not yet come to save him.

'He leaves us to die so that later he can claim Rome for himself. We should never have come up here. It's a death trap.'

When he tired of repeating that, he came to find Matthias and me and we retired to join Quinctillius Atticus in the law library, where Domitian passed the time rifling through the bronze tablets, reading old decrees passed centuries before he was born.

A knock rattled the door. Matthias ran to open it. Pantera stood on the threshold, with Sabinus a little behind him, and then Trabo. The brazier's red light showed them filthy, coated in ash and mud, scratched on arms and hands and face.

'My lord Domitian, my lady Caenis, Consul Atticus . . .' He nodded to each of us in precise succession although nobody made any pretence that any of us was in control of our defences: Pantera ruled us now. 'The Guards are mounting a diversionary assault on the front gate, but it appears they are also climbing up the Hundred Steps at the north side of the hill which, as we know, give access to the northern gates. We believe they may also be endeavouring to scale the tenements that lie against the temple walls on the forum side. Your lives are in danger. I know I argued that you should stay, but I believed Antonius Primus would be with us before this. If he comes now, he may well be too late. Accordingly, I would urge you to leave. We have found a way out over the wall behind the library, but those who are leaving must go now.'

'All of us?' I asked. 'You can get a thousand people out of here?'

'Not all. The emperor's family and immediate servants, and the consul. No more. And there is no time to waste.'

'I will not leave.' Sabinus was cloaked in calm. His words fell like the pronouncements of an Oracle. 'I will not abandon those who have placed their faith in my brother. Consul Atticus and I shall remain together and endeavour to negotiate with the Guard when they enter. If nothing else, it will give you time to get clear.'

'Sabinus!' Quinctillius Atticus fell on his knees. He has always been prone to over-dramatization and this was a splendid performance. 'We have to leave! If we go now, we can save our families. We can—'

'We are old men, Quinctillius. We will slow down the younger ones.' Sabinus' smile was peaceful, generous. 'Caenis of course must go. My brother would never forgive me if I kept her in danger.'

Pantera looked no happier than the consul. 'And your brother will never forgive me if I don't take you away now,' he said. 'I was sent to Rome with two tasks: the first was to take Rome bloodlessly, which I have manifestly failed to do. The second, and by far the more important, was to preserve Vespasian's family from harm.'

He quoted my love from memory, his eyes half shut, remembering. '"For if I am emperor and any one of them has come to harm, all the power in the world will not repair their loss." You are one of the three he holds most dear; you, his son and Caenis. Your safety is my first priority.'

'And yet if you tell him I ordered you to leave, and that I resisted all attempts to take me, he will understand.' Sabinus took Pantera by the arm, gently turned him round. 'We can stand here and argue, losing time, or you can accept what I say: that I will stay here with the consul and will negotiate with the officers of the Guard. If you have discovered – or created – a way out, you must use it now to take Domitian and Caenis to safety. I am the emperor's brother and I so order you.'

'They'll kill you.'

'They may not. Vitellius is a civilized man and he does still hold some sway with this rabble.'

Pantera's face was drained of colour, even in that place,

where the braziers turned everything red. He might have gone on arguing, but I said, 'Sabinus, are you sure?'

'I have never been more certain of anything. Go now. I will hold here. I served in Britain and that did not go altogether badly. We shall not give up without a fight and when we do, we shall demand our rights as civilized Romans.'

His brother had a stubborn streak and there was a painful familiarity in the man I saw before me now; never had he looked so much like Vespasian.

As Sabinus had done, I touched Pantera's arm. 'You'll have to take him by force if you want him to go and I think that may not be possible, if I understand how you plan us to leave?'

'No, my lady, it would not be possible.' Pantera swept his hands over his face. When they dropped again, the decision was made.

'My lord . . . Your brother will almost certainly crucify me, but I believe you are right. I honour your courage.'

'My dear.' Sabinus took my hand, drew me to him. 'We should have longer for this. Know that you have brought the light to my brother's life, and to mine, knowing him so happy. I would have liked to see you as his right hand on the throne, but you'll get there without me.'

'Sabinus . . .' I had known him since I was seventeen; the shy and distant boy of a not-quite-senatorial family who had become slowly, over decades, the big brother I never had.

We were too formal, too public. There should have been words, and there were so few, and all stuck.

'Brother . . .' My fingers cramped over his. 'He will know of this, and all else you have done for his cause.'

'I could ask for nothing more.' He pulled me into a quick, gruff embrace, a brief warmth and scents of smoke and sweat and home. I wanted to weep, but the moment was too great for that; it was not my place to spoil it.

'Go now,' he said. 'They are waiting.'

He gave a half-salute, such as men give on going to battle, and before I could say aught else I was being led at a half-run out of a side door in the library and we – Matthias, Domitian and I – were following Pantera westwards, to the wall that stood atop the precipitous eastern face of the Capitol.

We reached it swiftly, and without anyone seeing us. Trabo was there, and Borros, the big Briton. He stood wide-footed with his back braced against the wall and had made a stirrup of his looped hands.

Pantera said, 'Let me go up first.' He did so, and then sat astride with his legs dangling and leaned down.

'Caenis first. If it please you, my lady, Borros will lift you up until you can reach my hand.'

It didn't please me, but there was really no choice. The wall was ten feet high, if not more. Borros knotted his fingers into a platform and I took the same step Pantera had done and, stretching, was able to reach his hand. He gripped my wrist and hauled me up as if I were a sack of lamb. Scrambling, I made it up on to the curved top of the wall.

'If you sit on it, lady, you will be safest.' His eyes signalled an apology, but he was obviously right. I slid along to where he showed me and sat astraddle, in a way that would have scandalized the widows who were my neighbours and given them food for gossip for months. They were not the ones looking down the eastern face of the hill, at the sheer drop that fell away and away and away into the night. If we had tumbled then . . .

Domitian came next, and then Matthias and Trabo, who helped Pantera to haul Borros up.

'How are we to get down again?' I asked.

'There's a rope, lady. If I might climb past you?'

He had lizard feet, Pantera. He stepped lightly past me and went on a dozen paces and then lay on his belly on the wall and leaned down, and on the second or third try found what he sought. He whispered back, 'Borros!'

The big Briton made himself the anchor once again, and the rope dangled over the edge, down into the everlasting dark.

Domitian went first, stepping lightly down the wall with his legs braced against it. He seemed immune to fear that night. His father would have been proud of him. Trabo followed Matthias and then it was my turn. I couldn't move. I was frozen to the wall, staring at the height, terrified.

'My lady?' Pantera was behind me, standing on the wall's curved top. 'We need to lower you down. With your permission?'

He asked for my dignity, knowing I couldn't climb; of all the things I am grateful for that night, his care for me on that wall ranks amongst the highest.

He wrapped the free end of the rope around my waist and, with my feet braced against the stone, Borros and Pantera lowered me down until I felt Domitian's hands on my waist, helping me that last step, untying the rope that dug in beneath my ribs and made my breathing tight.

'Keep your back to the wall. Don't step forward. There is nowhere to go but down.'

I could feel it, the long drop to the foot of the Capitol. It sucked at me, sang to me siren songs of life swiftly gone, of an end to all care and fear and hope, for what use is hope when all is hopeless?

I thought of Sabinus and wished I hadn't. We were so close still to the temple; we'd have heard sounds of fighting if it had started, so it hadn't yet.

'Excuse me, my lady.' Shuffling past me on the tiny ledge, Pantera gave me a sickly grin. It felt better, knowing that he hated heights as much as I did.

With him in front, we all edged forward in the dark, testing each step as we went, keeping our right hands on the cold, slick stone of the temple wall and the other hand wrapped tight across our chests that we might not swing it out and pull ourselves over.

We reached a corner. Ahead, to our right, were the Guards who were assaulting the main gate of the temple. We had come round the side and there was a small gap before we reached the row of priests' houses, now largely burned out.

By the noise, there were Guards there in numbers greater than we had yet seen on the hill. They were not well ordered; I could hear the commands and counter-commands, but there was no doubt they were perfectly capable of killing us if they saw us.

Or they'd take us prisoner, which would be worse. Very badly, I didn't want to be the reason why Vespasian had to abandon his attempt, but I had no doubt, also, that he'd do exactly that if Domitian or I were to be taken by Lucius and threatened with harm.

They were a stone's throw away; less. Pantera drew Domitian, Matthias and me close and said, softly, 'Under the first of the priests' houses is a cellar room. The trap door has been badly burned but is still in place, and I think nobody will find it who doesn't know to look. The gap from here to there is ten paces.

'If I have timed it correctly, there will be a noise from inside the temple very soon. When this happens, you will keep your heads covered with your cloaks, your faces turned away from the light, and you will walk, not run, those ten paces on to the porch and in through the front door of the first priest's house.

'It will feel like a lifetime, but it is not. Borros, Trabo and I will protect you with our lives if the Guards see you. In that case, you will have to risk being seen. Run to the fifth house. It has a door in the back wall that leads out to a narrow path behind the row that leads down the hill. The silver-boys will hide you if you can get to the Street of the Lame Dog.'

'Pantera.' I caught his arm. 'If there is any chance of our being captured, I want your word that you will do for us what you did for Amoricus.'

He didn't know that I knew what he had done. His eyes swam with hurt. 'Lady, I can't—'

'You can. I order it. As your future . . .'

'As my empress,' he said, though we both knew I could never be that.

I said, 'I will not be used as a weapon against him. I would rather be dead. Is that clear?'

By way of answer, he slid his arm into his sleeve and brought out a small, wicked-looking knife, sharp on both edges of the blade and fining down to a narrow point.

'Take it.' He held it out, flat on his palm. 'For use in the last resort, if Trabo, Borros and I cannot help you.'

If we are already dead.

I had turned one of these down once, and regretted it. I took it. The hilt fitted perfectly into my hand. I prayed, briefly, to the gods whose temple we were leaving, that I would have the courage to use it at the right time.

As if in answer, a shout went up from behind the temple gates. A great ball of flame lobbed out, arcing up and over the wall, to fall down amongst the Guards. It was a barrel of pitch and it exploded as it hit the ground, sending hot tar over the nearest men. The noise, then, of screaming, shouting, weeping and cursing was like a wall of sound, crashing over us.

I barely heard Pantera's single word, 'Go', but I felt his hand in the small of my back and in my mind I repeated over and over, *Walk, don't run. Walk fast, don't run. Keep looking away. Don't look. Don't look. Don't—*

I was there, up the steps and in through the doorway. The

whole walk had been in shadow. The priest's house was a charred ruin, still smoking, still hot. I stepped in through a doorway that was little more than a pair of leaning doorposts with no lintel. Inside, the light of the blazing pitch barrel cast awkward shadows across the debris.

Domitian reached me, his face pinched and scared. He stared at me, hard, at the knife in my hand. 'Do you need to carry that?'

'For now, I do.' I had nowhere to put it, but even if Pantera had given me his little sleeve scabbard and strapped it on for me, I would have kept the naked blade in my hand. It was my touchstone for safety, my promise to myself.

Matthias came up on my right. His mouth moved in silent prayer. I realized I had no idea to whom he prayed.

Pantera joined us, then Trabo and Borros, together. 'This way.'

He led through the atrium into a small back room with a window that looked west, out over the cliff and down towards the city below where Saturnalia lights flared and flickered, tiny sulphur perforations in a sheet of night.

'Here.' Pantera knelt in the middle of the floor. The charred remains of a trap door stood upright on its hinges and below was a mellow light, as of a dozen wall lamps.

We descended down a ladder that had not been touched by the fire into a small room, half the size of my atrium, painted blood red on walls, floor and ceiling, with a statue on the northern wall of a young man killing a bull.

Two people were there ahead of us.

'Jocasta!' Trabo skidded down the last two rungs of the ladder and leapt towards her, his arms wide.

'Horus! I thought we'd lost you.' Domitian didn't run to the painted youth in the lilac gown, or embrace him, but I know that look, have felt it and given it, and his voice . . . I had never heard him sound mellow; always the opposite.

Just then, he was mellow. And he didn't so much as glance at Jocasta, which in itself spoke more than words could have done.

And so, and so . . . The trap door closed, softly. I glanced up and caught Pantera's eye and he gave a strange, quirked shrug that was at once apology and explanation. He knew and he hadn't told me. Very likely, he hadn't known what to say.

But he had sent these two ahead with orders to test the route, or on some other pretext, so that we were whole, and our hearts unbroken.

I said, 'What now?'

'We wait,' Pantera said. 'The force here are a diversion. The main attack is coming across from the tops of the tenements. They'll either open the gates and call these in, or call them back down the hill. We can hear them well from here. When they leave, we'll go out and down into the city. There are people there who will hide us.'

He was right, we could hear everything, there in the little Mithraeum.

And then, exploring, Domitian found a niche in the far wall from which arose a chimney that was not for fire, but for light. The priests of this place, perhaps fearing discovery – for what priest of Jupiter wishes it to be known that he secretly follows Mithras of the east? – had created an ingenious system of silvered discs set at angles that allowed us to see at least a measure of what was happening outside. Domitian said that Pythagoras had created such a thing, or perhaps it was Aristotle, he wasn't certain, but he knew how to angle the lowermost disc so that, by putting our eye to the gap and staring at the disc, we could see the feet and legs of the men who gathered in front of the row of priests' houses.

The rest of us found limited interest in the naked knees of Guardsmen, but Domitian stayed there, entranced by the mirrors and the ways they worked together, until his hoarse whisper filled the room. 'Fire! The temple's on fire!'

We all came to look then, and he was right, the temple was a great blazing beacon, shooting flame and sparks high into the night sky.

'Sabinus!' I wanted to go out, to shout at the Guard to let out the people trapped in the temple compound, but Pantera held me tight and would not let me go and after an age of desperate waiting Domitian said, 'They're coming out. Uncle Sabinus is with them. And the Guard, Juvens. Sabinus has surrendered to him in order that the people might be saved.'

We were proud of him then, you must understand that, even if it meant we were trapped. For of course we couldn't go out when a thousand people stood just outside the door, surrounded by the increasingly raucous Guards.

CHAPTER SIXTY-SIX

Rome, 19 December AD 69

Geminus

Nobody knows how the fire started in the temple on the Capitol hill. At least, nobody who speaks to me now, or who brought me messages at the time. It was the sacred heart of Rome; none of us wanted to live through what must happen to the empire if it burned to the ground.

Juvens' men say it was ablaze when they got there, that they organized bucket gangs to try to douse the flames. Those of Sabinus' contingent to whom I have spoken say that one barrel of fired pitch they threw out as a diversion was thrown back at them, and the temple, being old and dry and wrought of ancient wood, caught light like a tinder stack and the flames were unquenchable.

Reports from Juvens say he was on top of the tenements when he saw it, and knew what was needed. But it was eighteen storeys down to the nearest well and there was no way his own men were going to be able to stop the blaze.

It did mean, though, that he could abandon his earlier

secrecy. He spun to face his men, with the wild fire growing bolder behind him.

'Follow me! Find Sabinus and Domitian! Find the consul! Bring me anyone of consequence you can find. Don't let a single one escape or you'll answer to me!'

The flames had caught the temple, but the courtyard was still untouched. It was the work of moments for Halotus to throw their stolen door across from the third tenement to the wall and for Juvens to swarm across – *don't look down!* – and then on to the wall and down from it into the temple precinct. He was expecting a fight, and, indeed, Sabinus had marshalled the men inside and planned ways by which they might hold every entrance until morning.

The fire, though, had changed everything. As the temple blazed behind them, the assembled masses in the courtyard wanted nothing more than to open the gates and get out. They had nowhere to go, though, until Juvens arrived; Priscus' men held the Hundred Steps gate on the north side and the front gate had wood piled against it, leaving nowhere safe as an exit.

Juvens came over the wall to find silent, soot-speckled men and women waiting for him, standing in lines. One stepped forward; an elderly man, stooped a little, his hair dusted with ash.

'In the name of the emperor Vespasian,' he said, 'know that you are committing a crime against the state and will be punished for it.'

Juvens choked on a laugh. 'And you are?'

'I am his brother, Sabinus. And this is the consul, Quinctillius Atticus . . .' Sabinus signalled behind him. Any one of three or four men clustered at the crowd's head might have been the consul; he was certainly making no effort to be conspicuous.

Sabinus went on, 'We hold the rule of Rome until my brother's arrival, or that of his commander, Antonius Primus.

You have fired the Capitol, sacred heart of Rome, and for that you will answer. In the meantime, you have a duty to the people of Rome. We commend ourselves to your care.'

Juvens sucked in a breath. There was a protocol to be followed amongst men of noble blood. He said, 'Do you personally, Titus Flavius Sabinus, prefect of Rome, give yourself into my care?'

'I do.'

'Then if you wish to live, I would strongly advise you not to mention your brother's name or that of his generals in the presence of my men: too many of them remember the shame of Narnia.' He turned to his nearest officer. 'Halotus, put this man in chains. Find out which of those craven idiots is the consul and bring him too.'

'Where are we taking them?' Halotus was loyal, but not especially bright.

'To the emperor.' And then, because there was an un-forgivable flicker of confusion in the man's eyes – don't you *dare* ask which emperor! – 'To Vitellius. And you . . .' He rounded on a passing Guard. 'Find Domitian.'

'He isn't here,' Sabinus said.

'Not here in the temple? Or not here in Rome?'

'He has never been in the temple,' Sabinus said. 'And now he has left Rome.'

As Halotus led the older man off, the only certainty in Juvens' mind was that Sabinus had just lied to him. Which was why he was still with the mass of refugees he had herded out on to the Asylum, working his way personally through the sorry band of would-be rebels, hunting for the son of the usurper, when the catastrophe happened near the mint on the Arx.

He didn't see it, but he heard a cheer go up, of exactly the timbre and bloody enthusiasm of those in the circus when the beasts came out, or the gladiators fought to the death.

'Hades, no!'

He blasted away from the prisoners and sprinted down the slope and up the other side to the Arx, but he was too late to stop the frenzied stabbing, too late to stop Guards turned feral monsters from stripping the body of the man who had given himself freely into Juvens' care, too late to stop his desecrated corpse being flung to the foot of the Gemonian steps, the customary fate of convicted thieves and bandits.

He was in time to arrest the four men he had put in charge of the prisoner, but he didn't do it; there was no point, and he needed them: Halotus was the ringleader and the other three were amongst the bravest he had.

They hadn't killed Quinctillius Atticus, the consul, and so they were ordered to take him forthwith to the emperor, on the understanding that if he died they would watch the sun rise from the heights of a cross, and Juvens returned to the systematic search of the refugees, to be sure that Sabinus had not hidden his nephew amongst them.

He didn't find the boy before the heat of the burning temple forced him to bring the people away lest he roast them all. The courtyard acted as a kind of fire break, but in the temple itself the fire had become a monster, eating rock and wood and the bronze statues and laws and legacies beyond price. It destroyed centuries of Roman jurisprudence and the sanctity of Roman decency.

In the morning, he and I might hope to contemplate what it would take to rebuild it, but then, in the night, Rome was left to watch the biggest hill beacon in the history of her empire burn high into the sky.

That's when the war became real, I think, for the rest of Rome. They couldn't keep on pretending it wasn't going to touch them after something like that.

CHAPTER SIXTY-SEVEN

Rome, 19–20 December AD 69

Borros

After the fire-storm, the calm.

We huddled in that hidden underground shrine all night, with Domitian giving us a running commentary on what was happening outside.

We knew early on that they had killed Sabinus. We heard the animal shout – that light-tube brought sound to us too – but we didn't know what it was for until Juvens arrived at a flat-out run and began screaming abuse at his men.

Caenis took it particularly badly. She felt responsible, obviously, although there was nothing she could have done. Juvens should have controlled his men better; if anyone was to blame, it was him.

So we sat through the night and pretty much all we learned was that Pantera was virtually unbeatable at any game that involved bluffing, but he could be beaten at dice as long as it was only a straight roll and everything down to chance.

At a certain point, we nominated one corner to be a latrine, and all looked away as the ladies used it. The stink was vile. Being a slave, I was more used to it, but even so, three months of freedom had made me soft.

We thought we'd have to stay there through the whole of the next day while the temple on the hill burned out and probably we would have done, had not Juvens come back with about a thousand more Guardsmen and begun to forge a sense of order out of the chaos on the hill. Soon, the refugees had been herded down into the city until the place was empty.

We left after that, crawling out of our stinking hole, and scuttling the few dozen paces to the fifth house along, which had an exit in its back wall that gave on to a goat-path which led down the hill with a sheer drop on one side and the back walls of the houses on the other.

It was still dark, and on this side of the wall the blazing temple shed no light, so that we had to feel our way down in single file, one hand on the wall to our right, the other dangling out over nowhere. It wasn't as bad as the climb down from the temple wall had been, but all of us grew closer to our gods as we prayed for delivery from the certain death of a fall.

We were a subdued group who gathered at the hill's foot. Even the lady Jocasta was white and drawn and had no clever comment to make.

'Where?' she asked, as we reached flat ground. 'Where is safe?'

Horus said, 'The House of the Lyre.'

But Pantera said, at the same time, 'The Inn of the Crossed Spears.'

Given the choice, where would you have gone?

We all turned south, towards the House, but Pantera was in charge; he pulled us north, towards the Quirinal hill and the slums that run along the side. We were a sorry lot, slinking along the back alleys towards the inn.

The night was greying into dawn by the time we reached a hut three blocks from the inn. It was a ramshackle thing, with a goat-hide for a door that wouldn't have withstood even one Guardsman, but there was at least a bed, and water and food stored in a rat-proof barrel in the corner, and after the hole on the hill it felt like a palace. Domitian and Horus seemed to know it, and walked in as if it were home.

We drank and ate and laid Caenis down on the bed for rest, and then Pantera said to me, 'The next twelve hours are critical. Antonius Primus must be told what has happened. Will you come with me? Trabo can keep this place safe, with the help of the silver-boys. Trabo, if they whistle three short notes, rising, it means the Guards are coming and you need to get everyone out. Marcus will show you where to go. Follow him without question and do it fast.'

Trabo was as exhausted as everyone else, but he was more shattered by Jocasta's rejection of him than by the climb or the trek or the wait while the temple burned above us. He had gone down that ladder like a child expecting a gift and she had turned away from him, spurning him as clearly as if she had slapped him in the face.

I thought she might love Pantera, if any of us; certainly she never took her eyes off him and she had that look that women get sometimes, when they want to unscrew your head and lift out your brains and sift through them for all the hidden thoughts.

Anyway, Trabo was both desperately relieved not to be called away and desperately unhappy at being left with Jocasta. But he was a Guard at heart, for all he had tried to be a bandit, or a gladiator's cook. He needed people to protect and Pantera had just given him two women and the emperor's son to take care of. He didn't care about Matthias and could happily have lived without Horus, but it was clear that Horus and Pantera went back a long way and that to the spy the whore was as important in his way as Caenis or Domitian.

So Trabo sulked like a whipped child and stuffed his mouth with cheese and chomped on it miserably and, like that, we left them; a family flung together by fortune, and making the best of it.

Chapter Sixty-Eight

Trabo

O nce we were safe in the hut, exhaustion overtook us. Caenis was asleep on the only bed, blue prints of exhaustion layered under her eyes. Horus and Domitian sat with their backs to the far wall, propped on each other's shoulders, and they, too, were sound asleep. Matthias lay flat beside his mistress's bed and snored.

Jocasta and I were the only ones awake. If there had been another room, I would have gone to it: I couldn't bear the flat slide of her stare, the way it passed over me as if I didn't exist; worse, as if I were a slave who had let rip a particularly loud and noxious fart while serving dinner and was awaiting shipment to the circus.

I began to envy Domitian his ease in Horus' company. A whore is never going to cut you dead, even a highly paid one from the House of the Lyre. I took out my blade and began to scour it with the hem of my tunic; it wasn't useful, but it

471

was something to do. I felt Jocasta move across the room and come to rest beside me.

'Trabo?' She sounded doubtful. I kept my head down. She sat next to me; close. Her fingers caught my chin and turned my head so that I had to look at her. 'I'm sorry.'

'*What?*' Honestly, if Otho had come back from the grave, I couldn't have been more surprised. 'What for?'

She laughed, sadly. 'Everything. For the past days. For not being yours, or not obviously so.' She looped her arm through mine. I could feel the heat of her body, the rock of her breathing. I thought I had fallen asleep and was dreaming and didn't want to wake.

She said, 'What do you think Pantera is doing now?'

'I've no idea.' Nor did I care. She did, though, so I tried to concentrate. 'I'd say he's got out of Rome in some noxious garbage cart and is even as we speak relaying the details of Sabinus' death to Antonius Primus. He'll need to attack now, or we've lost all the momentum.'

'Pantera left you with Domitian?'

'Is that a problem?' I looked across at the sleeping boy. He looked like a child, and Horus the man.

'Only that you'll be blamed if Lucius were to find him.'

'Lucius is in the south. Pantera lured him down to Tarracina.'

'And you were taken there to prove it. And then brought back. Even so, Lucius still has agents here who do his bidding and he sends messages four times a day to Rome. What price do you think he would give for the chance to take alive Vespasian's son and his mistress? And, if not Pantera, then to take the spymaster who has worked against him from the start?'

Understanding snapped into place in my head. I should have known this. Why hadn't I? 'Are you the spymaster?' I asked.

'They call me the Poet.' She stared down at her fingernails. They were broken in places. I thought them beautiful. 'And Lucius knows it now.'

There was an accusation in her eyes that spoke more than her words. 'Pantera?' I couldn't believe it. '*Pantera* has betrayed you to Lucius? You can't be serious. They loathe each other. They've been prosecuting a proxy war with Rome as their battleground since he got off the boat last summer.'

'That's what everyone thinks, yes.'

'I don't understand.'

'From the beginning, from the day we met in Caenis' house, Lucius has been one step – one very small step – behind Pantera. All the way along, he knew where he was going and who he was going to see. Still, he didn't arrest him, or even have him killed, he—'

'Amoricus was captured alive. If Pantera hadn't killed him—'

'But he did. And we could all see how badly he was affected by it. Didn't we all grieve with him, didn't we all secretly want to take his arm, pat his shoulder, say don't worry, it wasn't really your fault; you did everything you could? Didn't we?'

'But why would he betray us? Why now, when he has been with us all summer?'

'Because there is no other time. If he waits a day longer, Vespasian might be emperor, Vitellius might be dead and Lucius with him, or exiled. And doubly now, because if you want truly to defeat your enemy, you have to let him extend himself to his – or her – fullest. He wanted to see what I knew, how much I could do, what lengths I would go to to get the right man on the throne. He thought he was going to be Seneca's successor. If he's going to kill me and take the network for himself, he needs to know as much about me as he can. Now, though, he has to act. What is the greatest prize in Rome just now?'

I was beginning to understand the way her mind worked. I looked across the room at the sleeping boy and the woman on the cot beside him. 'Them,' I said. 'Caenis and Domitian. If either or both is taken prisoner, Vespasian will offer any terms to get them back alive.'

'Well done.' She stood, held out her hand, lifted me up, kissed me, drily, lightly on the lips in a way that made my skin tingle. 'So let's get them out of here before someone comes to arrest us all. And don't imagine the silver-boys are on our side. I thought they were, but I have come to understand that their hearts belong to Pantera, and always have done.'

CHAPTER SIXTY-NINE

Rome, 20 December AD 69

Geminus

The burning of the temple was bad enough. We were all heart-sick at the sight of the blaze on the hill, smelling smoke in the air, tasting ash on everything we ate, wondering if the empire was coming to an end because of it.

Then Juvens came back in the dark time before dawn and brought with him news of Sabinus' appalling death and it seemed an omen too far: if the prefect of Rome could be slaughtered by a group of Guards running out of control, against the explicit order of their commanding officer, then truly the world had changed beyond all understanding.

I waited until after Vitellius had broken his fast to tell him.

He took it badly, as you'd expect. He also understood the extent to which his own life was even more precarious now: no chance of abdicating when his men had just slaughtered his rival's brother.

'We need to stop Antonius Primus.' He was pacing up and down the small audience room that had become his study, his dining room and his conference chamber, although he only conferred with me, Juvens and Drusus now. 'We need to take the heat out of this, for the sake of Rome. Who can we send to Antonius Primus? Who will he listen to? Not you,' he said to me and Juvens before we could answer. 'I need you here.'

'The Vestals?' I offered. 'No one will touch them, and it would not be the first time they've sued for peace in the name of Rome.'

He stared at me, frowning, with a look unnervingly like one Lucius might have given. Then he broke into a broad smile.

'Brilliant!' He clapped my shoulder. 'Arrange it in my name.'

He was direct now, succinct; the man he could have been if his mother and brother had not spent fifty years telling him how weak he was. 'And find Vespasian's kin; Caenis and the boy, Domitian. They'll be in the city somewhere, I feel it in my water. With Sabinus gone, they're our best chance of getting out of here alive.'

CHAPTER SEVENTY

Rome, 20 December AD 69

Borros

The early hours of the morning found Pantera and me in a side alley about three streets away from the hut where we'd left Trabo and the others; in essence, we'd run round a couple of corners and stopped.

Pantera had left me standing at the street's end with orders to keep a lookout, and then hopped on to a wall, and from there up on the rooftops where he dropped out of sight into some hidden hollow.

He returned some short time later, looking satisfied, and we walked on through the waking city, with every street lit by the burning temple, every house smeared with soot and ash.

We passed slaves and freedmen in the street, vendors and craftsmen, setting up for the day. None of them paid us any attention, nor we them until we came at last to a particular bakery where the ovens were already fierce and the scents warm, crisp and mouthwatering.

In the store room to one side we found Marcus eating newly baked cake; that was the blond-haired Marcus who led the silver-boys and had so discomfited Trabo earlier in the year.

I didn't listen to their conversation, but I can tell you it was short and swift and Pantera came out of this one, too, looking as if what he planned was going well.

'Do you suppose Cavernus is awake at this hour?' he asked.

'The entire staff of the White Hare was required to be up with the sun when I was there,' I said. 'On the day the temple burned down, I'd be surprised if they weren't up all night.'

'Then with luck we can go there and eat, and perhaps sleep. It's going to be a long day.'

'Antonius Primus . . . ?'

'Will hear what has happened from a dozen mouths. We don't need to speak to him personally.'

Pantera didn't look tired. He looked like a man whose life had suddenly sharpened, but I was exhausted and I wasn't going to turn down the offer of sleep. So we went to the tavern that had been my home for eighteen years and Cavernus greeted us like royalty — discreet royalty, which must be hidden, but royalty none the less — and gave us food and a little wine and a bed to sleep in and there would have been a girl to warm it if either of us had wanted.

For myself, unconsciousness came as I fell on the bed. Pantera, I think, made himself lie down and close his eyes as an act of will, but he was too vibrant to slip into sleep.

Marcus tapped on our door a couple of hours later, with news that Domitian, Caenis and the others had moved from the hut near the Crossed Spears and were believed to be heading in the direction of the Aventine.

Our task, I learned, was to find them and then follow them, discreetly. The silver-boys guided us with occasional whistles and many gestures, but our progress and theirs was hampered by the crowds who had emerged with the dawn. Some had come to stare at the fire, but most had gathered to watch the procession of Vestal Virgins make their way down from the emperor's palace on the Palatine, through the forum and down toward the Tiber. Rumour said they were going to meet Antonius Primus on the far side of the bridge on the Flaminian Way; he had come that close to the city.

We were near the forum when we first saw them: a column of women, dressed and veiled all in white, with white and red ribbons in their hair and criss-crossed on their bodices. They seemed to float, so slowly did they move, and in utter silence; they were attended by none of the horns and drums and pomp that customarily announced Roman ceremony.

Their bodyguards were vast men bearing bundles of rods and axes with which to deter the inappropriate attentions of lesser mortals, but even they kept a seemly distance from the white apparitions. The only people permitted to approach the Virgins were their hand-matrons; former Vestals who remained to serve their younger, still-chaste sisters. They, too, were dressed in white, but their ribbons were blue to show that they no longer tended the sacred flame.

They moved to and from the Vestals to the gathering crowd dispensing favours: dates and apples in accordance with the Saturnalia; small denomination coins; slips of paper with exhortations and prophecies: *Fortune favours you*; *Honour those who support you*; *Begin each day gladly, and it will end so.*

Simply to be gazed upon by a Vestal could free a condemned man from his execution. On the day after the temple burned, with the smoke still billowing up from the top of the Capitol hill, everyone wanted to fall under their stare. They were the nearest thing Rome had to living gods and we all needed their goodwill.

The mood of the crowd was strangely erratic. There wasn't

a man, woman or child there who didn't think Rome was on the road to certain ruin; the temple had gone and their emperor had all but abdicated, both things unheard of in the city's history. On the other hand, it seemed as if the gods had simply taken the inversions of Saturnalia and pushed them to their natural limit. The emperor was no longer ruler. The people were no longer safe. Anything was possible.

So the crush of the crowd grew denser with every passing heartbeat and we were caught up in it, helpless as a pair of corks in the ocean; for a while, it was all Pantera and I could do to keep sight of each other, never mind follow anyone else.

No one gave us any favours and we broke out eventually, but we had lost touch with Marcus in the chaos and when we found him again his cocky know-everything air had gone.

'We lost them.'

'What?' Pantera could make a single word sting like a sword cut. 'Where?'

'In the crowd. Not ten paces away. They were there, all of them, and then they were gone.'

Pantera's gaze cut us both equally. I had never been afraid of him, but I was then. 'Find them,' he said. 'Our lives and the future of the empire rest on it.'

CHAPTER SEVENTY-ONE

Rome, 20 December AD **69**

Trabo

In a city layered with a fine mist of ash, the silver-boys
were everywhere; I'd never known the streets of Rome
so infested with small boys. Every rooftop had one, every
side alley had two and their whistles meshed us in a net of
sound just as the falling ash from the temple fire meshed us
in filth.

We thought the Vestals had been sent by the gods to protect us from Pantera. The crowd around them was like an
army, the front row solid as a shield wall.

I was set to break through, with my shoulder angled down
and to the fore as we did in the Guards. Domitian was with
me; he must have read of the tactic, or seen his father show it
off, or his brother.

But Jocasta dodged into a side shop and came out with
cloaks and hoods – she must have paid for them, but the
bargaining was very brief – and said instead, 'The best place
to hide is in a crowd. All we have to do is change how we

look and we can get in amongst the people, become one of them. Do it quickly. The silver-boys are everywhere.'

I caught Domitian's eye and gave the nod, and together we pushed the crowd open a little to let us all in. As soon as the pressure was off, the mass of men and women closed again behind us, solid as a dungeon door, trapping us in, but trapping out Marcus and his light-footed spies.

We kept close in our pairs, me and Jocasta, Horus and Domitian, Caenis and Matthias. Of them all, Caenis and Matthias had been hardest to persuade into coming; Caenis would not have it that Pantera intended anything other than the best for her and Vespasian and, by inclusion, Vespasian's son. It took Domitian himself to point out that her house had been burned to the ground because Pantera had been seen going into it and that no decent man would have allowed that.

Bunched together, keeping watch each for the other, we were swept up by the crowd that surged in the Vestals' wake down the Palatine, and across the open space of the forum.

It was there, or close to it, that I saw Pantera standing on the margins with blond-Marcus to his one side and Borros to the other. He looked as thunderously angry as I've ever seen him, and he was clearly searching for us. I tipped my head down, let the hood of my cloak fall further over my face.

From the corner of my eye, I saw Jocasta's vindicated smile. 'I'm sorry,' I said.

'Don't be. Loyalty is a coin of infinite value, only some-times it needs to be spent with more care. Still, we need to get out of here. He'll work out soon enough how we got past him. I would.'

That was easy to say and harder to do. We were swept slowly out of the forum, leaving behind the temples and the ugly statue of Nero, and on down the Flaminian Way.

We passed on north, with the Aventine to our left, past

the circus and all the gladiator schools, past the temple to Claudius. We were heading out towards the markets that lined the Tiber, towards the bridge that was the front line of Vitellius' defences, when a flash of colour caught my eye: cowled robes in vermilion and midnight blue, worn by a huddle of shifty-looking individuals. Then one of them turned round and what I saw wasn't human.

'What the fuck is *that*?'

My voice was a squeak, my blade half drawn. Horus put a warning hand on my arm. 'Don't. They're priests. It's a mask.'

'Anubis,' Domitian said, in wonder. 'Dog-headed god of the Underworld. Are they Alexandrians?'

'They're priests of Isis,' Horus said. 'There's a temple behind the water tower that's said to have greater wealth than any other in Rome. They'll be taking it out of the city before Antonius' legions come in and decide to sack it.'

Jocasta said, 'And this is their best chance; nobody is going to commit acts of war while the Vestals are in procession. If they can leave now, they'll be safe. Shall we join them?'

Her smile was all challenge. Caenis saw it and bit her lip, but Domitian had begun to catch the fever of the day.

'Who has gold? Isis is only rich here because the priests love the sight of it.'

'I do.' Jocasta untied her belt. Along the back was sewn a pouch exactly like the one I had worn when I came into Rome. She hadn't used hers as a weapon, but she could have done; it was easily heavy enough. When she opened it, we saw gold glimmer softly inside.

'I have enough here to pay a dozen men for a year. Trabo, I believe you can match it?'

I could, and I did. There was something of an altercation when we first joined the group, much vermilion flouncing by the priests, whose dog-headed masks prevented them from offering coherent argument, but Jocasta opened her hidden purse and poured out her gold, and I joined her, and very swiftly the muffled grunting stopped.

A tall figure at the back spoke a sharp order in a language I didn't know and someone nearer to us lifted the mask, revealing a woman of mature years beneath.

'What for do you offer this?'

She wasn't Roman, clearly, but nor did she sound Alexandrian.

'For sanctuary amongst the people of Isis,' Jocasta said. 'We must leave Rome *incognito*. In the name of the Chosen, who is our personal friend, we would ask that you let us join your procession. When, in the coming days, the rightful emperor sits on the throne, your reward will be ten times what we offer now.'

Domitian started forward. 'My father—'

Jocasta's glance silenced him more effectively than anything I could have said, but still, in those two words he had revealed everything.

All the priests except the tall one at the back removed their masks then, and were exposed as men and women in equal numbers. Another short order came from the hidden one, at which the elderly priestess, with obvious regret, said, 'Keep your gold, lady. In the name of the Chosen, and of the god, we shall usher you in safety across the river. We go to our temple, which is some half mile beyond the bridge. Will that please you?'

'It will please us beyond saying.' Jocasta tipped her coins back into her purse. She nodded past the rest to the tall, masked figure at the back. 'We thank you.'

CHAPTER SEVENTY-TWO

Rome, 20 December AD 69

Geminus

How do you find one small woman and one youth in a
city of millions? How do you find them when there are
twenty thousand armed men standing at your gates waiting
to enter the city – and they will have no trouble at all finding
the man they seek because your emperor insists on staying in
his palace, which is the first place they'll look?

The Vestals had agreed to take our offer of terms to
Antonius, which had at least bought us time to look for
Domitian and Caenis, but we had failed to find them. And
then came the Vestals' answer, brought by one of the blue-
ribboned matrons and three monstrous lictors.

I relayed it to Vitellius in private.

'Antonius Primus says no. He has turned down the Vestals'
plea for peace. He says that all hope of armistice vanished with
Sabinus' death and he will attack today. To make it easier for
both sides to identify their own men, he has issued his forces
with blue armbands, that being the colour Vespasian favours.

They have sworn never to take them off in an effort to appear other than they are, even if they have been cornered by our men and are facing certain death. He suggests we colour our men green on the same basis. Accordingly, he has sent us three bolts of green silk as his gift.'

Vitellius stared at me flatly, running his tongue round his teeth. 'Pushy little man, as I remember,' he said. 'Did your men learn anything from their trip across the river?'

Eight of my men had dressed as lictors and accompanied the Vestals into Antonius' camp, to assess the enemy numbers and their dispositions, their morale. I said, 'They report what we already know: that Antonius Primus has at least twenty thousand men straining at the leash, in high morale, desperate to attack.'

'Nothing new, then.' Vitellius was sounding ever more like a general. His tone was dry and self-mocking, not the piteous weeping of the day before. 'Have we found the boy Domitian yet? Or Caenis?'

'Not yet, lord. And now it can no longer be our priority. I should be out there with the men. We have to hold Rome until Lucius gets here.'

'When will that be?'

'Three hours after our messengers reach him, I hope.'

Four had been sent, none had yet returned, nor had any others arrived to us from Lucius, but Vitellius didn't need to know that.

I said, 'He'll be here within the day. In the meantime, Drusus will take care of you. If—'

Drusus coughed discreetly from the doorway. 'Lord?'

He stepped back and a figure entered coated in fine white ash so that for a moment he looked like an albino. It wasn't until he stared at me and Vitellius simultaneously with his uneven eyes that I knew who he was.

'Felix!' I bounded forward. I could have kissed him: he was

one of the four I had sent to Lucius and I had despaired of ever seeing him alive. 'What news?'

The boy was fizzing with a strange kind of energy that I could not read. Vitellius could, though; he had grown up with Lucius and knew the signs.

'I think he has recently killed, is that not so, child?'

The boy flushed scarlet to the roots of his pale hair. 'There were more bandits on the road, lord. I had to—'

'I'm sure you did. Do you bring word from my brother?'

'I do. He had not time to write, but he entrusted me to say this to his brother, the emperor . . .' He screwed up his eyes and, in a voice not entirely unlike Lucius', said, 'Give my apologies to my dearly beloved brother, and tell him that I am in the midst of heavier fighting than I had anticipated, but that none the less I will be in Rome three days from now, perhaps sooner if all goes well.'

'Three days?' Vitellius gaped. 'Who is he fighting?'

Felix looked confused. 'Men, lord?' he offered.

'Men!' Vitellius laughed, hoarsely. 'Gods preserve us.' He looked at me, his eyes raw with loss. 'Three days until my brother comes. I make that about two and three-quarter days too late, wouldn't you say? Even if he wins against his so-tenacious rebels, which he may well not do.'

At least we knew. I said, 'Lord, you must leave. Go to the Aventine, if you will not flee Rome. You're offering yourself as a sacrifice if you stay in the palace and there's no point in that.'

'What will you do?'

'With your permission, I will join Juvens in defence of the city. I am more use out there than in here. I will keep an eye out for Domitian and Caenis, but only fools will be out in the streets with the fighting that is coming and they are not that. I beg you to let me go. Drusus will protect your person better than I ever could.'

My emperor was not a vindictive man, and he knew what I wanted. 'Go, then. Do what you must.'

He had an idea, then; I was learning to recognize the signs. I saw him think a moment, then take off yet another of his many rings and hold it out to Felix. 'Do you know how to talk with the silver-boys, child?'

A sudden craftiness entered Felix' features. 'It may be possible, lord.'

Lucius would have had him hanging from his wrists over a slow fire until he got the truth out of him, but we didn't care; this boy had got through to us when three others had failed. That his message was bad was not his fault, and personally I wouldn't have cared if he'd killed half the Guard to get it to us.

Ever aware of the power of gold, Vitellius placed the ring in the boy's grubby palm and folded his fingers over it.

'This and the titles that go with it are yours if you can talk to the silver-boys and get them to help you find Domitian, younger son of Vespasian. He's in the city somewhere and we would bring him to safety before the fighting starts. His life is at risk if he remains at large; tell him that.'

It was tactfully done. Felix clasped the ring to his chest, his pale eyes shining. 'Lord, I will find him,' he said, 'and make him safe.'

For a long time after he had gone, Drusus wore a small smile on his face, like a father whose favoured son has performed a deed of great valour.

Three being the number for luck, I wound my emerald-green scarf three times around my upper arm, which was fine, except that the flapping ends spooked the rangy bay gelding the stable master had sent for me.

Wincing, the boy who had brought him said, 'He's fast, master. You asked for the fastest. I could get something quieter . . .'

'No. It's fine. You did well.' I tossed out a silver piece as I mounted; when you may not see tomorrow's dawn, today's generosity is easy.

The boy's eyes shone. He threw up his hand in salute. I pointed the horse out of the gates and trusted its nerves to see me across the city.

I found Juvens in a sea of Guards, at the place where the Flaminian Way became Broad Street. He was organizing his cavalry across the road with his men behind.

Juvens' men were mine, too: men who had marched with us from the Rhine to the Tiber in support of their emperor; men who defeated Otho, who sacked Cremona the first time.

They were dressed for valour; none of the subtlety of the Guard now. They wore their tunics with their weapon belts in full display; great discs of silver that spoke of heroism and success to anyone who knew how to read them. Their helmets came from their war chests, not the plumed and polished frippery of parade, and, today, they had liberated their shields from the armoury; truly, they were legionaries once again, not Guards, and happier for it. Every one wore an emerald silk band about his arm with a pride and defiance that augured ill for Antonius' forces.

Juvens himself was on foot and helmetless, his flame-yellow hair visible across half the city. He looked dirty and tired and elated.

Nobody was proud of what had happened to Sabinus, but equally everyone was clear that the taking of the Capitol had been a tactical and strategic masterstroke and Juvens had organized it virtually single-handed. He basked in the glory, and his men – our men – basked with him.

It was noon. The Vestals had been back in the city for over an hour. Antonius' army was armed and ready and keen for blood.

'Where are they?' I asked.

Juvens nodded over my shoulder. 'Just across the bridge. They can see us; we can see them. The Blues can't cross the bridge yet: we're too many for them, but I'd bet my pension that they'll try a flanking move on one or other side. We have horn signals set in case they do.' He caught my eye and grinned. 'We didn't ask for this, but, Hades, I'm glad it's come.'

'You're not alone.' It wasn't just that our men were ready; the whole population had turned out for this.

All about, men, women and children sat in family groups on the balconies and rooftops, on the tenements and cottages and villas that clustered up to the river's edge. They were dressed in their multicoloured festival best, eating apples and dates and drinking wine, even the children. A small girl saw me looking and threw up her hand.

'Io Saturnalia!'

Her high, lark's voice carried over the street to the far side and was picked up by other children, and then their parents, uncles, aunts, cousins, friends; last, by our men.

'*Io Saturnalia!*'

'Roman fighting Roman. We're better entertainment than the circus, and in the right colours, too.' I fiddled with my green scarf, tucking in the loose ends. 'Where do you want me?'

'Wherever you'd like to be. We'll live or die where we stand. Nowhere is safer, or less safe, than anywhere else.'

'Then I'll stay with you, if you don't mind.'

I wasn't as well dressed as the men. My belt was plain leather, but that was all I needed; I had my gladius and some-one handed me a helmet. It slid over my head, cool about my ears, and I felt whole again, almost.

Chapter Seventy-Three

Caenis

You will know as much about our trip north across the river as I do: it was you who gave the order that we be taken across, was it not?

I didn't know you then, behind your mask. It was only today, remembering, that I realized where I had seen you before. Your voice, of course, is instantly recognizable, although it has taken me until now to realize that it was you who spoke to the priests and told them to take us. I had heard of Hypatia of Alexandria, of course, but I had never met you.

Does Pantera know you were in Rome? I thought not. And I suppose we shall never know if he would have acted differently if he had believed he had your support. Perhaps it is better this way; we knew, in the end, the lengths to which he would go to get what he wanted. The gods work to their own design, but we are grateful to yours for her care of us, never think otherwise.

So, as you will have seen, we walked sedately across the

491

river as part of the column of Anubis-priests and our disguise could not have been more complete.

We paid for our safety; the dog's-head masks stank of glue and sweat and paint. It was as hot inside as the steam room had ever been at the baths.

I couldn't see except in a line straight ahead, and even then sweat filled my eyes and blurred the road ahead. I carried a basket that clunked with every stride and felt as if it were filled with apples made of solid gold; I was never allowed to look inside.

Walking blindly, I followed the vermilion robes ahead, the high white ears of Jocasta's mask. She floated the way the Vestals had floated. I stumbled in her wake, but did not dare veer aside: I had no idea why she had done what she had done, but she had, in effect, taken custody of Domitian and I dared not let her out of my sight for fear of what she might do.

We passed through the lines of Vitellius' men, across the bridge – it echoed hollowly under my feet and we had to break step, as the legions do, not to cause it to collapse – and then through the lines of Antonius Primus' men on the far side. They were in high spirits, and desperate to fight, but we were priests of a god respected by both sides in this war, and no soldier was keen to incur divine anger in the hours before battle.

Guards stepped aside to let us pass and I saw the shimmer of iron, smelled the leather, felt the tense, dry-mouthed waiting.

We left the infantry behind, passed through the horse lines and then the cooks' lines, and finally turned off the road down a small dirt track that led, several tight turns later, to a temple built in the Alexandrian style, of white stone, with narrow, fluted columns and white-painted double doors that looked thick enough to withstand a year's violent siege.

Inside, we were divested of the hateful masks, shed our robes and stood around feeling awkward while the priests set about hiding their treasures in hollowed spaces under the floor pavings.

I saw statues of the goddess carved in the likeness of a young woman, images of Anubis, of Osiris, of the warrior goddess Sekhmet, depicted in her guise as a lioness. Not all were solid gold, some were crystal, ivory, ebony and marble; all were exquisite.

The interior of the temple was high-roofed and airy, hung about with silk banners in the same midnight blue and vermilion as our robes.

The priests didn't speak to us much. We had been offered sanctuary out of expediency, but now we were here, they didn't know what to say to us or we to them. We were offered a place to sit on white marble benches opposite the carved marble altar and did so, primly, not speaking. What does one say in the presence of a foreign god? I thought that Jocasta was more at ease than any of us, but even she was quiet.

I heard the trumpets sound the advance at the bridge and knew the fighting had started. I twisted round in my seat, trying to see out of the door. It was closed, but opened as I looked, so that I heard the first shouts of command, the first roar of battle, the clash of weapons, and death.

And then I saw who had stepped in through the open door, and it was not a priest.

Trabo saw him too. He erupted off the bench beside me, blade already slicing forward for the exposed neck. The intruder took a fast, fluid step to the back, to the side, out and round, and was behind him. 'Not me,' Felix said, quietly. 'I truly don't think you want to try to hurt me.'

There was a moment's shocked silence, then Jocasta said, 'That's true. We are your friends. Why would we hurt you? Trabo, if you please?'

Trabo was Jocasta's in soul and sinew; however unhappy, he didn't have the power to turn her down. He stepped away, half-formed oaths muddying the air about him.

Felix didn't move, but the look on his face was one Pantera could have modelled, just as the swift, clean disengage had been. Evidently, this boy was his master's apprentice.

'Did Pantera send you?' Jocasta asked.

'Vitellius sent me. I am sworn to find Domitian and make him safe.'

'Safe?' I gave a hoarse laugh. 'Vitellius wants to take him into custody so he can use him to keep the throne.'

'Still, he said he wanted him kept safe and I said I would.' The boy smiled, angelically. 'I didn't say I'd take him back. He forgot to ask me that.'

His uneven gaze roamed the benches, alighting briefly on each of our faces. He frowned. 'Borros isn't with you?'

'Borros is with Pantera,' Jocasta said. 'Did you not see him as you came through the forum? He was just behind us.'

'I didn't come through the forum. There were too many people. I knew you must try to flee Rome, so I came straight to the bridge and waited for you there.'

'And noticed us disguised amidst the group of priests.' Jocasta favoured him with a smile that made Trabo's bones melt. 'That was well done.'

She didn't ask him how he had picked us out when we had believed ourselves to be invisible. Clearly, she thought to let his pride do that for her.

But Felix was not like other men; he didn't need her approval, and did not respond to her tacit invitation, just stood there, still frowning, chewing lightly on his lower lip.

It took Domitian to get an answer from him. Vespasian's son said, conversationally, as to a friend, 'What did we do wrong? We thought we were invisible to anyone Vitellius might send.'

'You will have been.' Felix shrugged, loosely. 'But my lady Jocasta wears boots made by Leontus on the Aventine and there are few other tall women in Rome who do that, and none at all who walk side by side with a man of Trabo's stature who strides like a legionary on the march.'

Jocasta maintained an admirable composure. Trabo was visibly upset. They had thought the boy stupid because he had a squint, and were only now realizing their mistake.

'I'm sorry, my lord, lady . . .' Felix offered a sad smile to their discomfort. 'I don't think Vitellius knows it. Certainly, he didn't tell me how to pick you out when he sent me to look for you.' His gaze cleared. 'You will want to find Pantera? He was on the road north from the forum. I passed him.'

'No!' said Domitian.

But 'Yes!' said Jocasta at the same time. 'We would very much like it if you could help us find Pantera. Most likely, he will know where Borros is. Perhaps the lady Caenis and I could come with you? Trabo can remain here with Domitian, Matthias and Horus. We can bring Pantera back when we have found him.'

Was I a hostage? It certainly seemed like that. In one stroke, Jocasta was separating me from Domitian, so that I could not know what was done with him. I looked at her and received only a bland smile, which I returned in kind, saying, 'Certainly. That would be wise. Above all of us, Domitian must be kept safe.'

I could have challenged her, perhaps, but one of the things I learned in Antonia's court is that things gather a power of their own when they are spoken aloud. Let her think me compliant; let her underestimate me as she had done Felix; let her make just one mistake . . .

The priests came to see us leave, and to swear that their god would protect Domitian as long as he remained in their care.

The obvious corollary was that, in leaving the care of Isis, we three were putting ourselves in danger. We bowed and thanked them and promised gifts to the god on our return.

As we left the sanctuary of Isis' temple, Felix threw me a dazzling smile. I found him really rather charming, in his own strange way. Then we stepped out of the door and all we could hear was the battle for Rome, and the sounds of men dying.

CHAPTER SEVENTY-FOUR

Rome, 20 December AD 69

Geminus

'Step up! Shields locked! One step forward! . . . Hold that line!'

Days, months, years of training were tempered here, in the heat of battle. Men moved without thinking, their bodies responding long before their minds caught up, and the wall they made with their shields was flawless.

Against other legionaries, we would have been unassailable, but Antonius' blue-scarved cavalrymen brought their long spears when they came at us from the side – Juvens had been right about their flanking manoeuvre – and they drove them over the tops of our shields as if we were barbarian warriors, not fellow Romans.

I felt iron hiss past my right ear and jerked to my left, cracking my helmet hard against Juvens' – he had mirrored my move.

We bounced upright again, and ducked back down as the spears twisted and stabbed. Left and right, green-marked men were falling. Others stepped in to take their place, but there was only one way this could go if we stayed as we were.

'We need to move back!'

It was hard to be heard over the din of battle; iron clashed on mail, on iron, on flesh. The air flowed hot with lifeblood, the ground was a smear of ordure and spilled intestines.

I shouted it again, to my right this time, where the signallers stood. 'Sound the turn! We need to move back up the street. Form a square, wheel right, shields to the outside, back up the street. Can you do that?'

Even as I shouted, a spear thrust caught the signaller in the throat and he went down like a felled tree. The nearest legionary caught his horn almost as a reflex – it doesn't do to lose the signals in battle – but he was looking at it as if he had never played one in his life.

'Give me that!'

I grabbed the horn, put tight lips to a mouthpiece still warm from the man just dead, and prayed for help in remembering how to play.

The help came. I was rusty, but adequate, and the notes were a ripple of silver rising over the black mess of battle.

As before, decades of training paid off and our men spun and wheeled to my direction, but the enemy knew the signals just as well as we did and at every turn or counter-turn the blue cavalry was already waiting, and, soon, mass upon mass of infantry, as Antonius Primus loosed his reserve cohorts into the fray.

'Back! *Back!*'

Fighting, we fell back into the city. The enemy forces came at us like a flood. Every street was a butchery, every open square an ambush. The people were up out of harm's way, but we were left on the ground, caught in an orgy of killing.

I fitted my shoulder to Juvens' and hacked and hacked and—

'Shit! Disengage. Left in a hundred paces! *Now!*'

With me and Juvens were Halotus, Lentulus and Thrasyllus, whose father had disowned him for following Vitellius; good men, all of them; friends.

On my command, they disengaged and sprinted for the dark mouth of an alley ahead and to our left. The Blues-men we had been fighting saw the open street we had just abandoned and preferred it to a black, stinking alley that might have held a hundred of us. They forged on past, leaving us standing in the dark.

We watched their retreating backs. Juvens was half bent, with his hands propped on his knees. He peered up at me from below the flop of his hair.

'Why this way?'

'Because I just saw Jocasta come down here with Caenis, Vespasian's woman, and the boy who sold himself to us as a messenger.'

'Jocasta? You mean Lucius' lover?'

'Lucius' lover who also seduced Caecina before he marched north and defected,' I said, flatly. I had a very bad feeling about this, but that didn't matter compared to the prospect of catching Caenis. 'If we can take these three alive, we can secure the throne for Vitellius and his line for the next hundred years. They can't be far ahead of us.'

Juvens pushed himself upright. He straightened the flowing green scarf at his arm, re-tied the knot. 'That's easy then. We get into pairs and search every house in the row. If we can't catch two women and a youth barely shaving, we deserve to lose Rome.' He threw me a grin. 'Half a year's pay says that if Jocasta's here, then Trabo's not far behind. If he turns up, leave him to me. I have an oath to Jupiter, and after last night's fire now would be a good time to keep it.'

It was the closest I had heard him get to accepting responsibility for what happened at the temple, and by then it didn't matter.

CHAPTER SEVENTY-FIVE

Rome, 20 December AD 69

Borros

The rooftops of Rome were the only safe space that day. The entire population, those who weren't fighting, were up there in their festival finery, making the most of the novelty Saturnalia had brought.

At ground level, it was a different matter. Here, the green of Vitellius battled grimly with the oncoming tides of Antonius Primus' blue-marked men, cavalry at first, and then legionaries. The streets were a chaos of men stabbing, gouging, kicking, killing anyone whose colour differed from their own.

So the rooftops were the only safe place to be, which is why finding a route through wasn't easy.

'Excuse me . . . Thank you . . . May we pass . . . ? Thank you . . .'

Pantera was the soul of tact, but still, it was like fighting through mud and not helped by the fact that we weren't entirely sure where we were going.

The silver-boys were up here too. It must have felt odd for them to have their domain so entirely taken over by people who normally didn't venture higher than the steps up to the local Dionysian temple, but their whistles pierced the constant din of war. No doubt we weren't following them as well as we could have done, but we ended up in more or less the right place.

The first thing I knew of it was when Pantera grabbed my shoulder and forced me down on to the cold tiles of the roof.

'*There!*'

'What?'

Looking over the edge, I saw Guards fighting other Guards, which wasn't news by then.

'In that alley. There: at the far end. Geminus and Juvens are searching that street.' It took me a while to see where Pantera was pointing, to the dingy alley where yet more armoured men were flashing their swords at each other, except they weren't, they were opening doors and checking inside and not killing anybody. Yet.

'The enemy of my enemy is my friend.' Pantera threw me a fleeting grin. 'And they're not hunting us, so the next most likely quarry is Caenis and Domitian. We need to help them.' He was up, spinning on his heel. 'This way!'

Swift as a squirrel, he led me on to another rooftop, behind the fighting Guards, across the open street and up on to the rooftops on the far side. Here was as packed with people as everywhere else and we made the same slow progress until we came to the row of houses that backed on to those being searched.

'Excuse me . . . ? I'm sorry . . . Thank you . . . Are you for Vespasian or Vitellius?' And at the blank stare: 'Are you for the Blues or the Greens?'

'We're Blues-men!' This from a couple of youths no more than thirteen, making like men, but their elders nodded and

502

I saw a woman nursing a child at her breast, who grinned and pointed to the blue riband holding her hair. 'Blues all the way.'

'We may need your help shortly,' Pantera said. 'There are some Greens trying to get away from the Blues-men and they may be down in the alley. We'll send word if we find them.'

He spun a coin at the youngest of the boys and dropped down from the roof before they could start asking questions. I followed, fast.

A narrow alley separated the two rows of single-storey houses and we landed in it just in front of a battered door that yielded to two hard kicks from Pantera. Barging through, we found ourselves in a neatly kept small room with whitewashed walls that smelled faintly of mother's milk and baby-sick. In each back corner was a curtain. Pantera pushed one aside and I saw through into another room, the opposite of tidy, that smelled of old men.

'The whole street connects,' he said. 'If they're not in this side, we'll have to cross over and try the row opposite. If you have gods that you trust, start praying!'

We had gone through three rooms, all empty, when the Guards came in behind us.

Chapter Seventy-Six

Rome, 20 December AD 69

Geminus

We worked in pairs, swiftly, with one man always in the open street.

This was what we were good at. There's a routine to it that we followed here: kick in the doors and follow in fast and hard, shields up, blades to the front. Keep it sharp and loud and violent and anyone inside is already defeated before they even see you.

Except there was nobody inside: the entire fucking population was on the rooftops chanting the circus songs that went with the chariot races – and we'd been identified as Greensmen in a solidly Blue neighbourhood. Before long half of them were leaning over hurling insults, and I knew from experience that stones followed fast after the words.

I'd been the one keeping watch outside in case our quarry bolted, but now I barrelled after Juvens and Lentulus into a single-roomed dwelling, fastidiously neat, with whitewashed walls and the mellow-sweet-sticky smell of a nursing newborn. We were leaving when a flash of colour in the far corner caught my eye. In three paces, I'd found a blue pale curtain, lifted it and stepped into the next house along.

I didn't have to speak. Juvens ran outside and found Thrasyllus.

'They all connect. Take Halotus and go down the line as fast as you can. We'll take this side. Keep your head down any time you're outside. It's getting ugly out here.'

Juvens, Lentulus and I ran together, the rise and fall of the chariot songs over our heads not quite drowning out the sound of our nailed feet on the packed earth ground.

It didn't quite drown out the whisper of feet that started up ahead of us, either.

'*There!*'

You'd be amazed by how fast we ran, then.

CHAPTER SEVENTY-SEVEN

Rome, 20 December AD 69

Caenis

'Borros!'

'Felix!'

You'd think they were brothers, separated for years, the way they lit up when they saw each other.

With the Guards on our tails, there wasn't time to explain to either boy that Jocasta and Pantera were no longer on the same side, and even if one of us had tried I don't think Felix and Borros would have listened.

There was a brief, sharp moment, when both Jocasta and Pantera reached that same conclusion, and then Pantera said, 'Geminus and Juvens are three rooms behind us. We have to get out. Felix, climb up on to the rooftops and tell the Blues' supporters up there that Greens-men are in their houses trying to hide from the Blues. Tell them to whistle the Blues-men this way. 'Borros—' Pantera swung towards the big Briton. 'We're going to take a right turn out of the door, down to the end of the street, right again and up towards the forum. Can you carry the lady Caenis? We will have to move fast and you may have to shield her with your body.'

'Of course. My lady?'

He was huge. I couldn't have argued if I had wanted to; and I didn't want to.

He swept me up and carried me cradled in his arms as a child carries a wooden doll, and with as little effort.

In two sentences I was safe, and Felix, if he had been a danger, was neutralized. I saw sheer horror flash across Jocasta's face, saw her eyes narrow on a thought, saw her hand move to her girdle – and fall away again as Geminus and Juvens, two men I knew only in passing, burst into the other side of what was a very tiny room.

The only good thing was that they didn't carry spears.

We ran, just as Pantera had said we must, out of the door, right and right again at the end of the street.

By the time we turned right the second time, there were five green-marked men on our heels, howling.

CHAPTER SEVENTY-EIGHT

Rome, 20 December AD **69**

Geminus

So close!

We were yards from them. Feet, even. We nearly had our blades in their backs, but Hades they could run fast, and while we might have caught up with them on any normal day, on this day we were Greens-men in a ghetto that was solidly for the Blues and they had, as I'd thought, swapped their insults for stones, slates, vegetables, knives; anything they could lay their hands on that might slow us: and it did.

We ran through a hail of missiles, to which was soon added half a unit of blue-scarved men, drawn by the halloos of a bunch of youths who capered across the rooftops and drew them on to us. Amidst them, I spotted Felix, his near-albino colouring standing out like a beacon. I think it was then that I had the first inkling of how false was the path on which we had been led. There wasn't time to think of it, though: in one moment, we were chasing our fugitives; in the next, we were fugitives ourselves, hurtling down alleys, trying to escape the increasing mass of blue-marked men on our tails.

'Here!' I grabbed Juvens, pulled him down another lane, this one lined with tanneries. Like everywhere else, the tanners had climbed up, out of reach of the fighting men and, like everywhere else, they were against us.

'Here! Here!' They danced and whistled like overgrown silver-boys. 'Vitellius' officers! Here!'

CHAPTER SEVENTY-NINE

Rome, 20 December AD **69**

Borros

'W'here's Domitian?' Pantera asked.

We had slowed to a walk. I lowered the lady Caenis to the ground. She was bird light, and not hard to carry at all, but she thanked me kindly and did not seem overly flustered.

'Where's Domitian?' Pantera asked her again, trying not to seem impatient with her rearranging of her hair, her tugging down of her sleeves.

'With Trabo and Horus in the temple of Isis on the far side of the river.' She looked around. 'Where's Jocasta?'

'About two streets ahead of us,' Pantera said, grimly. He thrust blue scarves at us, taken from dead men as we escaped. 'Wind these on to your arms.' And to Caenis, 'Can you run?'

Caenis glanced at me, then bent down and took off her sandals. Barefoot, dust-lined, she looked like a slave until you saw the fire in her eyes. 'Let's go.'

*

'Pantera! Stop!'

Trabo stood outside the temple of Isis, his blade in his hand. He looked exactly like the men fighting in the streets, but bigger, and more angry, and all his ire was directed at Pantera. 'One step forward and you're a dead man.'

Pantera stopped exactly where he was told, about ten paces from the white marble steps leading into the temple. 'Is Jocasta inside?' he asked.

A flicker of panic in Trabo's eye betrayed him. He might have been a good legionary, but he would have been desperately bad at dice. 'She's not here.'

Pantera didn't call him on the lie. 'So why the blade?'

'You're working for Lucius. You'll take Domitian and hand him over and all our work will be for nothing.'

'And Jocasta, who isn't here, told you that?'

'She said it before she left.'

'Then I suggest you bring Domitian and Horus and come with us. We'll go somewhere safe. You can suggest the place and I'll come with you. I won't leave, I won't signal anyone. We'll sit in together and wait until Vitellius is deposed and Domitian can claim the throne. How does that sound to you?'

It sounded perfectly reasonable to me, but Trabo had gone beyond reason; he was in love with Jocasta and her lies had rotted his mind.

Pantera never took his eyes off him, didn't nod at me or wink or crook a finger, but I saw a shift in the set of his shoulders and it was signal enough.

'Haaaa!'

Trabo was a trained legionary, but I was bigger, and louder, and my father had been a warrior of the Ordovices; he had taught me all the moves a man might make against an armed opponent.

Trabo's blade slashed fast past my face but I had already ducked and swerved. I came in under his arm. My fist took him in the side of the head and my hip caught his, sending him crashing back on to the marble steps. He didn't make any attempt to rise.

'Is he dead?' Caenis asked.

'Not yet.' Pantera was kneeling at Trabo's side, his hand on his neck. He looked up at me and there was a respect in his eyes that made my heart sing.

'That was well done,' he said. 'Thank you.' And then, 'Jocasta's inside with Domitian. Felix went round the back.'

We burst in together, saw the blood together.

'Jocasta!'

'Felix!'

We threw ourselves forward, for it was Jocasta's blood that sprayed from a cut on her arm, but it was Felix who lay, purple-lipped, on the floor with no sign of life in his eyes.

I forgot about Domitian then; he might have been son of the emperor, but Felix had been my friend. I would have killed anyone who stood over him, and Jocasta must have seen that, for she whirled round, laughing, and leapt out of the back window, the one that Felix had come in through.

I held his hand, squeezed it, felt no squeeze back. His face was still, quiet, white. His uneven eyes were wide open, with the black points in them stretched as if he'd taken nightshade.

'He's dead. There was poison on the blade. See, where it entered?' Pantera was kneeling at Felix' side, his hand on his neck. 'Borros, I'm so sorry. We nearly had her there.'

'Do you want me to go after—' I waved a hand at the window, but in truth I wanted to stay with Felix. He looked so peaceful, so *young*.

'I'm sorry, we have to find Jocasta. She's taken Domitian.'

We found Horus cowering behind the open door, invisible until we closed it again. He had hidden there, it transpired, when he saw Jocasta coming.

Horus said, 'She would have killed me.'

Pantera was furious. He was on his feet and at the door but Horus caught his arm. 'You won't find her if she doesn't want to be found,' he said. 'She can vanish as easily as you can and Domitian with her. Keep the lady Caenis safe. She's the other half of the same coin.'

Pantera rounded on him, raging. I had never seen him angry before; it was a cold, fierce, frightening thing. 'Did she pay you to say that?'

I was aghast. I had thought Horus was Pantera's friend, but I watched the blood drain from his face and knew, then, that he was no friend. I stood, slowly; lifted my fist. If Felix had died because of him . . .

Horus whined like a struck hound. 'Don't! I am yours. I always was. When I wrote the letters, I didn't know what she planned. I have done nothing for her since. If you believe nothing else, know that I am loyal to Mucianus, and his goals are yours.'

They locked eyes for a moment, as deer lock horns.

Stiffly, Pantera said, 'We need to get Caenis to safety before Jocasta comes back with half of Vitellius' Guard. Will you provide sanctuary at the House? With Borros and your Belgian, it's probably one of the safest places in Rome just now.'

'Of course.' Horus leaked relief. He wept, silently, slowly. He looked like a bedraggled cat.

'Good.' Pantera looked my way. 'If I carry Felix back, can you carry Trabo as well as you did Caenis?'

Of course I could. Why ask? He was heavier, but he was only a man. I have carried whole oxen in my time. I would rather have carried Felix, but Pantera took him, gently, and we walked side by side.

CHAPTER EIGHTY

Rome, 20 December AD **69**

Geminus

'What I'd give now for a company of Scythian bowmen!'

The ironsmiths' boys were howling out our positions. The Blue Guards were racing at us as if we were the only men in Rome they had to hunt down. Bowmen would have been good, but we'd have needed a whole company, and if we had that we wouldn't have been where we were.

Juvens knew this part of Rome; I had hardly been in it. I said, 'Where do we go?'

'This way.' Juvens grabbed my sleeve and tugged me into an alley to our left. 'If we run, we can get to the barracks and make a stand there.'

A last stand, a hero's death; there was nothing else, now.

I said, 'We're south of the forum. It's a mile away and all uphill.'

'Then it's a good thing you haven't got soft on good living yet.' Juvens threw me a wild grin. 'Last one there pays the rest a month's wages each!' He smacked my arm, lightly, as children do, starting a race. 'Go!'

Heads down, arms pumping, we ran. Half a hundred men ran after us.

Somewhere near the forum, we lost Lentulus to bad luck and a thrown spear; if someone hadn't shouted his name, if he hadn't turned just as the spear was cast, if the aim had been less true . . . but he was dead and left lying, which was shameful, and nobody would speak of it.

We ran on.

I tasted blood in my throat. My windpipe was on fire, my lungs fit to burst. When I closed my eyes, my pulse flashed bright across the black inside my lids and we hadn't reached the steep part of the Quirinal yet.

Juvens was right; I had become soft in the few months in Vitellius' company. It wouldn't have mattered, but there was nothing soft at all about the blue-marked legionaries we faced, the men coming up the hill behind us, grim-faced and steady.

They were in no hurry; there was nowhere for us to go, except into the trap that was the barracks: one way in, one way out. And that exit could be blocked by a ten-man shield wall and held for as long as they felt like it once they had us trapped inside.

We had to stop for breath. I found I was leaning on a statue of Venus with my hand planted on her thigh, indecently high. I pushed myself away.

'A month's wages, you said?' And I was running again, driving myself as if I were in training, listening to Juvens' constant commentary on the men following us.

'Hades, they've brought up the cavalry. That means they've won at the Park of Sallust. Petilius Cerialis will have paid good gold to be allowed to go back there again and wipe out the shame of yesterday's defeat . . . Don't stop now, children, they're putting a push on . . . Look out—'

Eight of them came at us in a wall from the side. Iron flashed in the winter sun. I hurled up my shield, struck out in a curving arc with my blade, felt the clash of iron – and recoiled as scalding blood sprayed across my face. I tasted it. It blinded me. I heard the scream of a stricken man and in all the carnage around, all the screams and the hollered oaths, I recognized that voice, and the finality with which it was cut off.

'Juvens!'

I fought with my eyes shut, screaming; slashed out and felt the blade bite flesh, strike iron, heard it clang on a helmet, the impact so hard that it shocked me to the shoulder, but I felt my man go down and then Halotus was at my one side and Thrasyllus at the other . . . but no Juvens. He was lying to one side, sprawled in the filth.

I smeared my eyes clear, and, bending, saw the gash across his throat and the blood that foamed about it. He had clamped his mouth shut, but there was life still in his wide-stretched eyes.

'Fend them off!'

I grabbed Juvens under the armpits and dragged him back, kicked a door open behind me, hauled him inside.

Two men could hold that doorway with ease and Halotus and Thrasyllus did so with the ferocity of grief. I heard them kill at least three men. The rest stepped back and considered their courage. I knew then that they'd either leave us to get help or just leave. In that moment, I didn't care which.

I took a deep breath and choked on it, swearing; by bad chance, I had broken into a tanner's, ripe with the foul stink of curing hides and vats of rotting urine.

Kicking aside chairs, stools, workbenches, I laid Juvens on the floor. He tried to speak; blood foamed from the gash in his neck. His wild, beautiful face twisted with the effort.

'Don't.' I lifted his hand, squeezed it. 'There's nothing left to say.'

His eyes said there was. His fingers clawed tight around my wrist. His gaze hunted wildly round the room and came back to my face. He tried to speak without speaking.

'I don't understand. I'm sorry, I'm so sorry, but I'll meet you on the banks of the Styx before the day is out, which has to be worth more than a month's wages. I'll put silver on your eyes to pay the ferryman. It has been a good life.'

Juvens couldn't tut, but it was there, on his face, the upward twitch up his brows. He had never believed in the tales told to the credulous and he wasn't about to believe them now.

He still wanted to speak and had a moment's inspiration. Lifting his free hand, he wet a finger with his own blood. On the pale and costly fabric of my court tunic, bought and paid for by Vitellius from the imperial coffers, he drew a bloody letter, and another, and another.

He hadn't the strength to complete all he needed, but what he wrote was enough. FORGET OAT

'Forget my oath? You mean the one to kill Pantera? Or the one to serve the emperor?'

BOTH

LIVE

His hand reached up and stripped the scarf from my arm, or tried to. The knots were too tight, but the meaning was clear.

'What of honour? What of courage? What of all the things that bind the legions together?'

He gave a shrug and a nod together, and a faint grin that was all the old Juvens; wild, erratic, carefree. His tilted palm said, 'What of them? Life is too precious.'

His mouth framed the word Go. His eyes flicked to the door and back.

I tried to match his smile, and couldn't; my throat was too tight, my chest too full of hurt. Because he was right. I wondered how long I had known it. And yet—

'We both gave an oath in the temple of Jupiter,' I said, and my voice was dry as ash. 'But the temple is gone now, and the oaths burned with it. They were given to a poisonous man, for poisonous ends. I will not pursue Trabo, or Pantera. But I will go to the barracks and die with our men. Honour requires it. And I will join you by evening. Is that enough?'

It had to be enough because the light had gone from Juvens' eyes; no chance now for one last, mercurial thought, no smile, no wild idea.

The dying go so swiftly at the end. Always the speed of their leaving catches me unawares; so much left to say, to promise, to pray for.

I hadn't asked what to put on his monument, or even if there was to be one, and now I couldn't.

I smoothed his eyes shut with my hand, tipped coins from my belt-purse and laid them on the lids to hold them closed. I left silver; a fitting fare for a fitting man.

The freedom from my oath left me feeling unnaturally buoyant, as if someone had lifted leaden armour from my shoulders. I had no illusions about surviving the day, but I could die freed of petty vengeance; that much was good.

At the door, Halotus and Thrasyllus had killed two men each and the rest had run; the alley was clear.

I poked my head out, took a look round and up and got my bearings. We were perhaps three blocks south of the forum, with the Quirinal hill just behind and our barracks at the back of it.

At the door, I cleaned the grip of my sword on the hem of my tunic. The letters Juvens had drawn were clear across it. I had no time to wash them out, and didn't want to.

'To the barracks, then,' I said. 'A month's wages, I believe, paid out by the last one there.'

CHAPTER EIGHTY-ONE

Rome, 20 December AD 69

Marcus, leader of the silver-boys

The heights of Rome had been ours until this day, when every man and his son decided he owned them too.

Men, women and children were in places only silver-boys had been and so we had to get down to the ground where we were able to move about freely. The soldiers didn't attack us, and as long as we kept clear of the worst fighting there was profit to be made from doors left ajar and market stalls abandoned.

Early in the day, Pantera had sent me to Drusus, to find out how the emperor was. He didn't want him harmed, see, although he knew the risk. He said Vespasian wanted Vitellius kept safe and if he – Pantera – couldn't give him his brother alive, at least he would deliver his enemy still breathing.

So, through the day, whenever I had time, I went back to the palace and Drusus let me in and I knew when the emperor went to hide in his house on the Aventine, thinking at least the enemy soldiers might not look for him there, and then, later, when he returned again to the palace, thinking it better to stay there. He knew they were going to kill him, I think: he didn't want to die like a rat in a hole.

I took that information myself to Pantera; he was coming out of the House of the Lyre, where another Marcus was working as his runner.

He shook his head when he heard my news. 'The man is mad. He has absolutely no sense of self-preservation. Geminus should never have left him.'

'Geminus is near the forum,' I said. 'I saw him as I came to you.'

'Did you? That was well done.' Pantera's smile grew wide at that. 'Could you find him again? Take him a message?'

'Of course. This is Rome. I can do anything.'

Chapter Eighty-Two

Geminus

We ran covertly, keeping to side streets and back alleys, dodging into doorways to avoid the hunting packs of Antonius' men and the rooftop vigilantes who were all howling for Blue now: the mob will always support the winning side and we were so clearly losing.

We turned a corner and saw a flow of townspeople crossing our path; a sea of ardent faces. 'Come on!' I found a last burst of speed and turned tightly, to cut behind them. Behind me, Halotus was breathing like a narwhal. Thrasyllus trailed us, too far back to be heard.

A burst of whistles rose over the street, a brief chorus of songbirds in the afternoon, which was odd, but there wasn't time to contemplate its meaning because a small street boy with dirty blond hair had swooped down from a wall to stand in my way, and then three others.

They formed a line across the road.

'Get out of the way! Clear the road!' I was not so desperate yet that I would have killed a child to reach my goal, but I wasn't far off.

The boy didn't move. He was small; you could have crushed his hand in your own, easy as a fistful of spring walnuts. 'You are Geminus,' he said. 'I am Marcus. Pantera sent me with a message for you.'

'Pantera?' I stopped, hard, in front of the boy. 'What message?'

He closed his eyes, reciting from memory. 'I am to tell you that your emperor was taken safely to his house on the Aventine, but that he saw the condition of the warring cohorts and believed that they would soon engulf his house, and that his presence was a danger to his wife and children. Accordingly, he has returned to the palace, which is commendable, but not safe. If you turn back now, I can show you a way that will get you to him ahead of the people. If they take him, they will kill him, but if he comes out the back way we may yet keep him safe for you.'

'*You* will keep him safe for *me*?' I laughed, hoarsely. Halotus had joined me, and Thrasyllus. Either one of them was likely to bring his sword out shortly and use it. The boy was nine years old at most, and fearless. 'Why should we trust you? Or Pantera?'

'He said when you asked that, I was to show you this.' The boy held out one dirty paw. On his hand lay Lucius' ring. The shining emerald was a feral eye, fixed on me.

He went on, 'I am to tell you that help is not coming, but you must know this by now. I am also to say that the lord Domitian, in the name of his father, wishes you and Vitellius no harm. There is still time for your lord to walk free as he was promised, but only if you move swiftly. If the crowd reaches him first, neither you nor Pantera has the power to turn them.'

'We don't, do we?' I could have stood there for the rest of

the day, mesmerized by that ring. I had still hoped; against all evidence, against sanity, I had still nurtured a hope that Lucius and his cohorts might come to our aid. And now the ring.

'Is Lucius dead?'

The boy shrugged. In the alleyways, where the silver-boys reigned and he so evidently their king, they neither knew nor cared what happened in the palaces of power.

I reached into my purse and found one of Vitellius' new denarii, the same coin that I had laid on Juvens' eyes. I flipped it to Marcus who caught it on a flat palm and held it there; he had no need to make it vanish as the other boys did.

I said, 'We'll bring our emperor out of the palace by the slaves' door. Tell Pantera that if he spares Vitellius, I will spare him.'

'You'll need to wear this.' The boy held out a blue scarf, free of bloodstains; I would bet a year's pay that it had not yet been worn.

'No. Not now.' Not yet. I looked left to Halotus and right to Thrasyllus.

'Go,' I said to them. 'Go to the barracks. I'll catch you up when I've seen the emperor safe.'

That was a lie, but they wanted to be there. We could hear the beginnings of battle and any man not inside when the gates closed faced the prospect of being cut to pieces by the clear-up teams afterwards.

We made our farewells and, free of the other two, I followed Marcus and his boys down alleys so dark they felt like tunnels, twisting and swerving, and always overhead the high, fierce whistles guiding us as the horn guides the legion: left, here, up the hill, left again, second right; no, stop and turn back, take another right, sprint fast along here and out . . .

And stopped.

'We're too late.'

The palace was ahead, but between it and us the broad swathe of the Aventine Way was packed, from side to heaving side, by the people of Rome, come down off the rooftops and into the streets again.

'Hades!' I heard shock in my own voice. 'Are they all here? Has every single Roman come to see him brought down? It's worse than the circus.'

It wasn't really any worse; just that while the emperor – any emperor – provided his population with bloody entertainment, none had ever before taken the starring role himself, and the promise of exactly this had brought everyone out to watch.

Vitellius was taller than any of those around him; it was easy to keep track of him in the centre of the sea of jeering humanity. His captors were Guards all marked with blue. They had tied his hands and put a cord round his neck and were leading him towards the forum like an ox to sacrifice.

A dozen armed men circled him, of whom I recognized only Marcus Claudius Placidus, a junior officer prone to pandering to the masses.

'Where's Drusus?' I asked aloud. 'Did they kill him?'

Marcus was with me still; glued like a bur to my leg. 'Vitellius sent him away,' he said. 'He sent everyone away. He would have sent you away too. His wife and children have been sent south to Lucius.'

I snorted. 'Lucius, whose ring you have?'

'She's safe. Pantera did not intend this.' The boy's face was grave. 'You are too late to help, but you can watch if you want, from the rooftops. Nobody's up there now. Everyone's in the street, wanting to touch him as he passes.'

He was right; the rooftops were almost bare. And so, like the citizens who had so recently taunted us, we climbed on to a pig sty and from there on to a thatched roof and crawled along, keeping our heads low, as the mob descended the hill to the forum.

A statue crashed from its plinth below us; an image of Vitellius that flattered him in all aspects. It broke on the ground and a child tried to pick up the head, cut her fingers, and started to wail. Others picked it up for her, and used it as a missile to topple other statues, until 'collecting the heads' became a game much as it had done with Nero's effigies eighteen months before.

Vitellius wouldn't look; he stared solidly at the ground, his jaw working, but half the citizens around him were armed with the blades that the emperor had himself issued from his armoury to help in the defence of Rome. Oh, the irony . . . Those nearest leaned in, leering, and jabbed him under the chin.

'Look! See how the mighty fall!'

It was shameful and that idiot Placidus was doing nothing to stop it. I began to slither back down the roof. 'Someone needs to put a stop to this.'

'You can't rescue him.' The boy, Marcus, caught my sleeve. 'There's no point in dying for— What's Drusus doing there?'

The crowd parted, as before a stampeding horse, and Drusus was there, piling through them, big as a bear, and as terrifying. Men and women flung themselves out of his path and he had a clear route all the way to the emperor.

'Oh fuck, oh fuck, oh *fuck*! He's trying to rescue him. Drusus, you fool! You can't save him single-handed.'

'He isn't trying to save him,' Marcus said, in a thin, tight voice. 'He hates Vitellius for ordering his brother crucified. I think he's trying to kill him.'

'Drusus hates— But . . .'

Marcus was right. Whether it was out of mercy, or an act of personal vengeance, Drusus aimed himself like a bull at the emperor, with a massive blade held high in his hand.

Nearly. So very nearly. But Placidus was an idiot, not a complete incompetent, and Drusus was only one man. The emperor's head swung up and he faced his death bravely, but there was a fence of iron around him and three blades countered Drusus' one.

The giant German's momentum carried him on and spun him round and his sword sliced down the side of Placidus' head, carving away his ear in a gout of blood. Placidus fell away, screeching.

Eight men ran Drusus through.

'*Drusus!*'

'No!' Marcus was weeping, but he grabbed my shoulders with both hands. 'You can't stop it. They'll kill you if you try.'

I hadn't been aware that I'd moved, but I looked down and found that, though I had been safely a dozen feet from the edge, now I was at it, poised to leap.

Marcus was right: I would have died had I gone down there, either crushed underfoot or slaughtered, exactly as Vitellius was being slaughtered.

He died with all his wounds to the fore, and in silence, but he died, all the same.

Drusus' actions had pushed the mob past their boiling point and what had been contained ridicule descended fast into uncontained violence and eight men were not nearly enough to protect the emperor.

They didn't even try; without Placidus to command them, they lowered their blades and backed away. If I were Vespasian, I'd have had them all flogged and dismissed for dereliction of duty. They stood by and watched the mob rip Vitellius apart.

He died under a dozen savage blows and then, with no one to stop them, the mob stripped his hacked and bleeding body and dragged it to the foot of the Gemonian steps, where lately Sabinus' bloodied corpse had been left. There was a ghastly symmetry that was lost on no one. Somewhere, the gods were balancing the fates of the mighty, and laughing.

'He's dead.' Marcus was holding me still; a boy, holding a man, talking sense to the senseless. 'They're both dead. Drusus and Vitellius are both dead. Please will you stop. Which one was it you cared for?'

'Vitellius,' I said. 'And Drusus. Both.'

I was numb, dead inside. I should have been with my men at the barracks, but I could hear the noises of battle from the camp behind the Quirinal hill and knew that I was too late; the gates had closed and there, too, the slaughter had begun. My men were dying bravely, and I was not with them.

Pantera had kept me from that. Dully, I wondered why, and had no answer, although somewhere the shade of Juvens was pleased.

There was only one place left I could go and salvage any honour, any pride. Slowly, I unwound the green scarf from my arm and took the blue one Marcus had offered me earlier.

Tying it on under his too-adult sardonic stare was as hard as anything I had done, but necessary. After, I took his small fist, prised it open and tipped the contents of my belt pouch on to his flat palm. If nothing else, I had the momentary satisfaction of seeing the boy's jaw go slack.

'All of this,' I said, 'if you can get me out of the city and on the road south to where Lucius is.'

Indecision flickered for a moment across Marcus' face, then he smiled a true smile that showed a different boy inside.

He handed back all but one new-minted silver piece. This one he held in the flat of his palm, dull in the late afternoon sun. He slid me a look. 'One more like this when we reach the south gates.'

Solemnly, I spat on my hand and held it out. 'Two if we can reach there before nightfall.'

CHAPTER EIGHTY-THREE

Rome, 20–21 December AD 69

Horus

The House folded its silk welcome around us, warm, safe, homely; an antidote to Jocasta's poison.

Word had come ahead of us of Drusus' death; Segoventos, the Belgian who had taken his place as our doorman, was beside himself with grief and the rest of the House was subdued and sad even before we arrived with Felix' body and news that Domitian had been taken by Jocasta.

It's hard to know which part of that was hardest. We did not know Felix well, but Drusus had been our brother, our friend, and we mourned him. Then again, everyone had come to like Domitian in the time he had spent with us and all of us knew by then that he was the new emperor's son – if he lived.

I ordered wine for everyone and locked the doors and had them hang white banners from the windows to show we were in mourning and promised that there would be no work tonight, or tomorrow.

The lady Caenis, it hardly needs saying, was a model of

composure. We offered her a bed, alone, of course, and the opportunity to bathe, but she sat with the rest of us as we gathered news from the night.

She kept close to Borros, feeling, I think, a measure of responsibility for his grief; or perhaps she simply liked him. Together, they oversaw the laying out of Felix, ensuring he was accorded all honours as one who had given his life in defence of the new emperor; he was treated as a hero.

Trabo, of course, did not believe the evidence of his eyes. In his mind, Pantera was the threat and Jocasta the injured victim. In the end, we gave him poppy to calm his rantings, which worked for a while.

He recovered his wits around midnight, and I set a girl to tend him: Tertia, the one Pantera had paid for and ordered and sent to him in the summer, to see to his needs when Jocasta was not with him. Bizarre though it sounds, she had grown fond of him, I think. Certainly she cared for him, and soothed him, and let him work out his anger in safer ways.

Of us all, Pantera was least readily contained. I've known him almost all my life and never been afraid of him, but I was afraid that night. He didn't rant or scream, or even speak much, but he gave off a kind of white-hot fury that stunned everyone to silence. Even the lady Caenis was subdued in his presence.

As soon as he could, he left, taking Marcus-who-served-with-us and together they called up every silver-boy they could reach – which was all of them, given that he had taken half of my gold stocks as payment. They were set to work with explicit instructions, but scour the city as they might they couldn't find Jocasta or Domitian.

After midnight, when the noise of fighting had died away, Pantera sent Marcus back with news that the barracks had fallen: two thousand men bravely dead with their wounds all to the fore. Soon after, another boy brought word that

Antonius Primus had occupied the palace formerly used by Vitellius and was holding it in Vespasian's name while his men conducted a street by street clear-up of the city.

Nobody knew where Lucius was, except that he wasn't in Rome. Pantera believed that he was marching up from Misene and would be on us within a day, and that Jocasta had gone to join him.

Near dawn, Pantera came back with word that a woman fitting her description had taken two of Vitellius' horses and paid for them with coins cut in Vitellius' likeness. It wasn't proof, but it was as close as we were likely to get.

Pantera roused Caenis and told her that he, personally, was going to lead the legions that were about to march out to face Lucius. He knelt before her and swore that he would bring Domitian back to her alive, or die in the attempt. He chose not to leave her in my care, but took her to Antonius Primus, who could provide half a legion to protect her.

Then he came back for Trabo.

CHAPTER EIGHTY-FOUR

Rome, 21 December AD **69**

Trabo

Iwoke to a stunning headache and the stench of burning men. I opened my eyes slowly, closed them, opened them again at the feel of soft breasts pressing against my arm.

I thought *Jocasta* and was full of hope and joy. And then I remembered. I made myself focus, strove for a name.

'Tertia?' I blinked and it was still her. 'What are you doing here?'

'She works here,' said a man's voice behind me. 'Four denarii a night.'

Four denarii? *Four?* I'd paid her two sesterces a month and she'd had to buy food for us out of that.

And then I recognized the voice. I sat up, fast, and fell back against the wall at the bed's head. 'Where's Jocasta?'

'She's gone south, we think.' Pantera moved round to stand in front of me. 'Do you feel well enough to ride?'

'South? You think she's gone to Lucius? I don't believe you.'

I couldn't stand, but lifted my head to look at where Pantera had sat down, cool as you like, on a pale blue satin couch. We were in the whorehouse and the whole place was done out in pastel shades and smelled of roses.

Looking down, I found I was lying on a bed with silk sheets in three different shades of lavender. More than the stench of funeral pyres, that drove me to my feet. I swayed and caught the wall to hold me.

'Ride where?' I asked.

'Down the Appian Way. Lucius' cohorts are advancing on Rome. Unless we want a repeat of yesterday, and I don't think we'll find a soul alive in Rome who wants that, it will be necessary to meet him in force. Antonius Primus is sending three legions south to stop him. They leave by the second call. If you want to see Jocasta alive, you'll be ready to leave with them.'

I had no idea what time it was, only that there were chinks of daylight under the door and so it must have been after dawn.

'She isn't a traitor,' I said.

He blew out his cheeks. He was grey at the edges, like a man who has had little sleep and much commotion. 'You won't know if you don't come.'

He pushed himself to his feet. I don't think he liked the couch any more than I did. It smelled of sex. Come to that, so did I, but mine wasn't scented sex.

Stiffly, he said, 'You are offered the lead of the army riding south. If you don't take it, someone else will. So your choice is this: do you want to face Lucius and his cohorts and the risk of meeting Jocasta, or would you rather stay here and fuck Tertia at my expense?'

I could have hit him. Perhaps I could. But Borros was there and my head still hurt and he looked more than ready to hit me again.

Without a word to either of them, I turned and began to dress. I am not a coward, but I choose my battles and this was not one worth fighting.

Outside, the air was foul with the scent of burning flesh. Greasy soot fell in soft flakes, staining everything.

At the barracks, there were more men bearing bodies in funeral parties than there were in the columns of tired-faced men lined up ready to march out, and everyone was sunk into despond by the pyres that ranged behind the wall. They didn't want war any more than I did, but nobody, either, wanted Lucius to descend on the city with his cohorts thirsting for blood, so they were there, ready; brave men all.

At Pantera's orders, someone brought me a horse marked with Vitellius' brand, but wearing trappings hurriedly cobbled together that showed the oak branch in leaf and nut that was Vespasian's livery.

Someone else handed me a helmet with a fresh scarlet plume, and as I rode up the ranks the men who knew me stared and then cheered: I was Trabo, whose name had been in the lottery, and here I was, alive, ready to lead them. Those few who had never heard of me took longer to understand who I was, but before I reached the head of the column they were cheering too.

I waved: it was expected of me. I hated it.

'I'm a fraud,' I said bitterly to Pantera, as he rode up beside me.

'No. You're the man who fulfilled his oath to Otho and survived the depredations of the false emperor. Don't belittle yourself.'

It was on the tip of my tongue to ask him just what he thought he would achieve by going out with three legions against Lucius' three cohorts, but there was something in his eyes that warned me off. He was in a rare mood: tight and taut with a sense of impending explosion. It left me jittery, and in any case my head still hurt from Borros' attentions; this, too, wasn't the fight I wanted to have.

We two rode in sullen silence and the men, feeling it, were quiet; nobody raised a marching song. If they were like me, every sinew ached, every bone felt bruised. Less than a day before, I had been desperate for battle; all that running around in dog-headed masks had driven me mad. Now, I never wanted to lift a sword in anger again.

I tried to remember if I had felt like this when Otho was beaten, but the past was a haze and all I could recall were the faces of the recent dead. Their shades walked with me in columns on either side, mourning their own passing. Someone said that Rome had lost fifty thousand men in the past month, which had to be the most monumental exaggeration, but even if it was a third of that number, it was too many.

Just before noon, on Pantera's advice – his order, if we are honest – we halted in the open land between the Alban and Volscian hills. The rhythms of the legions were returning to me. Pantera may have given the order, but I saw it carried out and found the first beginnings of joy in the snap of command and response. At my signal, muted trumpet calls moved the men about: the cavalry to the higher ground, the legionaries into blocks in the centre with their banners brought down and kept tight so that they might not be readily seen from a distance.

The breeze lifted the horses' manes, fluttered the ends of the coiled flags. Men stood in silence, scanning the horizon, but it was the cavalry, mounted on the higher ground, with the double advantage of height, who first saw the advancing cohorts and called out.

We waited until the mass of moving men marching north up the Appian Way was obvious to us all. Even this close, perhaps a dozen spear-casts away, they showed no particular sign of having seen us. We had the advantage of the sun behind us, and the folds of the land to protect us.

I waited until they had closed to half the distance before I gave the command for the companies to raise their banners aloft.

Then they noticed us.

It must have been a spectacular sight; the horizon suddenly forested with standards. A shudder rippled down the oncoming cohorts, of recognition, disbelief, despair. Lucius might have known already that Rome was lost, but from the look of things he hadn't told his troops; they had believed they were marching back to victory, or at least to fight for a city that might still be taken.

Silence spread across them as they stamped to a halt, five spear-casts away. Their faces were a pale blur, but it was possible to see the images of Vitellius that remained on their standards, the only ones left anywhere near Rome.

Lucius rode a big bay horse that was already patched black with sweat as he paced it forward from the front ranks. Three figures followed him; one was an officer: Geminus, the second his prisoner – that must have been Domitian. There was a chain from his neck to Geminus' saddle. The third wore a silk robe that blew in the breeze; a priest, perhaps, or an oracle.

'Will he fight?' I asked. My mouth was dry.

'I hope not.' Pantera was as grimly white as he had been in the morning. 'Geminus was given help to escape from the city last night after he witnessed Vitellius' death. He will have been the most credible of witnesses: not even Lucius could accuse him of lying. My hope is that, knowing his brother is dead, and seeing by how much he is outnumbered, he'll realize that the only choice is surrender. Unfortunately, being Lucius, we can't depend on his reason. We should go forward to meet him. Tell the men to hold.'

535

I did and they did and we nudged our horses forward across the close-cropped winter turf. The robed priest lifted his head and Pantera's horse napped savagely, as if jerked hard in the mouth.

'If I die,' Pantera said, without warning, 'tell Caenis . . . tell her that Seneca's network is hers, that she knows all she needs to make it work, and that Horus will have the answers to any questions she may have.'

'Seneca's network? But it is Jocasta's.'

'It was,' said Pantera, tight-voiced. 'Not any more. If I am dead, it will be because Jocasta has killed me. And you are going to have to kill her.'

'But—'

'Trabo, *look!*' The word stung like a slap. 'The robed rider with Lucius – it's Jocasta.'

CHAPTER EIGHTY-FIVE

Rome, 21 December AD **69**

Jocasta

If Trabo didn't recognize me before Pantera pointed me out, he was deceiving himself.

I didn't care at the time, either way. Trabo was only a small part, a counter to be discarded for the wider game. Pantera was the one who mattered, the one for whom all this had been played out. Since Seneca's death, we had been manoeuvring around each other. Now, finally, we could be open.

I smiled at him, as I had at that first meeting, back in Seneca's house, with the old man recently dead and the ink newly dry on the forged letter that made me leader of the entire Senecan network.

Horus wrote it for me, yes. Few men in Rome could have reproduced Seneca's hand so accurately, or his voice.

Horus is not as straightforward as he would have you believe. His first loyalty is to Mucianus and then himself. Everything else depends on who pays and I have always had deeper pockets than Pantera, even when he had Vespasian's backing. Vespasian, as I'm sure you know, has never been what you might consider wealthy. It will be different now, of course.

So Pantera was never sure who wrote that letter. It might have been real, you see. It was very close to the original, and he had that strange mix of certainty and insecurity that made him a good spy: he didn't know if it was his own arrogance that said he should have been named leader over me.

And I was not a bad spymaster. Given free rein, I could have been the best.

Approaching, Pantera's eyes fastened on my face, searching for some sign as to the depth to which I had deceived him. Even then, I think, he hoped for less, or more, than the truth.

I gave Trabo barely a glance, and oh, how that wounded him. He had been relaxed, riding towards us, slightly melancholy, as men are after the killing is over, but now he was spear-stiff and bristling with righteous anger. He had been in love; probably he still was – is – which was what made it all so very dangerous.

They stopped at a sensible distance. Close enough to speak without having to shout, not quite within sword reach. Geminus had been given clear orders. He brought Domitian up to stand on my left, with Geminus on his left and Lucius on *his* left. We made a line, with me at the far right of it.

'Jocasta.' Pantera made a bow, palm to breast, as the Alexandrians do. 'You honour us with your presence.'

'Do I?' I gestured to the boy at my side. He sat stiffly, not only for the chain at his neck that fixed him to Geminus' saddle. 'My blade has on it a different poison from that used on Felix. If scratched, Vespasian's son will fall into near-death, but will continue to breathe. I can, of course, provide an antidote which will ensure his recovery, but only at great cost. It would be better for all of us if he were never touched.'

Pantera bowed his understanding. Seneca had taught him

well; never speak when you don't have to. Never give the enemy words to work with.

We studied each other in silence. If I hadn't slept much, neither had he. I recognized the signs in him by then; nothing so dramatic as dark smudges under his eyes, but a shortness of temper signalled by tension in the lines at his mouth, at the corners of his eyes. I wanted more than that. I wanted him to know how soundly he had been deceived.

'When did you know?' I asked.

He shrugged, loosely. 'As soon as Sabinus died. While he was alive, there was always a chance it could have been him. My lord Domitian, of course, has always been blameless.'

That was a lie. He had suspected Domitian from the start; too much gold, too many contacts with the silver-boys. I tried to catch his eye, to show him I knew that, but he was watching my hands, not my face. He was clever, always. And right.

'Jocasta?' At his side, Trabo's horse was stuttering backwards, held on too-tight reins. He kicked it forward, savagely. A bruise on the side of his face was colouring deeply in purple and black. 'What could Sabinus have been?'

'My informant in Pantera's group,' Lucius said coldly from my left. 'They are congratulating each other on their cleverness. It was obvious from the summer that Pantera and I each had someone who was privy to the other's most secret thoughts, but neither of us knew the identity of the other's informant. Much of the past half year has revolved around us each protecting our source, while trying to find the name of the one sent against us.'

'And we succeeded,' Pantera said. 'Was it worth the cost?'

I had posed that same question to Lucius not long before. He said now what he had said to me in the tent in that last, long night of intimacy.

'I let Caecina defect to protect Jocasta; I allowed her to

poison Valens; I let her give gold to Domitian and encourage him to the House of the Lyre, so that it might seem as if he was selling stories for sex. I have no doubt you did things that were likewise dangerous. You let me kill a hound, although in retrospect I should have killed its master. Who betrayed me? Was it Geminus?' He looked sideways at Geminus, who had come to us in the night and was still as doggedly loyal as ever. 'Should I have killed him when he came to us last night with news of my brother's death?'

'I shouldn't, if I were you,' Pantera said. 'Geminus is as loyal to you as he has always been.'

That was clever. From the little I know of him, Geminus' first oath was to Vitellius and he cleaved to Lucius only because he was the emperor's brother. Now that another man had been named emperor . . .

'It was Drusus,' Pantera said.

'Drusus?' Lucius laughed. 'The German masseur? I don't believe you.'

'You should; he did his utmost to kill your brother yesterday.'

'We knew that.' Lucius' jaw clamped shut. 'At your order?'

'No. Your brother was not a monster; he could have lived, and at worst deserved a decent death. Drusus had his own oath to fulfil and thought others might get in ahead of him.'

'And you let him?'

'I couldn't stop him.'

Across from me, perhaps a dozen paces away, Trabo was still coming to terms with reality. He wouldn't look me in the eye and his head was clearly addled from the blow that had knocked him flat the day before.

Unexpectedly, he looked up. 'Jocasta, why?' So much pain in his voice.

'Yes, why?' Pantera's horse took an uneasy step sideways. 'You could have thrown the whole of Seneca's network behind

Vespasian and I would have gladly followed your lead. Why did you not? You can't have thought *Vitellius* would have made the better emperor?'

'Vitellius was never emperor.' I heard the acid in my own voice, but was too shaken to make it mellow; we were beyond that.

My gaze skidded over Pantera's face. I was studying his hands, just as he was still studying mine, trying to see where the knife was hidden. Like lovers lately parted, we knew each other too well. He was up to something . . . I just couldn't tell what.

I said, 'Lucius has ruled since before his brother reached Rome. If you hadn't tried to impose your provincial soldier on us, Vitellius would have died by now of a surfeit of eels or bloody flux, or something equally certain.'

'But then his son would have taken the throne,' Trabo said.

'Don't be ridiculous!' I snapped, I admit it. 'The boy was far too young to rule. After Nero, nobody is ever again going to let a child take the throne of Rome. He would have been dead within days of his father.'

'And what of the men who had been loyal to Vitellius? What of Geminus and his Guards? Were you expecting them to transfer their oaths to Lucius without demur?'

'When one emperor dies, their oaths are given to the new one,' Lucius said. 'It has always been so.'

'And is so now, with Vespasian.' It was the middle of winter and the wind was cold, but still, I saw Pantera wipe a trickle of sweat from the side of his face. He kept one hand on the reins; the other fell to his side.

He said, 'You can't fight on. We have three legions, you have a handful of cohorts and your men must know that Vitellius is dead. They won't fight, even if you ask them to. My "provincial soldier" has won, and not yet set foot on Roman land.'

Carefully, carefully . . . this last was a taunt, thrown in my face, but I didn't have to rise to it.

I smiled, and made no comment. He thought he had won, but I knew that victory could be pulled from defeat more certain than this. An emperor who was locked in Alexandria was not a real emperor.

Pantera pushed on, needling at what he thought were sore points.

'That's the truth of it, isn't it? You couldn't bear the idea that a rustic provincial, with only one generation in the senate, could take the throne?'

'No.' I gave him a look to freeze his blood. 'I don't care about that. I'm sure Vespasian will make a perfectly good emperor, I never disagreed with you on that. But he wasn't *my* emperor and never would have been. He was yours. You made him. I made Lucius. I brought Seneca's network to him. You tried to give it to Vespasian instead. And that I could not bear.'

The last words were flung at him, and my knife behind them, and however much he was expecting it, he could never have been completely ready.

CHAPTER EIGHTY-SIX

Rome, 21 December AD **69**

Geminus

'*P*antera!'
Domitian shouted, but the spy was already moving, launching himself left, because she threw right-handed and he must have known how the knife would fly. He soared out in an arc from his horse, tucked his head in, pulled his arm in, ready to roll.

His horse was not trained for this. It shied and kicked him in the chest, a glancing blow, but it drove the wind from his lungs and he messed up the roll and landed awkwardly and we all heard something snap, high up, by his shoulder, while over his head Trabo was proving that it had been right to bring him along, that he could think and act properly even when his heart was so clearly broken.

There was a lick of winter sun across a blade and the slam-sigh of iron on bone. Somewhere, a man called out. It might have been Trabo, I don't know, because Jocasta was not my problem, and never had been: Lucius was mine to deal with; my pleasure, my duty.

You see, Pantera might have been goading Jocasta, but his gaze had held mine when Lucius spoke: *When one emperor dies, their oaths are given to the new one. It has always been so.*

And about Pantera's wrist, revealed beneath his sleeve as he had raised his hand to wipe imaginary sweat from his cheek, was a silver wristband with the sign of the house of Vespasian engraved on it.

His thumb had pointed back to his legions and my eye had followed the line. Every single horse I could see, every banner, had the livery of the oak branch in fruit and leaf. Some of those men were mine; I knew their cohort colours.

They had sworn to the new emperor; it's what we do and the gesture said, as clearly as if Pantera had spoken, *Vespasian is your emperor now. All other oaths are void.*

They didn't have to be. I could have carried on serving Lucius, but really, what sane man would want to serve him? In that one single, liberating moment, I was free and my soul sang.

So when the moment came and Jocasta made her move – really, it wasn't a surprise to any of us – I unclipped the chain holding Domitian, left Jocasta to Trabo, and spinning my horse let my blade sing out and slice hard, fast, horizontal, across the place where Lucius' neck had been.

And still was.

His throat came apart cleanly, in a wash of blood. He fell like a stone and I did not do him the honour of bending to hold his hand or to hear his last words. In the heart of my mind, I heard Juvens say, 'Nicely done!' I had already turned back, to signal to the cohorts behind not to move, that we had surrendered to Vespasian's men. In truth, they were relieved, let no one tell you otherwise; they were outnumbered ten to one and they had heard of the slaughter in Rome. What point in fighting for a dead man? Vespasian was their emperor too now, one we could all respect.

And so I turned again, to see Jocasta not dead, but unconscious, lying flat, with a great gash on her forehead where Trabo's sword hilt had taken her, and him on the ground, holding Pantera's head, saying his name, hitting his face.

'Pantera . . . Pantera. Don't die on me now, you bastard. You've got too much explaining to do. Wake up, man! You are not going to fucking die now . . .'

I came to kneel behind him, to find out where the wound was, for I saw only a scratch across the back of his hand where he had thrown up his arm to protect his face. There was no other blood. Nor was his neck at a false angle, as it might have been if he had broken it.

I knelt and reached for her blade, which lay a short distance away.

'Don't!' It was Domitian whose hand clamped on my arm. 'Don't touch it. The bitch has used poison. She killed Felix like this.'

I had hardly known Pantera, and yet his name had dominated my life since July. I felt his loss as keenly as I felt Juvens'. 'Is he dead?'

'Oh, no. Not yet. You heard her. She's far cleverer than that. When she comes round, she'll be ready to bargain with us; his life for hers.'

The new emperor's son lifted his head. Already there was a gravitas to him, a dignity that only royalty can confer. 'It would please me, and so my father, if you and Trabo together could take care of her interrogation. I wish this man to live. I owe him my life, many times over.'

CHAPTER EIGHTY-SEVEN

Rome, January, AD 70

Hypatia, Chosen of Isis

This concludes the witness statements of the events leading to the death of Vitellius, the burning of the temple and the death of the emperor's brother, Titus Flavius Sabinus.

From these, we may conclude that, by his actions, Juvens caused Sabinus' death and the fire that accompanied it. As to who killed Vitellius, that was the mob, spurred to it by the actions of Drusus, a German.

Both of these men are dead, as is Lucius, who may fairly be said to have engineered both his brother's rise to fame and his downfall.

The woman Jocasta remains in custody awaiting your decision. She acknowledges that she used poison on the knife that struck the spy Pantera, and she has offered to trade: in exchange for her safety she can supply us with that which will give him life, instead of the endless sleep that now afflicts him.

There are those in your service, Domitian amongst them, who suggest that there are means by which such a curative may be drawn from her by force, but Caenis has pointed out that if she gives another, lethal, recipe first, under duress, we may lose him altogether.

Thus we await your decision in this as in many other affairs of state. Geminus serves as tribune of the Guard. Trabo is your Master of Horse. My lord Mucianus has order of Rome and your son Domitian is a willing pupil, ably learning the reins of state from one who understands what must be done. Those who need to die are dead, save for the woman Jocasta, whose fate remains uncertain.

We await your order.

EPILOGUE

Rome, September, AD 70

The Emperor, Vespasian

It ends as it began, with the scent of wild strawberries filling the throne room.

I could smell it when I entered this morning, and can smell it still now, when everyone else has left us. We are here alone, just me and Caenis; the emperor and his woman, who can never be his wife.

It's the first time we've been alone together since I landed. Being a soldier was my life and I was moderately good at it. Being emperor will be my future and perhaps, having taken the wolf by the ears, I will learn how to ride it. But today I am a man long separated from his woman, and the petitioners and robe-makers and goldsmiths can all wait.

As the last grovelling senator leaves, I open my arms. She steps slowly into my embrace, as if she, or I, were too fragile for sudden moves.

'What?' I know her every frown, every line about her mouth. I kiss them, each one, gently, with lips tired from talking. She tastes sweet as nectar, ripe, perfect. She is Diana, Isis, Astarte, Demet—

'There is one more,' she says. 'One more to see, to talk to, before today is done.'

'Oh, please . . . Must we?' I am beyond tired. I have fought battles that lasted from dawn until dusk and felt less exhausted after them than I do today, when I have done nothing more than ride up from Misene to Rome, and there met with my senate and all who serve my state.

But I know that look. I close my eyes. 'Who?'

'Look,' she says, softly, and I do, and there is a man standing before me who was not there when I turned my head away.

'Pantera.'

Am I glad to see him? I am certainly surprised. I am surprised first that he is able to walk when I had heard he was still on a nodding acquaintance with death, and second that he looks so thin, so hollow, so unlike the man I knew.

Except he doesn't, really. His eyes are the same, and the dry, knowing intelligence that burns at their core.

'I believe I owe you my throne,' I say; an exaggeration, but not by a great deal. Antonius Primus claims that distinction for himself. Mucianus claims it, louder, as his own. Nobody has claimed it for Pantera, but he is here, which is perhaps claim enough.

I glance at Caenis; she knows why he is here, and I don't. 'Yes?' I ask.

She says, 'He won't take Seneca's spy network on my command. I thought your word might do it.'

Pantera is smiling; however blue his lips, however haggard his cheeks, however thin his arms, he can still make me feel like a child in front of a stern parent.

'You don't want it?' I ask.

He bows, just a little. 'Lord, I am not fit to take it, on any level. The lady Caenis would do far better.'

'The lady Caenis,' says the lady Caenis, crisply, 'has absolutely no wish even to attempt such a thing.'

My spy (is he mine? Ever? Truly?) casts me a glance that says *Is she always uncontrollable?* and since she is there seems little I can do. I am not prepared to become caught between these two who ran Rome while I was locked in Alexandria, hearing of my war at second hand.

But there is, possibly, a way through.

I say, 'But perhaps my lady could organize the administration under Pantera's direction until he is well enough to take up the reins fully? He, meanwhile, can recuperate at our expense, since his . . . affliction was garnered in our defence.'

Myself, I think this is an ideal solution. They both look at me sourly, at each other, open their mouths to protest.

I hold up my hand. 'I order it,' I say. 'There will be no discussion.'

They both look surprised and I have no doubt I will pay later, but there are advantages to being emperor and I could begin to enjoy this, given time. These two, between them, might give me the time.

There is nothing else to say, and I am a man who has not seen his woman in nearly two years. I turn to her, take her into my arms again, and she resists only a little.

'You may leave,' I say to the man who still waits.

'Lord.'

Pantera turns and walks out of the room. Gods be thanked, he doesn't back away bowing.

'Stop.'

He is near the door. He stops. I say, 'The woman Jocasta, who poisoned you, what happened to her?'

'Trabo killed her,' he says. 'Not on our orders. But she could not have been let loose in the world and we all knew it. I think he did it at her request, or at least her instigation. He has not been disciplined, but he has been permitted to retire from army life. The Guard was not big enough for him and Geminus together and neither could readily have been demoted to a legion.'

'Good.' All good, all wise. I will need this wisdom in the years ahead. I wish . . . it doesn't matter what I wish. What matters is what I have. Which is a great deal.

I wave a hand and he departs, and I am left with Caenis, my Caenis, who smells of wild strawberries, whose smile can lift me over seas and over nations, who will reign with me in all but name for as long as we both may live.

Author's Note

Few periods of ancient history have been described in such depth and detail as the eighteen months from Nero's death to Vespasian's eventual assumption of the throne: the period that we now term the Year of the Four Emperors.

While much of our ancient history comes from a single literary source – Tacitus, say, or Josephus – and was often written long after the fact at fourth or fifth hand, the Year was documented as it happened by men who took part in it and then within a few years by the great historians of that time: Tacitus, Josephus, Plutarch, Suetonius and Cassius Dio.

Much of what they wrote is missing – the only ones of Plutarch's *Lives* to survive are those of Galba and Otho, for instance, when we know he wrote from Augustus through to Vitellius – but what remains has been enough to keep academics in cheerful disagreement for centuries.

This kind of half-fleshed detail is, of course, a fiction writer's dream. As long as I don't put Otho before Galba in my lineage of emperors, or stick stirrups on the saddles of my cavalry; if, in other words, I commit no gross anachronistic errors, and keep to the time frames that are common to all our sources, then I can weave my narrative amongst the many pillars of accepted 'fact'.

I can also – and this is a great deal harder – endeavour to find a sense of structure in a time that was, from a Roman perspective, utterly chaotic. As Tacitus says (and I paraphrase), emperors were made in Rome, they weren't 'discovered' by distant legions who then put their man on the throne. But the realization by those legions that they could do exactly that changed for ever the relationship between the rulers and their legions. The balance of power shifted and it never truly shifted back.

In addition, as Tacitus also points out, the premium on blue blood dropped with each successive emperor in this Year of Four, with the result that the man who, at the start, would never have been considered an option ended up as the last man standing in the war of attrition that saw all the others dead.

Vespasian was not another Corbulo: there is every evidence to suggest that he truly had no ambition to take the throne and he took a lot of persuading into the role. The attempted assassination is cited as one of the persuading factors – but the fact that someone bothered to persuade him at all leads me to think that someone had a vision of who he could become, if he were given ultimate power.

It would be convenient if that same someone had maintained a consistent vision from the time of Vespasian's declaration: as a fiction writer, having an overall 'intelligence' to drive the narrative would have made life a lot easier. The sad fact is that, in this particular year, that was so manifestly not the case that to try to fit the facts to easy fiction would have been a travesty of history.

No sane man (or woman) would have set up the double destruction of Cremona, and even if he had it would have taken a tactician of rare imagination to expect one army to *run* eighteen miles in (we assume) full kit and then insist on fighting a pitched battle when they reached their destination, against equally willing opponents who had just force-marched a hundred miles in a handful of days, and all at a small town that had already been sacked by one side in the previous battle for the throne.

In truth, the entire Year was a highly complex series of accidents where the bullish soldiery of the legions led by men of spectacularly venal ambition was interspersed by treachery, blackmail, double- and triple-dealing and sheer luck, good and bad; fortune favoured neither side in particular.

The best anyone could have done was to remain fluid and make the most of those opportunities that presented themselves, while having some kind of strategy to deal with the disasters – at the kind of remove forced on the players by the slow transfer of orders and messages.

Given all of this, the best a novelist can do is try to make sense of the nonsensical with the proviso that it needs all to be coherent. Otherwise, as Lindsey Davis so wisely pointed out in her *Course of Honour,* we risk going into great depth to describe battles fought by people we've never heard of, in places we've never been.

At the end, though, we can believe that the right man won. Otho might have made a good emperor; certainly his selflessness in committing suicide rather than forcing men to fight on in his name foreshadows a degree of decency remarkable in the ancient world, but Vespasian was one of the best things to happen to Rome.

It wasn't just his age that made him right – Galba was older and manifestly unsuited to the role; as is said of him, everyone thought he'd make an excellent emperor until he actually got the job, at which point everyone except the man himself realized it was a catastrophe.

Nor was it merely Vespasian's able command of the legions that made him so suited to power: Vitellius was a general, although not a very good one, and Vitellius was a disaster of an emperor.

It was that Vespasian had been a good general in an era

when those could be numbered on the fingers of one hand (Julius Caesar, Corbulo, Vespasian, Hadrian, Trajan – a long span and you'd be hard pressed to add to that number). We might conclude that good generals learn things in battle that lead them not to take life too seriously, but also not to throw it away without good cause.

They learn the management of finances – Vespasian was very much in the Democratic mould of balancing the books rather than the Neronian/Republican one of throwing the entire treasury at pointless wars and then blaming everyone else when the cupboard was bare – and they learn how to manage men efficiently.

And at the heart of it all lies one of the greatest love stories of the ancient world. It does seem that Vespasian fell in love with Caenis when she was still a slave girl, or at the very least newly freed – and that love lasted for the remainder of their natural lives.

Roman law forbade a senator from marrying a freed-woman, so Vespasian had to marry and get his children elsewhere – a rather crowded marriage, we might presume – but he returned in the end to his true love and lived with her in all respects as if she were his wife until the end of her life. That alone put him in a league quite different from the majority of the Julio-Claudians, and if it didn't set a precedent for later, we can hardly hold him accountable for that.

For those who care about such things, you should know that the four emperors and their immediate adherents are all based in fact, while Pantera, Jocasta, Geminus, Trabo, Horus, the Marcuses, Felix, Borros and Amoricus are not.

The basic skeleton of the narrative is all based on our ancient sources, from the declaration of Vespasian by the eastern legions through Antonius Primus' naked ambition, from Caecina's outstanding generalship in putting Vitellius on the throne to his apparently easy conversion to Vespasian's side afterwards. The supposed 'suicide' of the centurion who fell on his sword because Vitellius wouldn't listen to his tales of Caecina's defection is true, as is the detail of the last five days when Antonius Primus had brought his legions to Rome's gates, and sent Valens' head to his former comrades on a pole. Vitellius' dithering, his three meetings with Sabinus, the siege on the Capitol and the later conflagration, Sabinus' death, and Vitellius' . . . all these are based on the ancient sources.

What I have done is to flesh out the bare skeleton, but for those who want to read further into the history I can heartily recommend *69AD, The Year of the Four Emperors* by Gwyn Morgan and *The Year of the Four Emperors* by Kenneth Wellesley; the latter's detail concerning the topography of the route marches is invaluable.

Anyone interested in the day-to-day living of those not at the top end of Roman society would find *Invisible Romans* by Robert Knapp a fascinating read, I certainly did; and for those who want a coherent synthesis of the primary sources, the biography of Vespasian by Barbara Levick knows no peer.

As always, this book has been a journey and I would like to offer wholehearted thanks to Mark Lucas and Bill Scott-Kerr for joining along the way; long may we travel. Thanks are due also to Nancy Webber and Vivien Garrett for outstanding help with the editorial process; to Phil Lord for design; to my colleagues and friends in the Historical Writers' Association who have made the process of writing so much more social; to Tilly for keeping me moving; to the members of Rule of Three for keeping me sane; to Lauren and Lee for teaching me things I may one day remember; and, as always, to Faith for sharing home and hearth and life.

Shropshire,
21 September 2012

ABOUT THE AUTHOR

M. C. Scott taught veterinary surgery at the universities of Cambridge and Dublin before taking up a career as a novelist. Now founder and Chair of the Historical Writers' Association, her novels have been shortlisted for the Orange Prize, nominated for an Edgar Award and translated into over twenty languages. In addition to the bestselling *Boudica* series, Scott is the author of an acclaimed sequence of Roman novels featuring the emperor's spy, Sebastos Pantera.

Visit: www.mcscott.co.uk